THAT TEXAS BLOOD

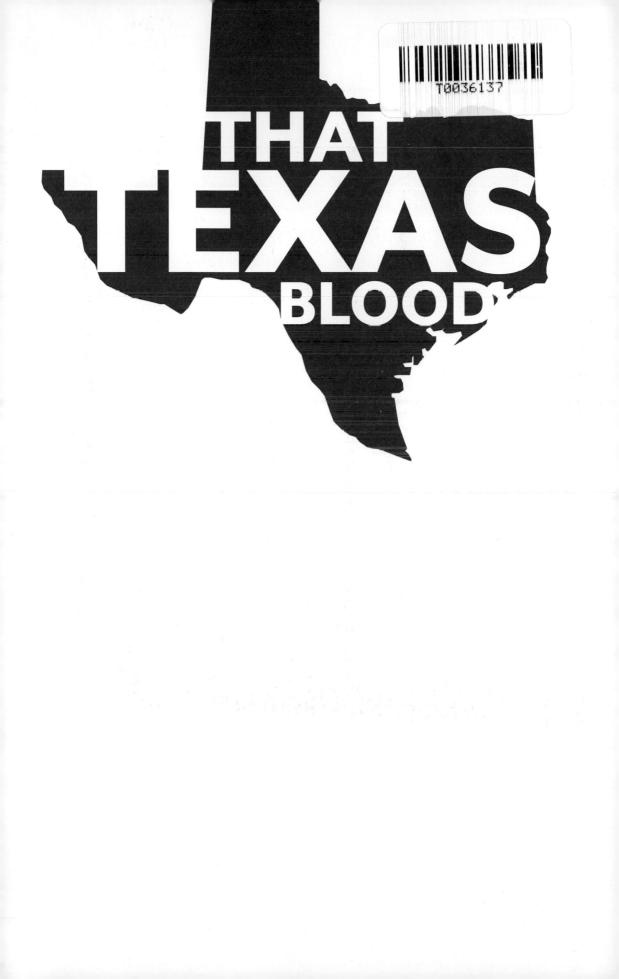

Color Assistant Pip Martin

IMAGE COMICS, INC. • Robert Kirkman: Chief Operating Officer • Erik Larsen: Chief Financial Officer • Todd McFarlane: President • Marc Silvestri: Chief Executive Officer • Jim Valentino: Vice President • Eric Stephenson: Publisher / Chief Creative Officer • Nicole Lapalme: Vice President of Finance • Leanna Caunter: Accounting Analyst • Sue Korpela: Accounting & HR Manager • Matt Parkinson: Vice President of Sales & Publishing Planning • Lorelei Bunjes: Vice President of Digital Strategy • Dirk Wood: Vice President of International Sales & Licensing • Ryan Brewer: International Sales & Licensing Manager • Alex Cox: Director of Direct Market Sales • Chloe Ramos: Book Market & Library Sales Manager • Emilio Bautista: Digital Sales Coordinator • Jon Schlaffman: Specialty Sales Coordinator • Kat Salazar: Vice President of PR & Marketing • Deanna Phelps: Marketing Design Manager • Drew Fitzgerald: Marketing Content Associate • Heather Doornink: Vice President of Production • Drew Gill: Art Director • Hilary DiLoreto: Print Manager • Tricia Ramos: Traffic Manager • Melissa Gifford: Content Manager • Erika Schnatz: Senior Production Artist • Wesley Griffith: Production Artist • Rich Fowlks: Production Artist • IMAGECOMICS.COM

Ⓢ Publication design by Sean Phillips.

THAT TEXAS BLOOD

Volume Three
by Chris Condon
& Jacob Phillips

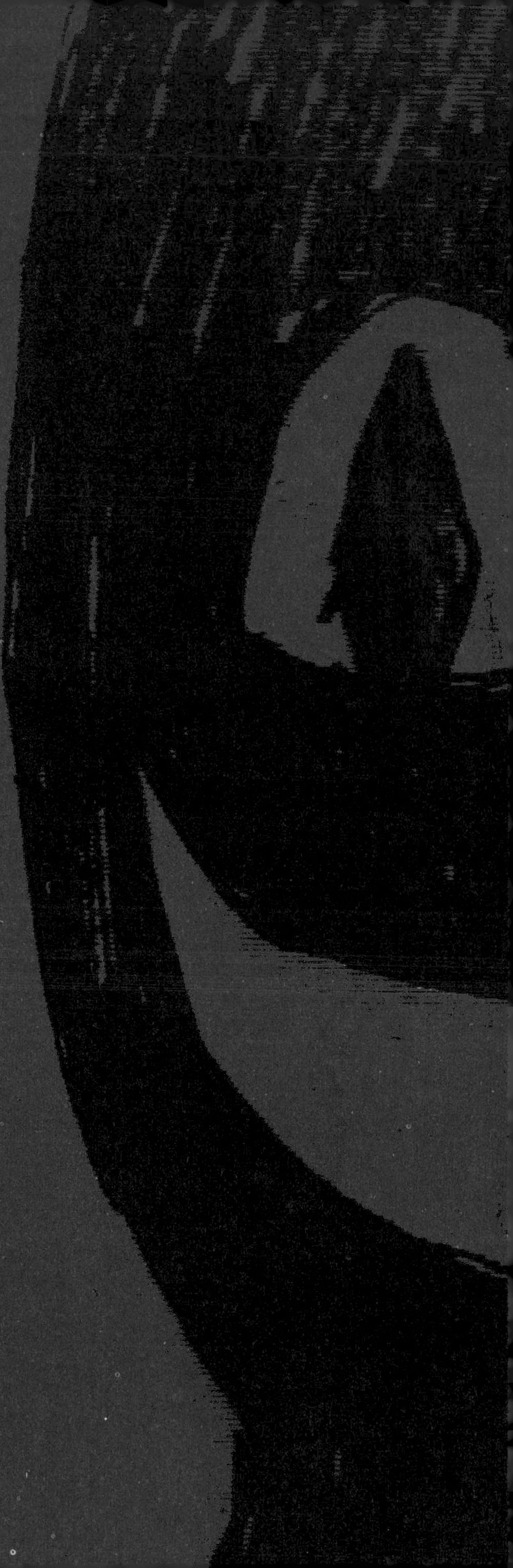

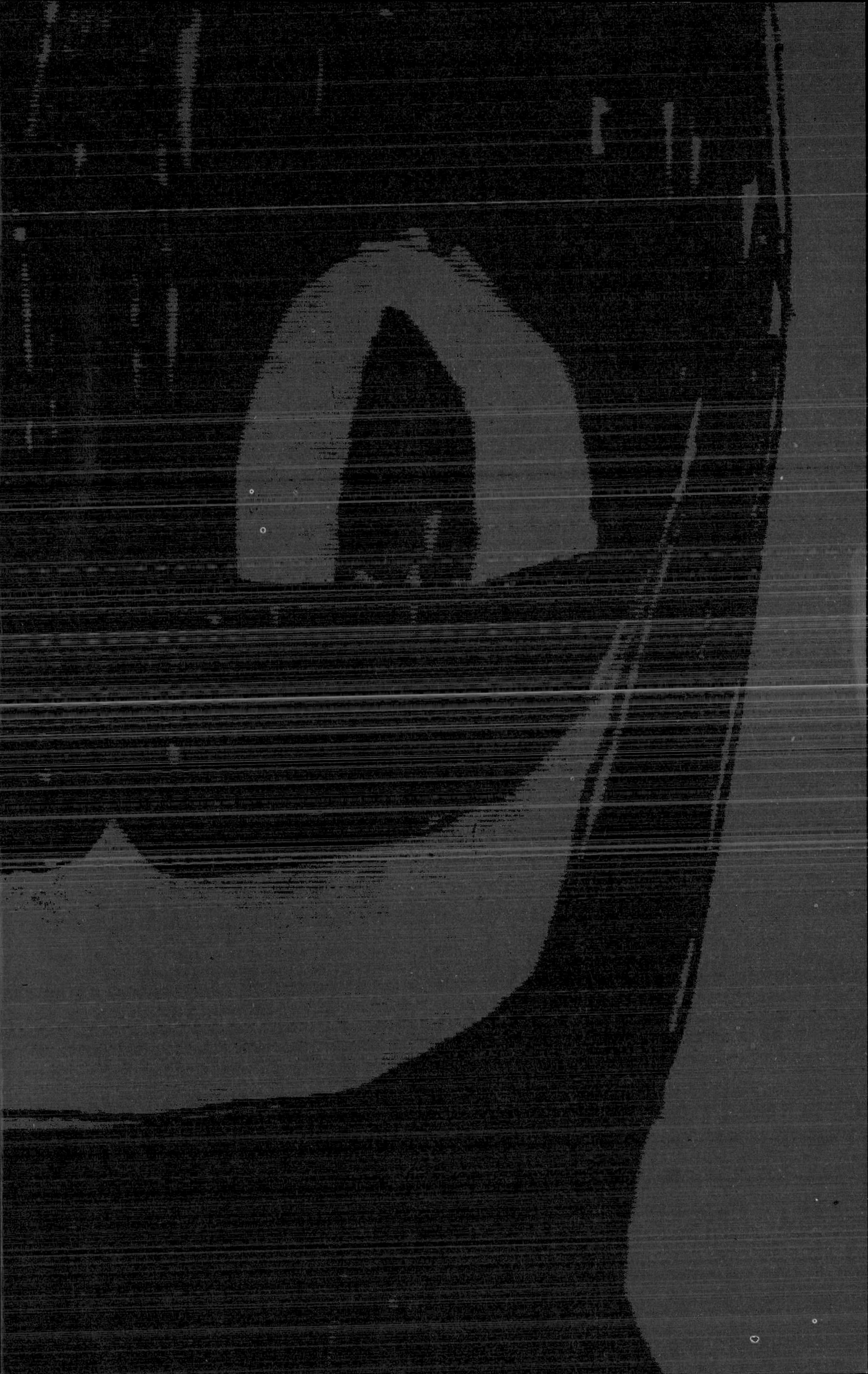

PATTI DOYLE AND THE BAD BLIZZARD OF '92

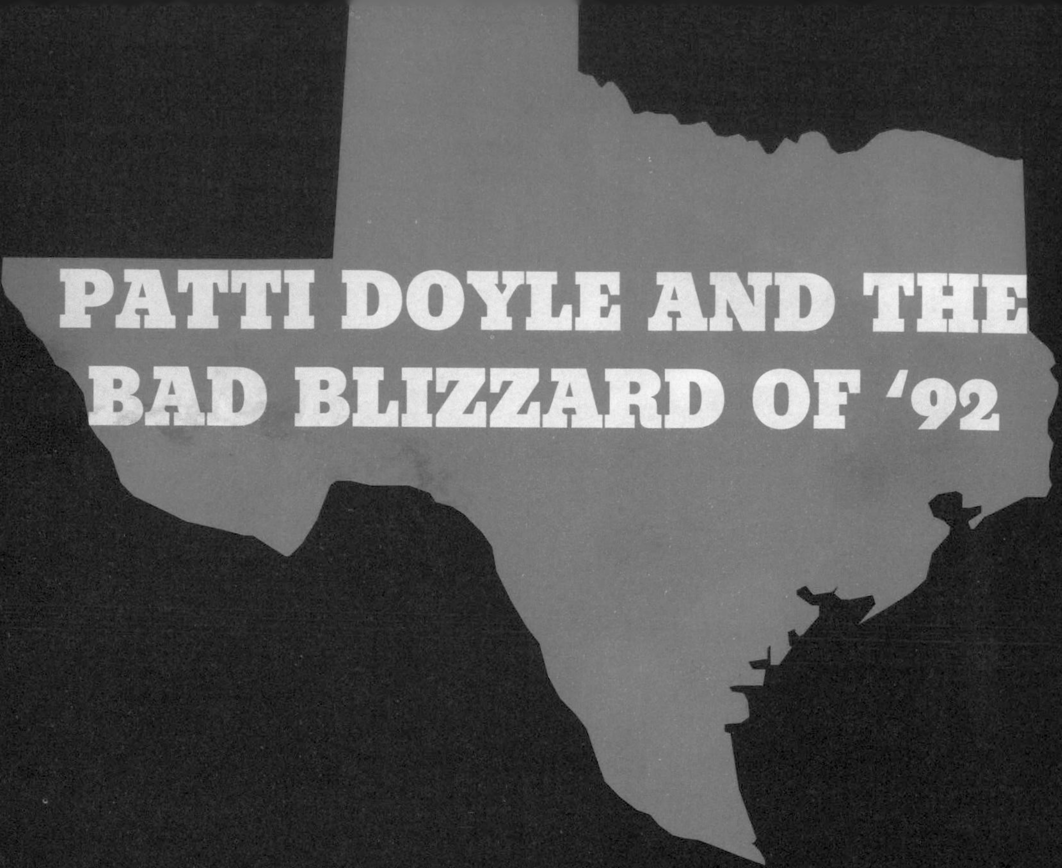

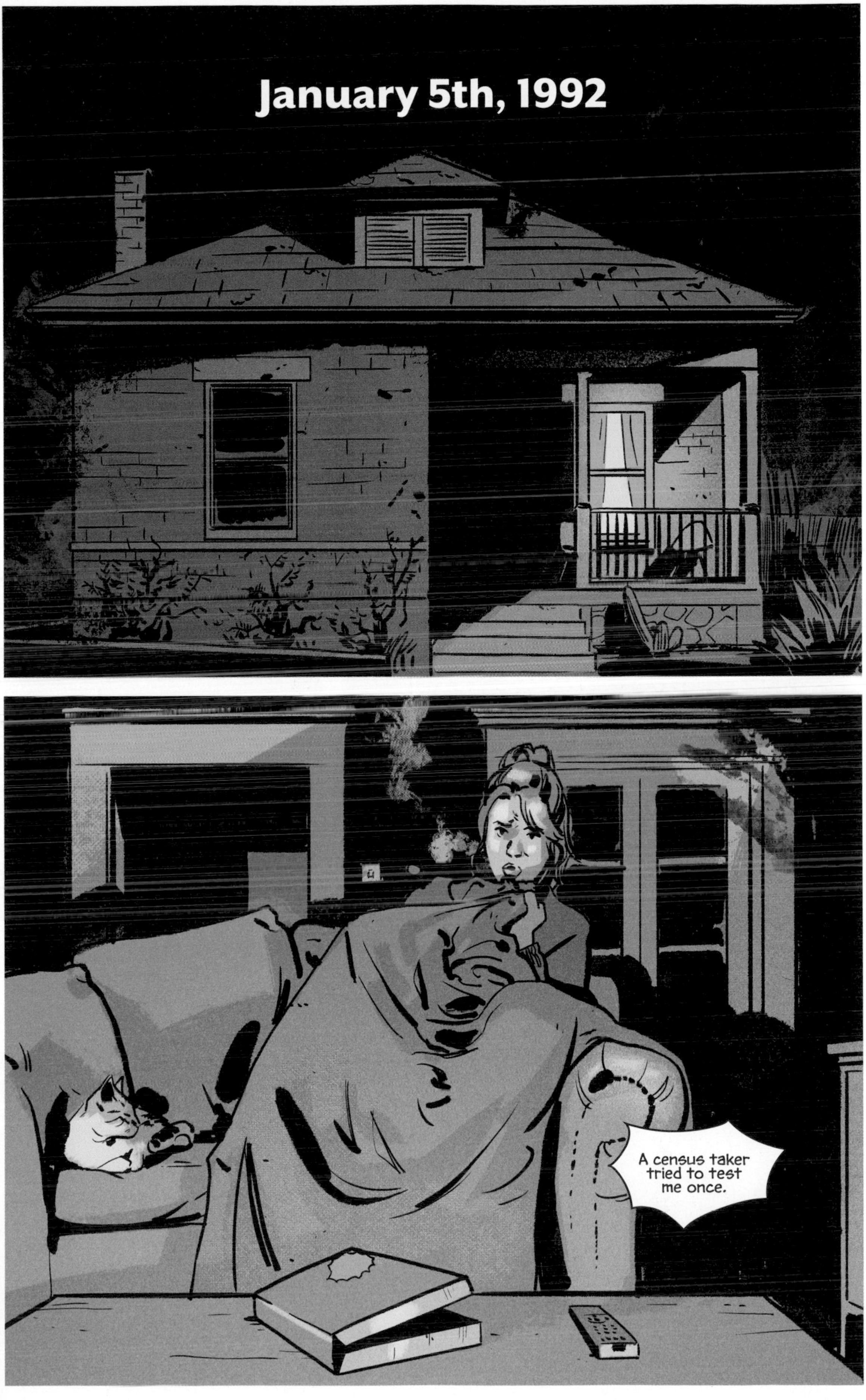
January 5th, 1992
A census taker tried to test me once.

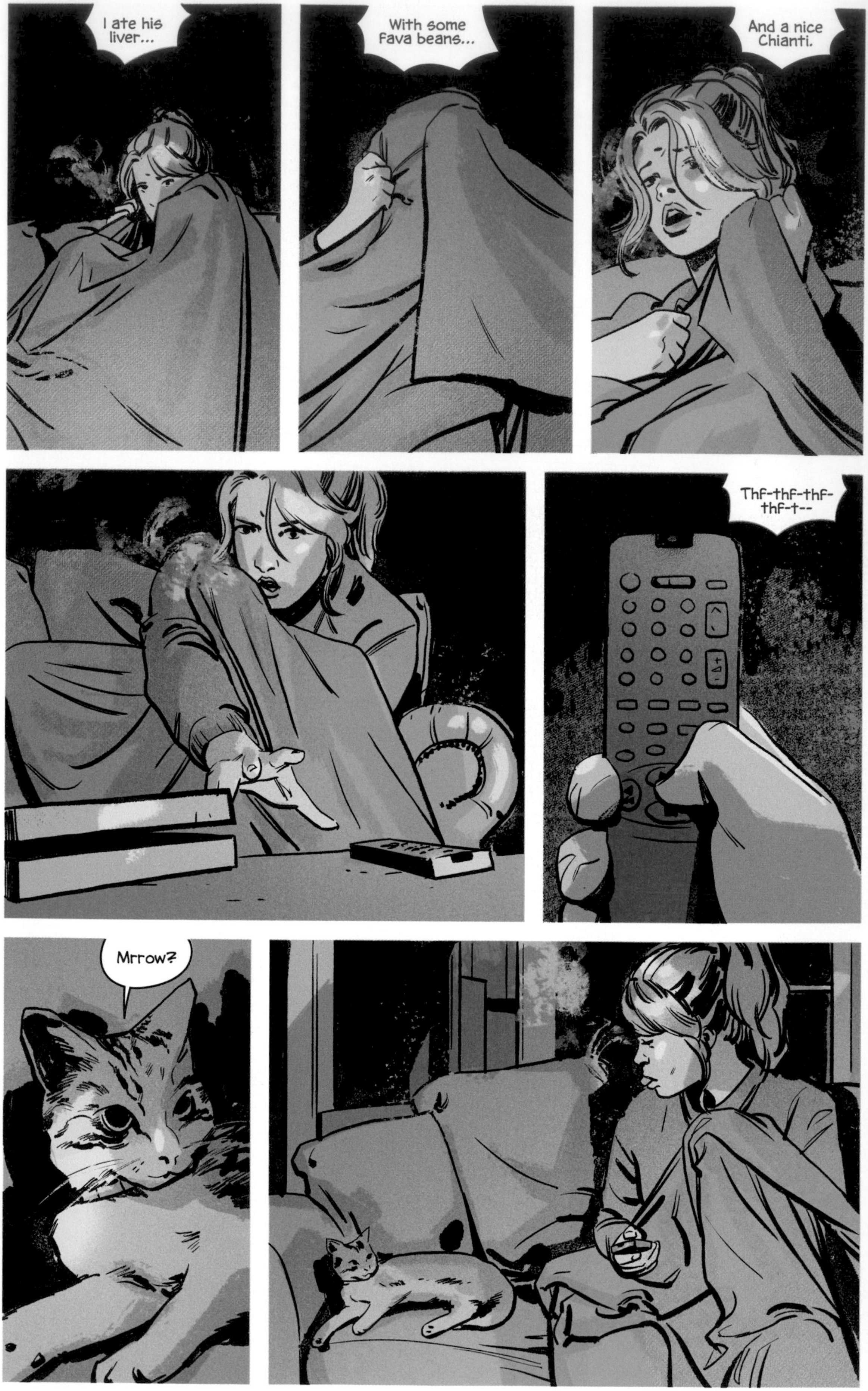
I ate his liver...
With some fava beans...
And a nice Chianti.
Thf-thf-thf-thf-t--
Mrrow?

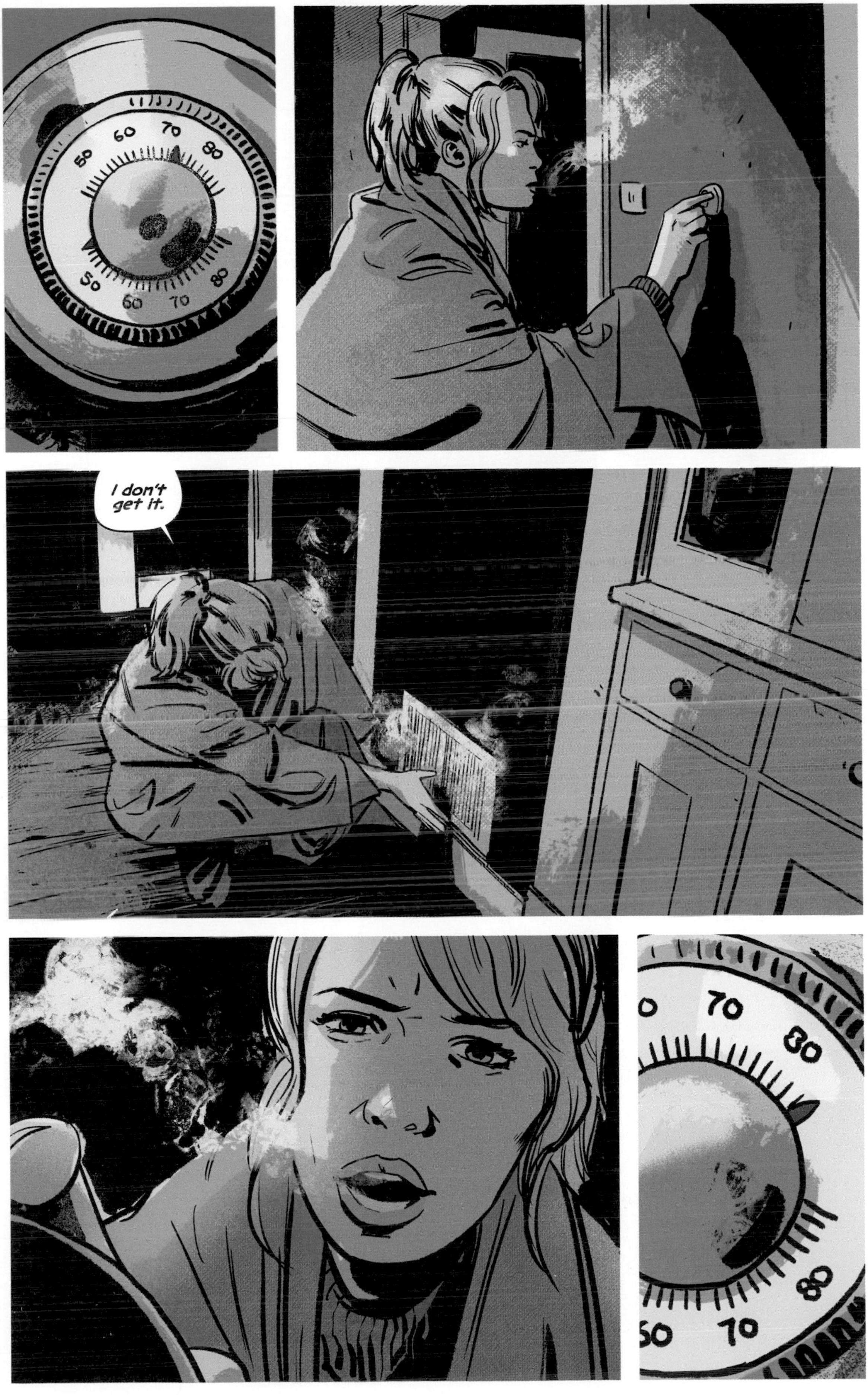
50
60
70
80
50
60
70
80
I don't get it.
70
80
80
50
70

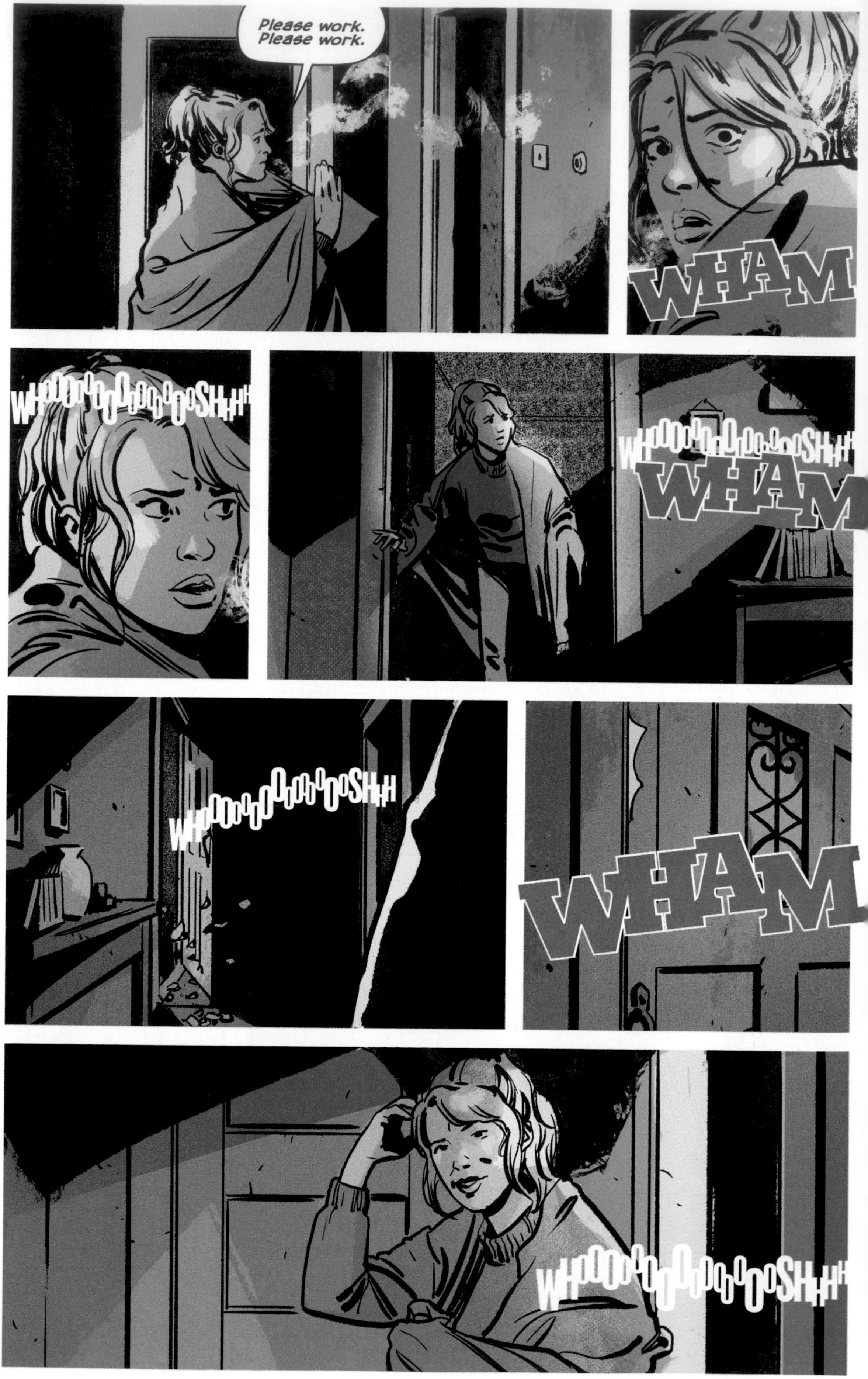
Please work. Please work.
WHAM
WHOOOOOOOOOOOOOOSHHHH
WHOOOOOOOOOOOOOOSHHHH
WHAM
WHOOOOOOOOOOOOOOSHHH
WHAM
WHOOOOOOOOOOOOOOOOSHHHHH

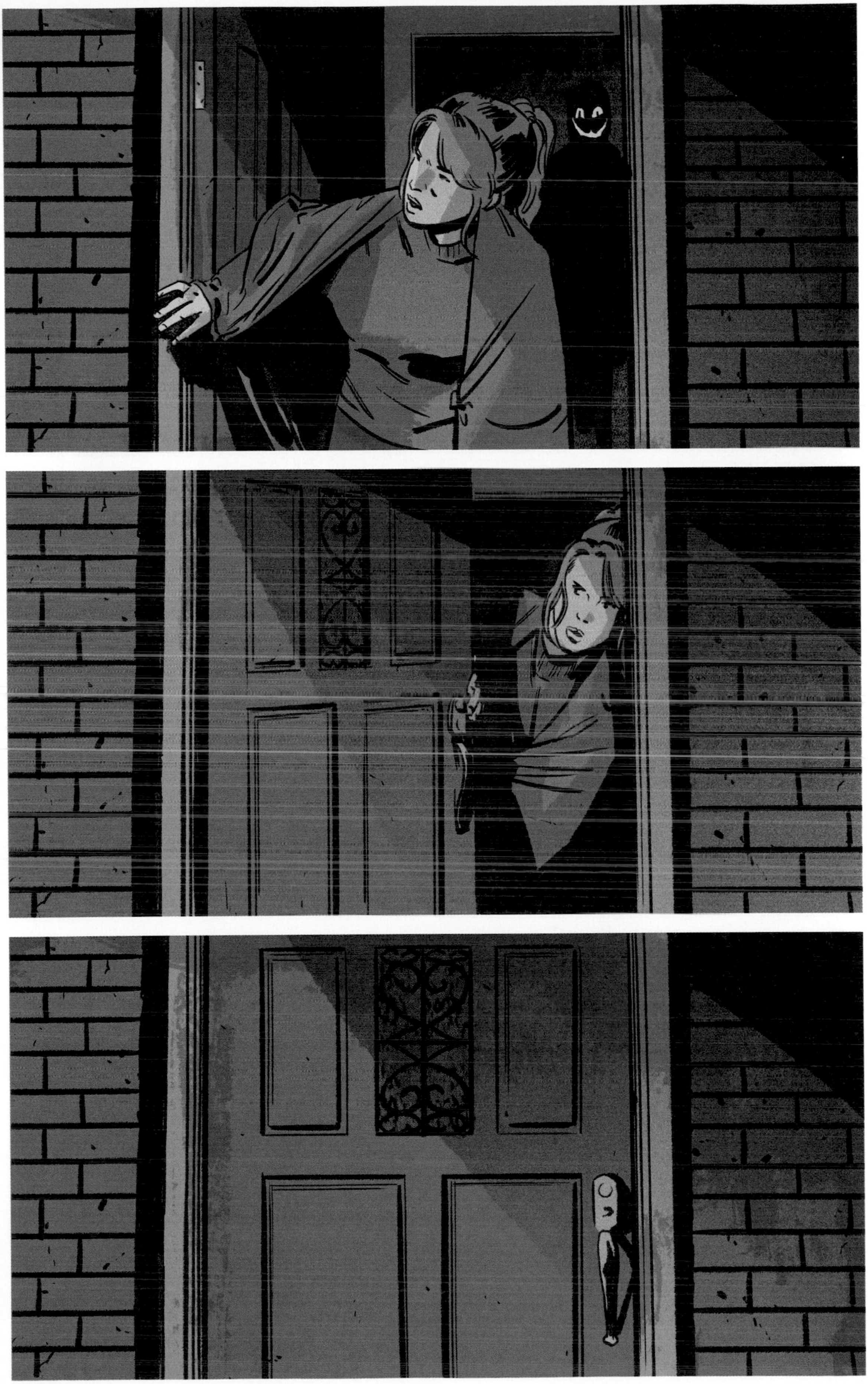

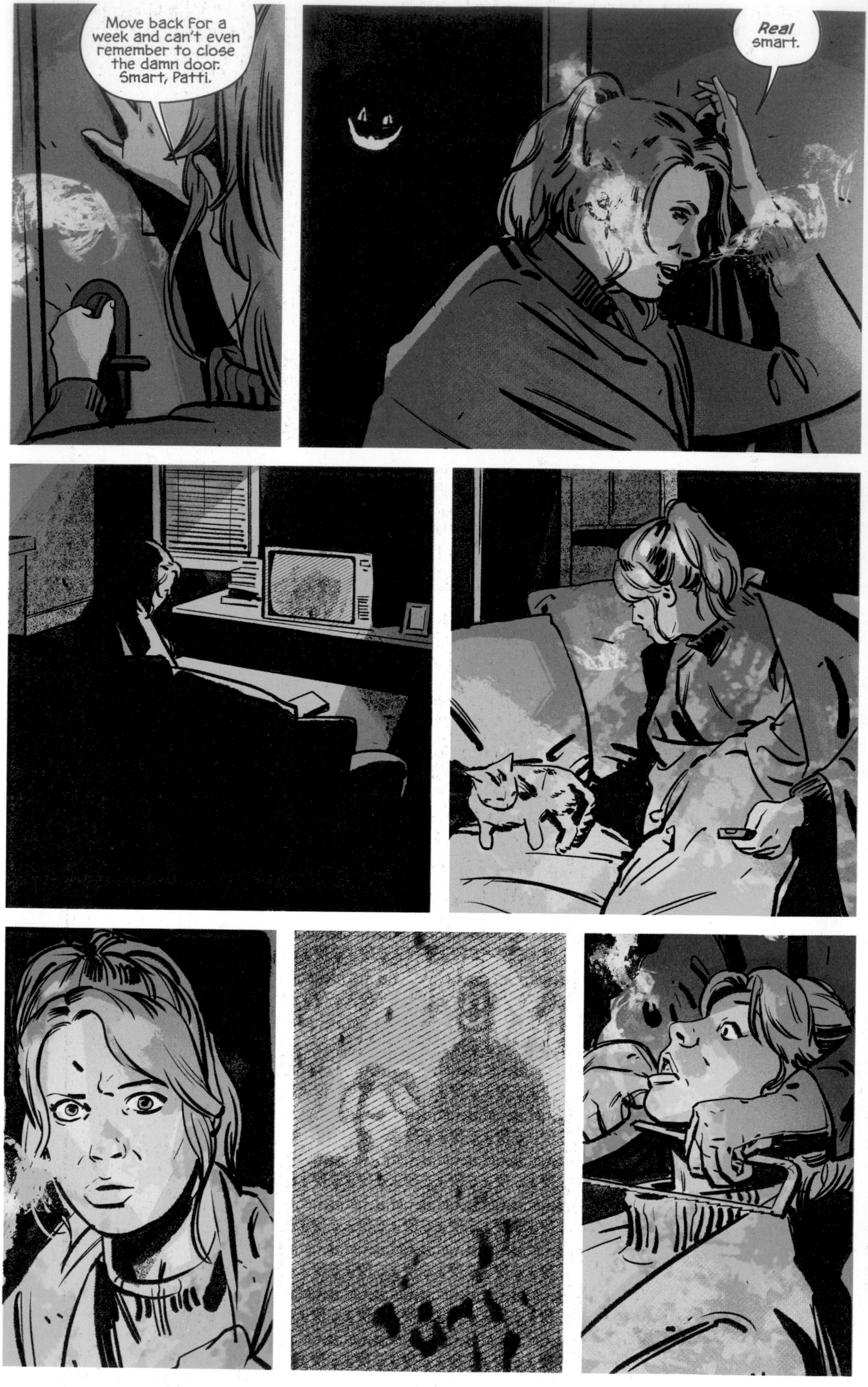

Move back for a week and can't even remember to close the damn door. Smart, Patti.
Real smart.

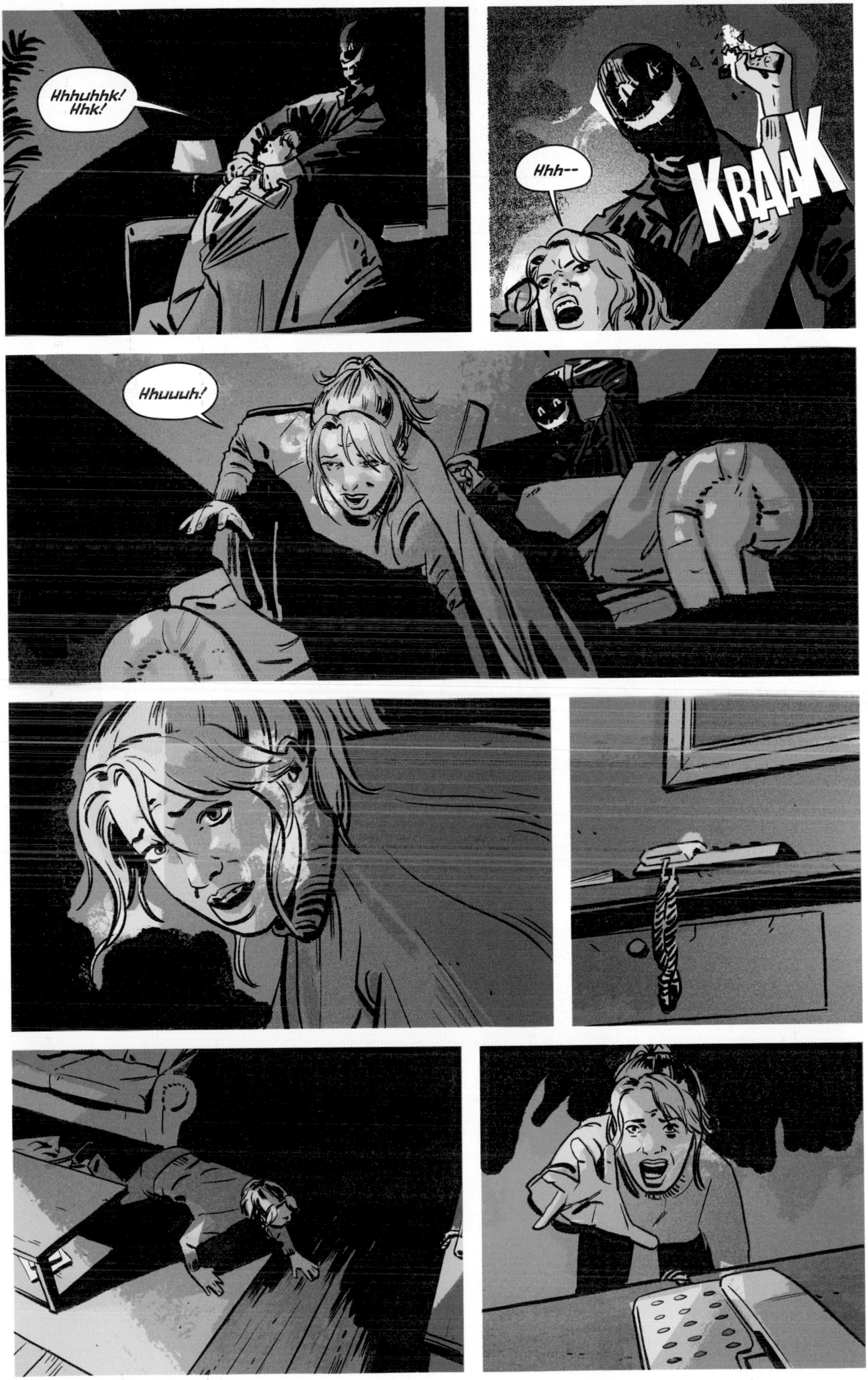
Hhhuhhk! Hhk!
Hhh--
KRAAK
Hhuuuh!

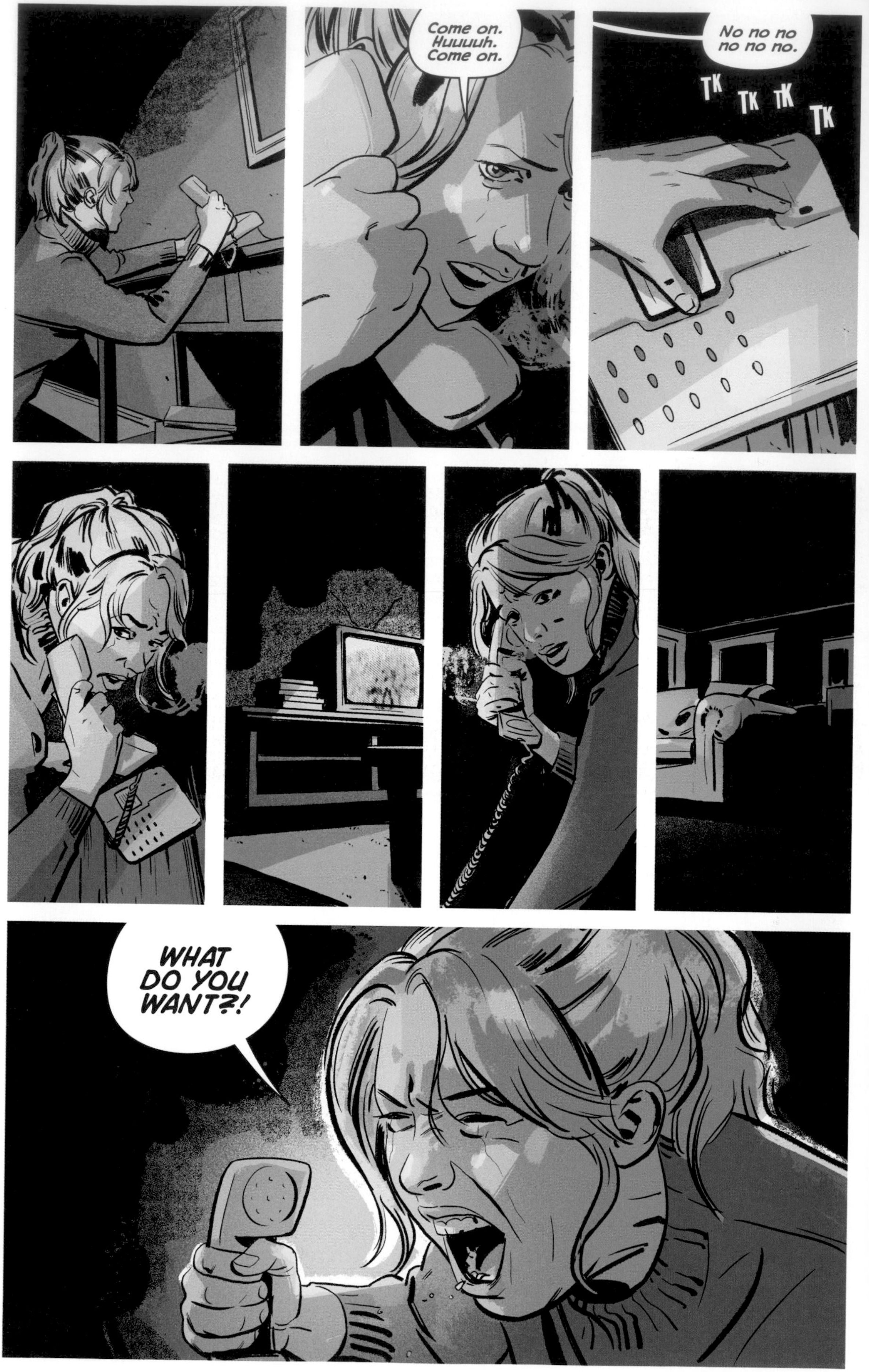
Come on. Huuuuh. Come on.
No no no no no no.
TK TK TK TK
WHAT DO YOU WANT?!

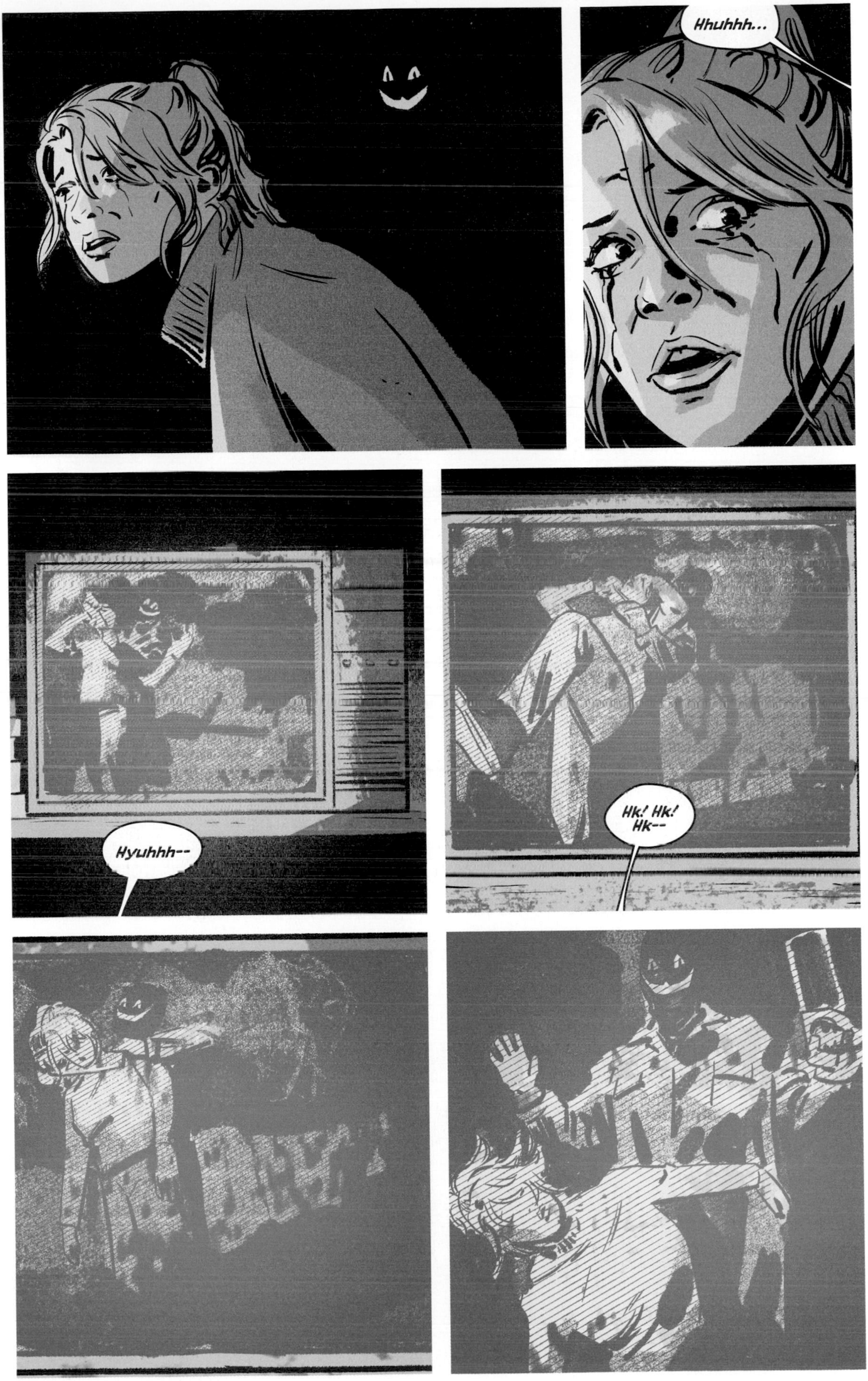
Hhuhhh...
Hyuhhh--
Hk! Hk! Hk--

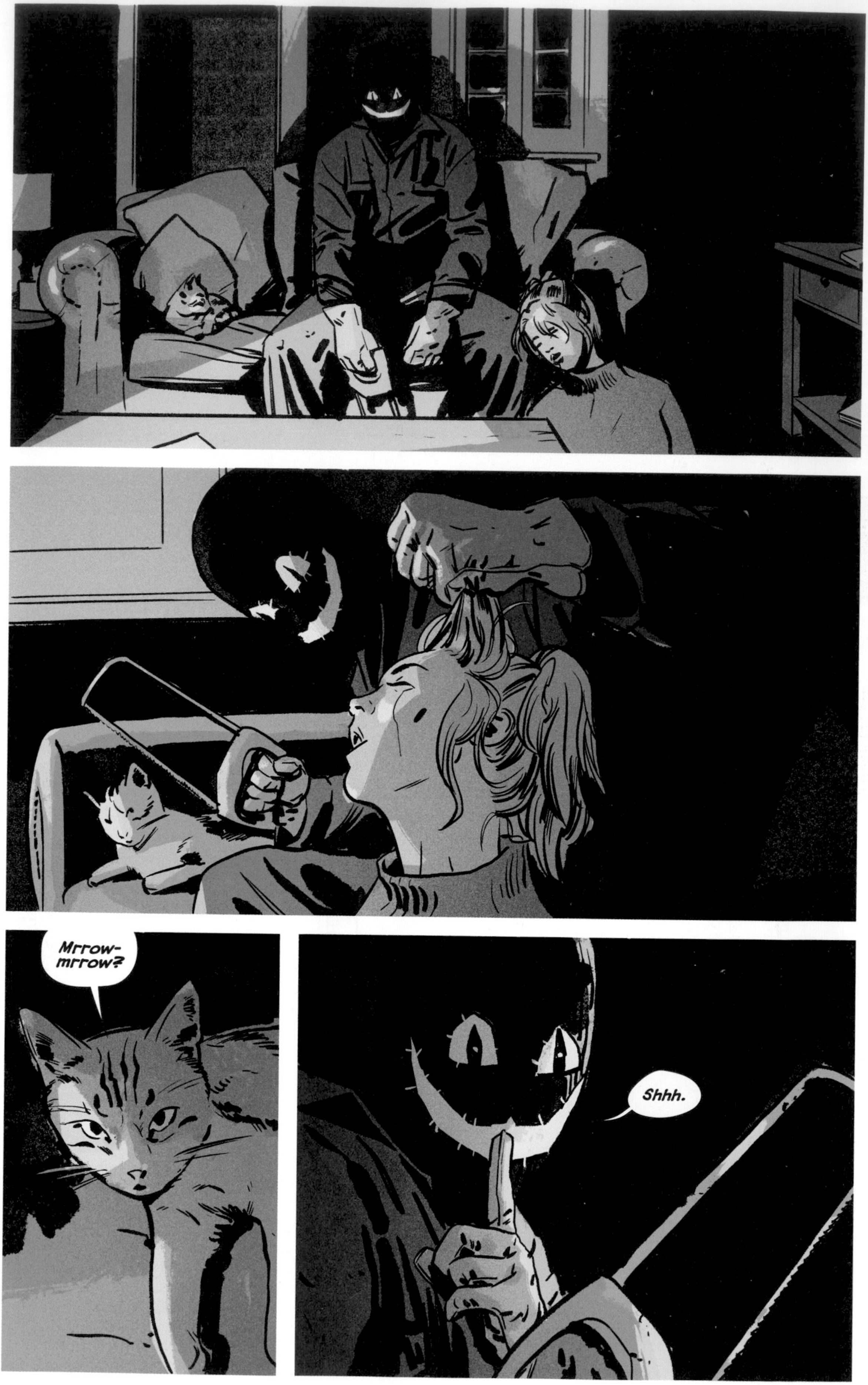
Mrrow-
mrrow?
Shhh.

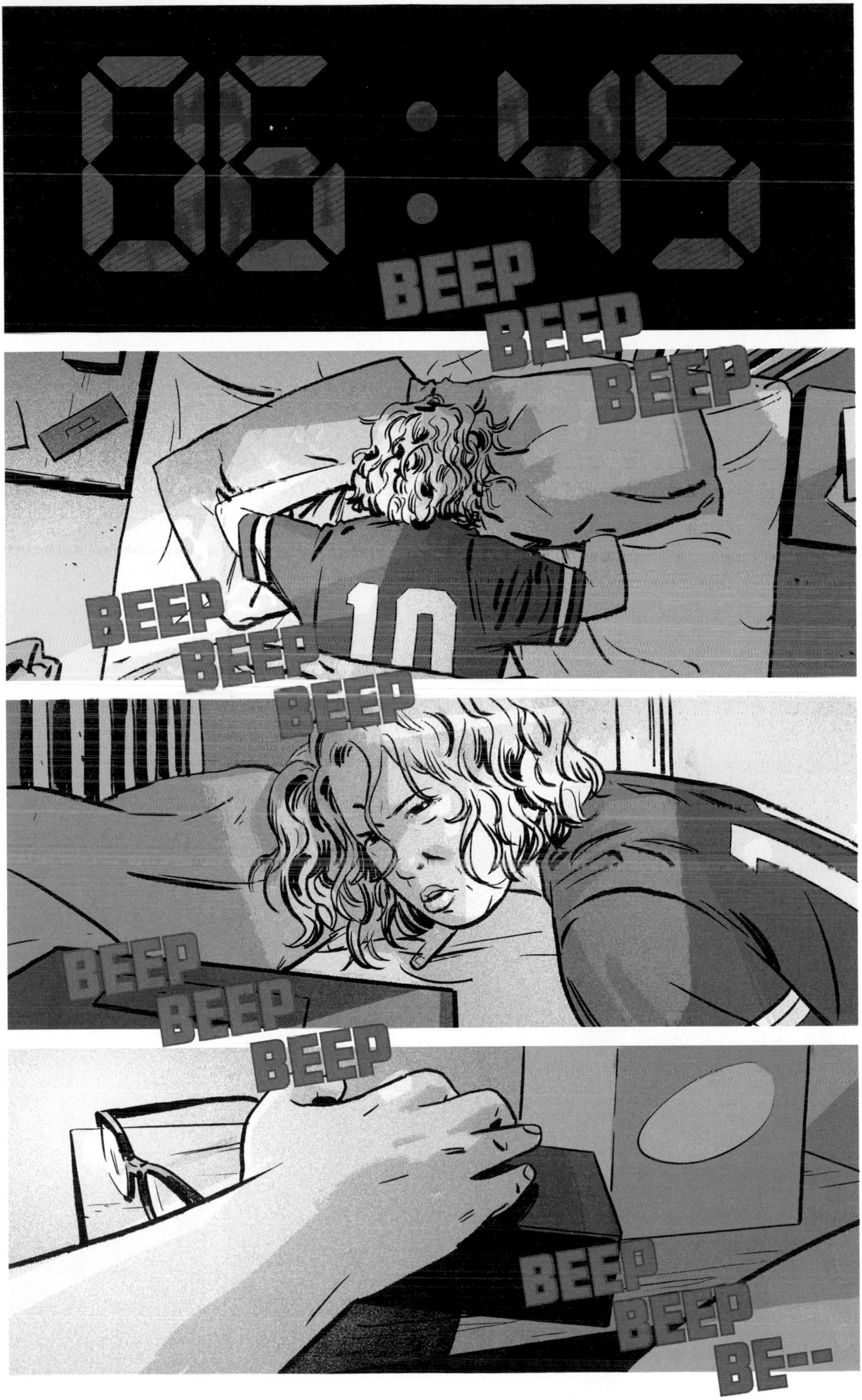
06:45
BEEP
BEEP
BEEP
10
BEEP
BEEP
BEEP
BEEP
BEEP
BEEP
BEEP
BEEP
BE--

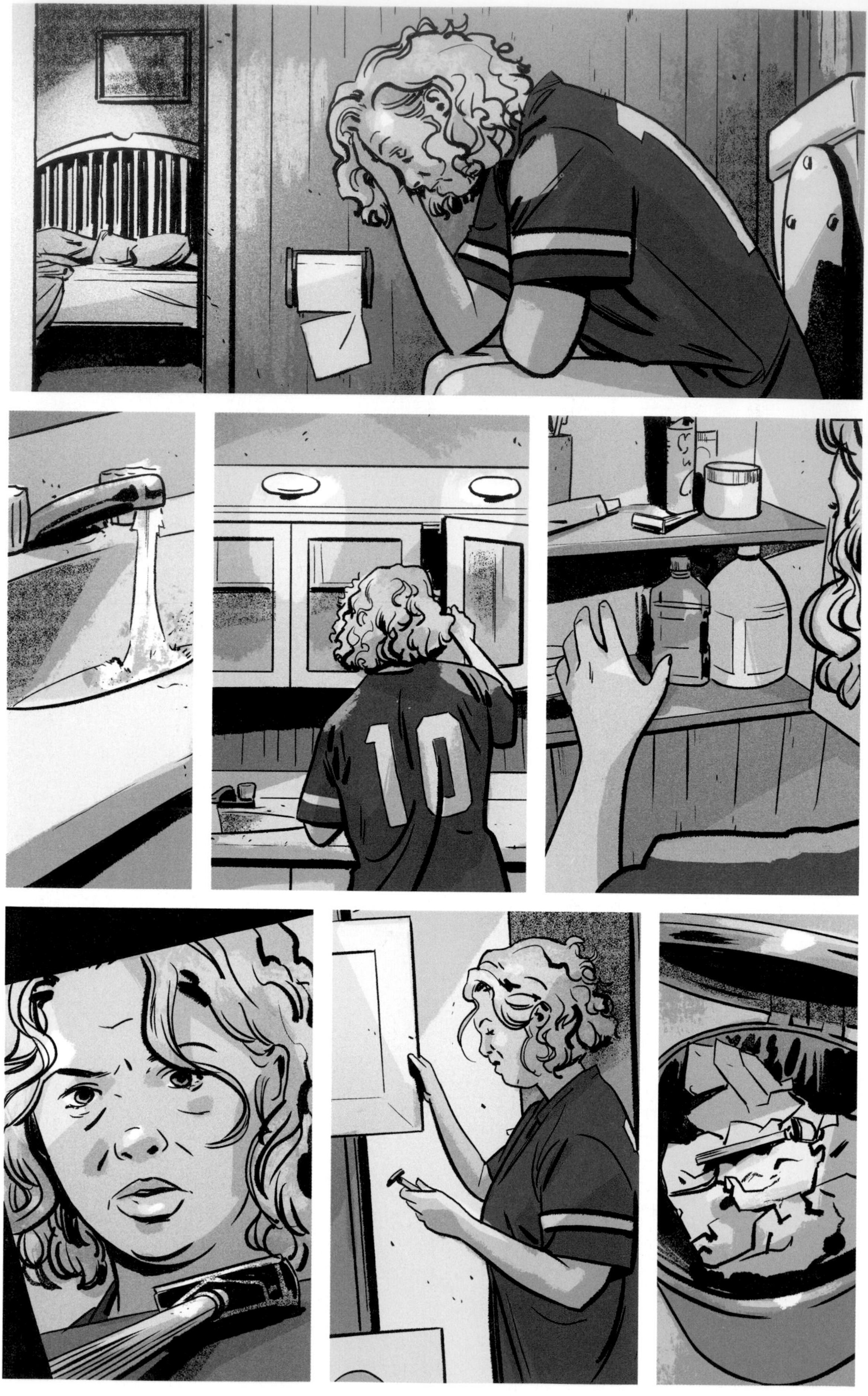
10

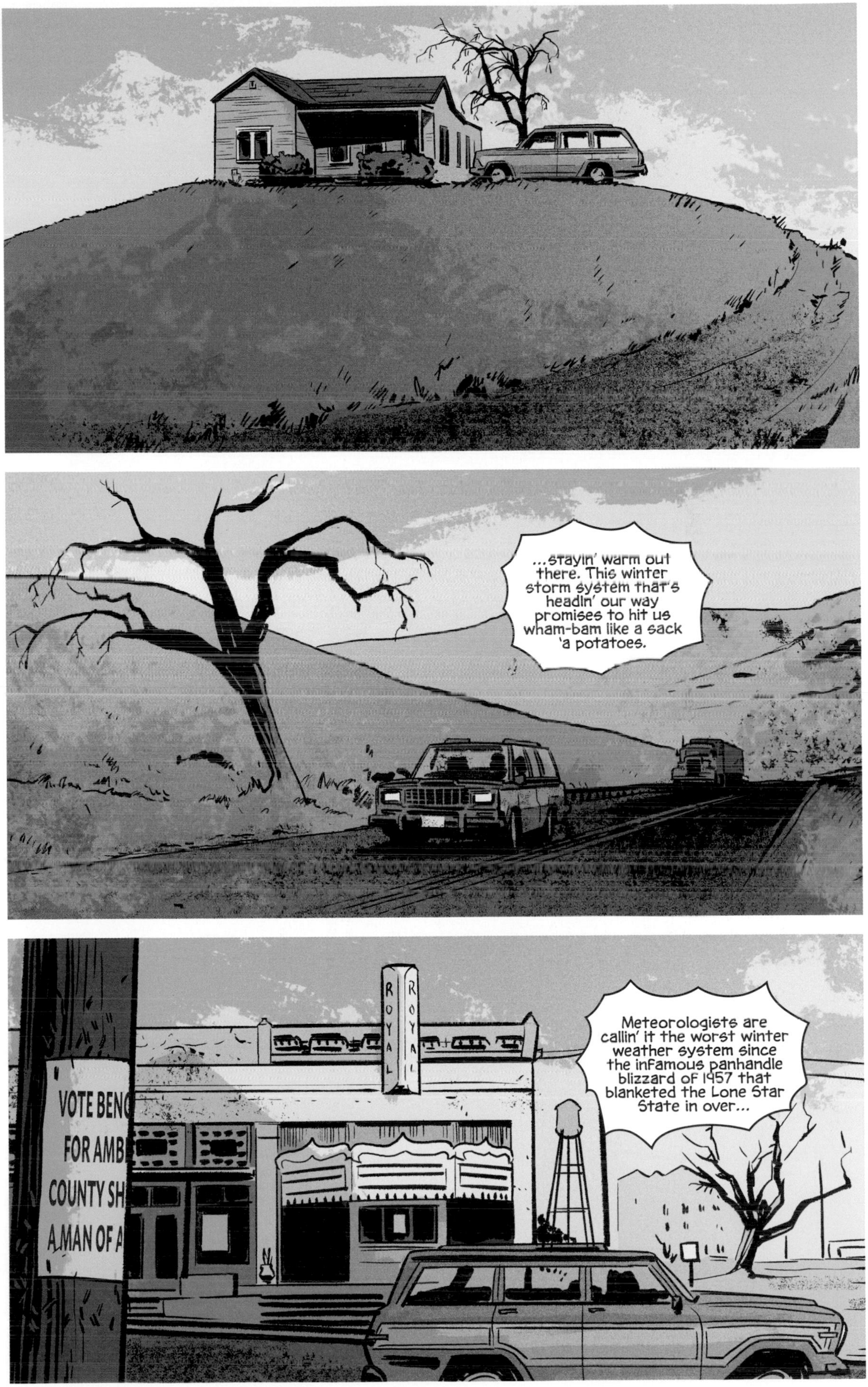
...stayin' warm out there. This winter storm system that's headin' our way promises to hit us wham-bam like a sack 'a potatoes.
ROYAL
ROYAL
VOTE BENG
FOR AMB
COUNTY SH
A MAN OF A
Meteorologists are callin' it the worst winter weather system since the infamous panhandle blizzard of 1957 that blanketed the Lone Star State in over...

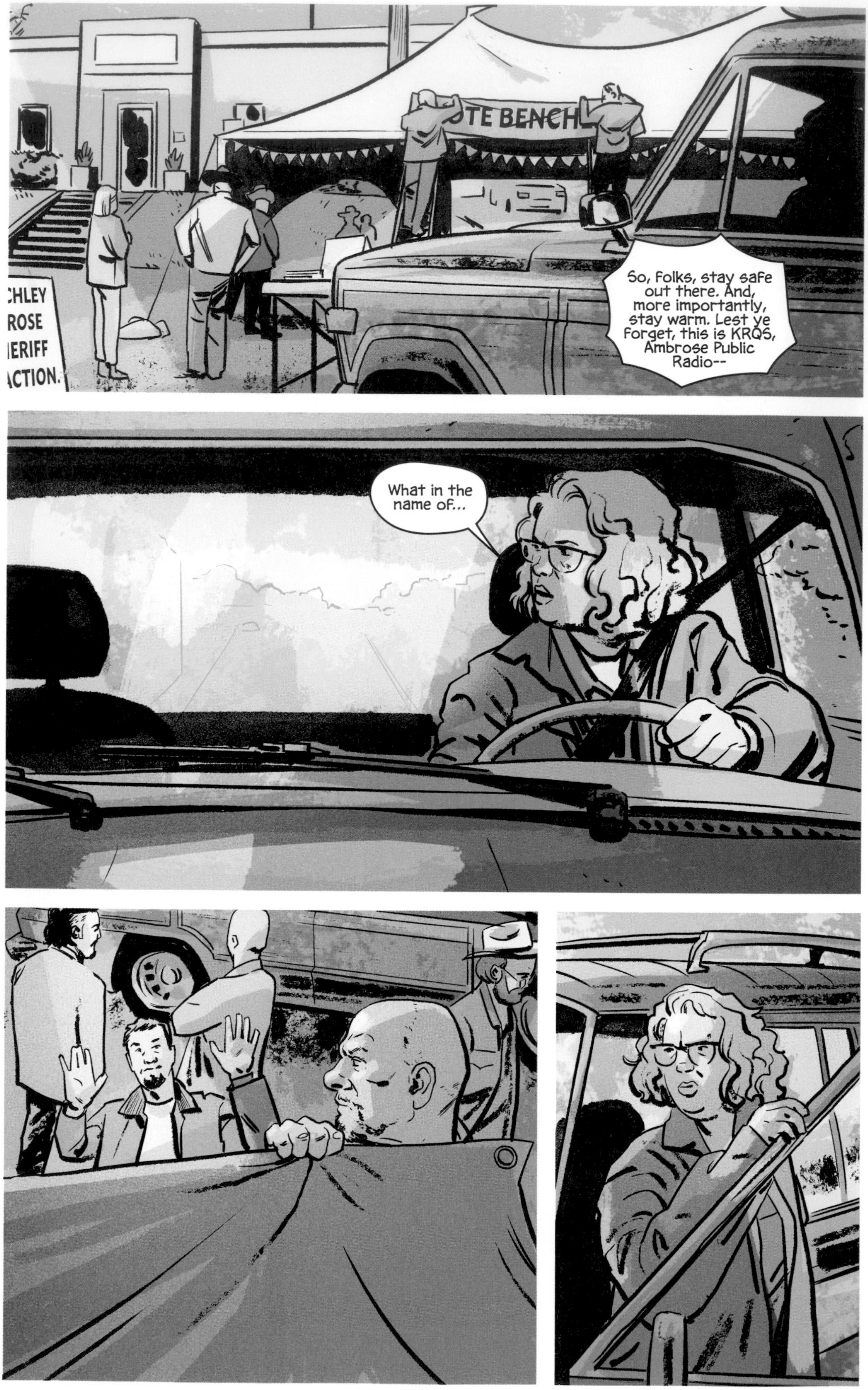

OTE BENCH
CHLEY
ROSE
IERIFF
ACTION.
So, Folks, stay safe out there. And, more importantly, stay warm. Lest ye forget, this is KRQS, Ambrose Public Radio--
What in the name of...

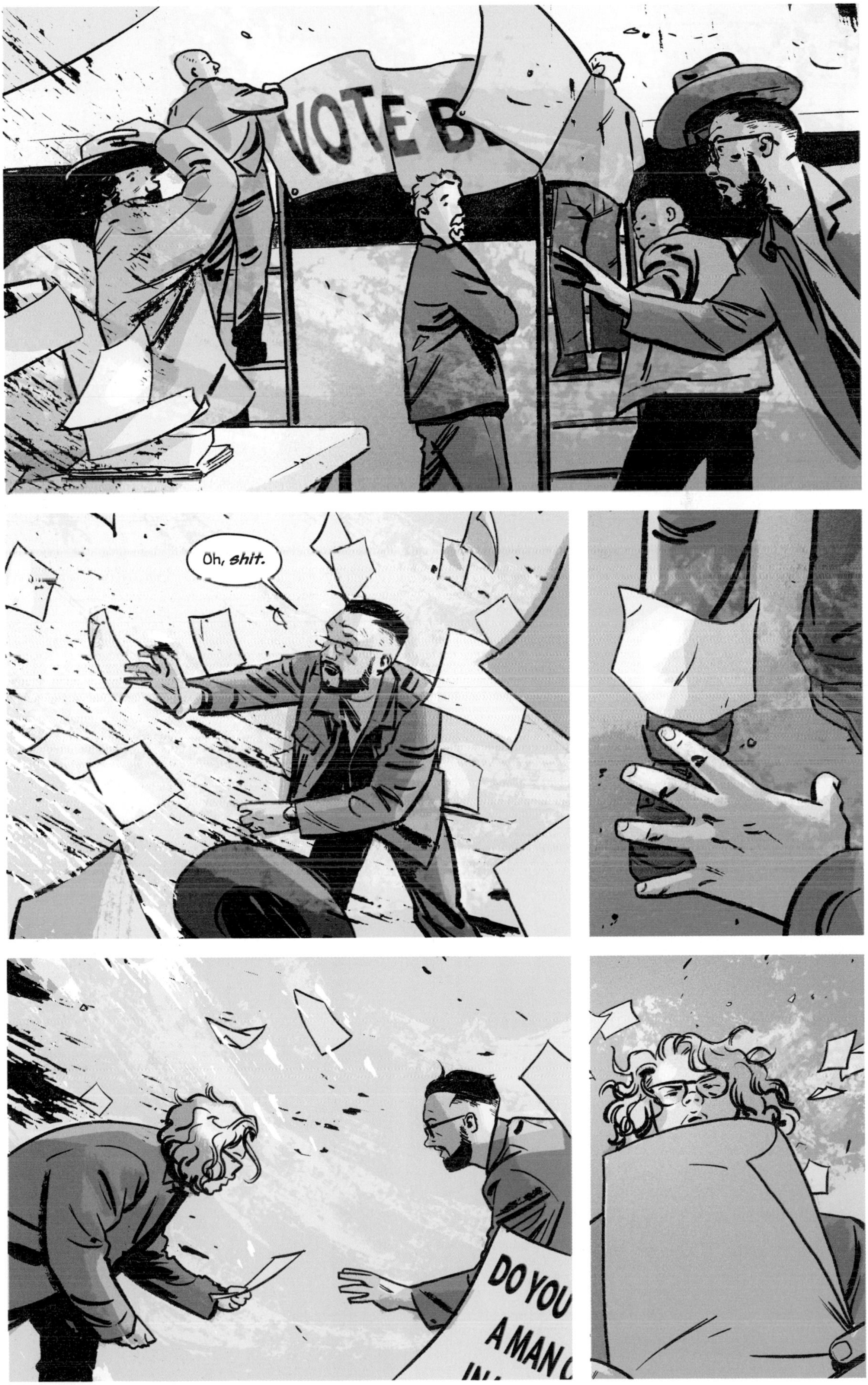
VOTE B
Oh, shit.
DO YOU
A MAN

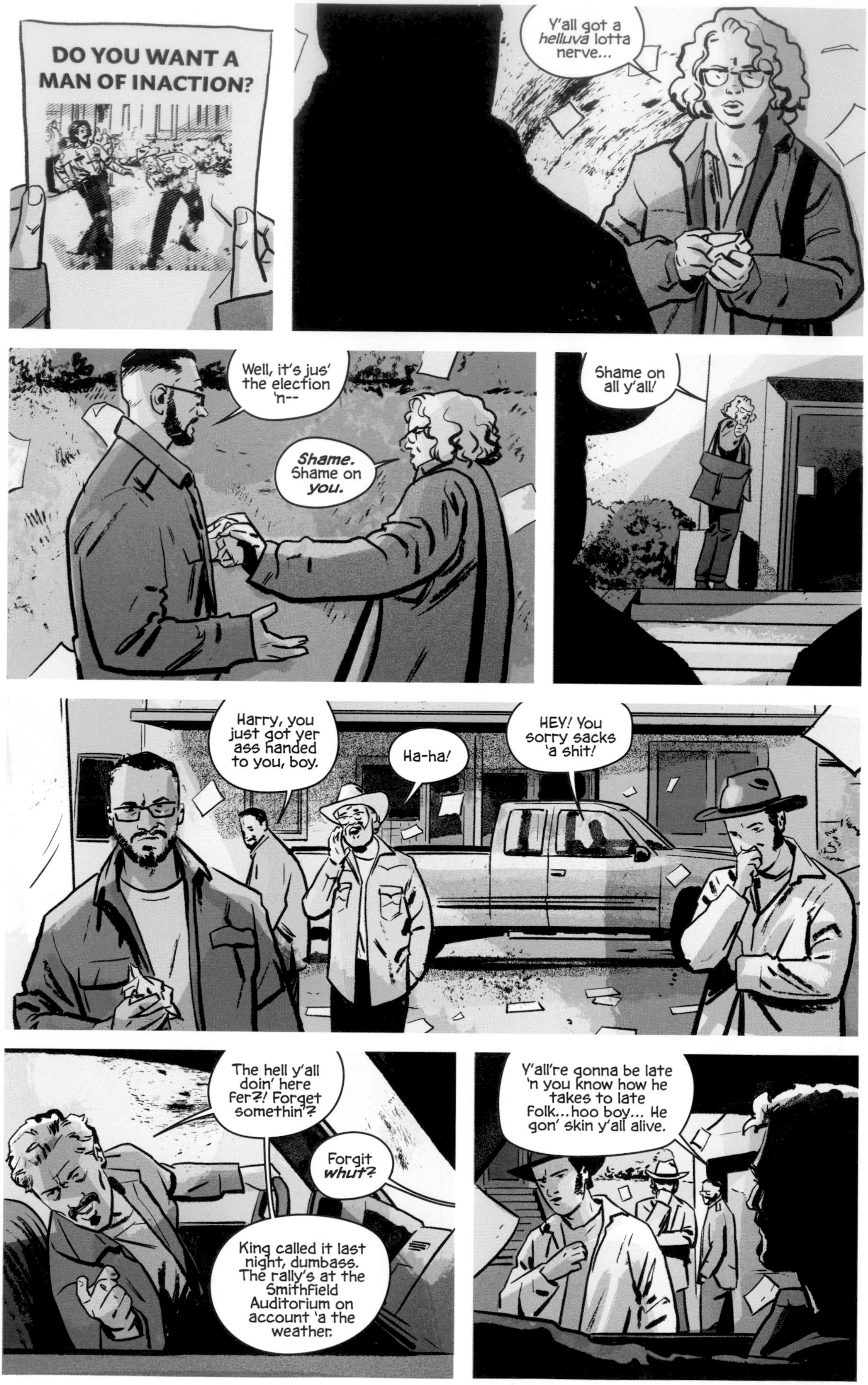
DO YOU WANT A MAN OF INACTION?
Y'all got a *helluva* lotta nerve...
Well, it's jus' the election 'n--
Shame. Shame on ***you.***
Shame on all y'all!
Harry, you just got yer ass handed to you, boy.
Ha-ha!
HEY! You sorry sacks 'a shit!
The hell y'all doin' here fer?! Forget somethin'?
Forgit ***whut?***
King called it last night, dumbass. The rally's at the Smithfield Auditorium on account 'a the weather.
Y'all're gonna be late 'n you know how he takes to late folk...hoo boy... He gon' skin y'all alive.

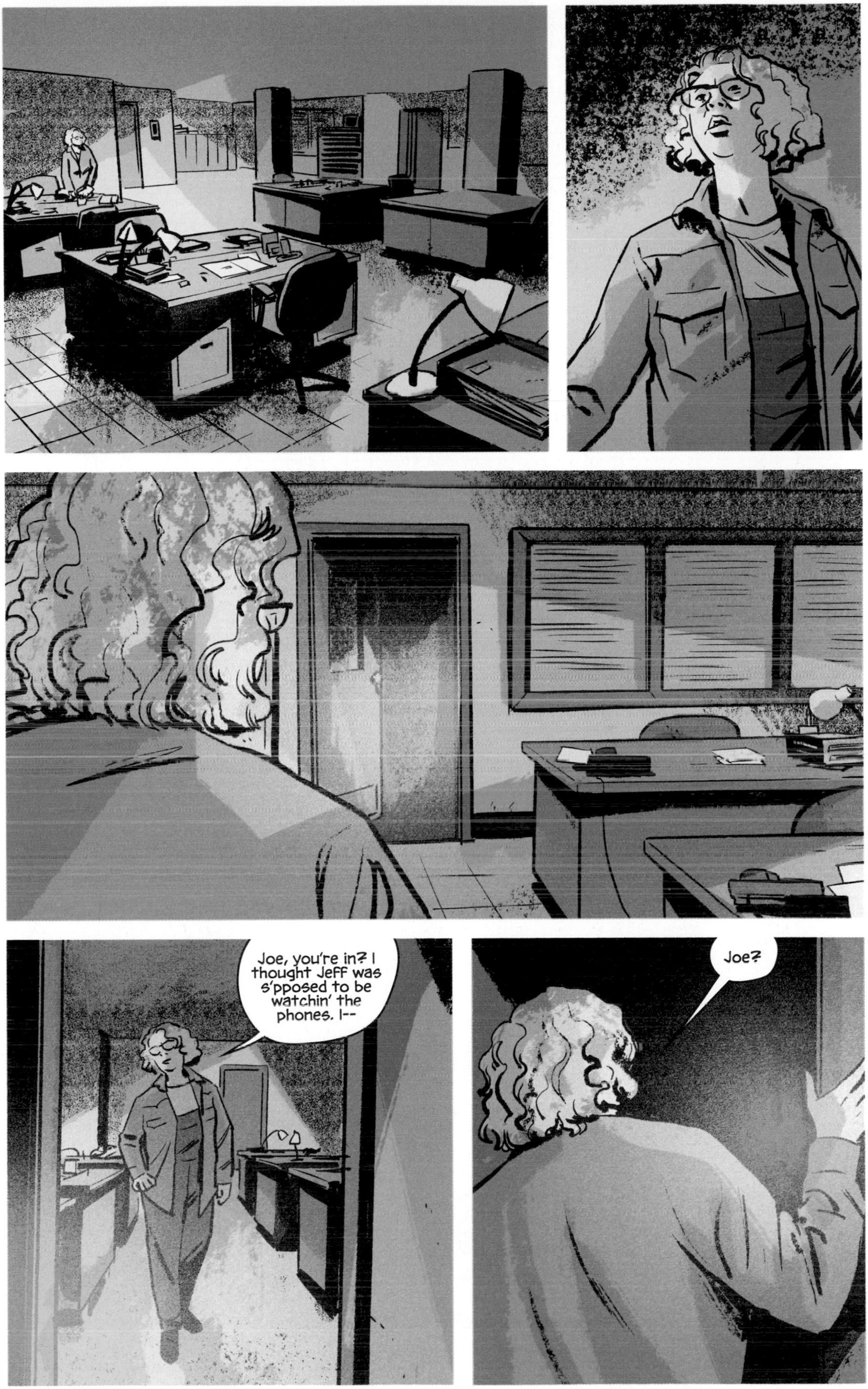
Joe, you're in? I thought Jeff was s'pposed to be watchin' the phones. I--
Joe?

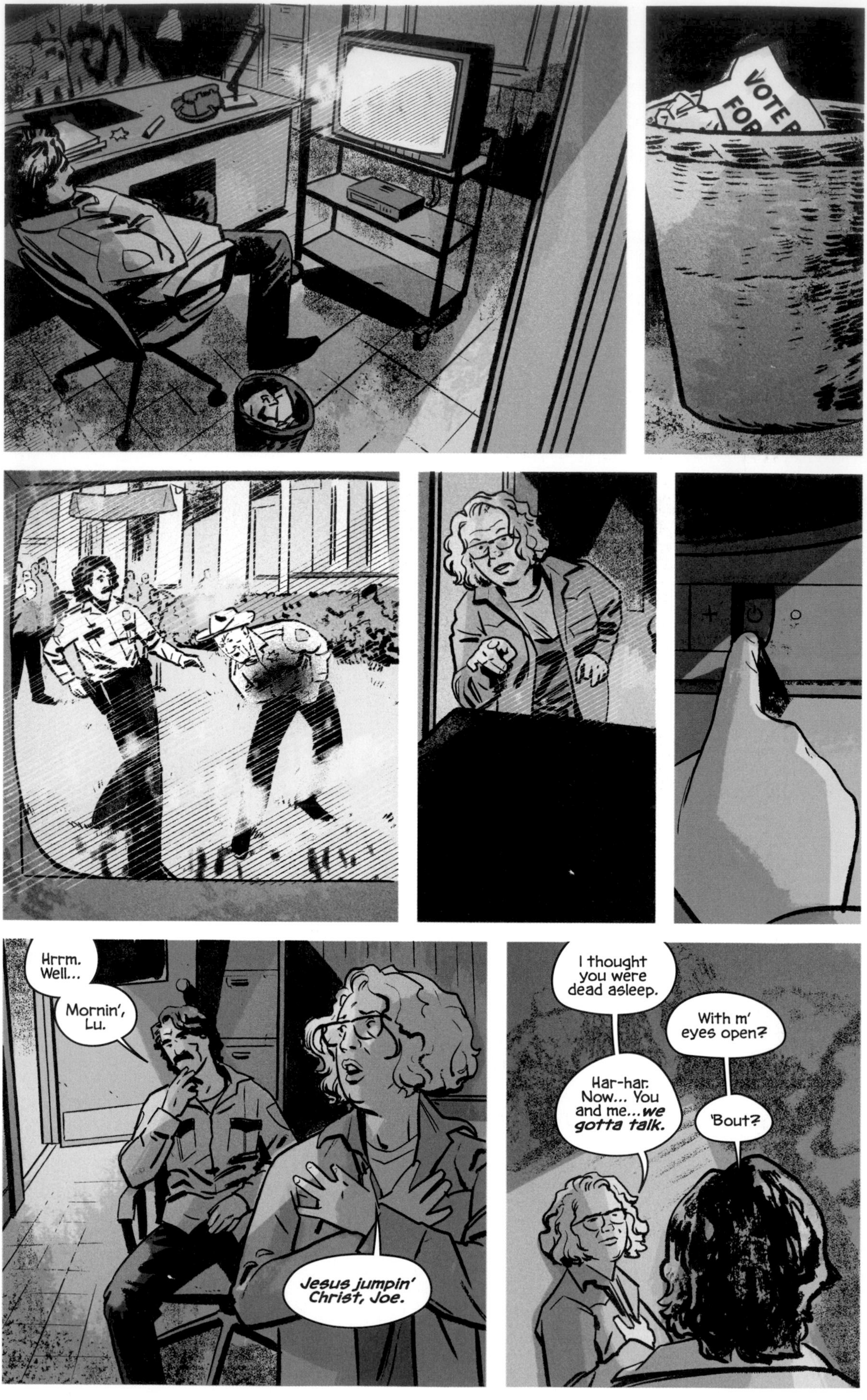
VOTE
FOR
Hrrm. Well...
Mornin', Lu.
Jesus jumpin' Christ, Joe.
I thought you were dead asleep.
With m' eyes open?
Har-har. Now... You and me...*we gotta talk.*
'Bout?

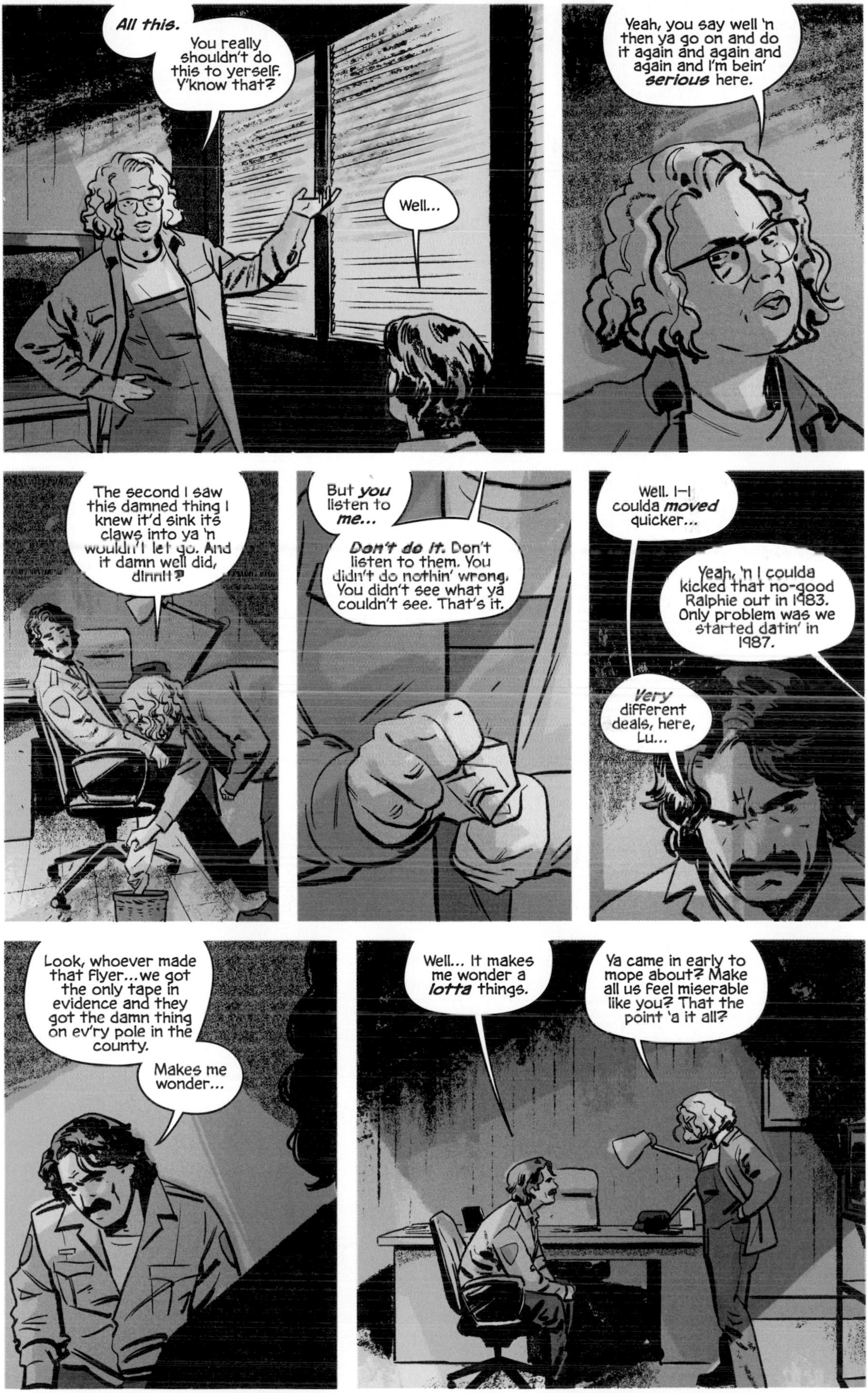
All this.
You really shouldn't do this to yerself. Y'know that?
Well...
Yeah, you say well 'n then ya go on and do it again and again and again and I'm bein' serious here.
The second I saw this damned thing I knew it'd sink its claws into ya 'n wouldn't let go. And it damn well did, dinnit?
But you listen to me...
Don't do it. Don't listen to them. You didn't do nothin' wrong. You didn't see what ya couldn't see. That's it.
Well. I—I coulda moved quicker...
Yeah, 'n I coulda kicked that no-good Ralphie out in 1983. Only problem was we started datin' in 1987.
Very different deals, here, Lu...
Look, whoever made that flyer...we got the only tape in evidence and they got the damn thing on ev'ry pole in the county.
Makes me wonder...
Well... It makes me wonder a lotta things.
Ya came in early to mope about? Make all us feel miserable like you? That the point 'a it all?

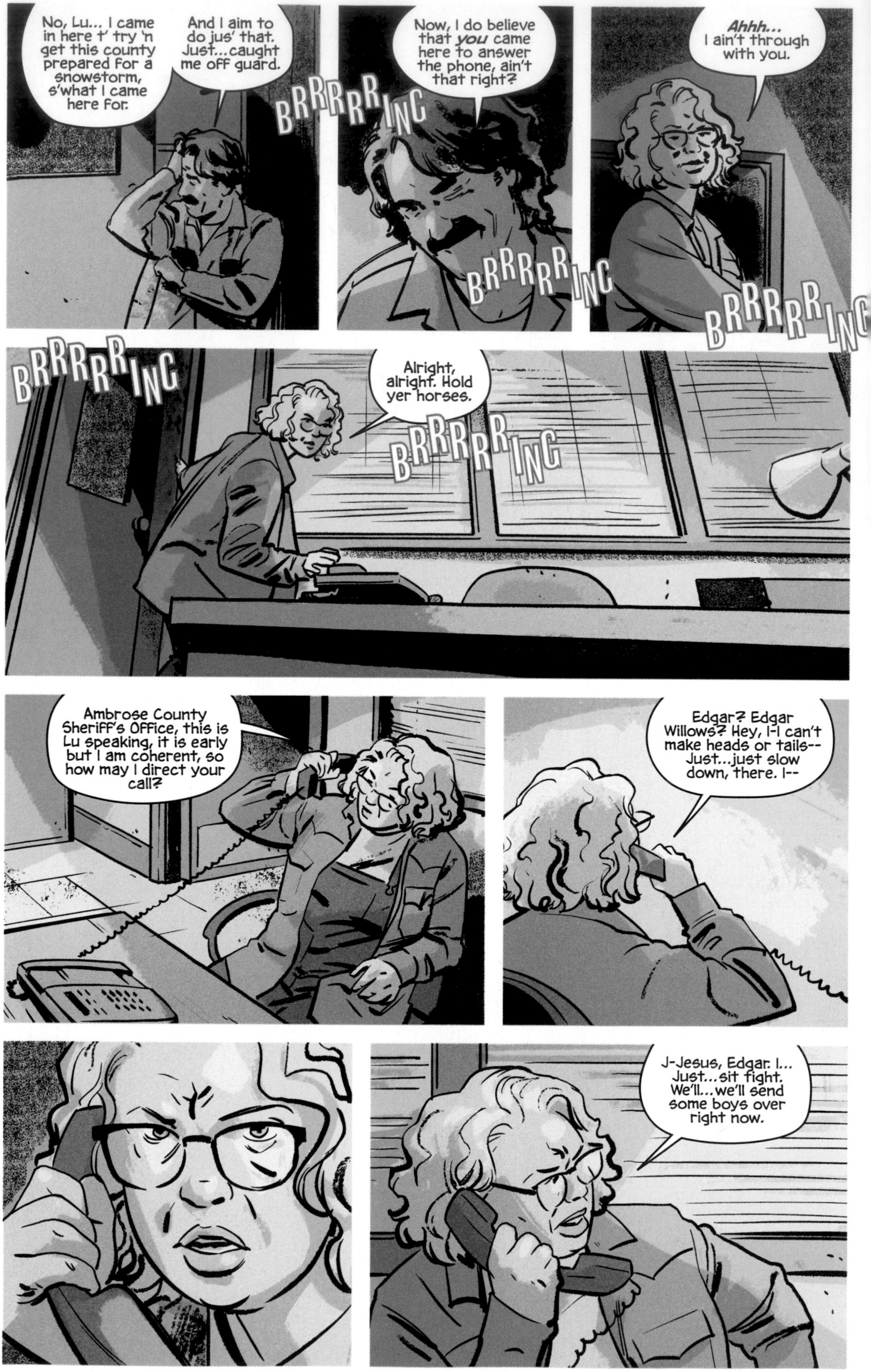
No, Lu... I came in here t' try 'n get this county prepared for a snowstorm, s'what I came here for.
And I aim to do jus' that. Just...caught me off guard.
BRRRRRING
Now, I do believe that *you* came here to answer the phone, ain't that right?
BRRRRRING
Ahhh... I ain't through with you.
BRRRRRING
BRRRRRING
Alright, alright. Hold yer horses.
BRRRRRING
Ambrose County Sheriff's Office, this is Lu speaking, it is early but I am coherent, so how may I direct your call?
Edgar? Edgar Willows? Hey, I-I can't make heads or tails-- Just...just slow down, there. I--
J-Jesus, Edgar. I... Just...sit tight. We'll...we'll send some boys over right now.

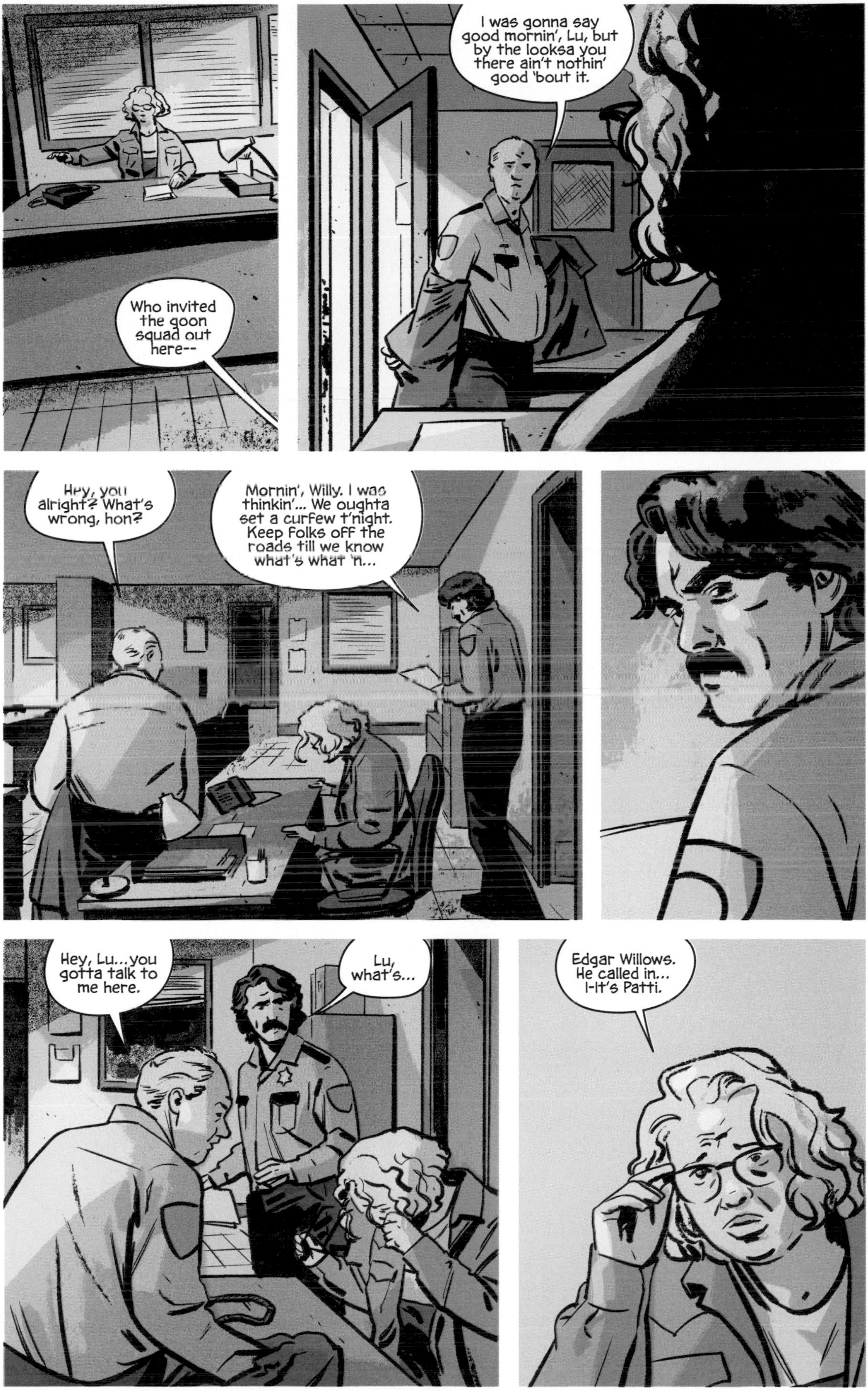
Who invited the goon squad out here--
I was gonna say good mornin', Lu, but by the looksa you there ain't nothin' good 'bout it.
Hey, you alright? What's wrong, hon?
Mornin', Willy. I was thinkin'... We oughta set a curfew t'night. Keep folks off the roads till we know what's what 'n...
Hey, Lu...you gotta talk to me here.
Lu, what's...
Edgar Willows. He called in... I-It's Patti.

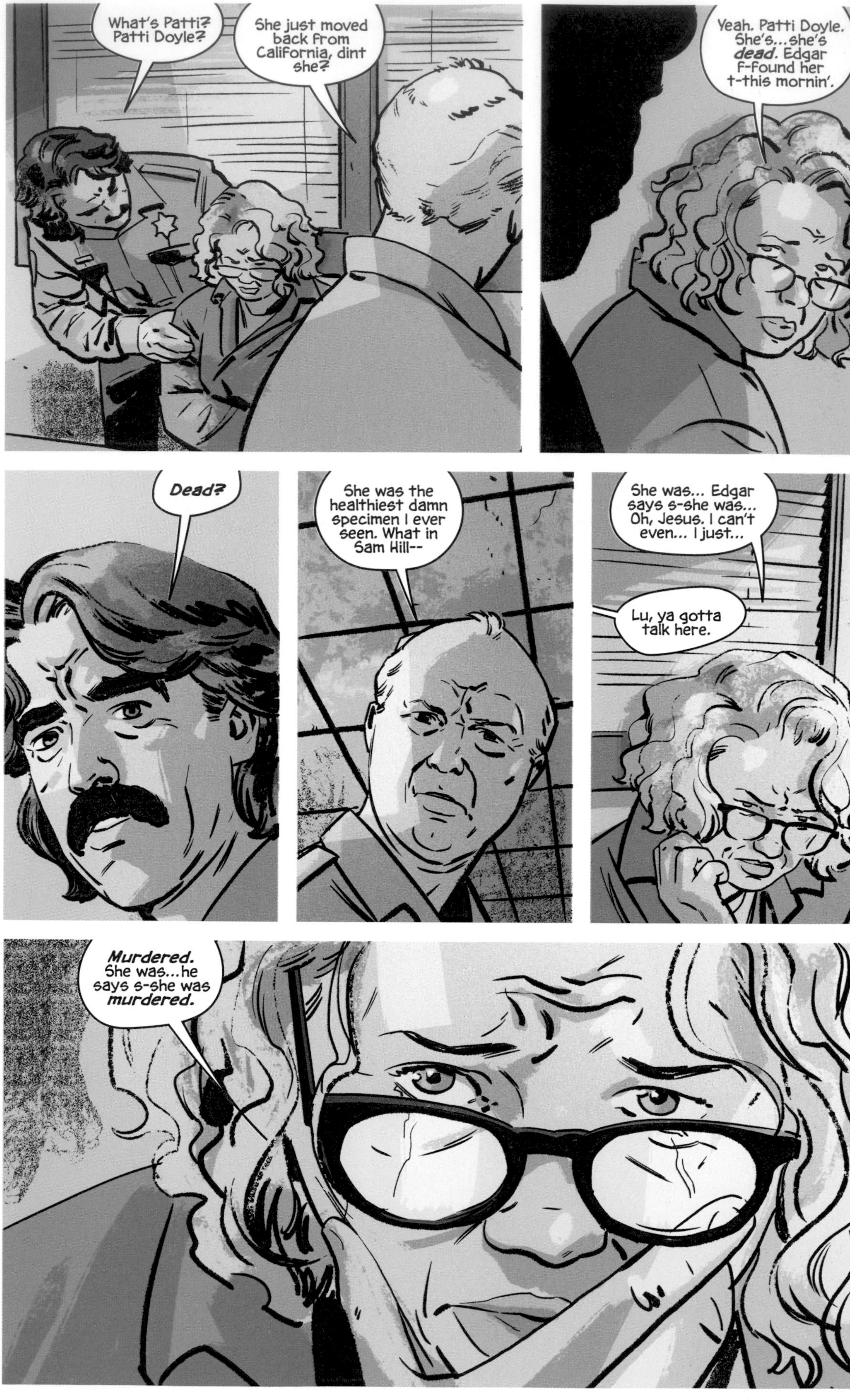
What's Patti? Patti Doyle?
She just moved back from California, dint she?
Yeah. Patti Doyle. She's...she's *dead.* Edgar f-found her t-this mornin'.
Dead?
She was the healthiest damn specimen I ever seen. What in Sam Hill--
She was... Edgar says s-she was... Oh, Jesus. I can't even... I just...
Lu, ya gotta talk here.
Murdered. She was...he says s-she was *murdered.*

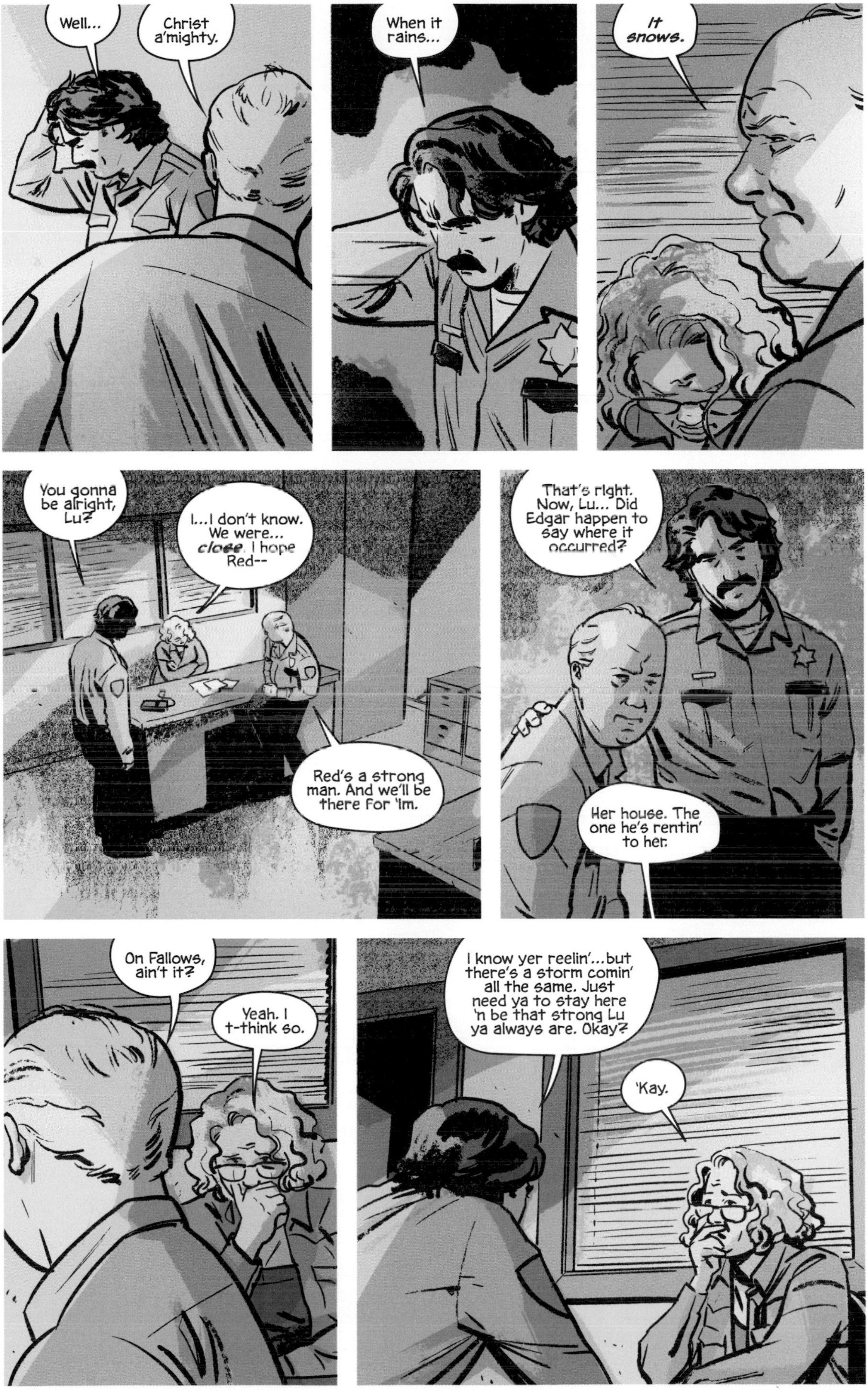
Well...
Christ a'mighty.
When it rains...
It snows.
You gonna be alright, Lu?
I...I don't know. We were... close. I hope Red--
Red's a strong man. And we'll be there for 'im.
That's right. Now, Lu... Did Edgar happen to say where it occurred?
Her house. The one he's rentin' to her.
On Fallows, ain't it?
Yeah. I t-think so.
I know yer reelin'...but there's a storm comin' all the same. Just need ya to stay here 'n be that strong Lu ya always are. Okay?
'Kay.

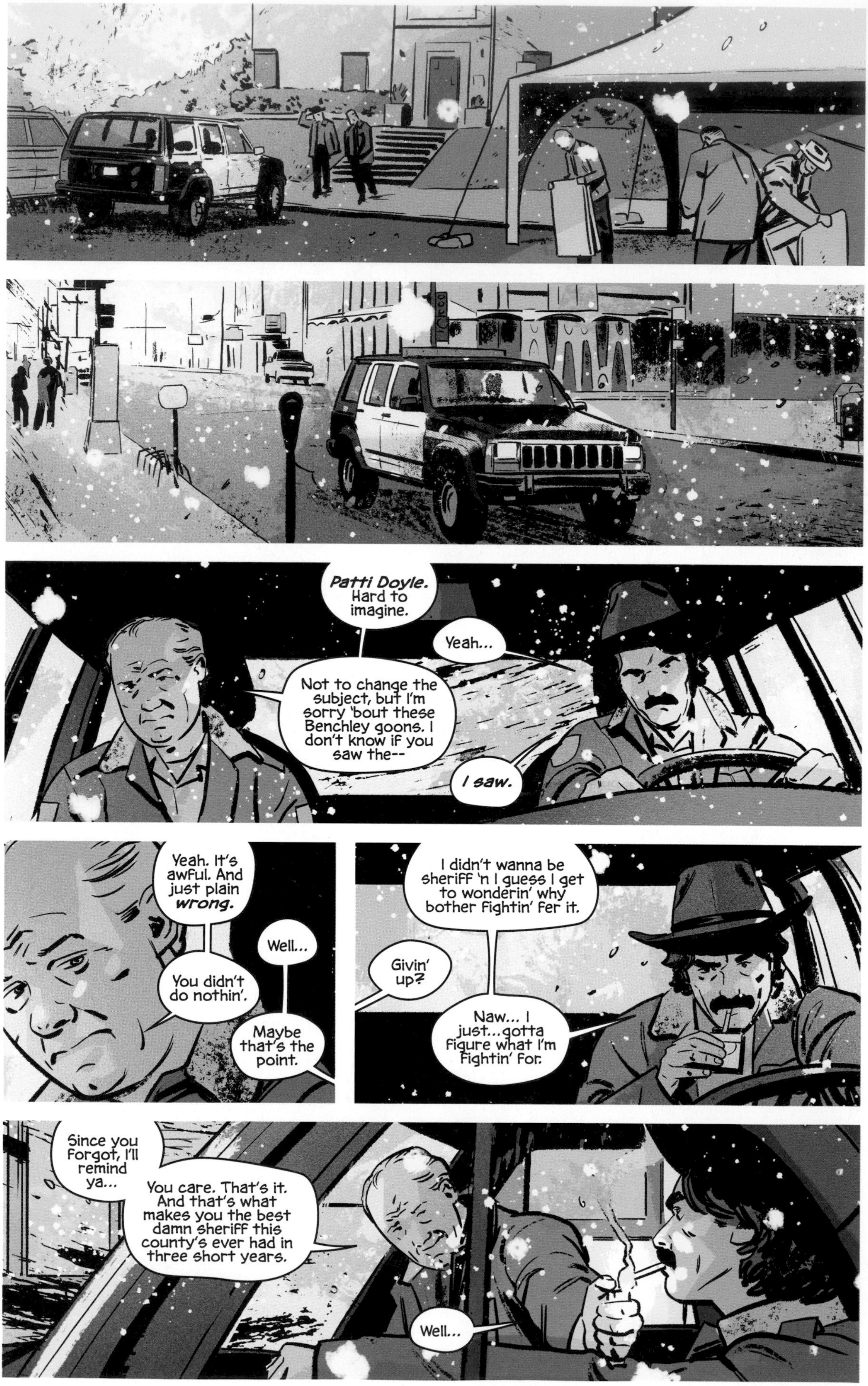

Patti Doyle. Hard to imagine.
Yeah...
Not to change the subject, but I'm sorry 'bout these Benchley goons. I don't know if you saw the--
I saw.
Yeah. It's awful. And just plain *wrong.*
Well...
You didn't do nothin'.
Maybe that's the point.
I didn't wanna be sheriff 'n I guess I get to wonderin' why bother fightin' fer it.
Givin' up?
Naw... I just...gotta figure what I'm fightin' for.
Since you forgot, I'll remind ya...
You care. That's it. And that's what makes you the best damn sheriff this county's ever had in three short years.
Well...

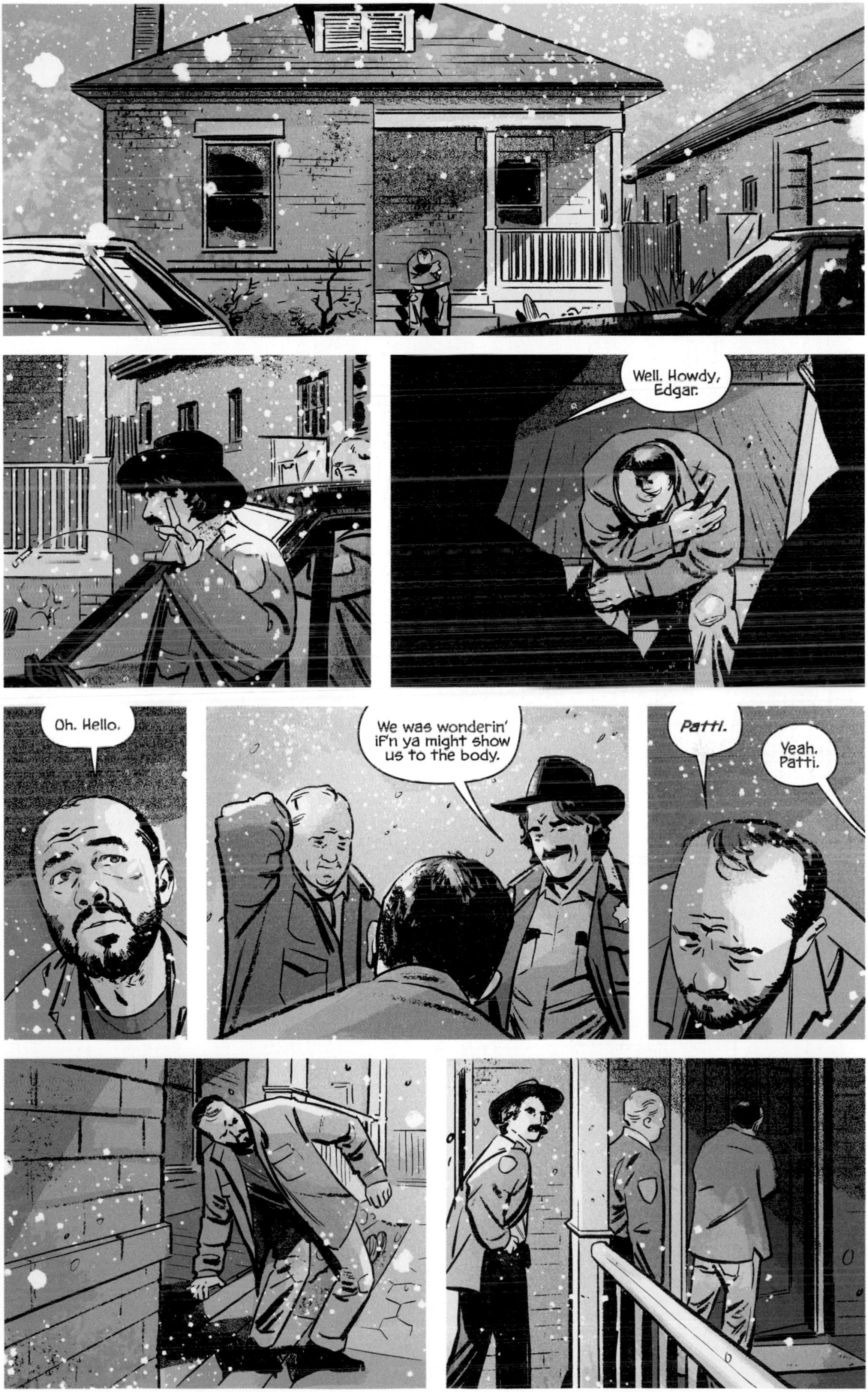
Well. Howdy, Edgar.
Oh. Hello.
We was wonderin' if'n ya might show us to the body.
Patti.
Yeah. Patti.

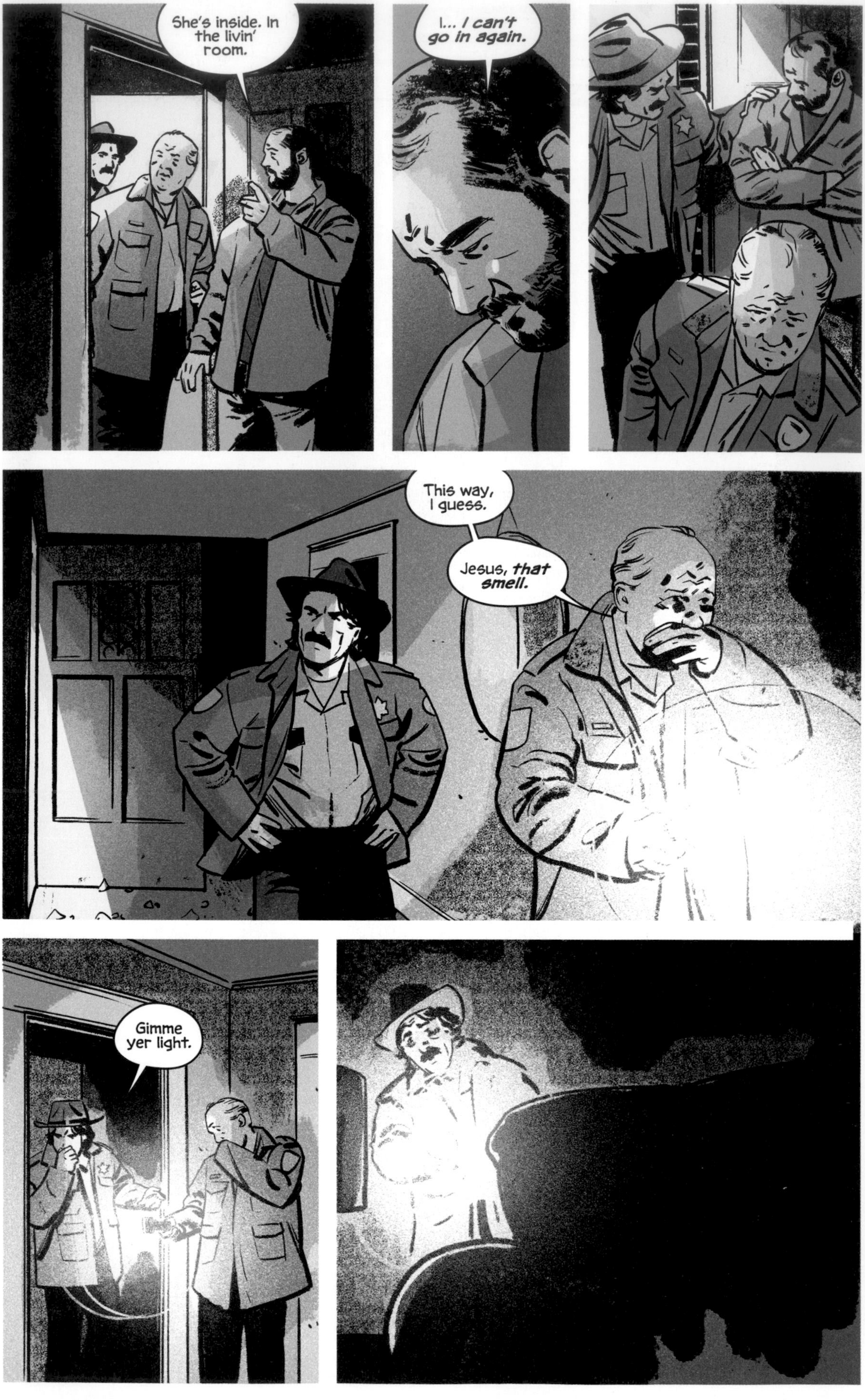
She's inside. In the livin' room.
I... *I can't go in again.*
This way, I guess.
Jesus, *that smell.*
Gimme yer light.

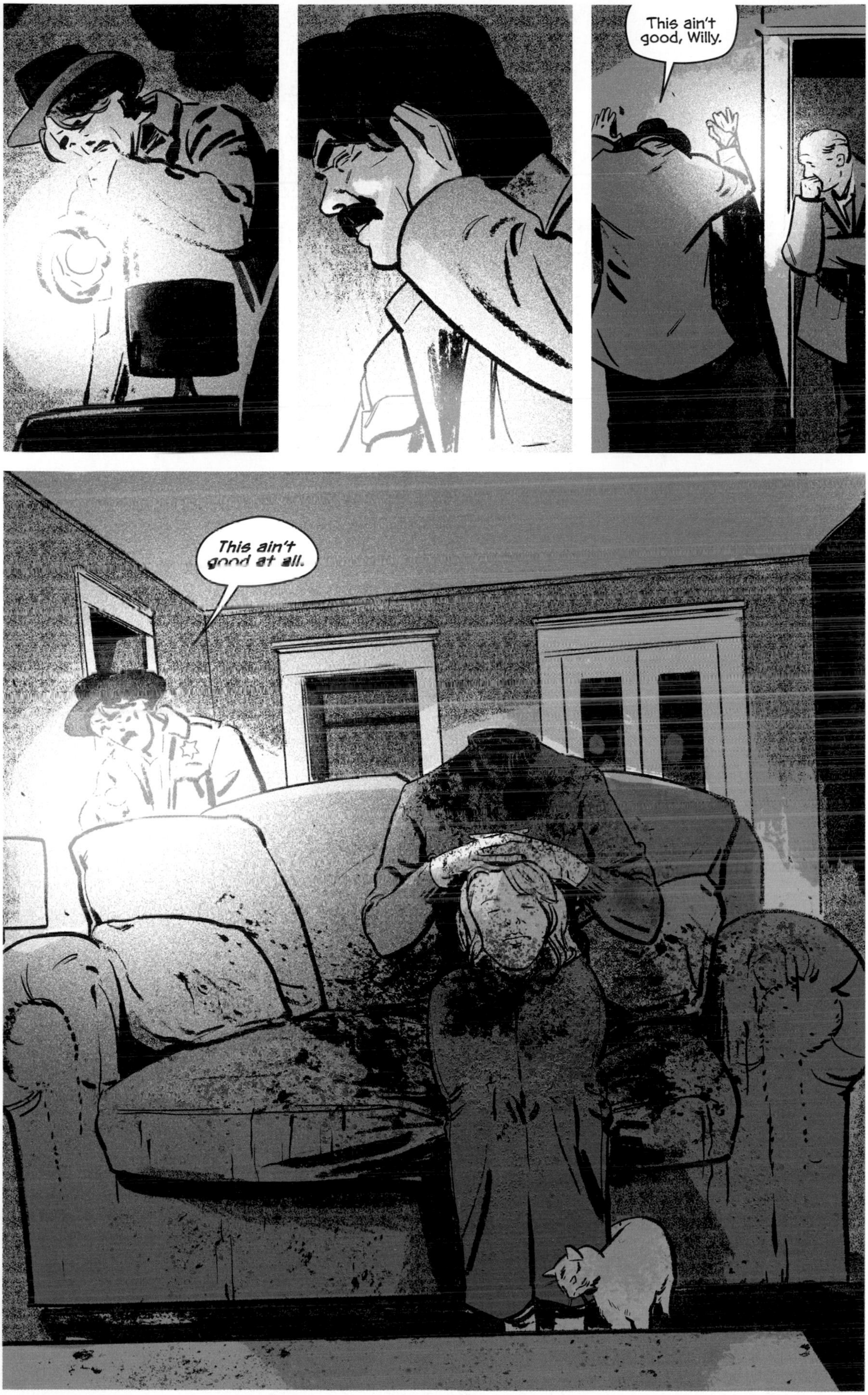
This ain't good, Willy.
This ain't good at all.

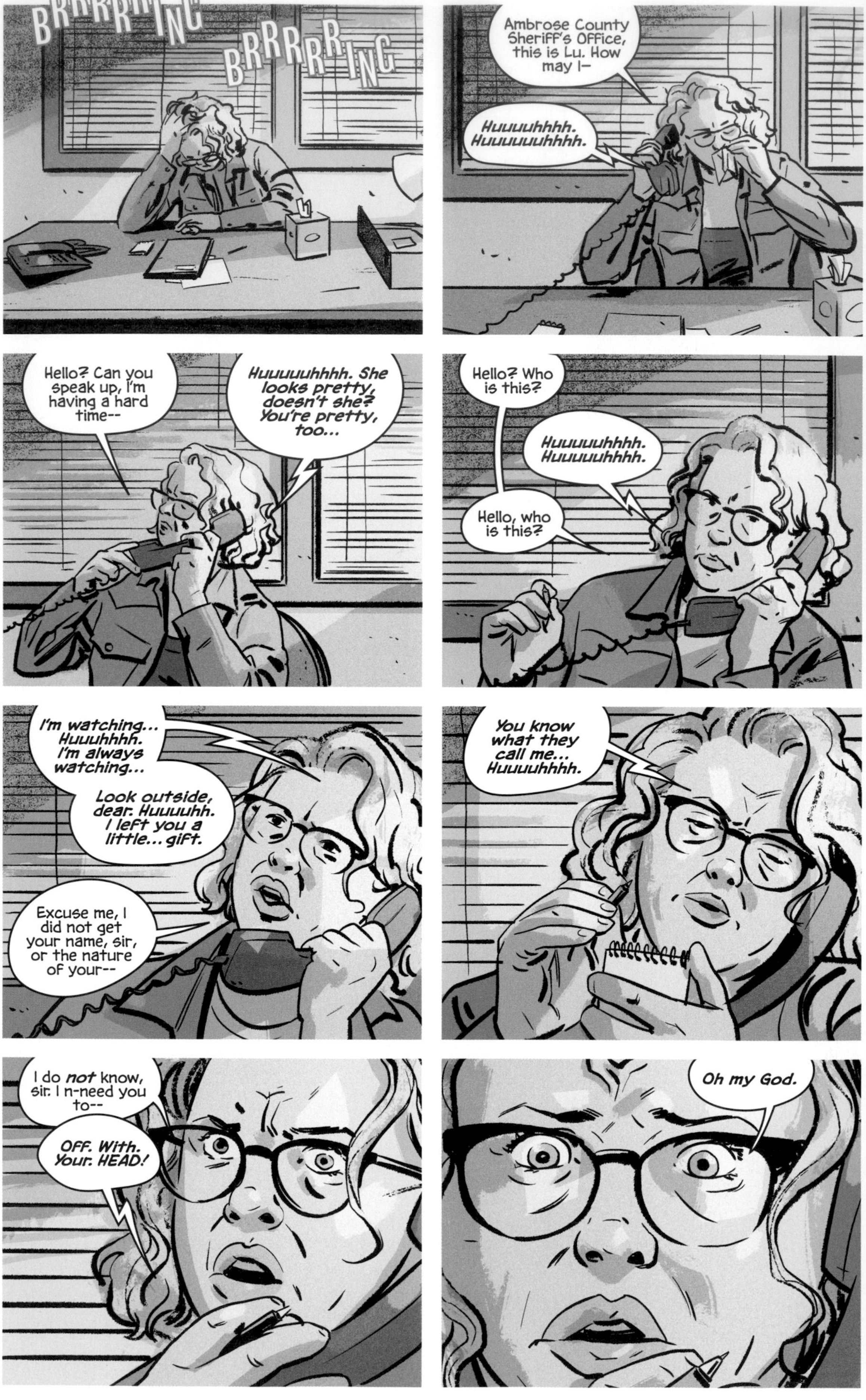
BRRRRRING
BRRRRRING
Ambrose County Sheriff's Office, this is Lu. How may I–
Huuuuhhhh. Huuuuuuhhhh.
Hello? Can you speak up, I'm having a hard time--
Huuuuuhhhh. She looks pretty, doesn't she? You're pretty, too...
Hello? Who is this?
Huuuuuhhhh. Huuuuuhhhh.
Hello, who is this?
I'm watching... Huuuhhhh. I'm always watching...
Look outside, dear. Huuuuhh. I left you a little... gift.
Excuse me, I did not get your name, sir, or the nature of your--
You know what they call me... Huuuuhhhh.
I do not know, sir. I n-need you to--
OFF. With. Your. HEAD!
Oh my God.

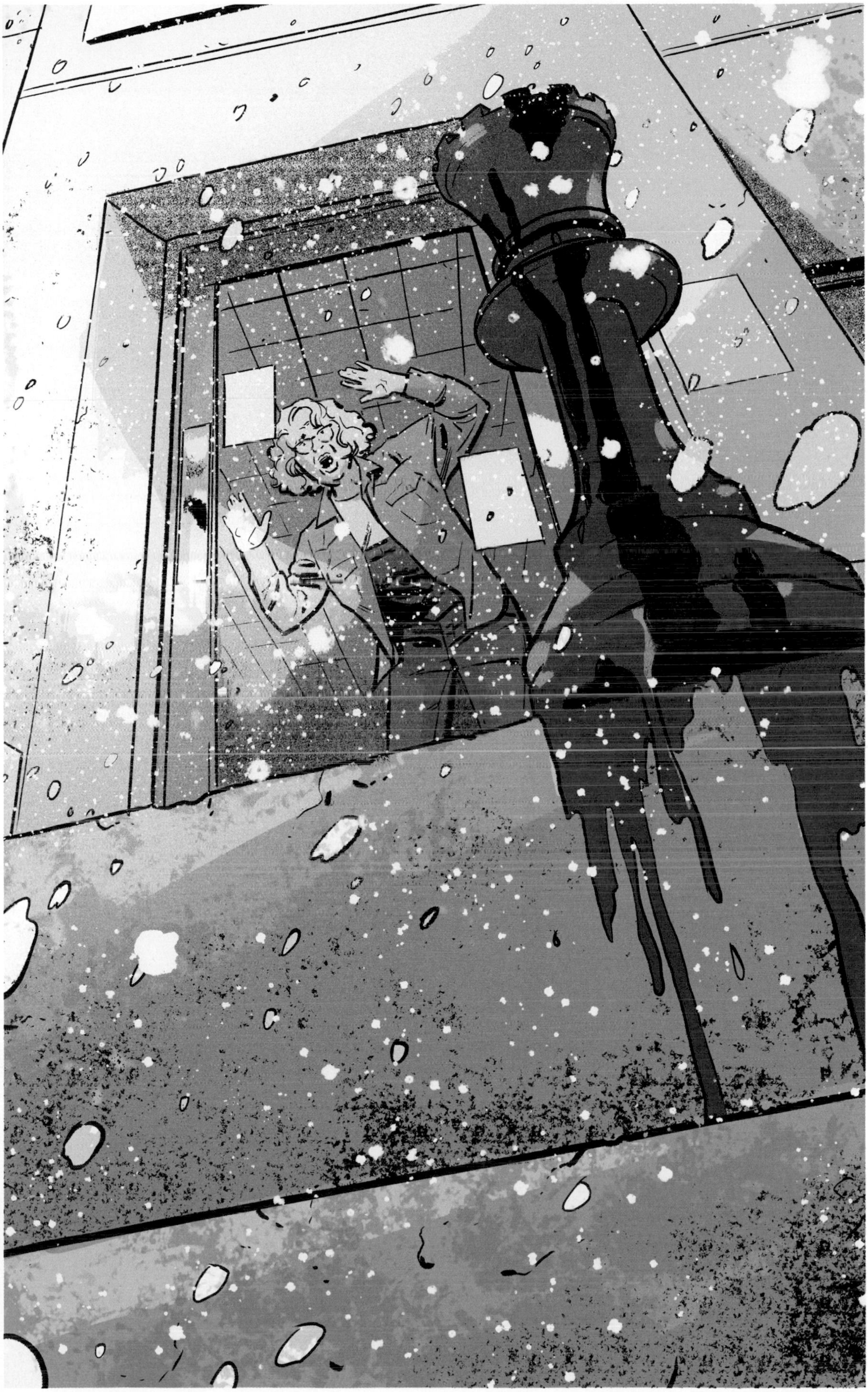

BAD NEWS AND THE RADIO PLEA

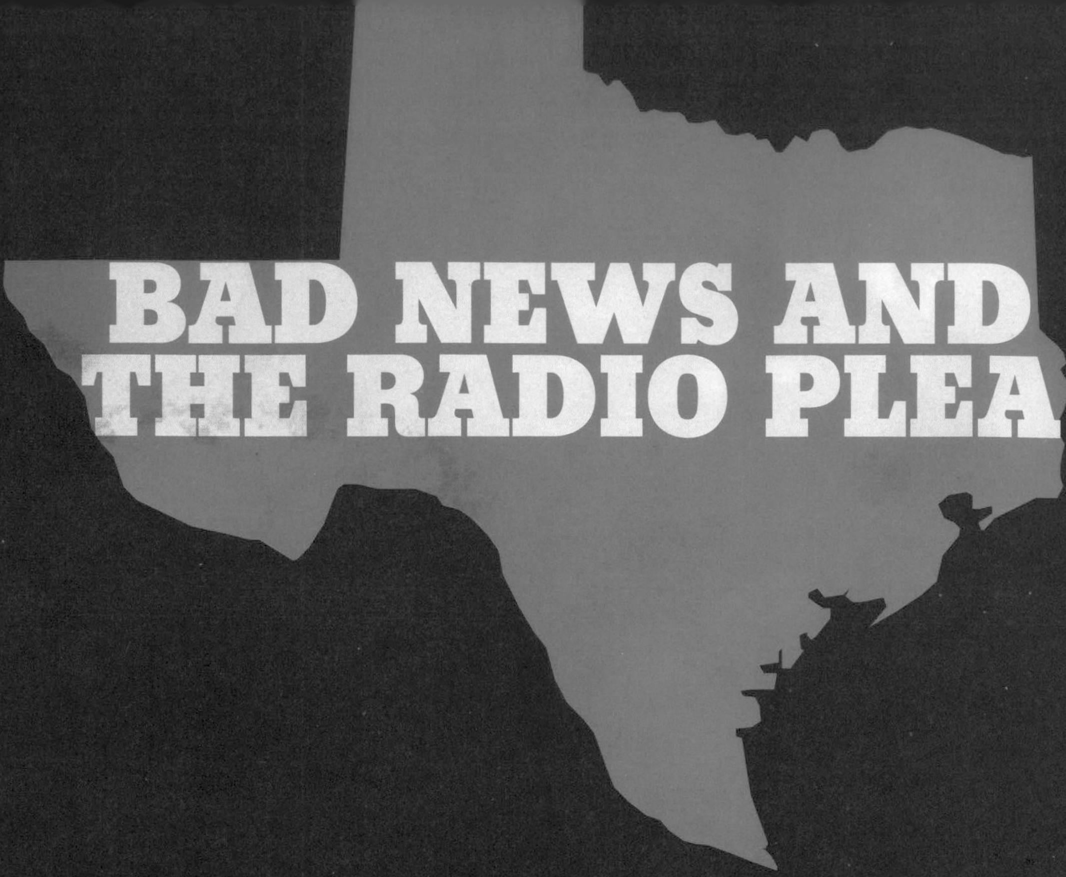

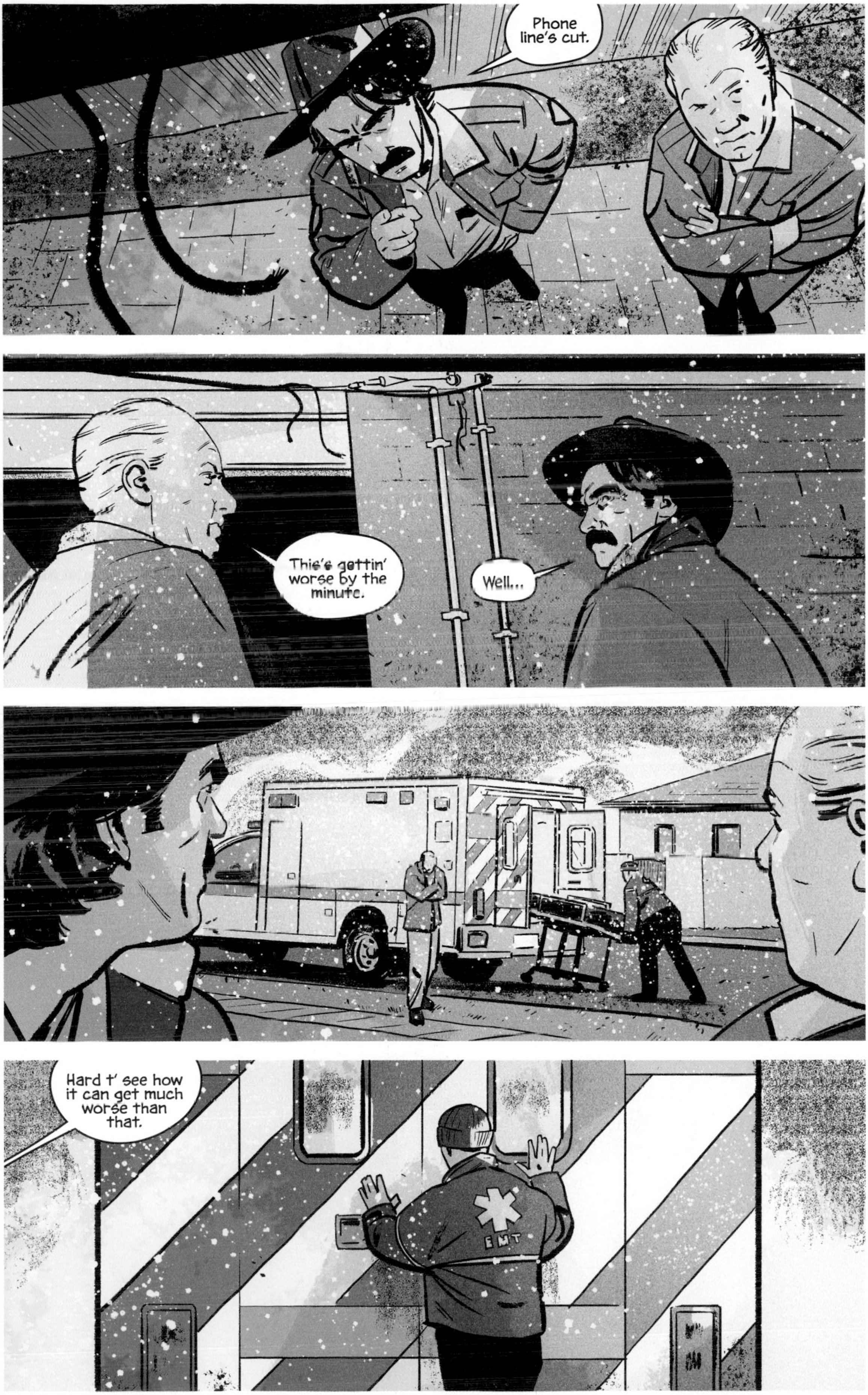
Phone line's cut.
This's gettin' worse by the minute.
Well...
Hard t' see how it can get much worse than that.
EMT

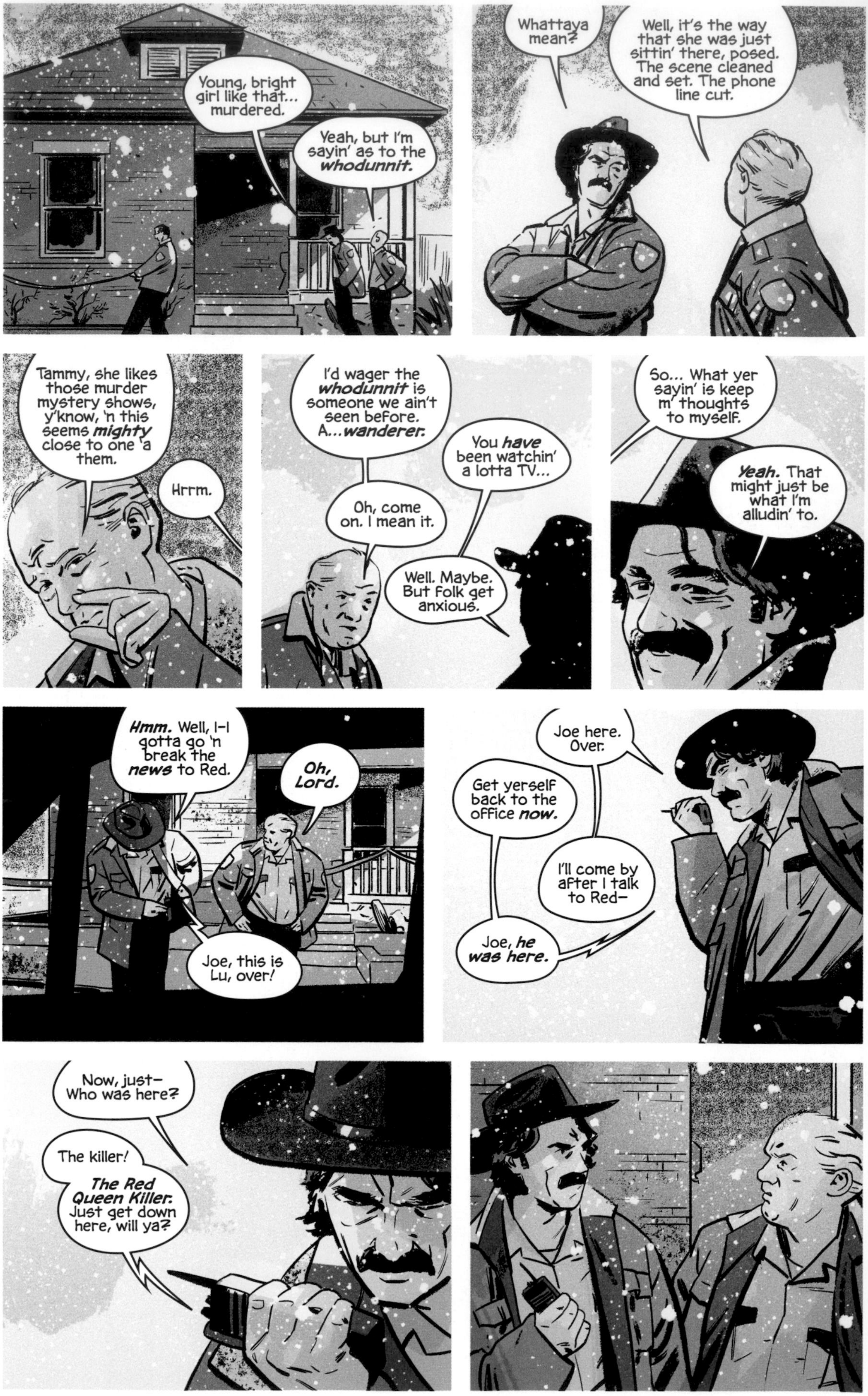

Young, bright girl like that... murdered.
Yeah, but I'm sayin' as to the *whodunnit.*
Whattaya mean?
Well, it's the way that she was just sittin' there, posed. The scene cleaned and set. The phone line cut.
Tammy, she likes those murder mystery shows, y'know, 'n this seems *mighty* close to one 'a them.
Hrrm.
I'd wager the *whodunnit* is someone we ain't seen before. A...*wanderer.*
You *have* been watchin' a lotta TV...
Oh, come on. I mean it.
Well. Maybe. But folk get anxious.
So... What yer sayin' is keep m' thoughts to myself.
Yeah. That might just be what I'm alludin' to.
Hmm. Well, I-I gotta go 'n break the *news* to Red.
Oh, Lord.
Joe, this is Lu, over!
Joe here. Over.
Get yerself back to the office *now.*
I'll come by after I talk to Red—
Joe, *he was here.*
Now, just— Who was here?
The killer!
The Red Queen Killer. Just get down here, will ya?

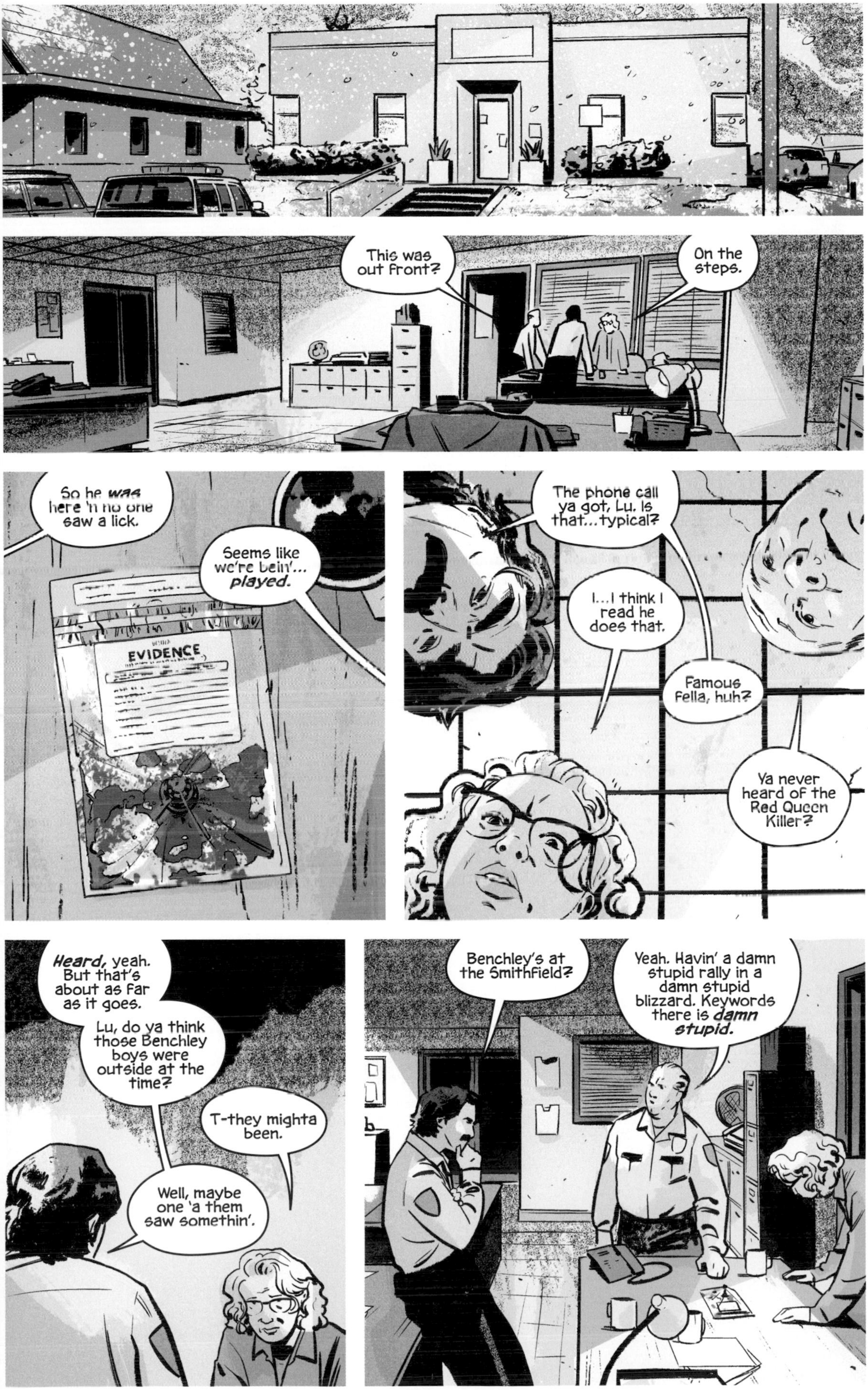

This was out front?
On the steps.
So he *was* here 'n no one saw a lick.
Seems like we're bein'... *played.*
EVIDENCE
The phone call ya got, Lu. Is that... typical?
I... I think I read he does that.
Famous fella, huh?
Ya never heard of the Red Queen Killer?
Heard, yeah. But that's about as far as it goes.
Lu, do ya think those Benchley boys were outside at the time?
T-they mighta been.
Well, maybe one 'a them saw somethin'.
Benchley's at the Smithfield?
Yeah. Havin' a damn stupid rally in a damn stupid blizzard. Keywords there is *damn stupid.*

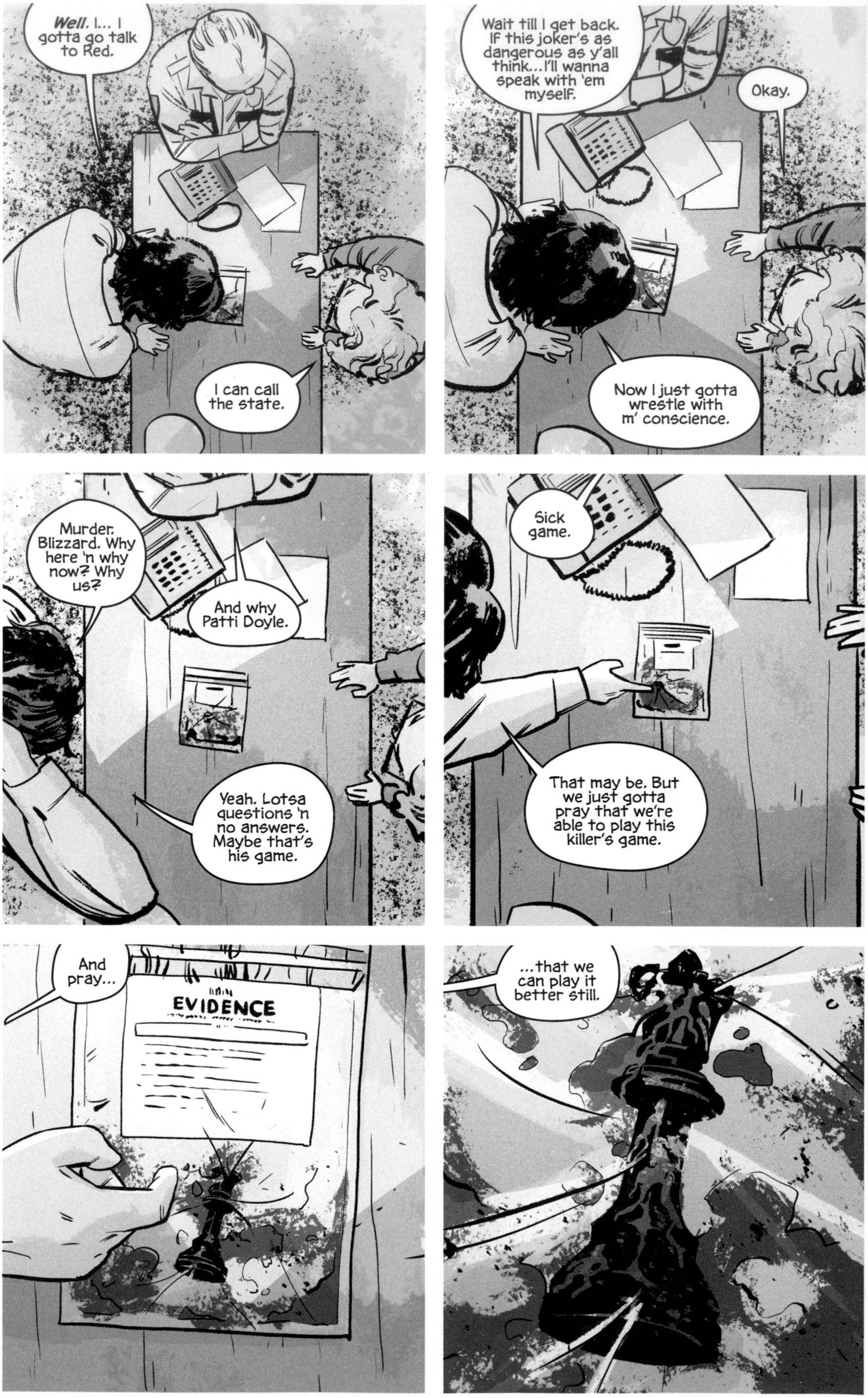
Well. I... I gotta go talk to Red.
I can call the state.
Wait till I get back. If this joker's as dangerous as y'all think... I'll wanna speak with 'em myself.
Okay.
Now I just gotta wrestle with m' conscience.
Murder. Blizzard. Why here 'n why now? Why us?
And why Patti Doyle.
Yeah. Lotsa questions 'n no answers. Maybe that's his game.
Sick game.
That may be. But we just gotta pray that we're able to play this killer's game.
And pray...
EVIDENCE
...that we can play it better still.

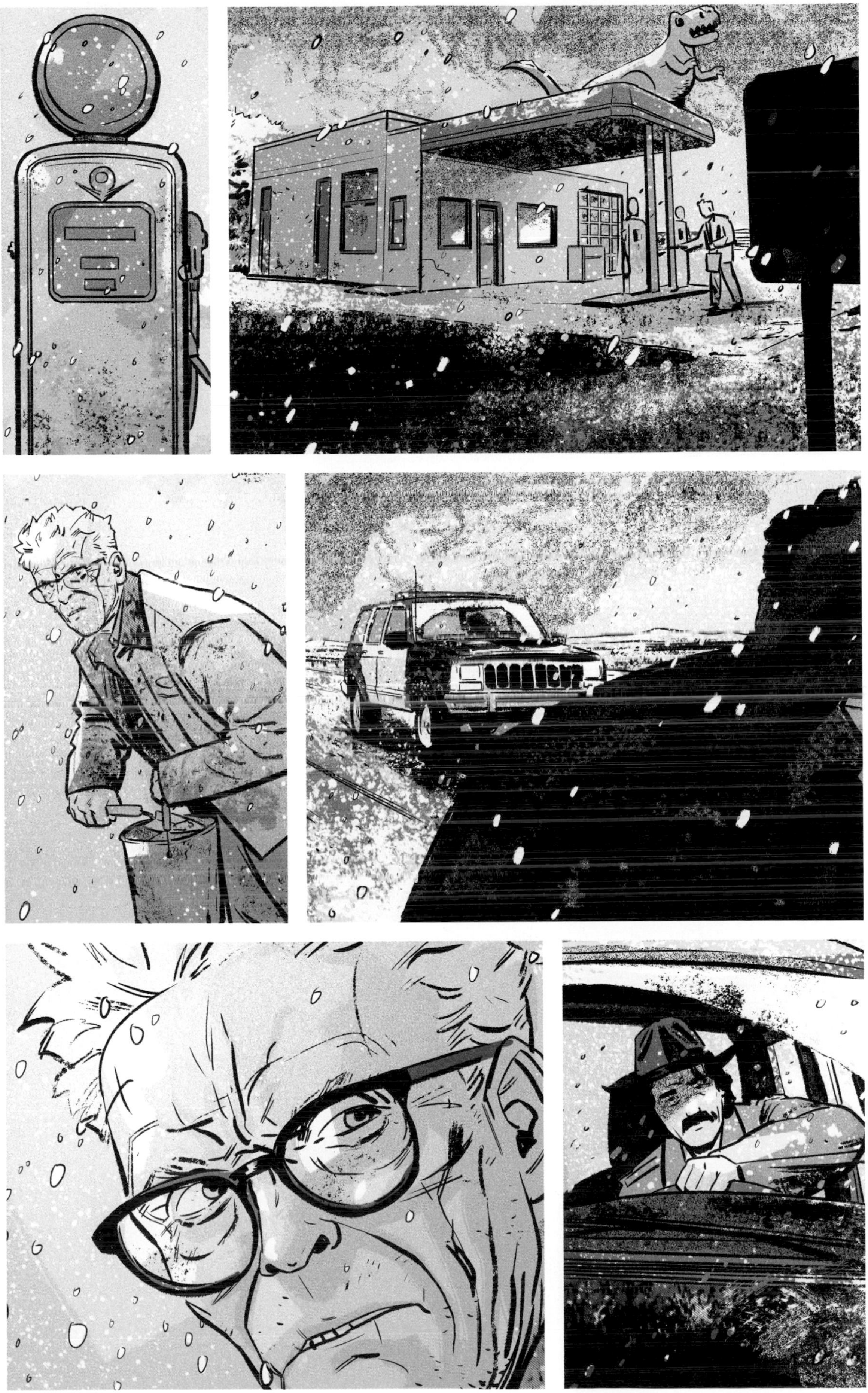

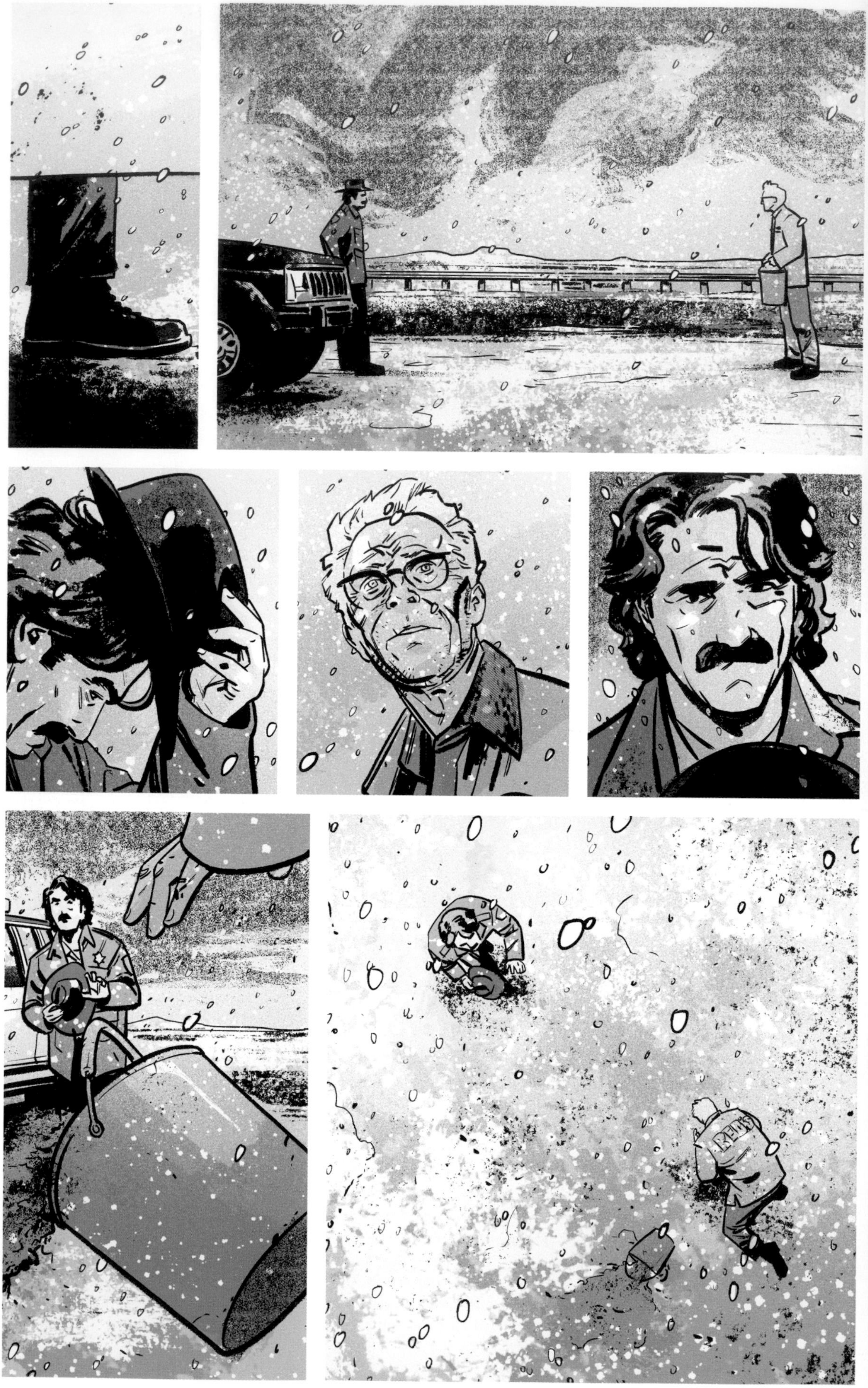

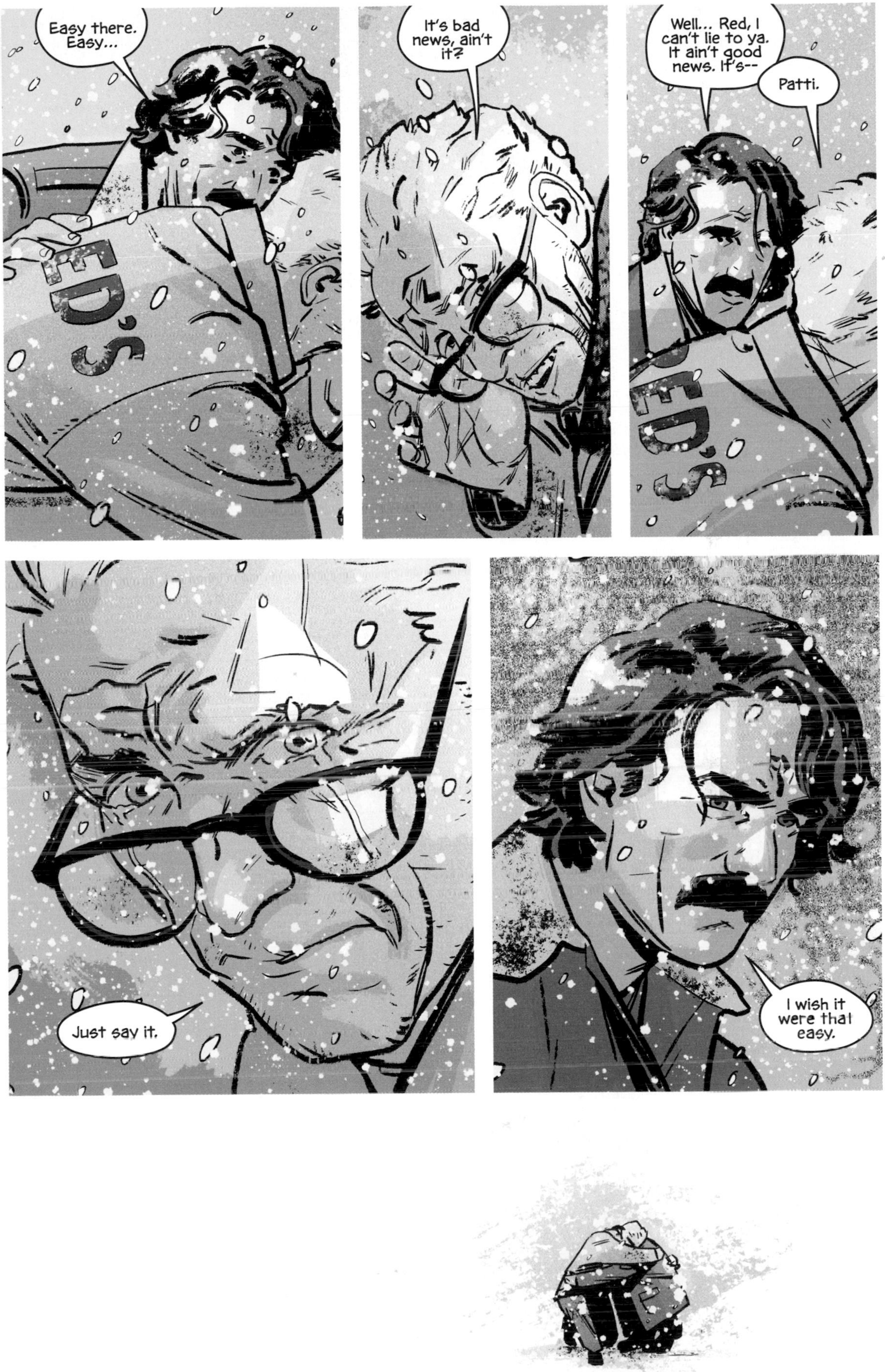
Easy there. Easy...
It's bad news, ain't it?
Well... Red, I can't lie to ya. It ain't good news. It's--
Patti.
Just say it.
I wish it were that easy.

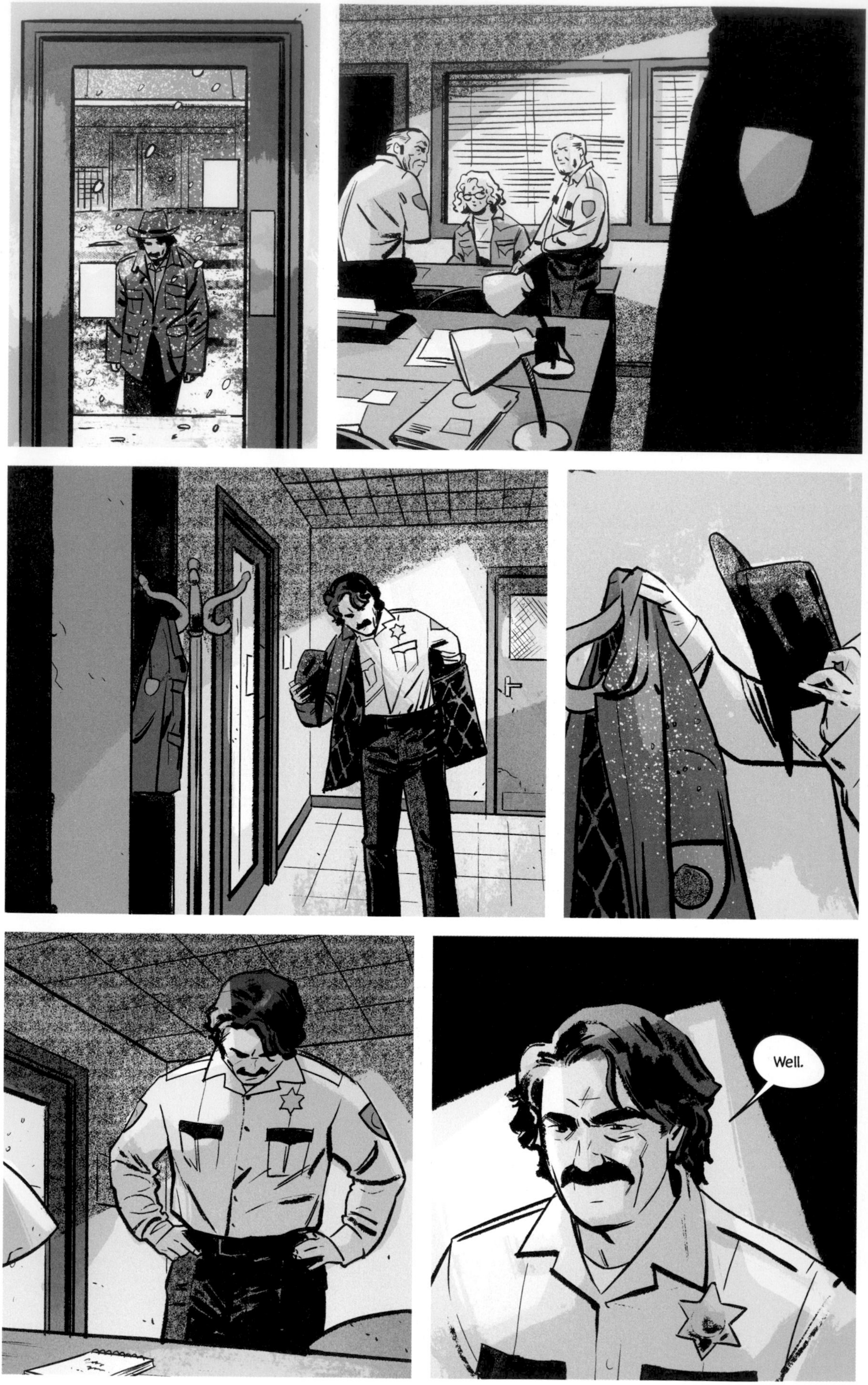
Well.

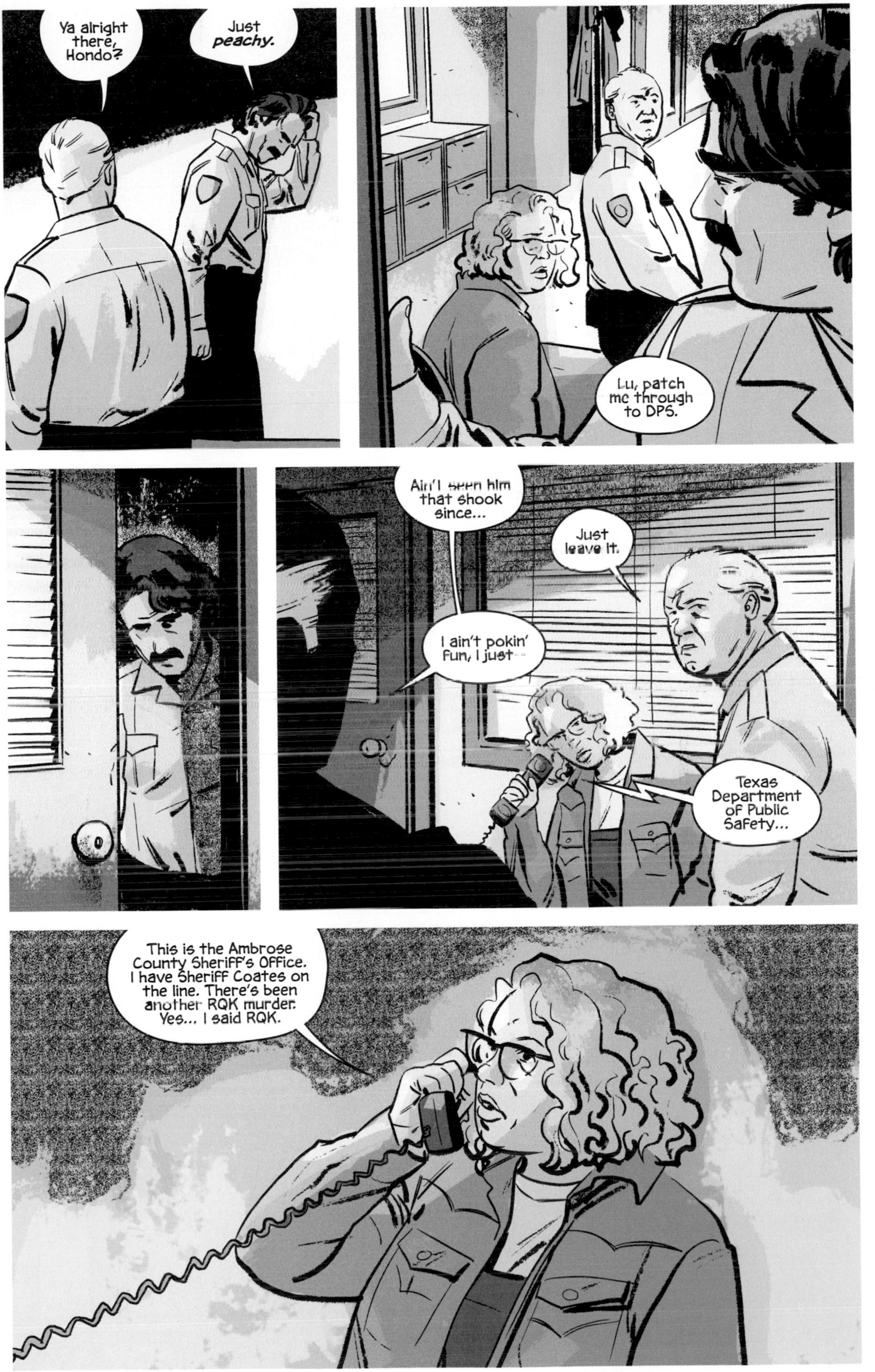

Ya alright there, Hondo?
Just *peachy.*
Lu, patch me through to DPS.
Ain't seen him that shook since...
Just leave it.
I ain't pokin' fun, I just--
Texas Department of Public Safety...
This is the Ambrose County Sheriff's Office. I have Sheriff Coates on the line. There's been another RQK murder. Yes... I said RQK.

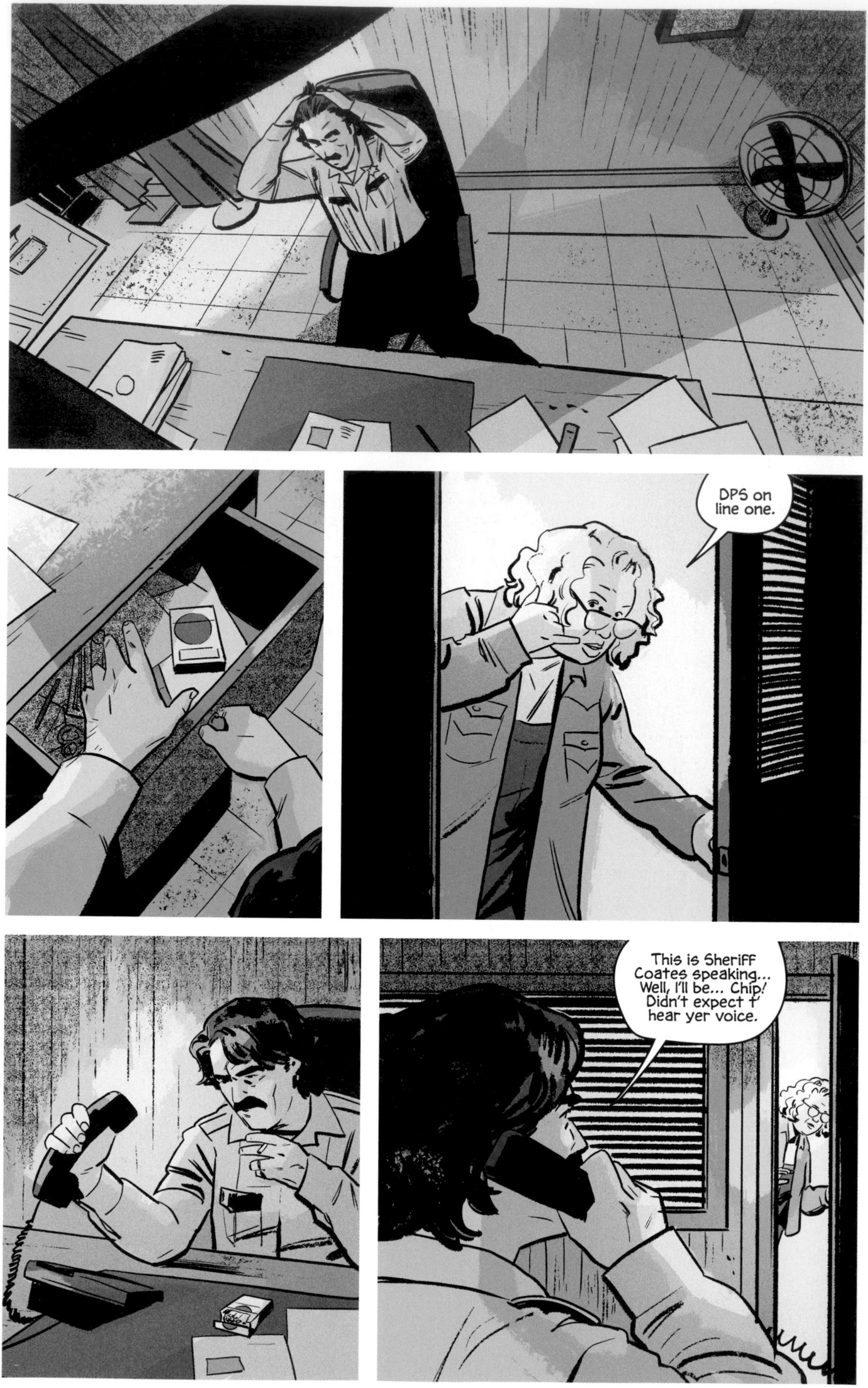
DPS on line one.
This is Sheriff Coates speaking... Well, I'll be... Chip! Didn't expect t' hear yer voice.

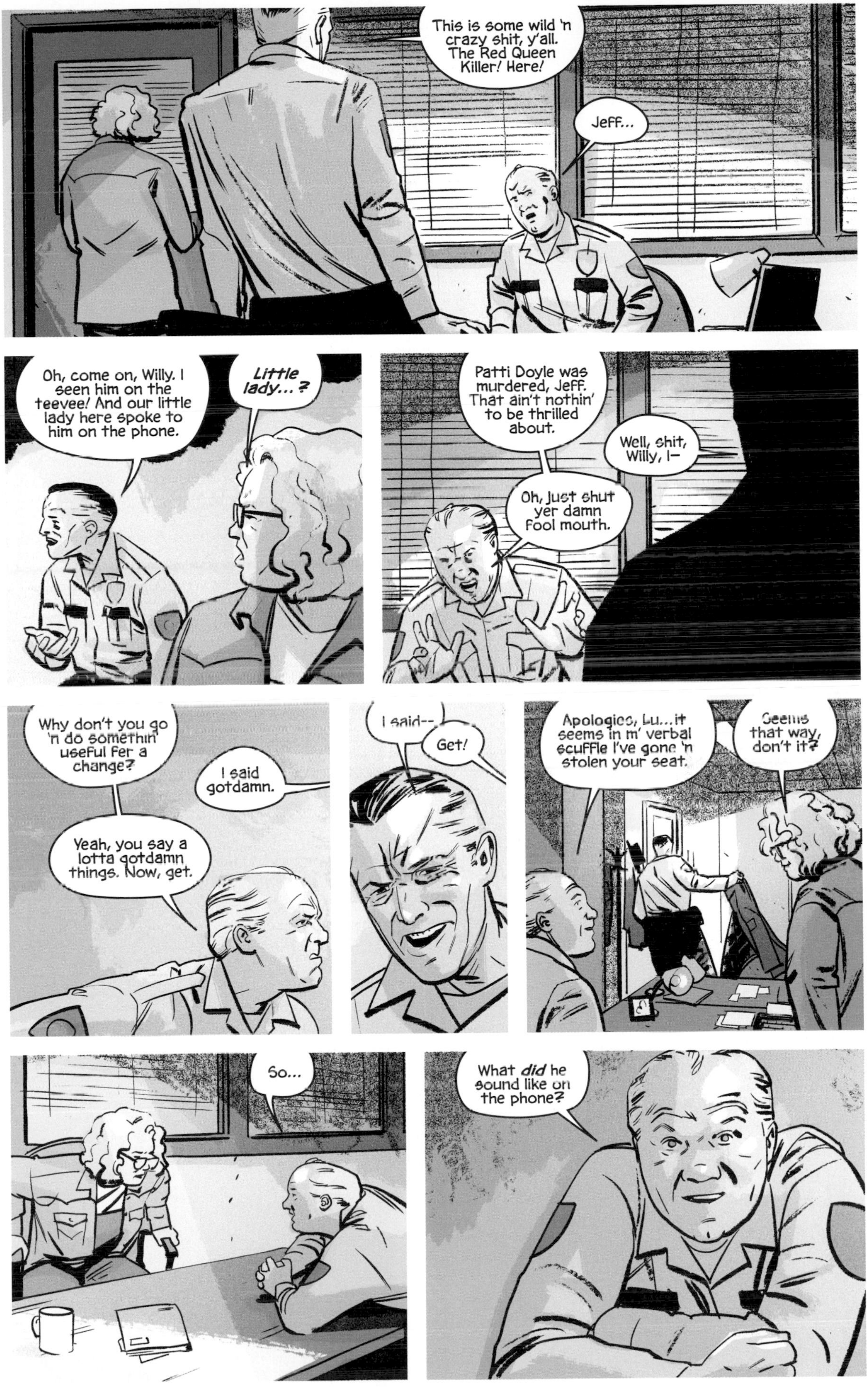

This is some wild 'n crazy shit, y'all. The Red Queen Killer! Here!
Jeff...
Oh, come on, Willy. I seen him on the teevee! And our little lady here spoke to him on the phone.
Little lady...?
Patti Doyle was murdered, Jeff. That ain't nothin' to be thrilled about.
Well, shit, Willy, I–
Oh, just shut yer damn fool mouth.
Why don't you go 'n do somethin' useful fer a change?
I said gotdamn.
Yeah, you say a lotta gotdamn things. Now, get.
I said--
Get!
Apologies, Lu...it seems in m' verbal scuffle I've gone 'n stolen your seat.
Seems that way, don't it?
So...
What *did* he sound like on the phone?

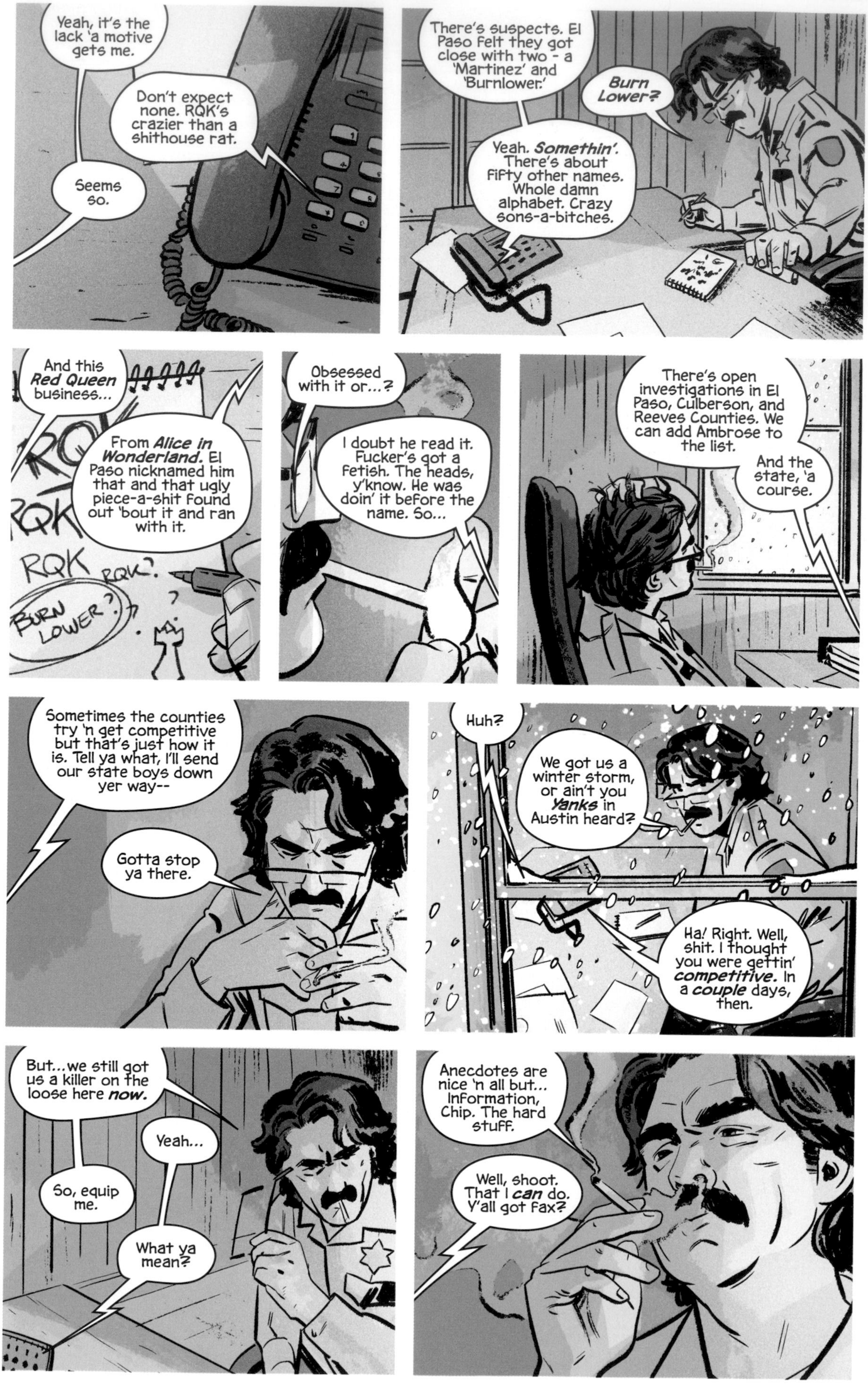
Yeah, it's the lack 'a motive gets me.
Don't expect none. RQK's crazier than a shithouse rat.
Seems so.
There's suspects. El Paso felt they got close with two - a 'Martinez' and 'Burnlower.'
Burn Lower?
Yeah. Somethin'. There's about fifty other names. Whole damn alphabet. Crazy sons-a-bitches.
And this Red Queen business...
From Alice in Wonderland. El Paso nicknamed him that and that ugly piece-a-shit found out 'bout it and ran with it.
RQK
RQK
RQK
RQK?
BURN LOWER?
Obsessed with it or...?
I doubt he read it. Fucker's got a fetish. The heads, y'know. He was doin' it before the name. So...
There's open investigations in El Paso, Culberson, and Reeves Counties. We can add Ambrose to the list.
And the state, 'a course.
Sometimes the counties try 'n get competitive but that's just how it is. Tell ya what, I'll send our state boys down yer way--
Gotta stop ya there.
Huh?
We got us a winter storm, or ain't you Yanks in Austin heard?
Ha! Right. Well, shit. I thought you were gettin' competitive. In a couple days, then.
But...we still got us a killer on the loose here now.
Yeah...
So, equip me.
What ya mean?
Anecdotes are nice 'n all but... Information, Chip. The hard stuff.
Well, shoot. That I can do. Y'all got fax?

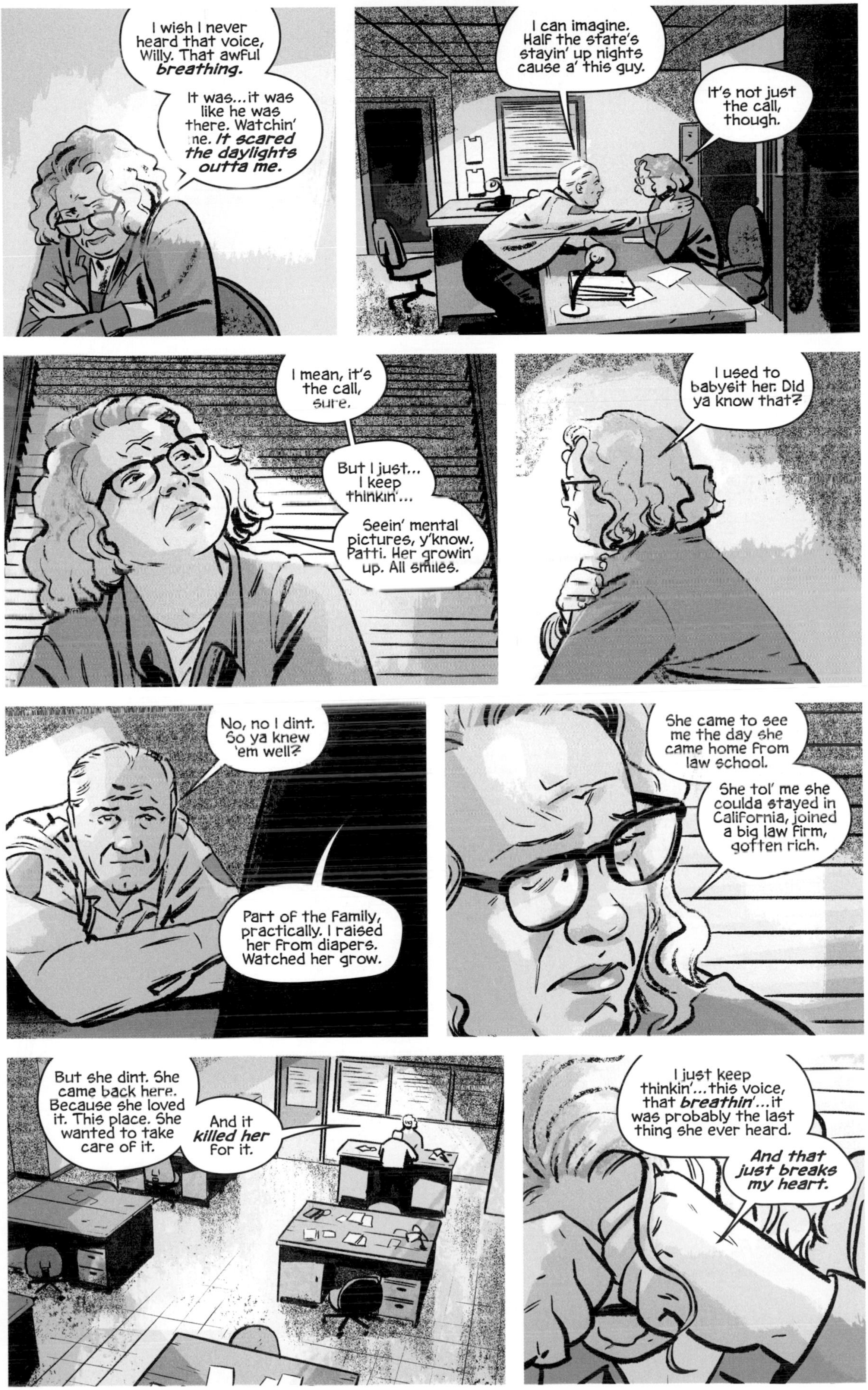
I wish I never heard that voice, Willy. That awful *breathing.*
It was... it was like he was there. Watchin' me. ***It scared the daylights outta me.***
I can imagine. Half the state's stayin' up nights cause a' this guy.
It's not just the call, though.
I mean, it's the call, sure.
But I just... I keep thinkin'...
Seein' mental pictures, y'know. Patti. Her growin' up. All smiles.
I used to babysit her. Did ya know that?
No, no I dint. So ya knew 'em well?
Part of the family, practically. I raised her from diapers. Watched her grow.
She came to see me the day she came home from law school.
She tol' me she coulda stayed in California, joined a big law firm, gotten rich.
But she dint. She came back here. Because she loved it. This place. She wanted to take care of it.
And it ***killed her*** for it.
I just keep thinkin'... this voice, that *breathin'*... it was probably the last thing she ever heard.
And that just breaks my heart.

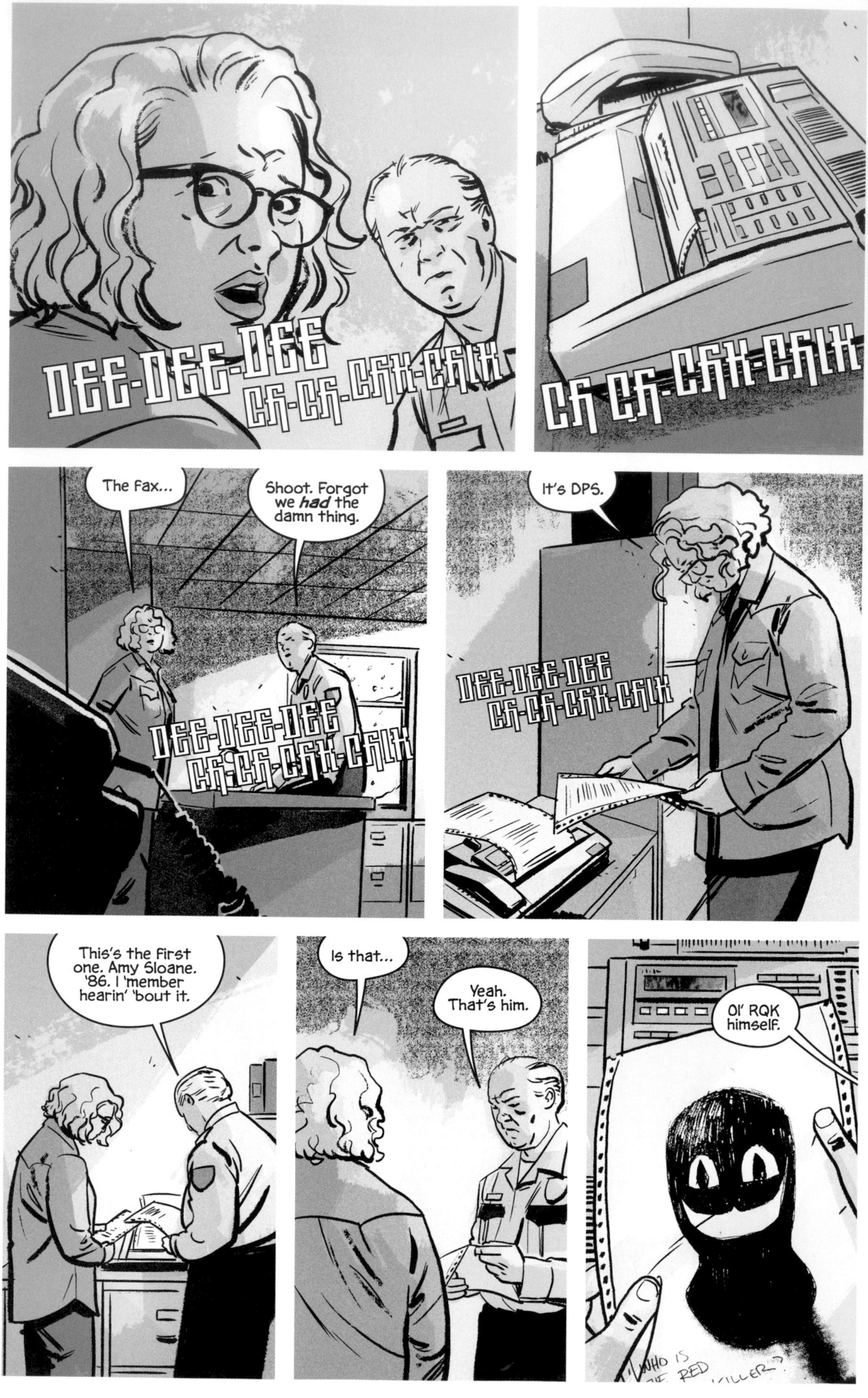
DEE-DEE-DEE
CH-CH-CHK-CHLK
CH CH-CHK-CHLK
The fax...
Shoot. Forgot we *had* the damn thing.
DEE-DEE-DEE
CH-CH-CHK-CHLK
It's DPS.
DEE-DEE-DEE
CH-CH-CHK-CHLK
This's the first one. Amy Sloane. '86. I 'member hearin' 'bout it.
Is that...
Yeah. That's him.
Ol' RQK himself.
WHO IS
RED
KILLER?

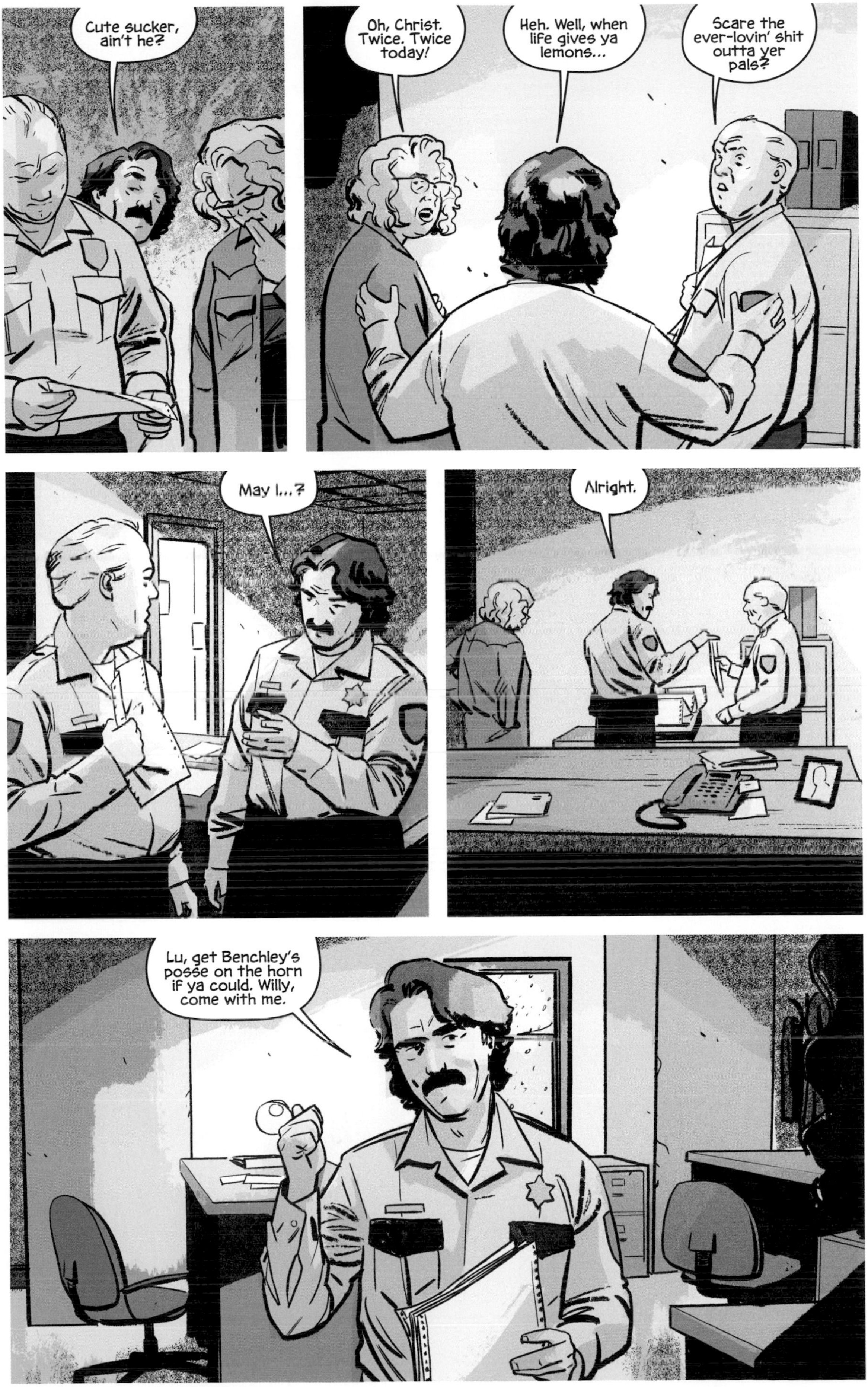
Cute sucker, ain't he?
Oh, Christ. Twice. Twice today!
Heh. Well, when life gives ya lemons...
Scare the ever-lovin' shit outta yer pals?
May I...?
Alright.
Lu, get Benchley's posse on the horn if ya could. Willy, come with me.

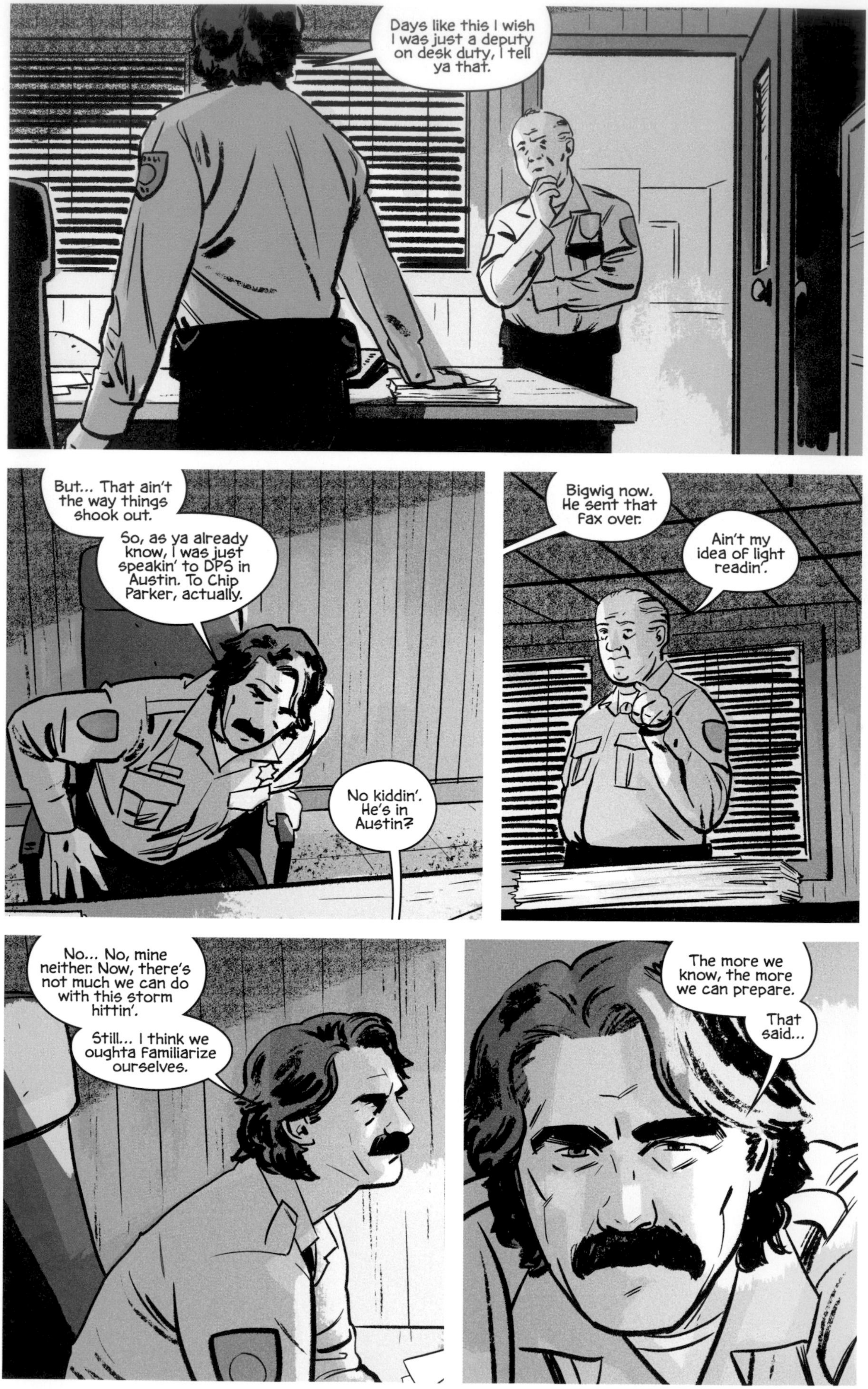

Days like this I wish I was just a deputy on desk duty, I tell ya that.
But... That ain't the way things shook out.
So, as ya already know, I was just speakin' to DPS in Austin. To Chip Parker, actually.
No kiddin'. He's in Austin?
Bigwig now. He sent that fax over.
Ain't my idea of light readin'.
No... No, mine neither. Now, there's not much we can do with this storm hittin'.
Still... I think we oughta familiarize ourselves.
The more we know, the more we can prepare.
That said...

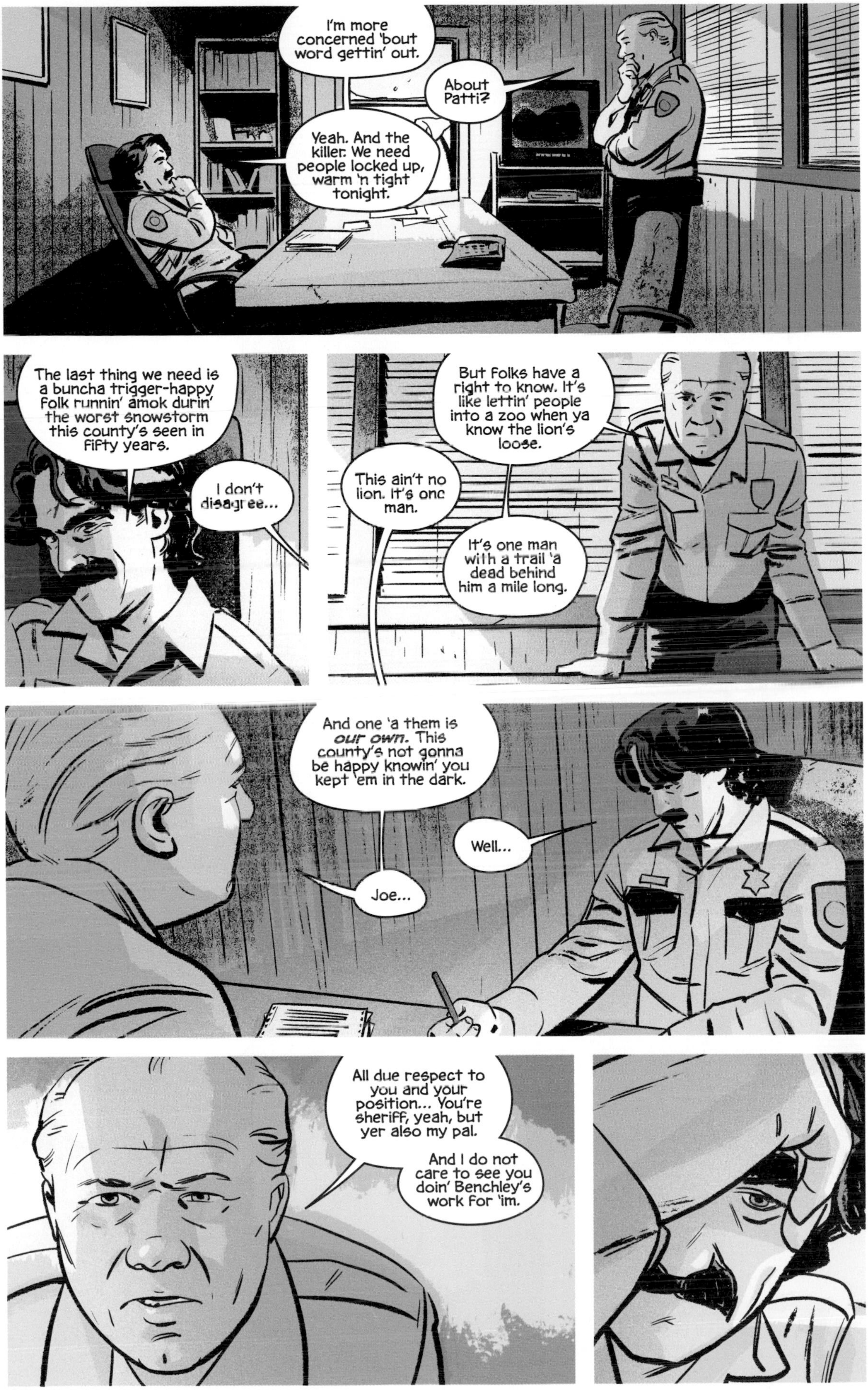
I'm more concerned 'bout word gettin' out.
About Patti?
Yeah. And the killer. We need people locked up, warm 'n tight tonight.
The last thing we need is a buncha trigger-happy folk runnin' amok durin' the worst snowstorm this county's seen in fifty years.
I don't disagree...
But folks have a right to know. It's like lettin' people into a zoo when ya know the lion's loose.
This ain't no lion. It's one man.
It's one man with a trail 'a dead behind him a mile long.
And one 'a them is *our own*. This county's not gonna be happy knowin' you kept 'em in the dark.
Well...
Joe...
All due respect to you and your position... You're sheriff, yeah, but yer also my pal.
And I do not care to see you doin' Benchley's work for 'im.

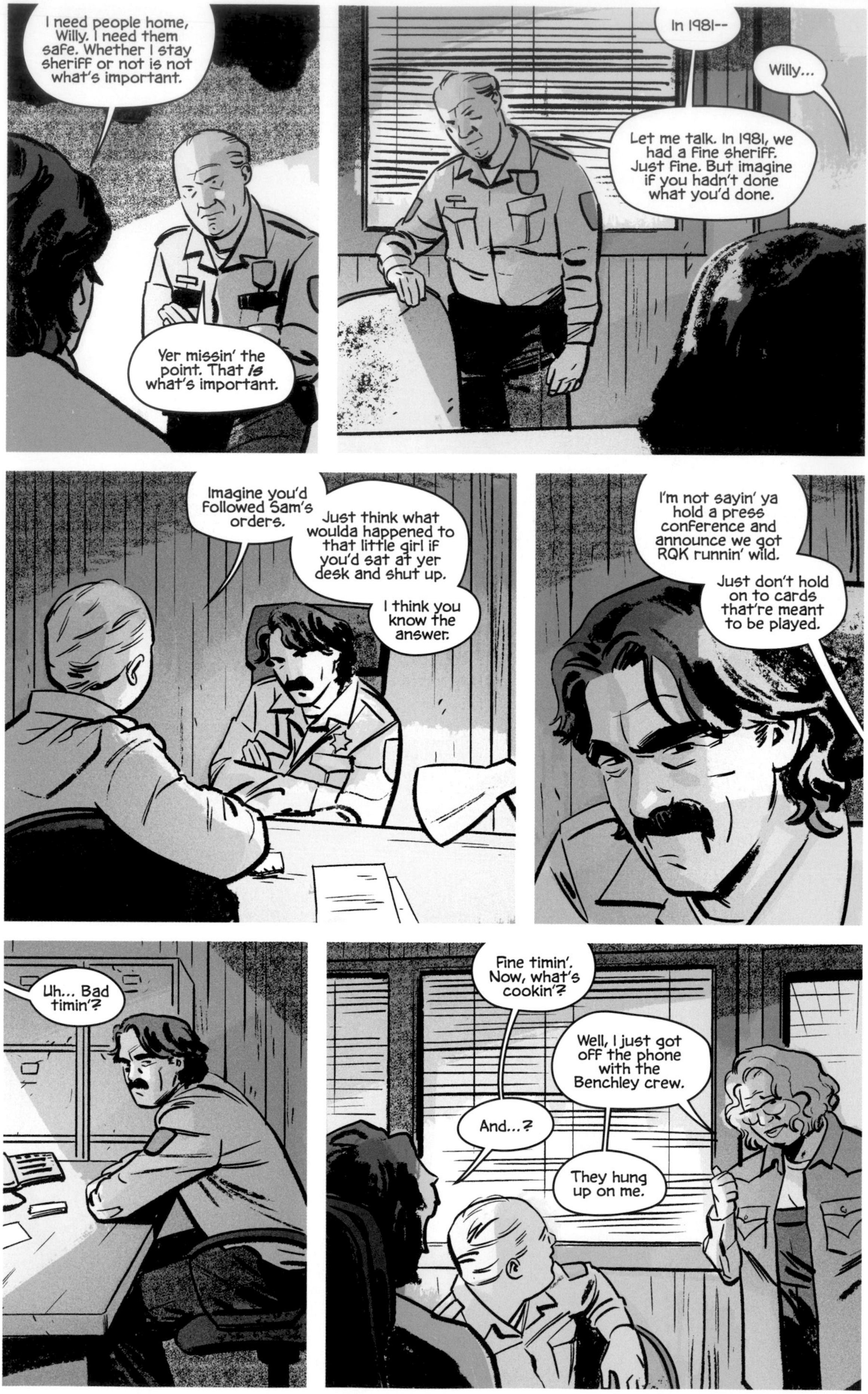
I need people home, Willy. I need them safe. Whether I stay sheriff or not is not what's important.
Yer missin' the point. That *is* what's important.
In 1981--
Willy...
Let me talk. In 1981, we had a fine sheriff. Just fine. But imagine if you hadn't done what you'd done.
Imagine you'd followed Sam's orders.
Just think what woulda happened to that little girl if you'd sat at yer desk and shut up.
I think you know the answer.
I'm not sayin' ya hold a press conference and announce we got RQK runnin' wild.
Just don't hold on to cards that're meant to be played.
Uh... Bad timin'?
Fine timin'. Now, what's cookin'?
Well, I just got off the phone with the Benchley crew.
And...?
They hung up on me.

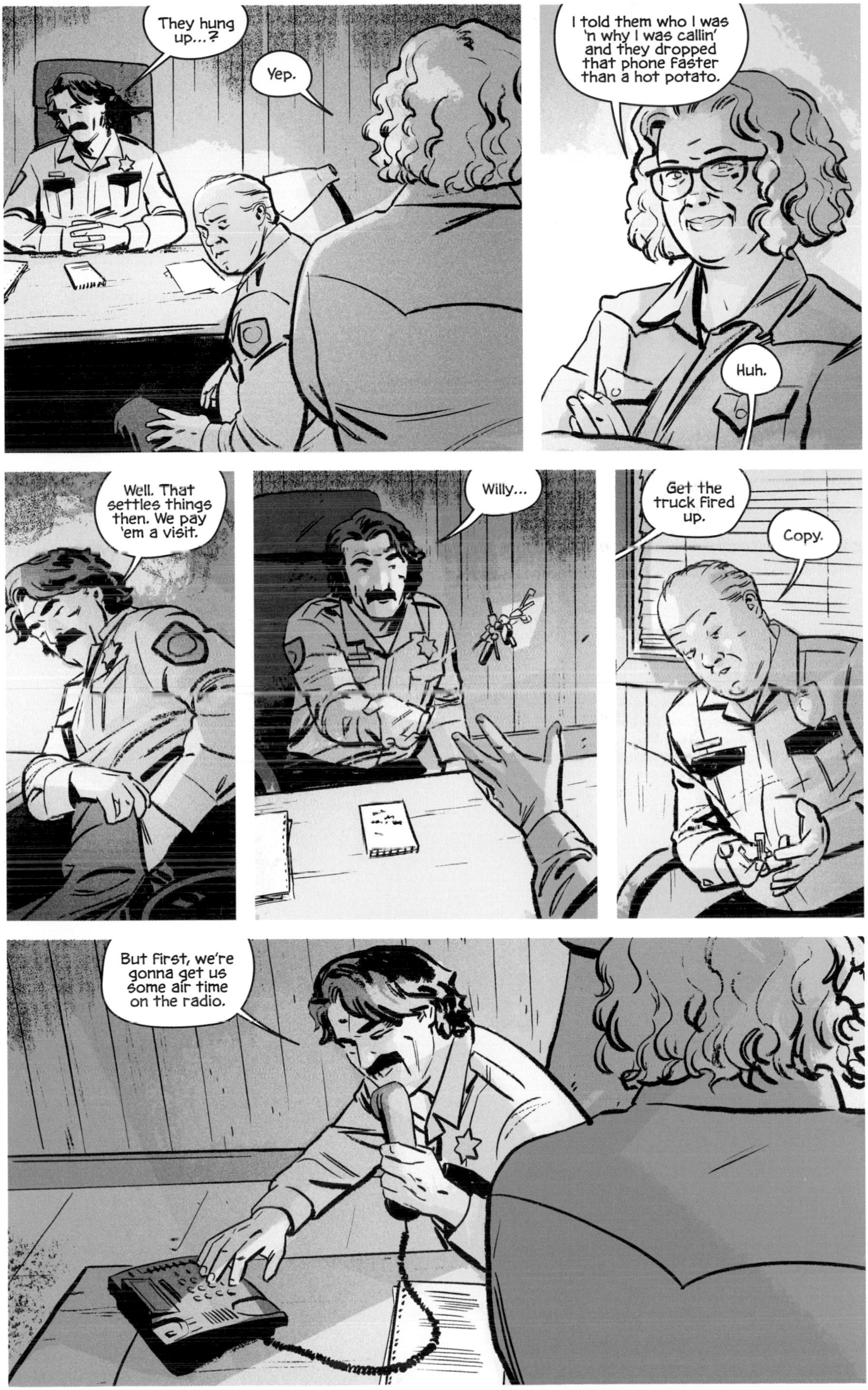
They hung up...?
Yep.
I told them who I was 'n why I was callin' and they dropped that phone faster than a hot potato.
Huh.
Well. That settles things then. We pay 'em a visit.
Willy...
Get the truck fired up.
Copy.
But first, we're gonna get us some air time on the radio.

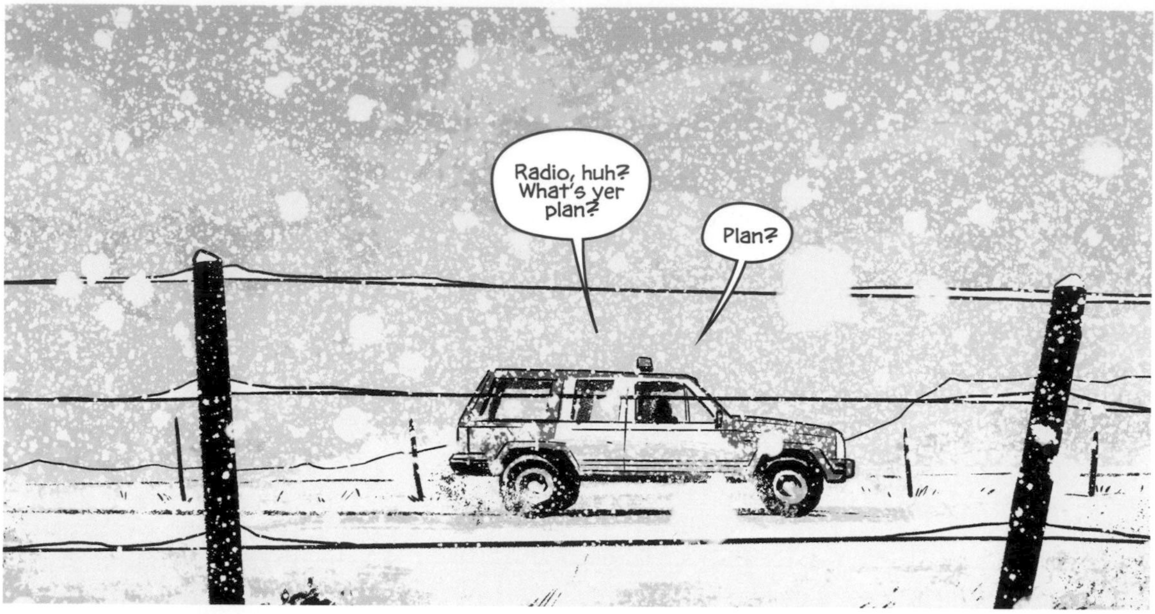
Radio, huh? What's yer plan?
Plan?
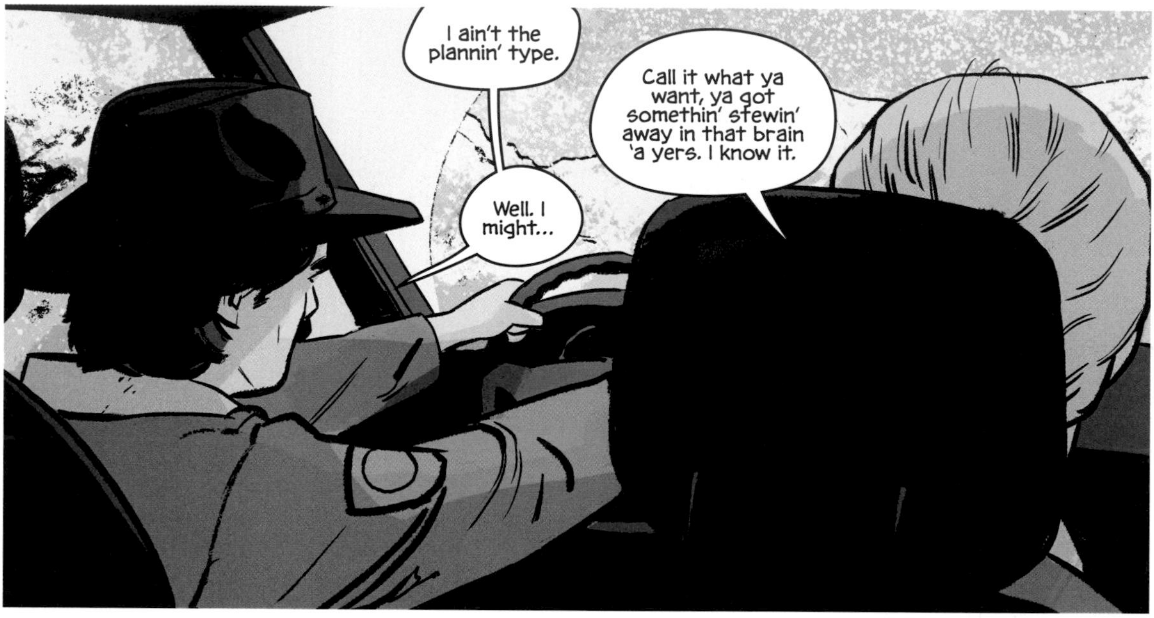
I ain't the plannin' type.
Call it what ya want, ya got somethin' stewin' away in that brain 'a yers. I know it.
Well. I might...
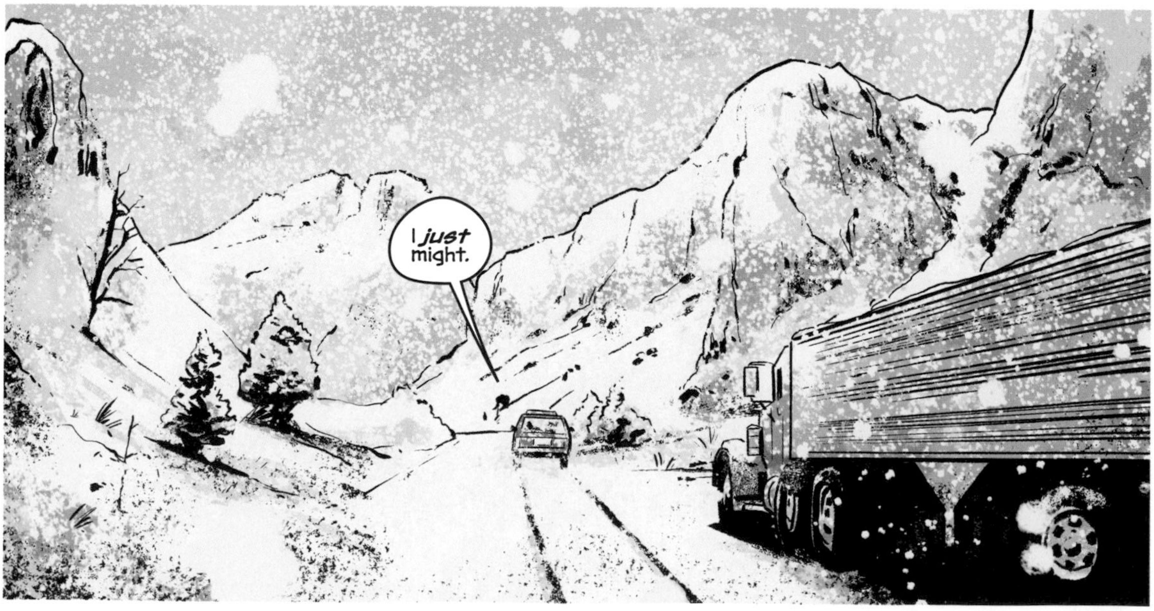
I *just* might.

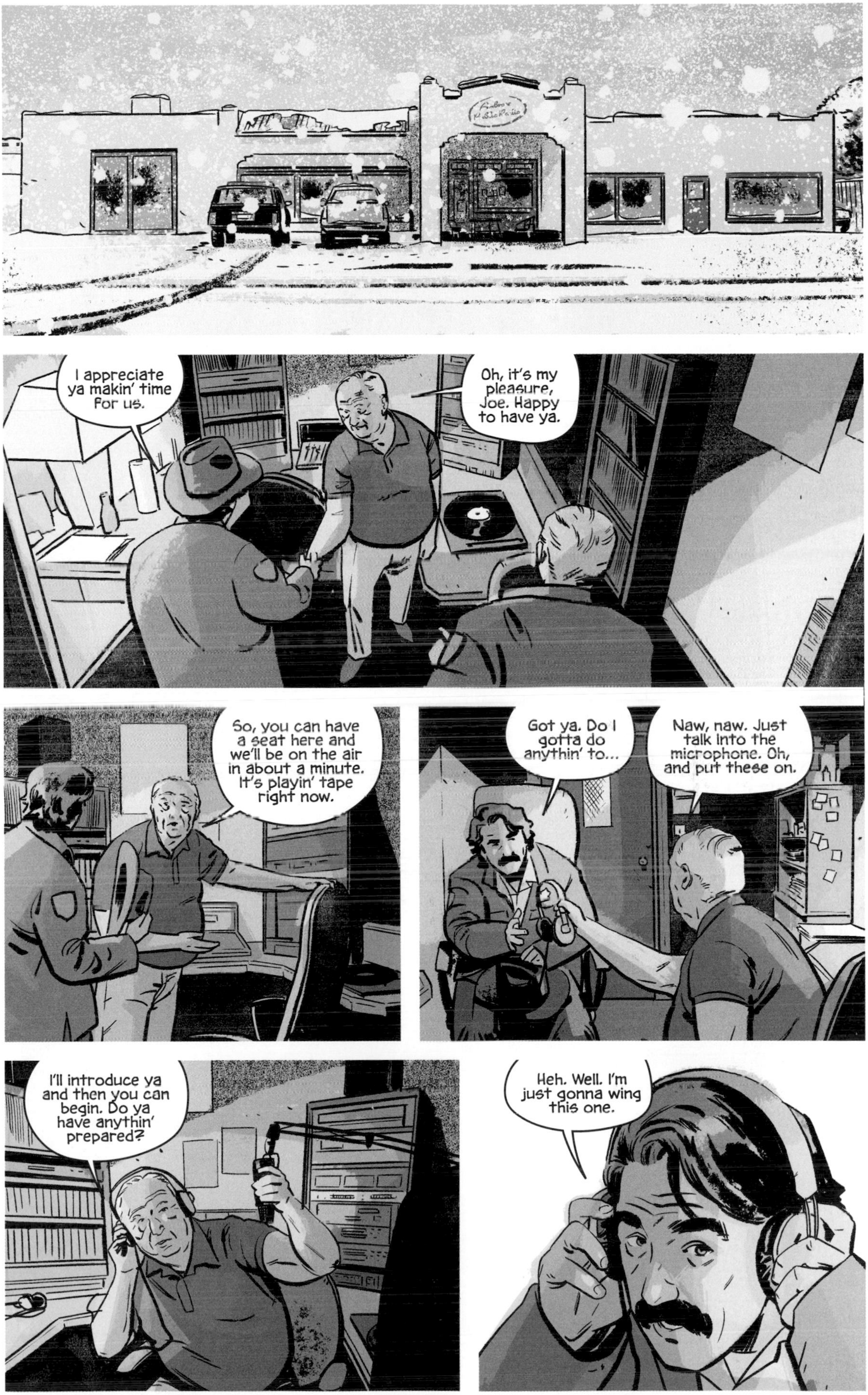
I appreciate ya makin' time for us.
Oh, it's my pleasure, Joe. Happy to have ya.
So, you can have a seat here and we'll be on the air in about a minute. It's playin' tape right now.
Got ya. Do I gotta do anythin' to...
Naw, naw. Just talk into the microphone. Oh, and put these on.
I'll introduce ya and then you can begin. Do ya have anythin' prepared?
Heh. Well. I'm just gonna wing this one.

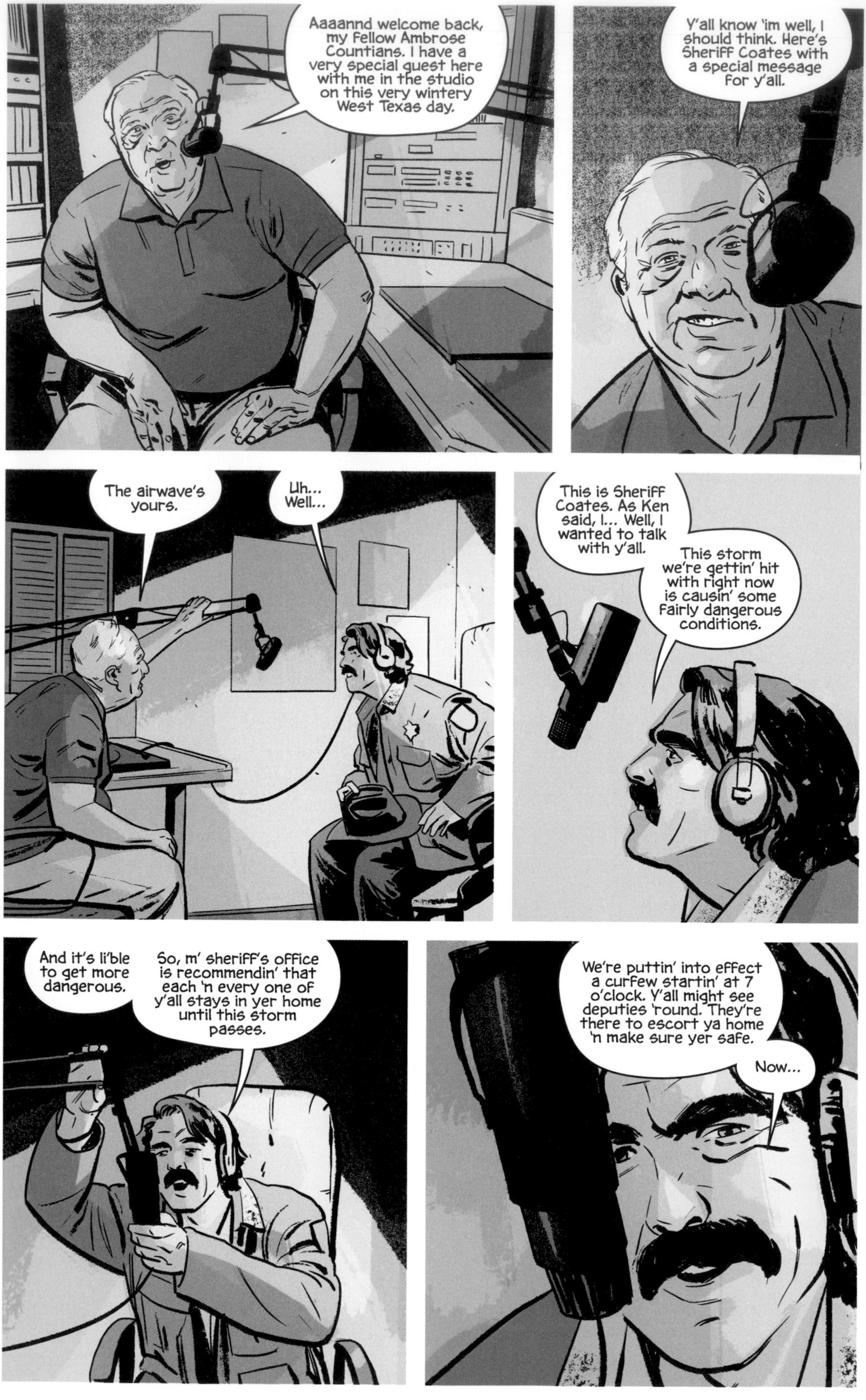
Aaaannd welcome back, my Fellow Ambrose Countians. I have a very special guest here with me in the studio on this very wintery West Texas day.
Y'all know 'im well, I should think. Here's Sheriff Coates with a special message for y'all.
The airwave's yours.
Uh... Well...
This is Sheriff Coates. As Ken said, I... Well, I wanted to talk with y'all.
This storm we're gettin' hit with right now is causin' some fairly dangerous conditions.
And it's li'ble to get more dangerous.
So, m' sheriff's office is recommendin' that each 'n every one of y'all stays in yer home until this storm passes.
We're puttin' into effect a curfew startin' at 7 o'clock. Y'all might see deputies 'round. They're there to escort ya home 'n make sure yer safe.
Now...

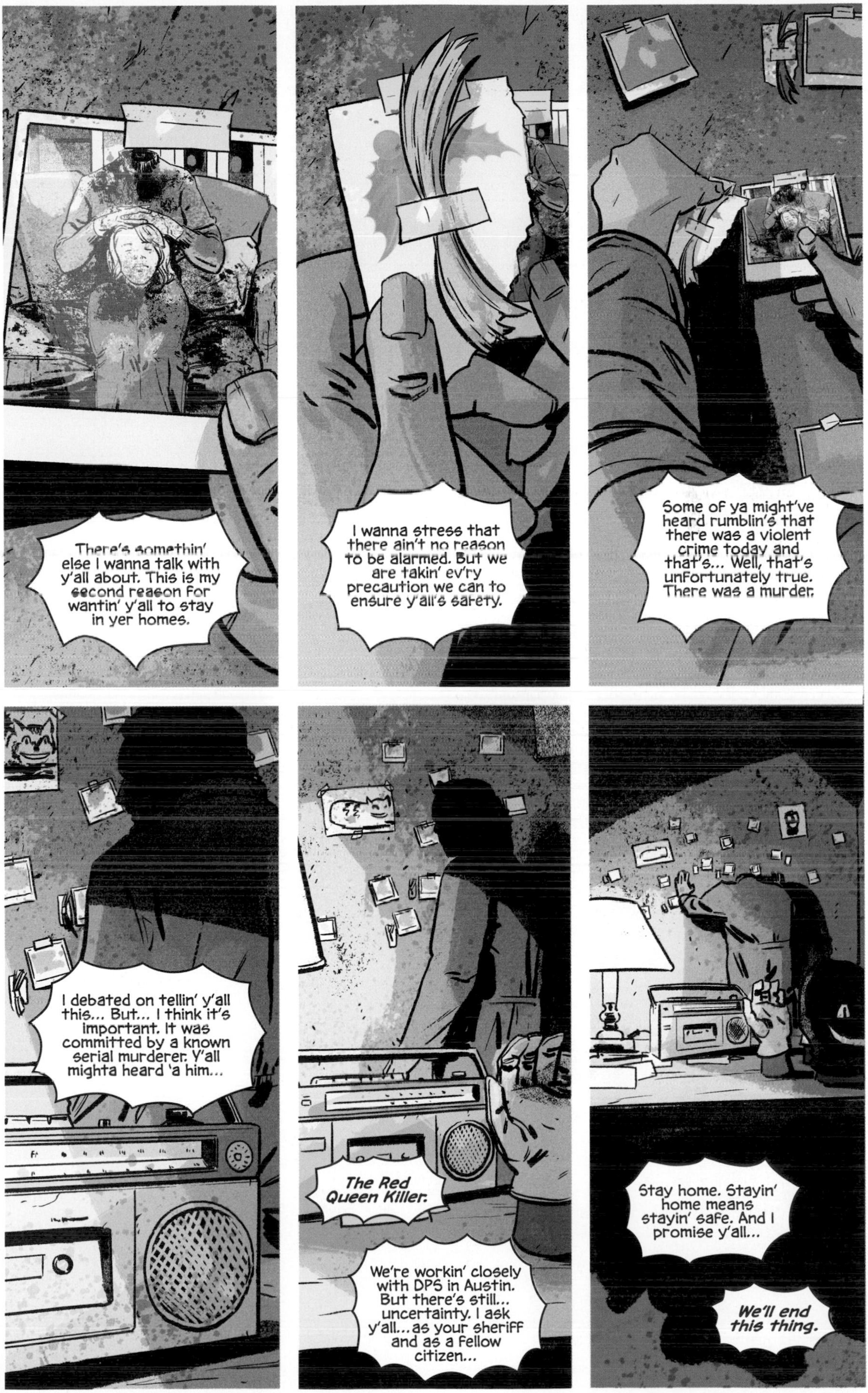
There's somethin' else I wanna talk with y'all about. This is my second reason for wantin' y'all to stay in yer homes.
I wanna stress that there ain't no reason to be alarmed. But we are takin' ev'ry precaution we can to ensure y'all's safety.
Some of ya might've heard rumblin's that there was a violent crime today and that's... Well, that's unfortunately true. There was a murder.
I debated on tellin' y'all this... But... I think it's important. It was committed by a known serial murderer. Y'all mighta heard 'a him...
The Red Queen Killer.
We're workin' closely with DPS in Austin. But there's still... uncertainty. I ask y'all...as your sheriff and as a fellow citizen...
Stay home. Stayin' home means stayin' safe. And I promise y'all...
We'll end this thing.

THE ABANDONED TRUCK AND THE DAMN STUPID RALLY

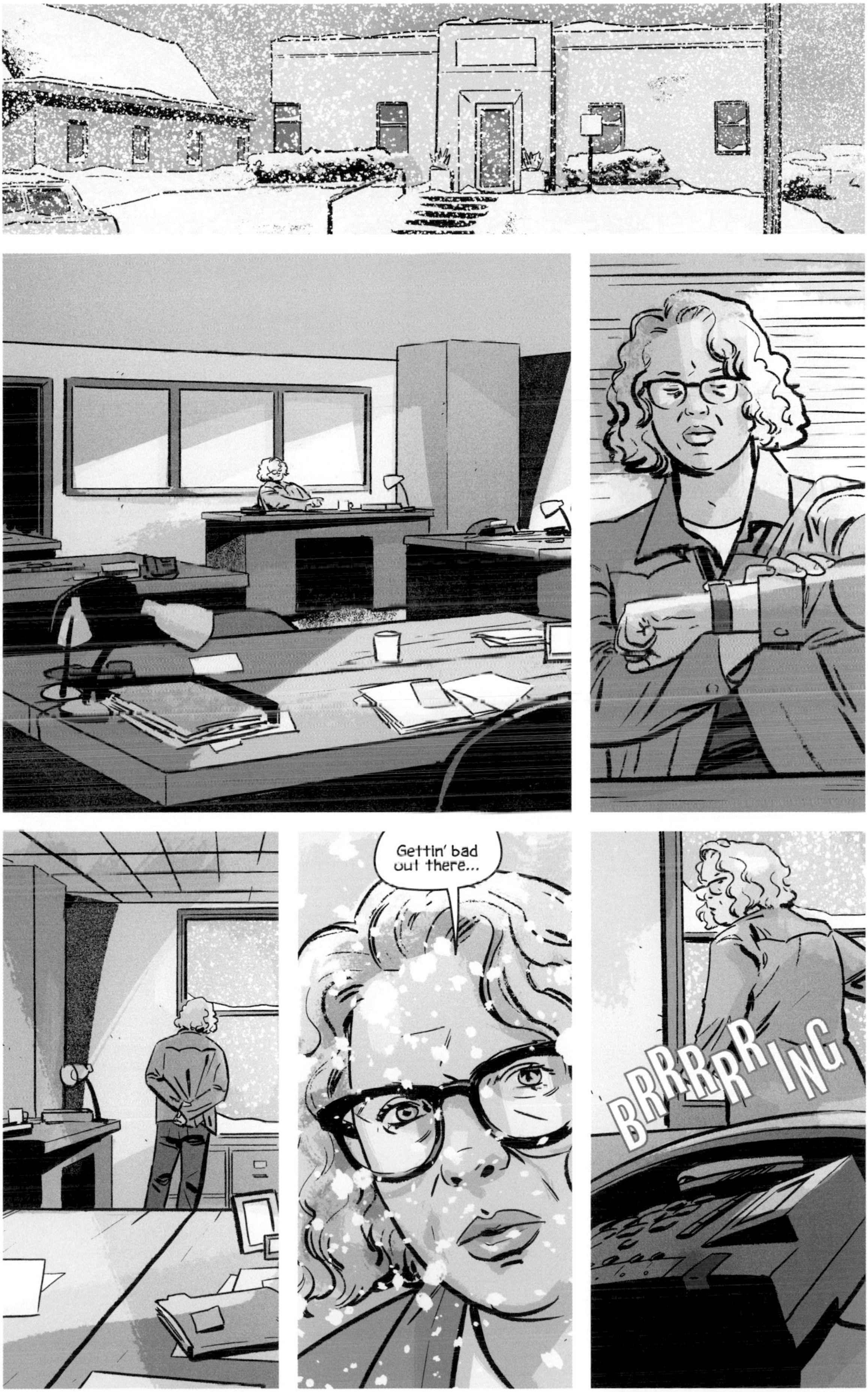
Gettin' bad out there...
BRRRRRING

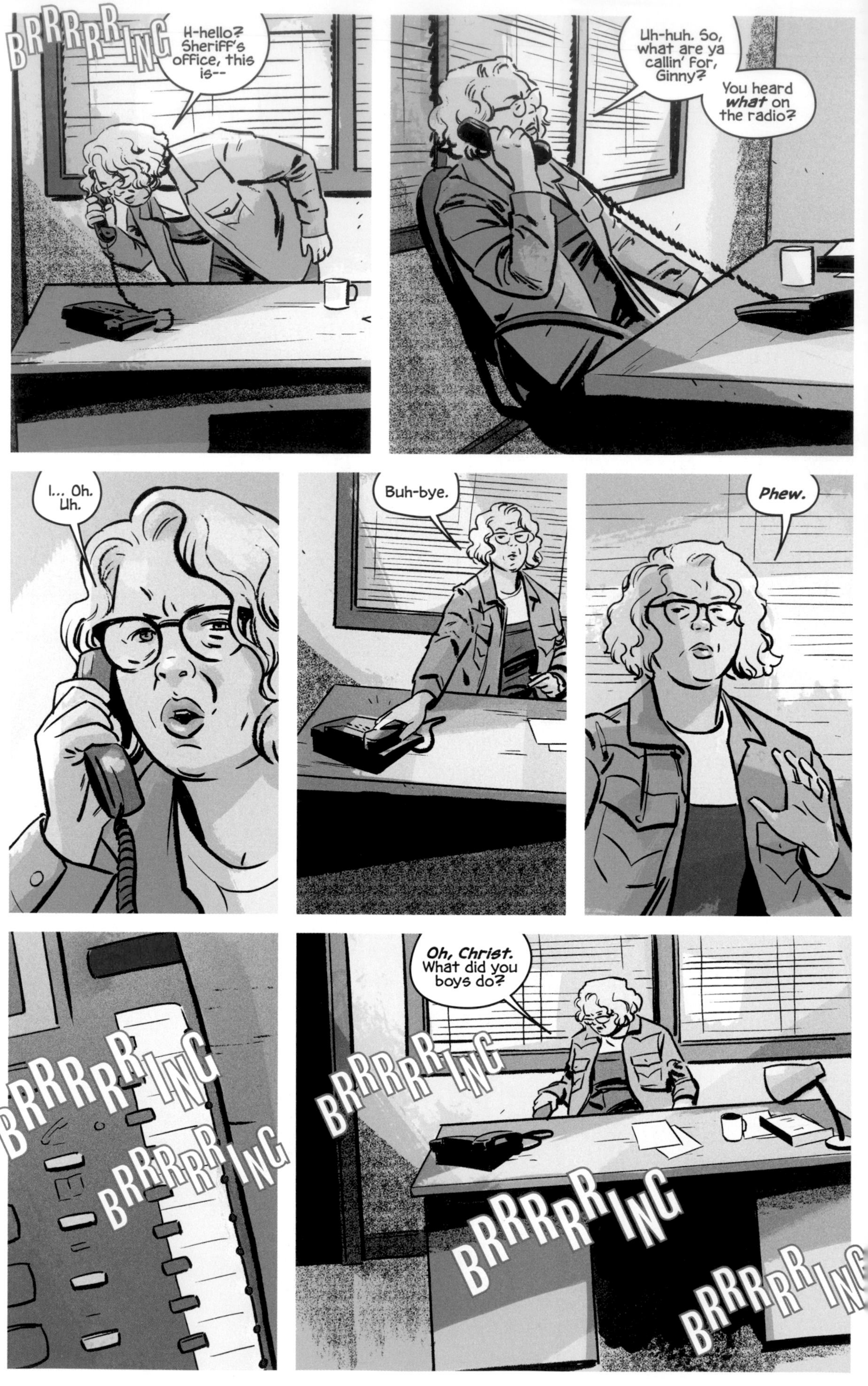
BRRRRRING
H-hello? Sheriff's office, this is--
Uh-huh. So, what are ya callin' for, Ginny?
You heard what on the radio?
I... Oh. Uh.
Buh-bye.
Phew.
BRRRRRING
BRRRRRING
Oh, Christ. What did you boys do?
BRRRRRING
BRRRRRING
BRRRRRING

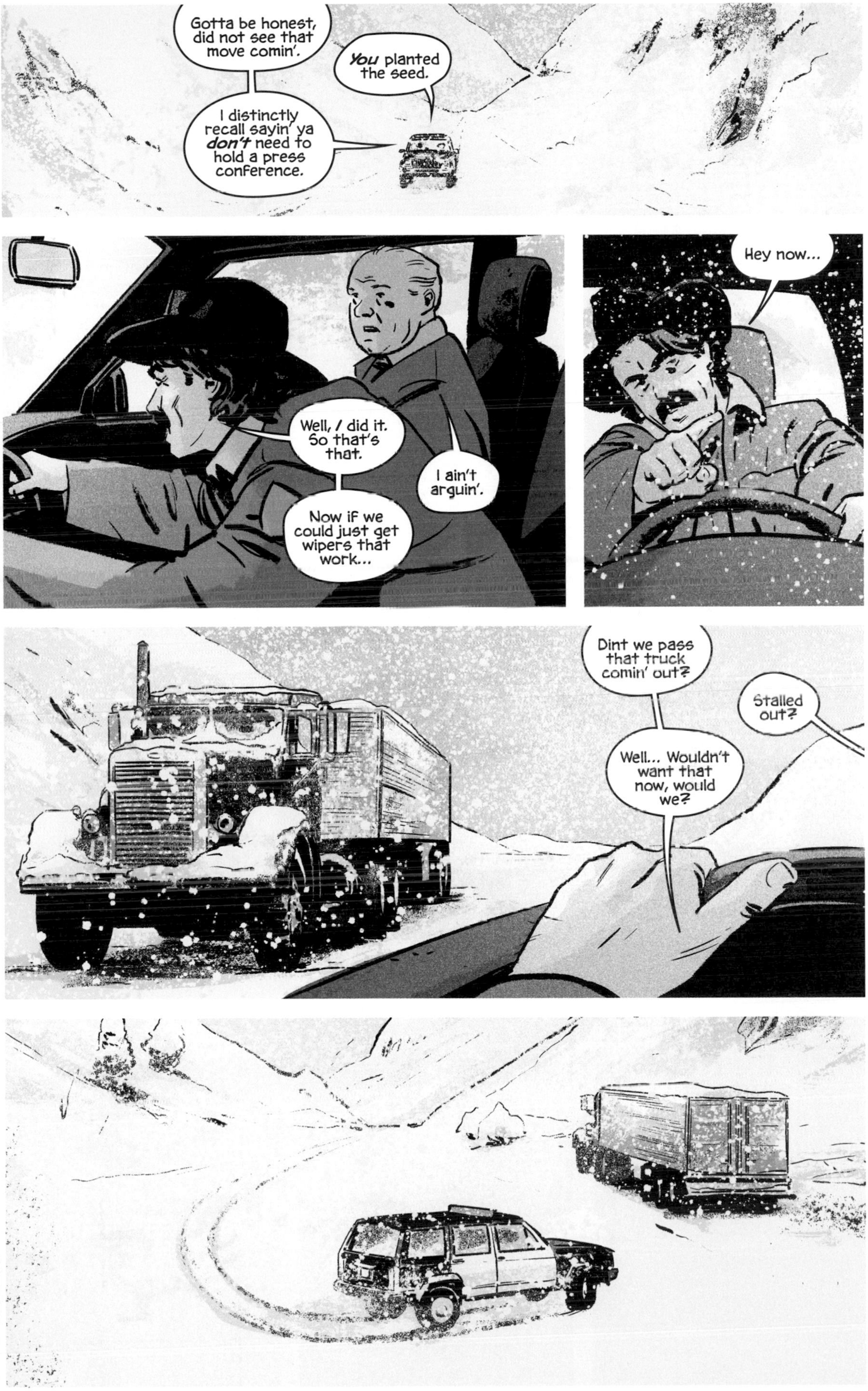
Gotta be honest, did not see that move comin'.
I distinctly recall sayin' ya *don't* need to hold a press conference.
You planted the seed.
Well, *I* did it. So that's that.
Now if we could just get wipers that work...
I ain't arguin'.
Hey now...
Dint we pass that truck comin' out?
Well... Wouldn't want that now, would we?
Stalled out?

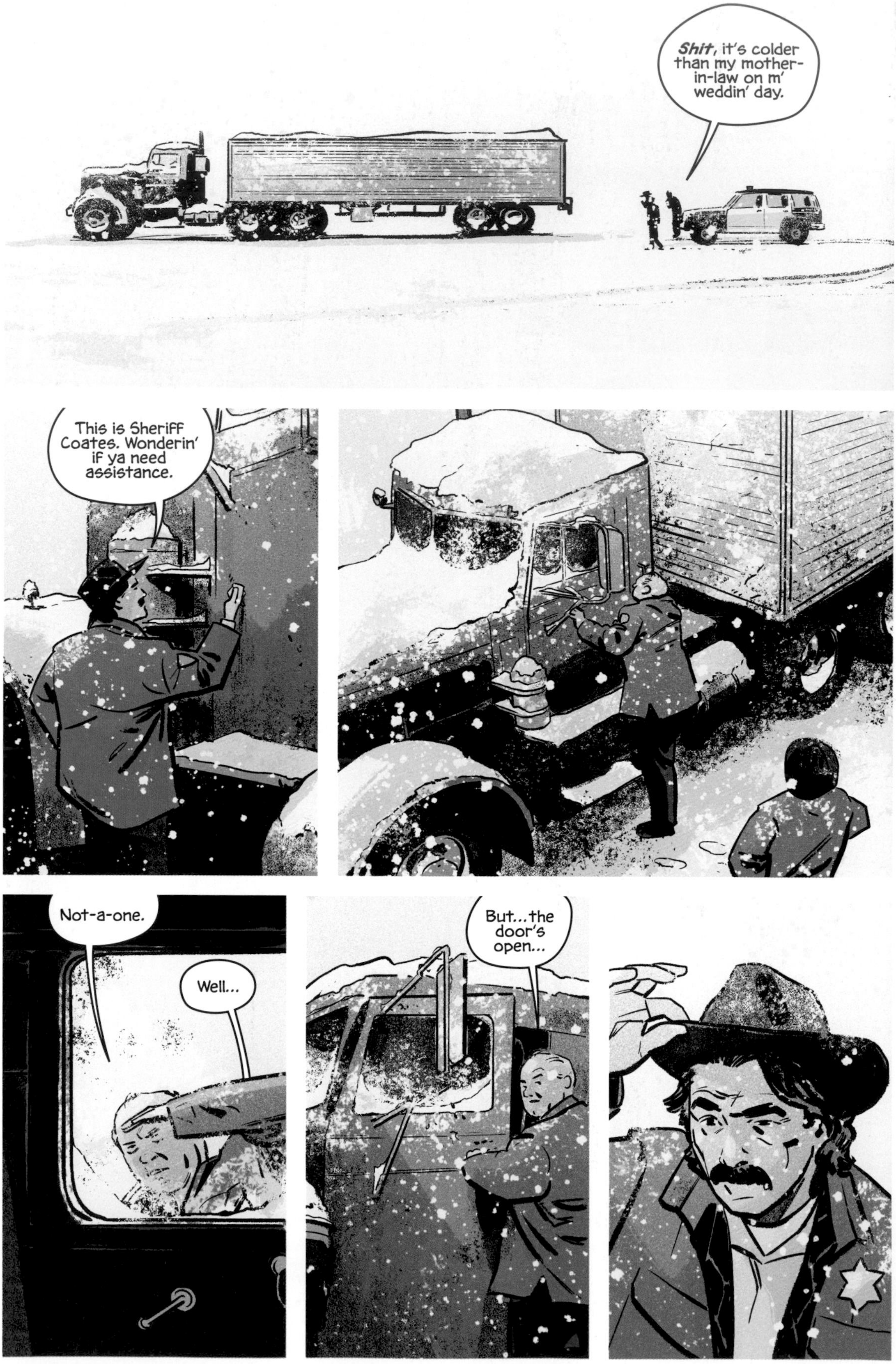
Shit, it's colder than my mother-in-law on m' weddin' day.
This is Sheriff Coates. Wonderin' if ya need assistance.
Not-a-one.
Well...
But...the door's open...

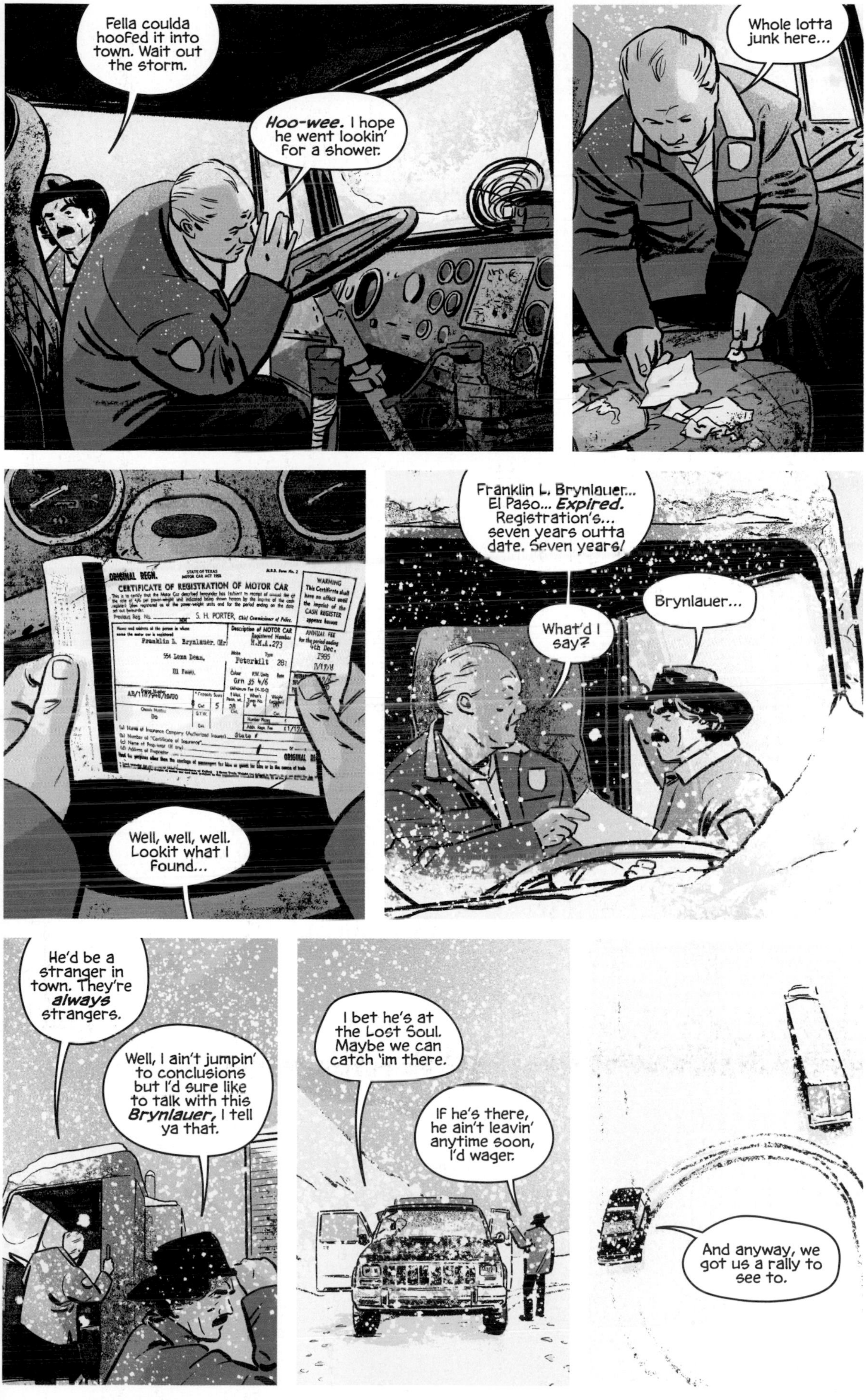
Fella coulda hoofed it into town. Wait out the storm.
Hoo-wee. I hope he went lookin' for a shower.
Whole lotta junk here...
ORIGINAL REGN.
CERTIFICATE OF REGISTRATION OF MOTOR CAR
Well, well, well. Lookit what I found...
Franklin L. Brynlauer... El Paso... *Expired.* Registration's... seven years outta date. Seven years!
What'd I say?
Brynlauer...
He'd be a stranger in town. They're *always* strangers.
Well, I ain't jumpin' to conclusions but I'd sure like to talk with this *Brynlauer,* I tell ya that.
I bet he's at the Lost Soul. Maybe we can catch 'im there.
If he's there, he ain't leavin' anytime soon, I'd wager.
And anyway, we got us a rally to see to.

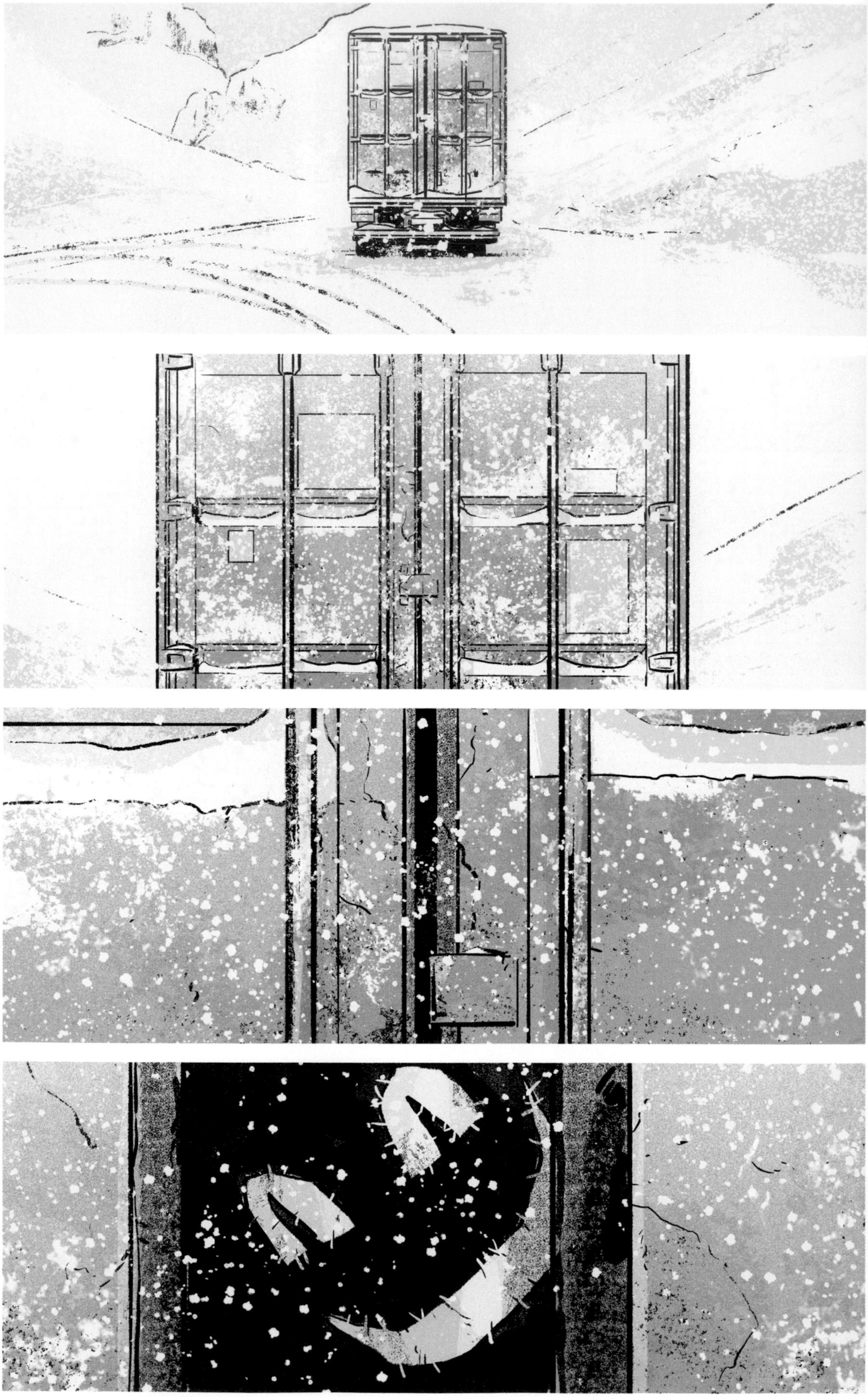

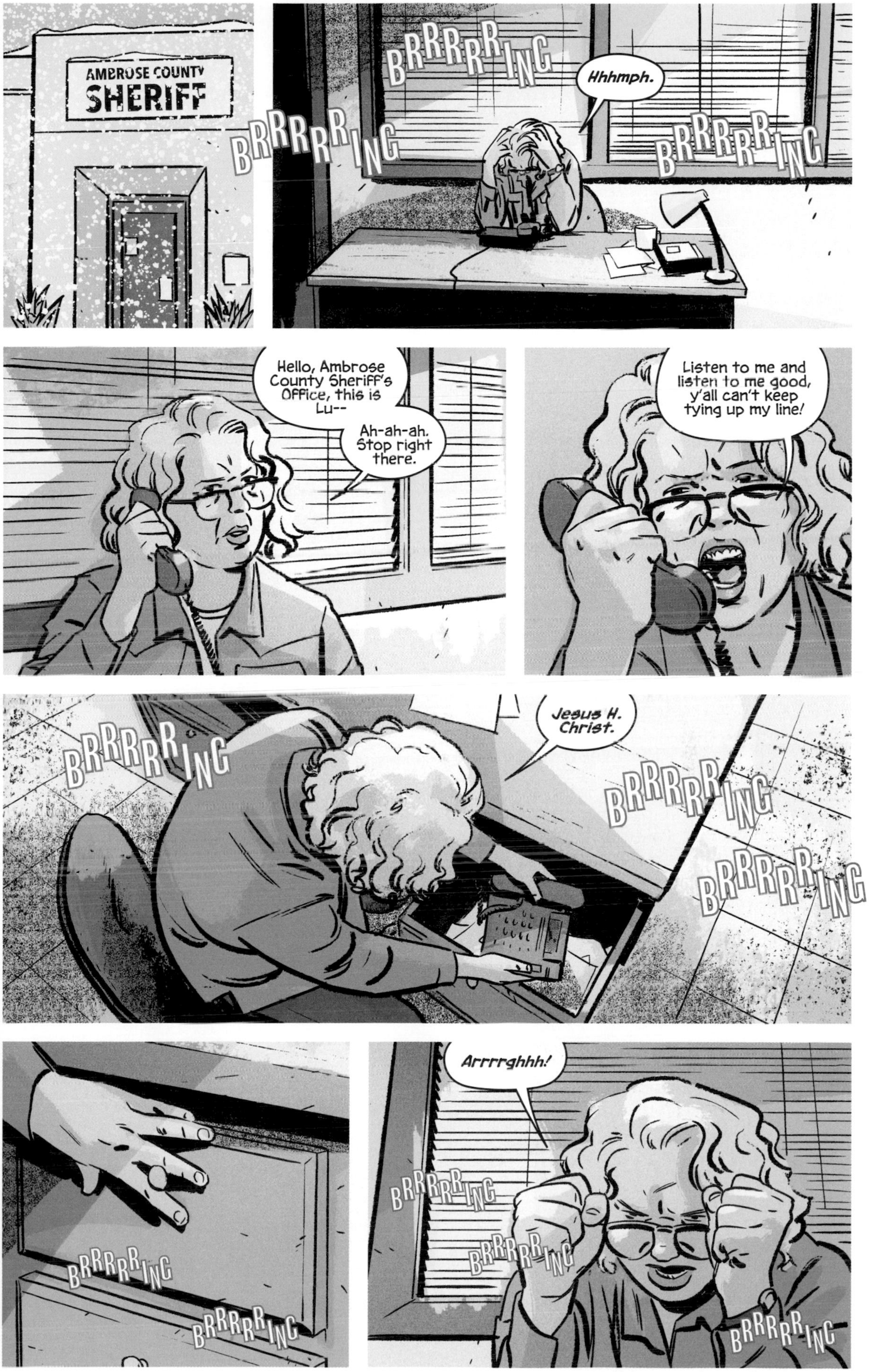
AMBROSE COUNTY
SHERIFF
BRRRRRRING
BRRRRRRING
Hhhmph.
BRRRRRRING
Hello, Ambrose County Sheriff's Office, this is Lu--
Ah-ah-ah. Stop right there.
Listen to me and listen to me good, y'all can't keep tying up my line!
BRRRRRING
Jesus H. Christ.
BRRRRRRING
BRRRRRRING
BRRRRRING
BRRRRRING
Arrrrghhh!
BRRRRRING
BRRRRRING
BRRRRRING

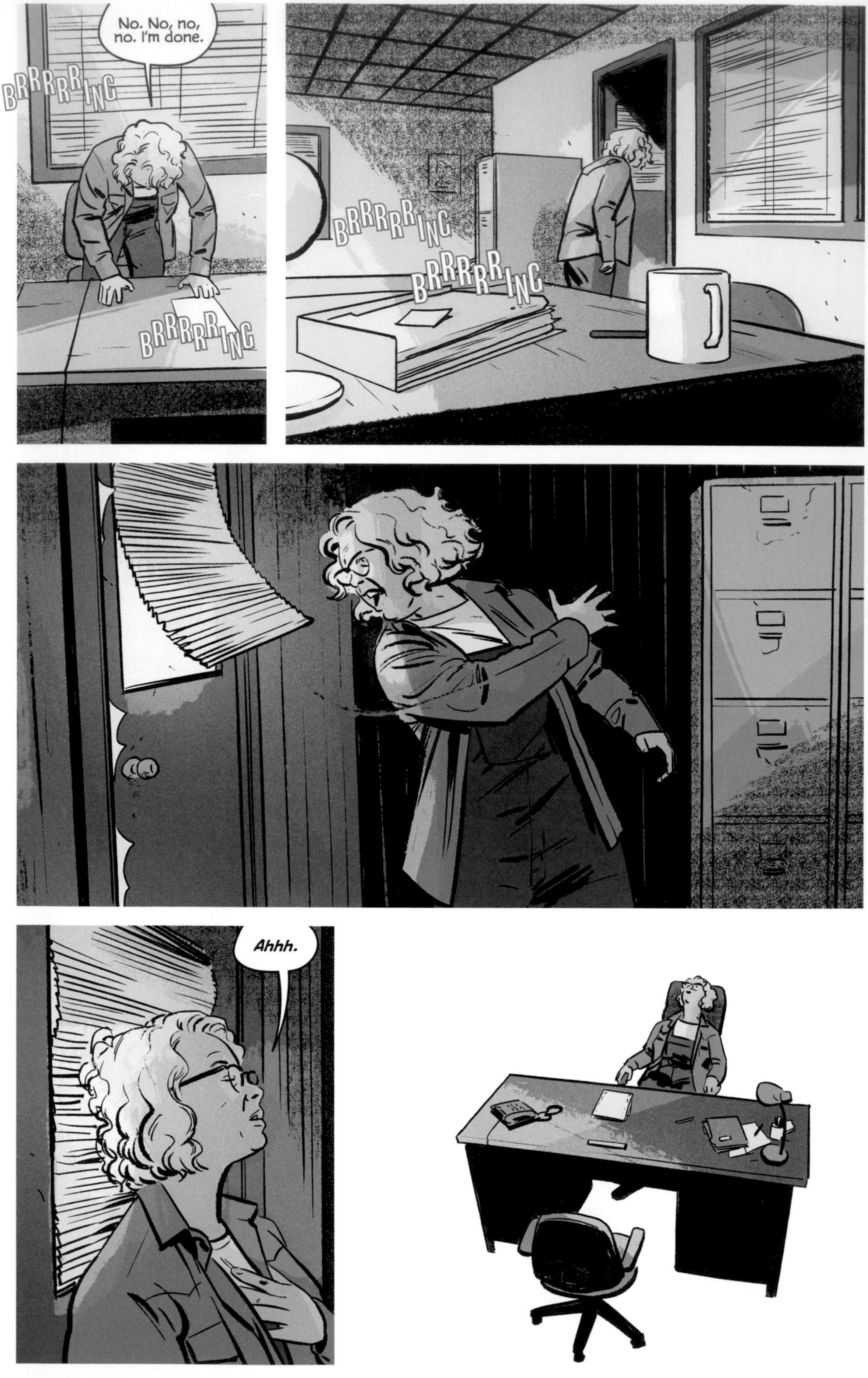
No. No, no, no. I'm done.
BRRRRRING
BRRRRRING
BRRRRRING
BRRRRRING
Ahhh.

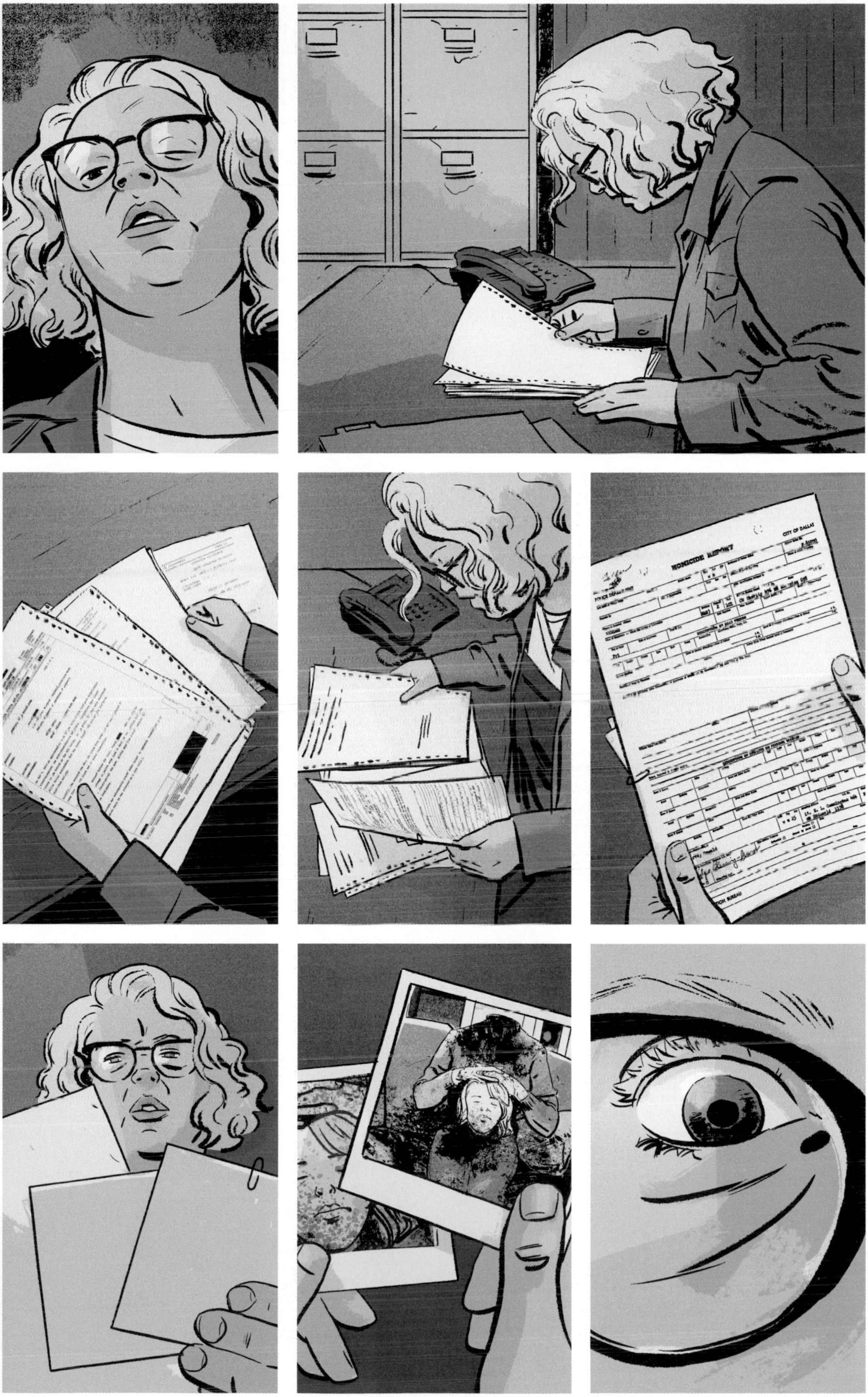

HOMICIDE REPORT
CITY OF DALLAS
POLICE DEPARTMENT

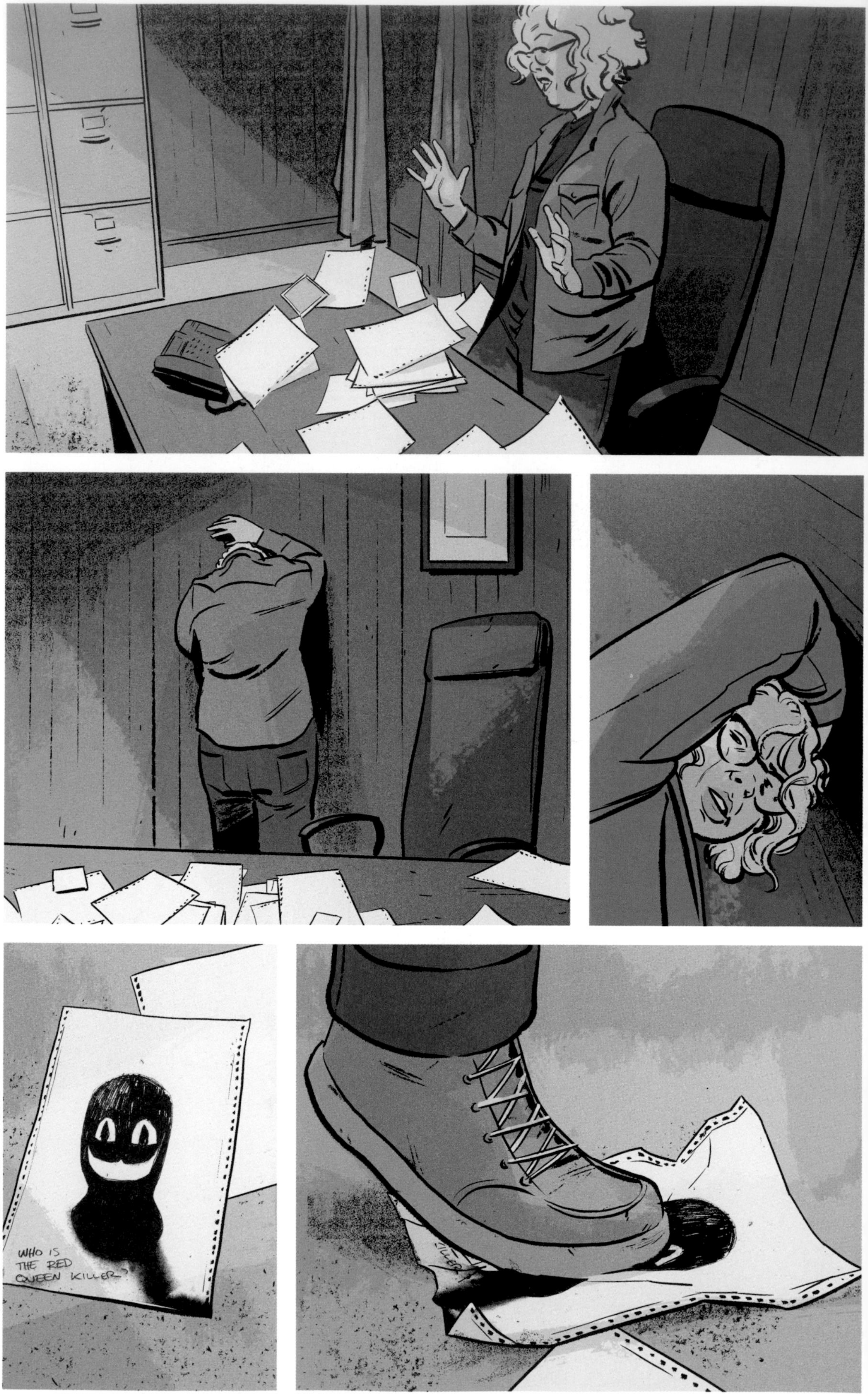
WHO IS
THE RED
QUEEN KILLER?
KILLER

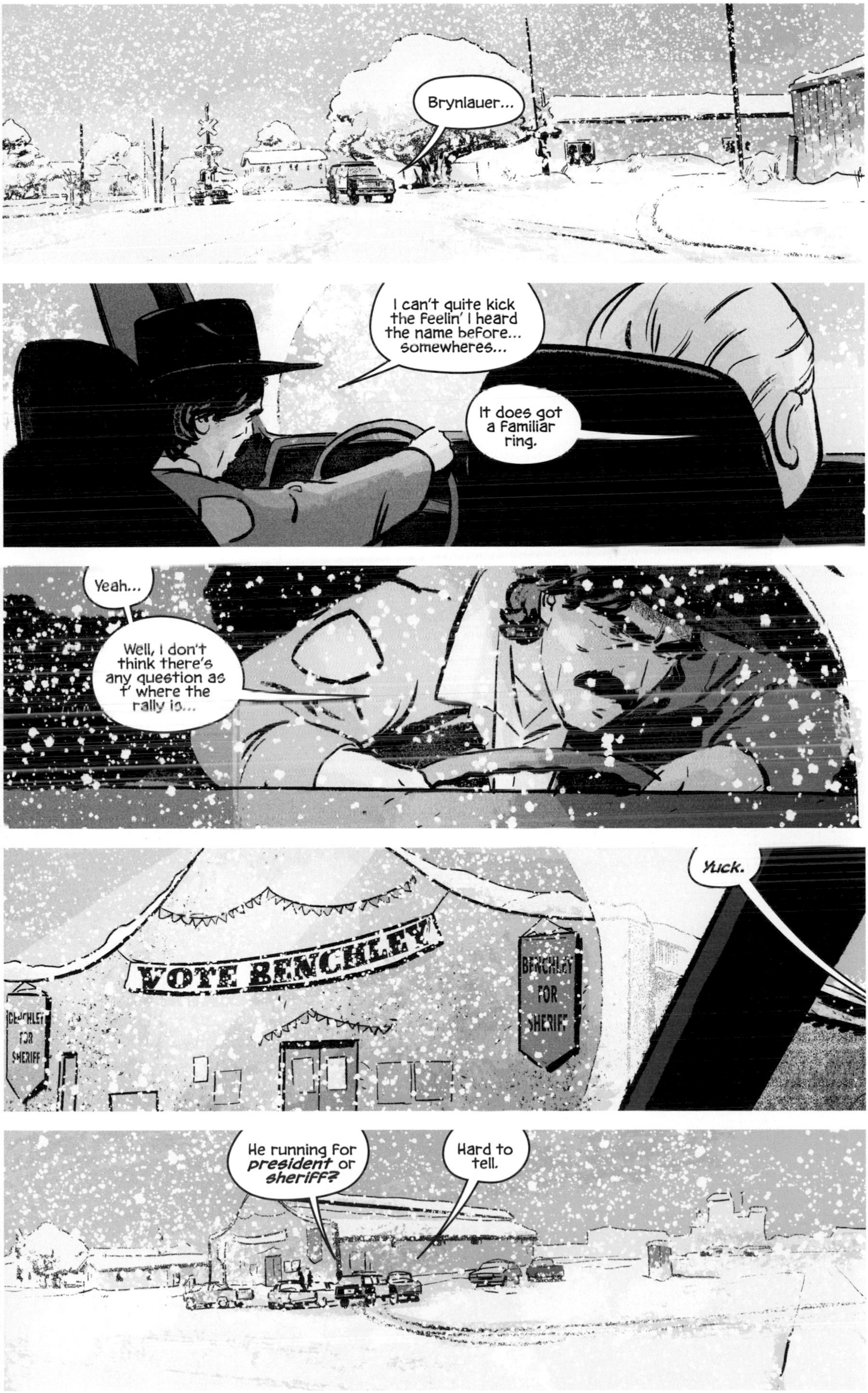
Brynlauer...
I can't quite kick the feelin' I heard the name before... somewheres...
It does got a familiar ring.
Yeah...
Well, I don't think there's any question as t' where the rally is...
VOTE BENCHLEY
BENCHLEY FOR SHERIFF
BENCHLEY FOR SHERIFF
Yuck.
He running for *president* or *sheriff?*
Hard to tell.

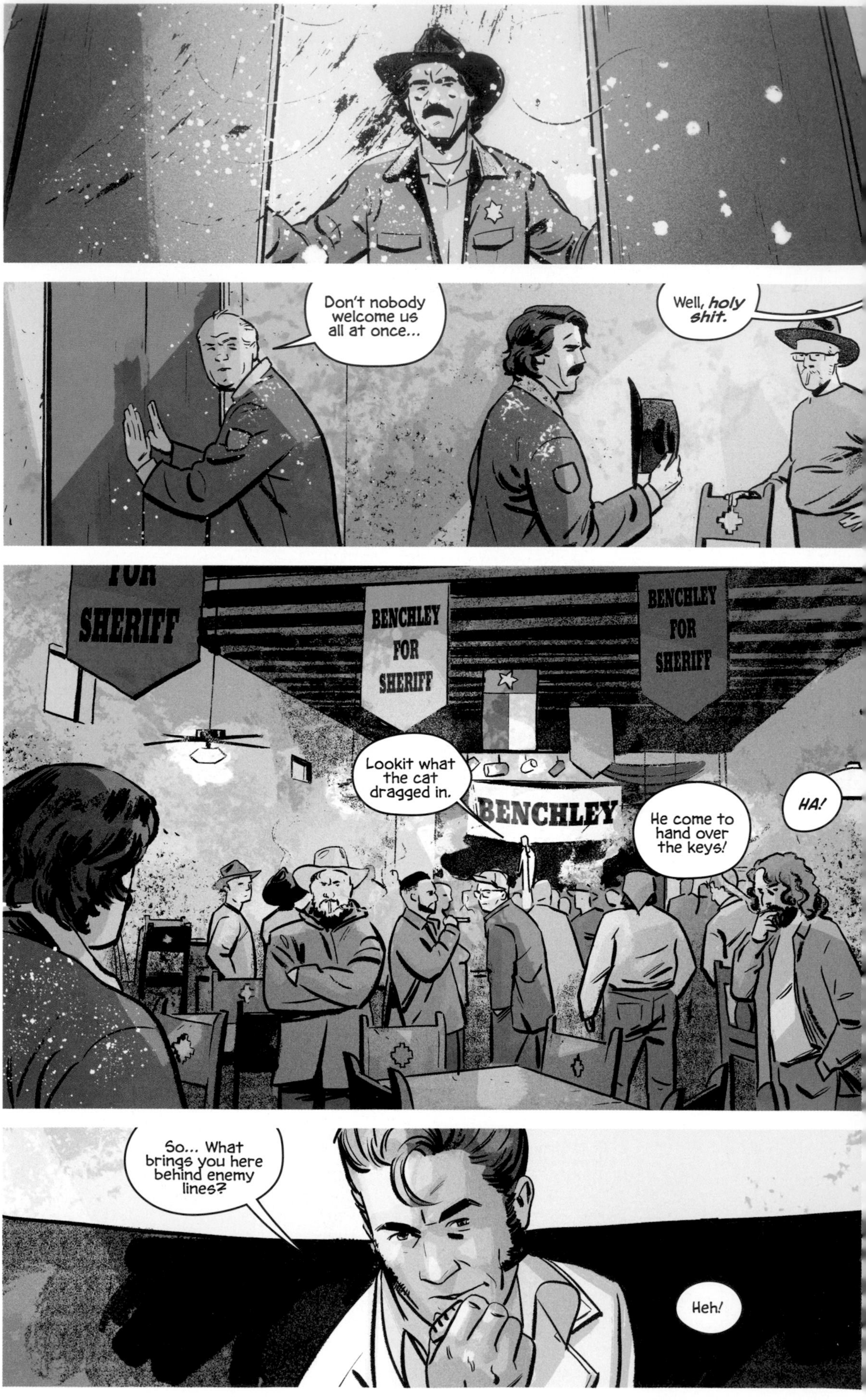
Don't nobody welcome us all at once...
Well, *holy shit.*
FOR SHERIFF
BENCHLEY FOR SHERIFF
BENCHLEY FOR SHERIFF
BENCHLEY
Lookit what the cat dragged in.
He come to hand over the keys!
HA!
So... What brings you here behind enemy lines?
Heh!

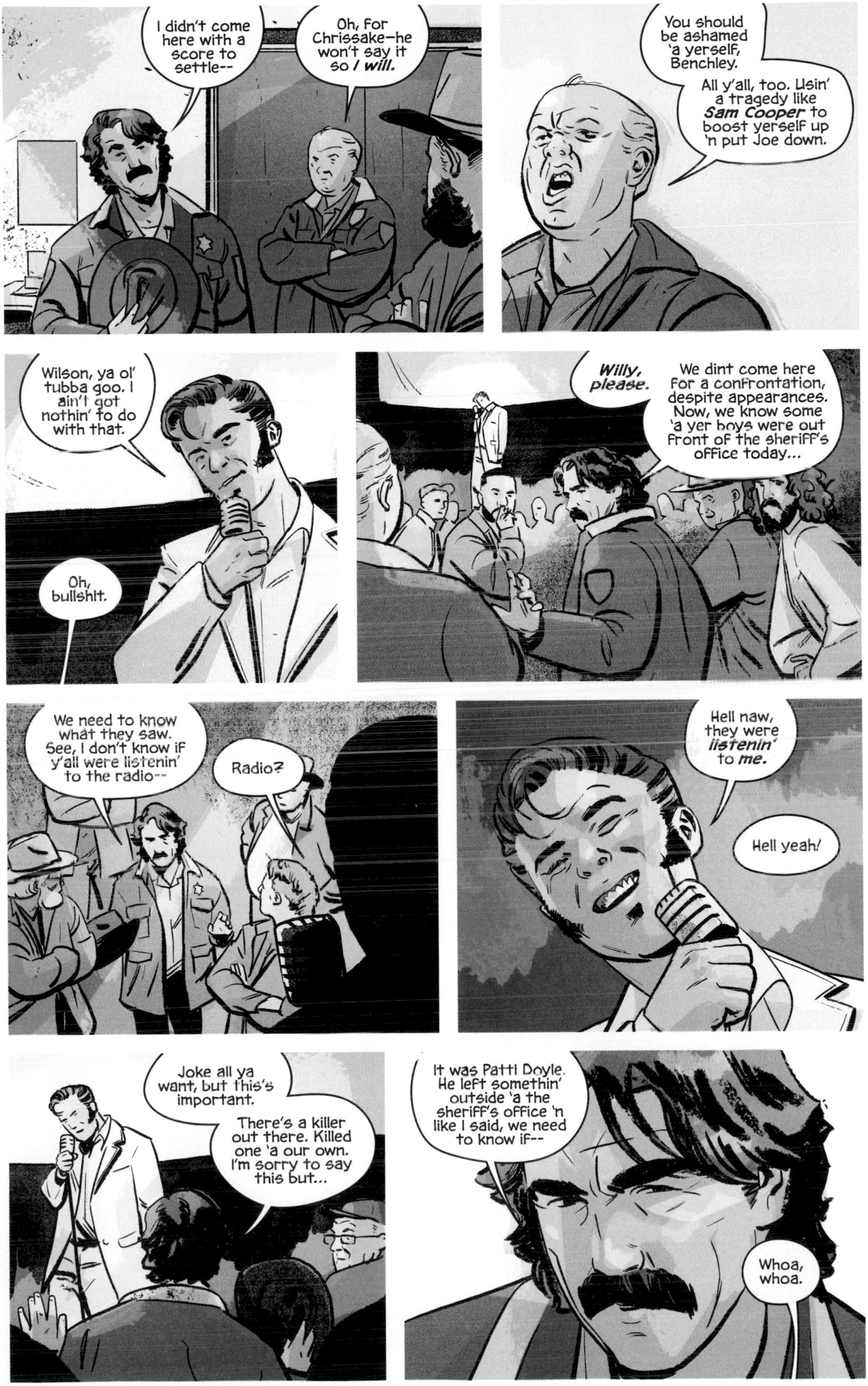
I didn't come here with a score to settle--
Oh, For Chrissake—he won't say it so *I will.*
You should be ashamed 'a yerself, Benchley.
All y'all, too. Usin' a tragedy like *Sam Cooper* to boost yerself up 'n put Joe down.
Wilson, ya ol' tubba goo. I ain't got nothin' to do with that.
Oh, bullshit.
Willy, please.
We dint come here for a confrontation, despite appearances. Now, we know some 'a yer boys were out front of the sheriff's office today...
We need to know what they saw. See, I don't know if y'all were listenin' to the radio--
Radio?
Hell naw, they were *listenin'* to *me.*
Hell yeah!
Joke all ya want, but this's important.
There's a killer out there. Killed one 'a our own. I'm sorry to say this but...
It was Patti Doyle. He left somethin' outside 'a the sheriff's office 'n like I said, we need to know if--
Whoa, whoa.

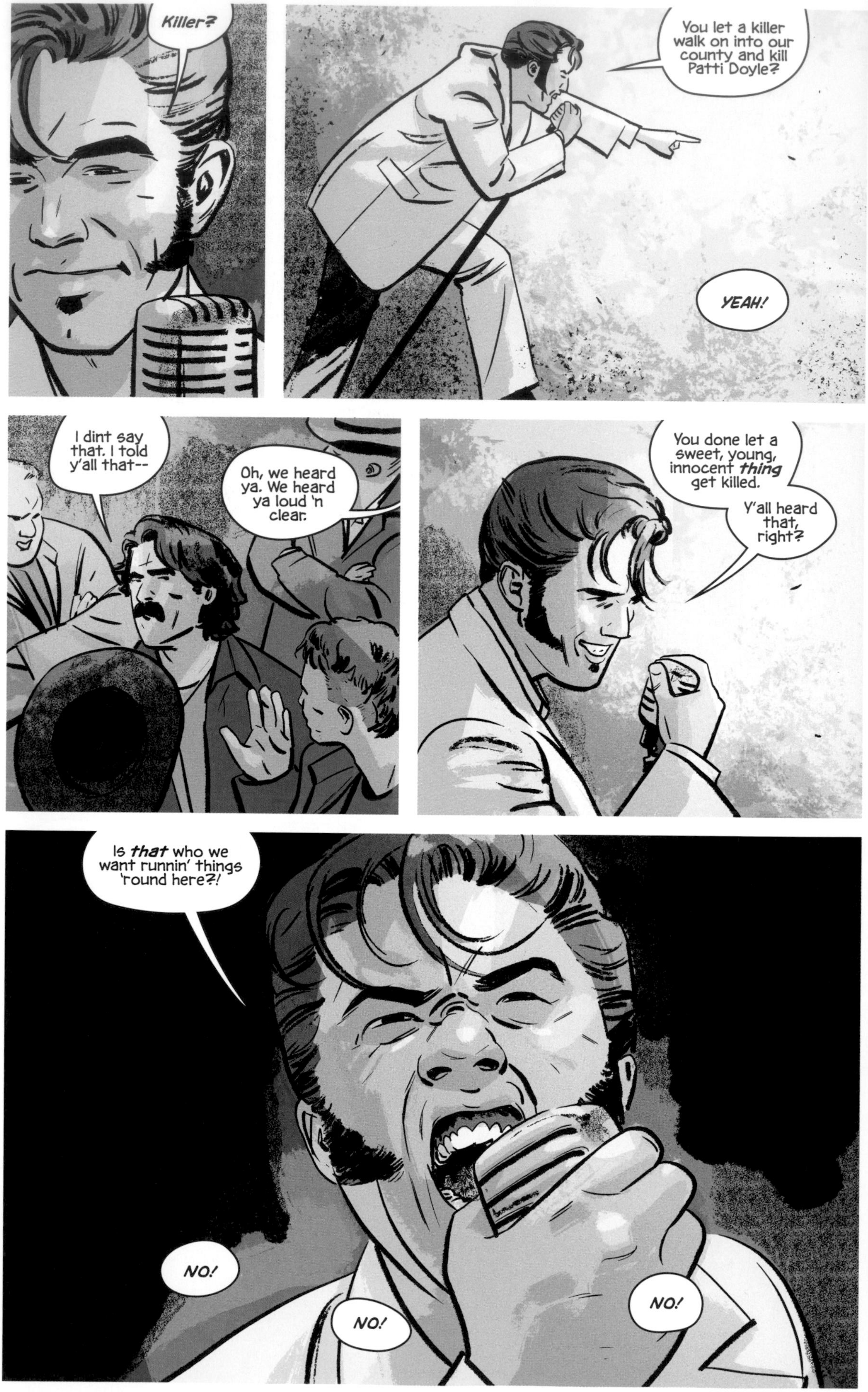
Killer?
You let a killer walk on into our county and kill Patti Doyle?
YEAH!
I dint say that. I told y'all that--
Oh, we heard ya. We heard ya loud 'n clear.
You done let a sweet, young, innocent *thing* get killed.
Y'all heard that, right?
Is *that* who we want runnin' things 'round here?!
NO!
NO!
NO!

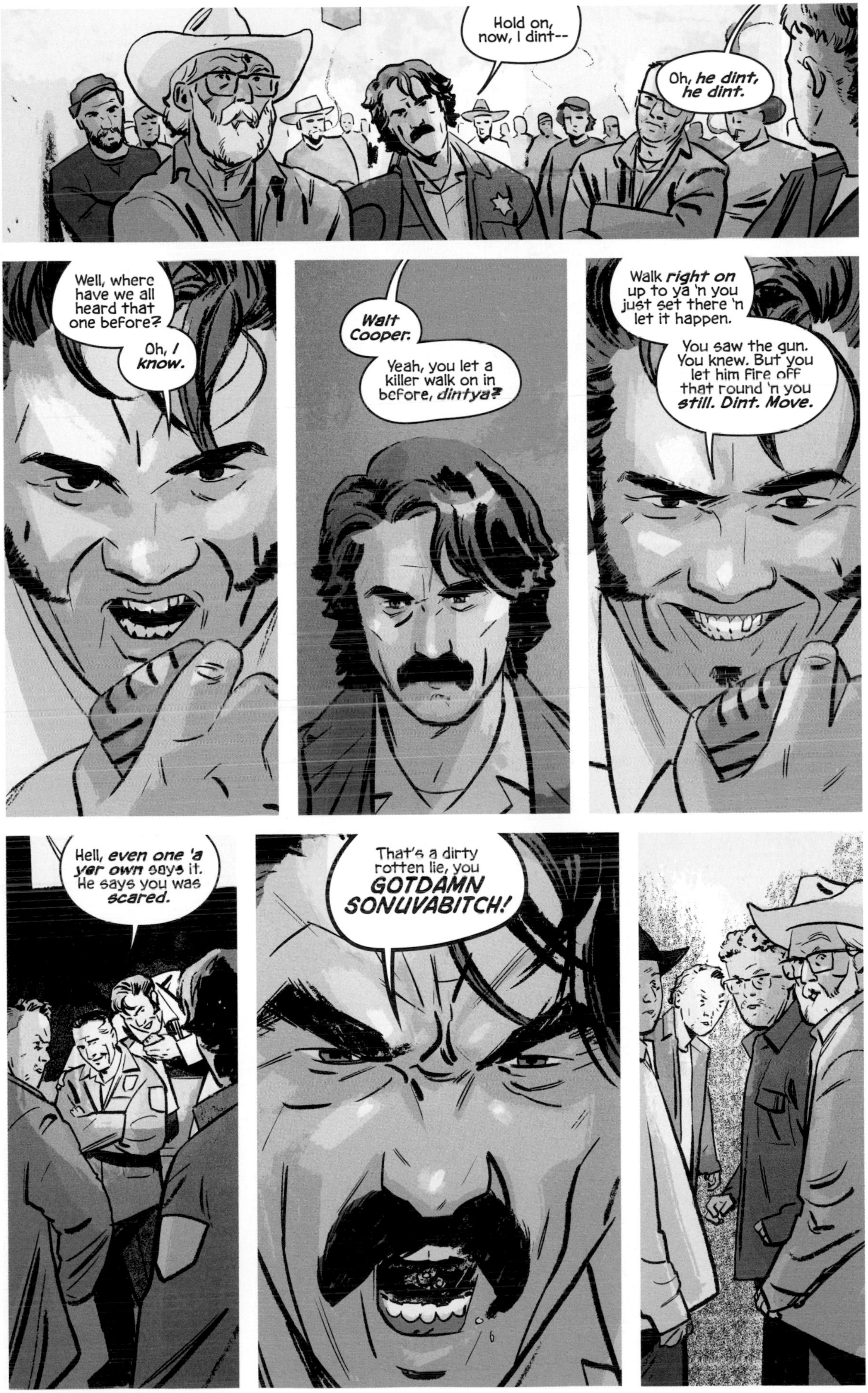
Hold on, now, I dint--
Oh, he dint, he dint.
Well, where have we all heard that one before?
Oh, I know.
Walt Cooper.
Yeah, you let a killer walk on in before, dintya?
Walk right on up to ya 'n you just set there 'n let it happen.
You saw the gun. You knew. But you let him fire off that round 'n you still. Dint. Move.
Hell, even one 'a yer own says it. He says you was scared.
That's a dirty rotten lie, you GOTDAMN SONUVABITCH!

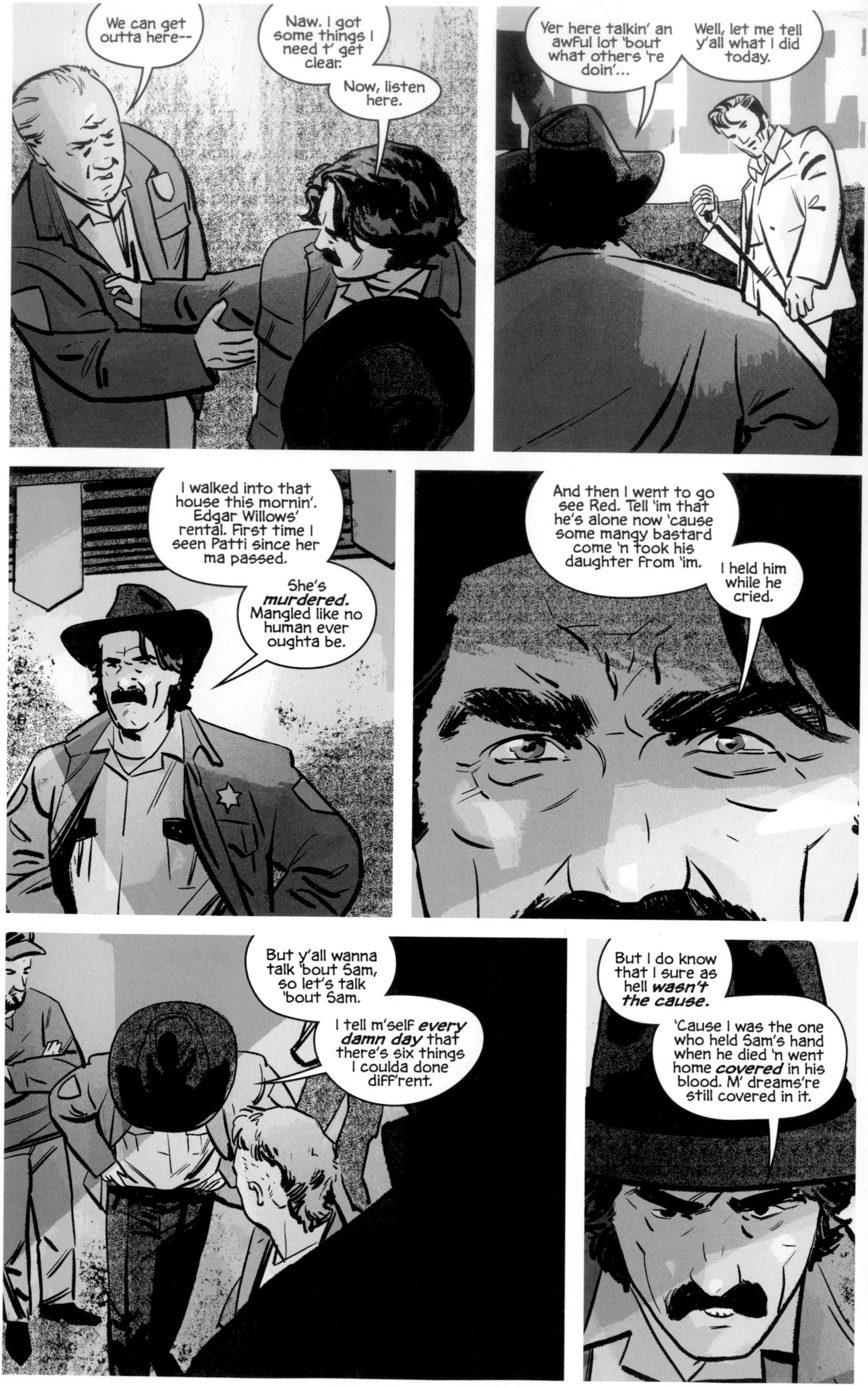
We can get outta here--
Naw. I got some things I need t' get clear.
Now, listen here.
Yer here talkin' an awful lot 'bout what others 're doin'...
Well, let me tell y'all what I did today.
I walked into that house this mornin'. Edgar Willows' rental. First time I seen Patti since her ma passed.
She's *murdered.* Mangled like no human ever oughta be.
And then I went to go see Red. Tell 'im that he's alone now 'cause some mangy bastard come 'n took his daughter from 'im.
I held him while he cried.
But y'all wanna talk 'bout Sam, so let's talk 'bout Sam.
I tell m'self *every damn day* that there's six things I coulda done diff'rent.
But I do know that I sure as hell *wasn't the cause.*
'Cause I was the one who held Sam's hand when he died 'n went home *covered* in his blood. M' dreams're still covered in it.

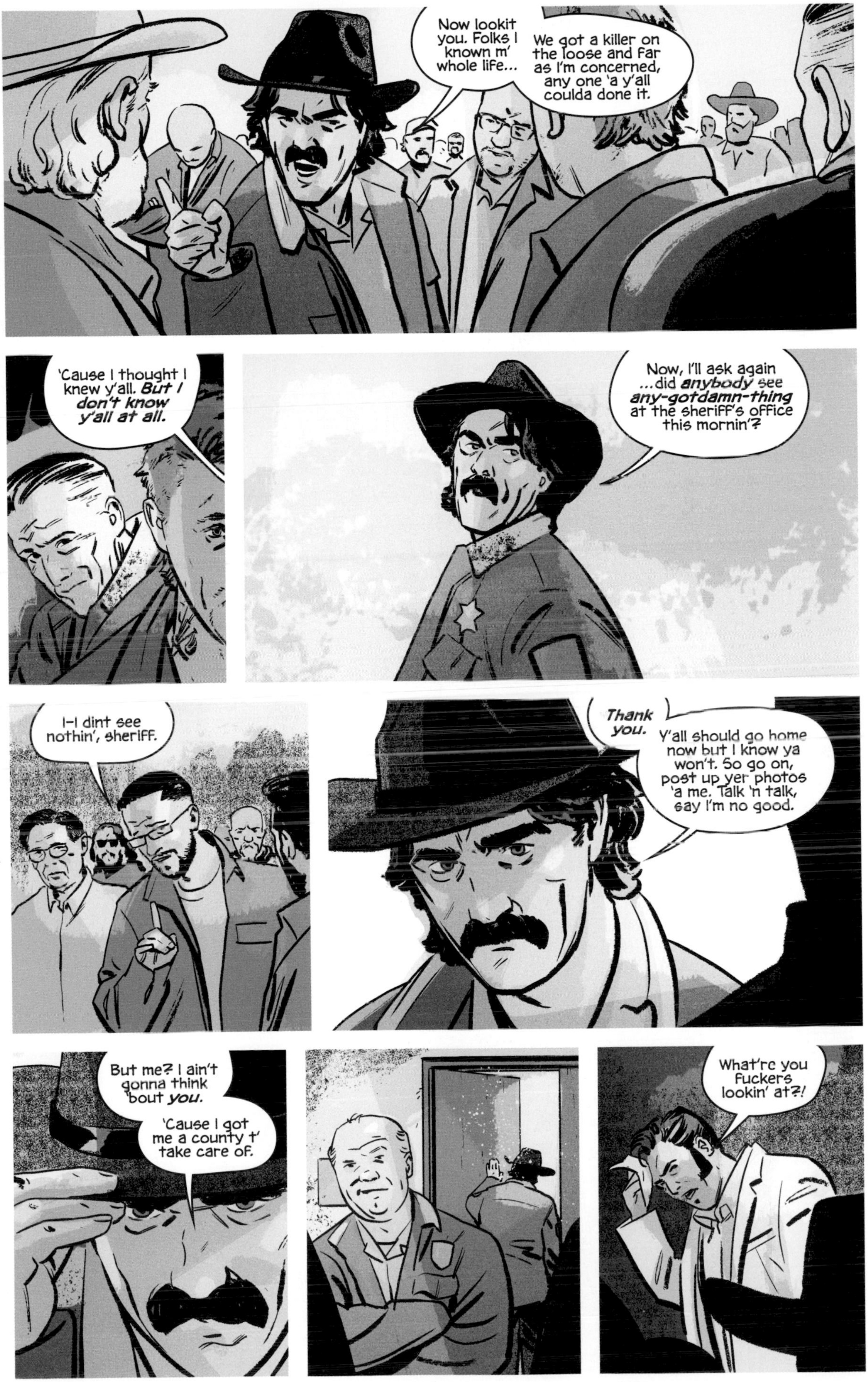

Now lookit you. Folks I known m' whole life...
We got a killer on the loose and far as I'm concerned, any one 'a y'all coulda done it.
'Cause I thought I knew y'all. *But I don't know y'all at all.*
Now, I'll ask again ...did *anybody* see *any-gotdamn-thing* at the sheriff's office this mornin'?
I-I dint see nothin', sheriff.
Thank you.
Y'all should go home now but I know ya won't. So go on, post up yer photos 'a me. Talk 'n talk, say I'm no good.
But me? I ain't gonna think 'bout *you.*
'Cause I got me a county t' take care of.
What're you fuckers lookin' at?!

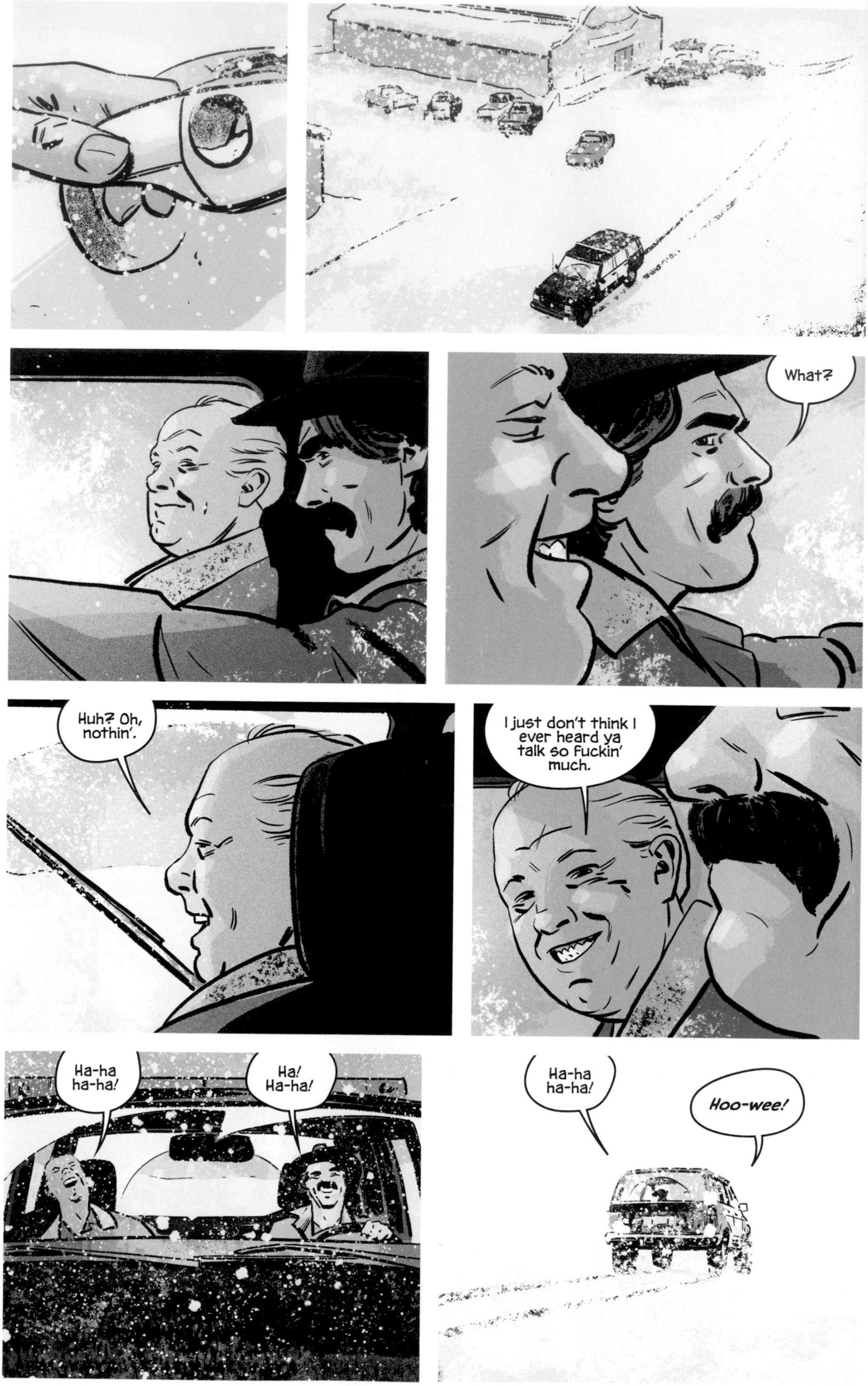
What?
Huh? Oh, nothin'.
I just don't think I ever heard ya talk so fuckin' much.
Ha-ha ha-ha!
Ha! Ha-ha!
Ha-ha ha-ha!
Hoo-wee!

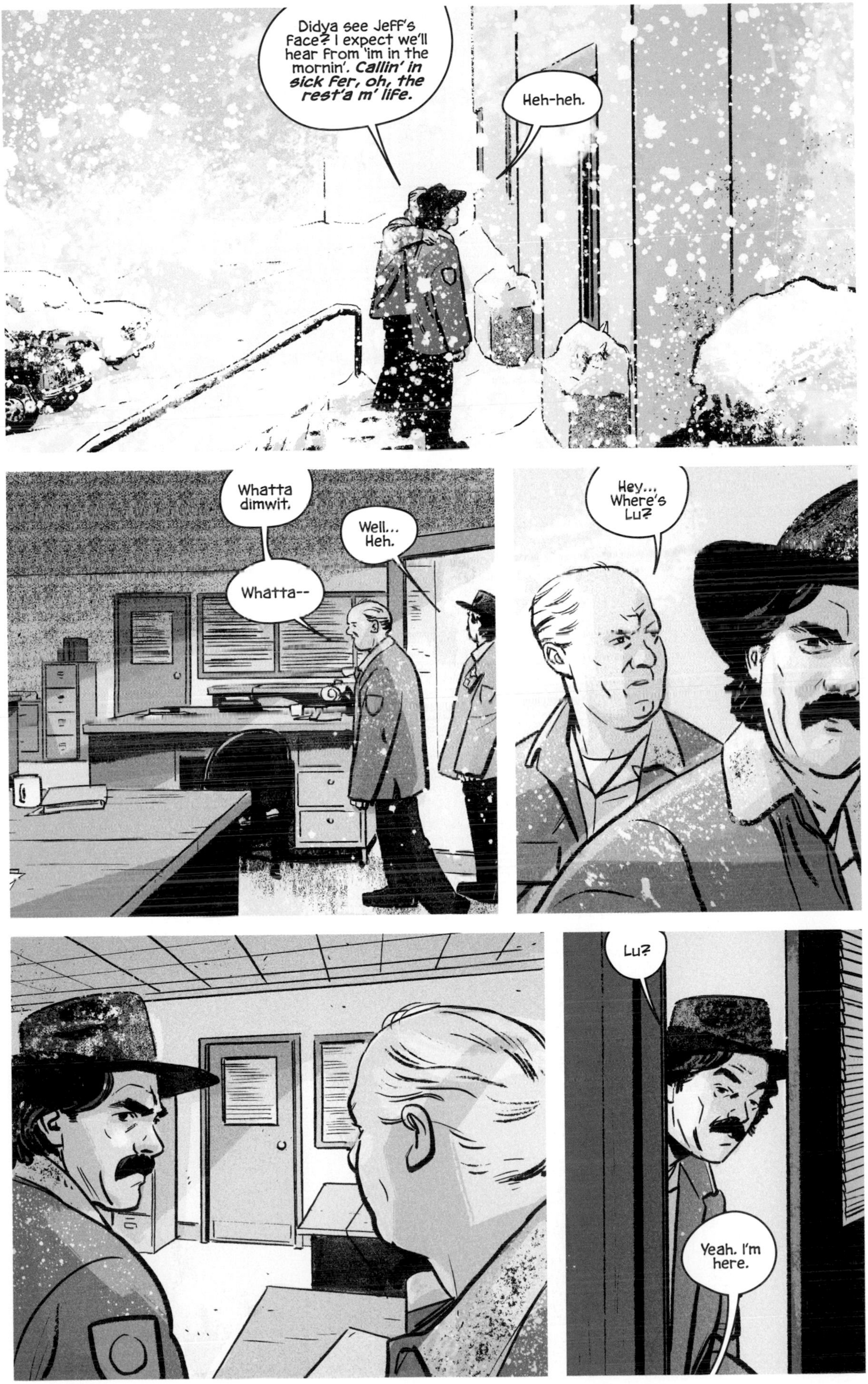
Didya see Jeff's face? I expect we'll hear from 'im in the mornin'. *Callin' in sick fer, oh, the rest'a m' life.*
Heh-heh.
Whatta dimwit.
Whatta--
Well... Heh.
Hey... Where's Lu?
Lu?
Yeah. I'm here.

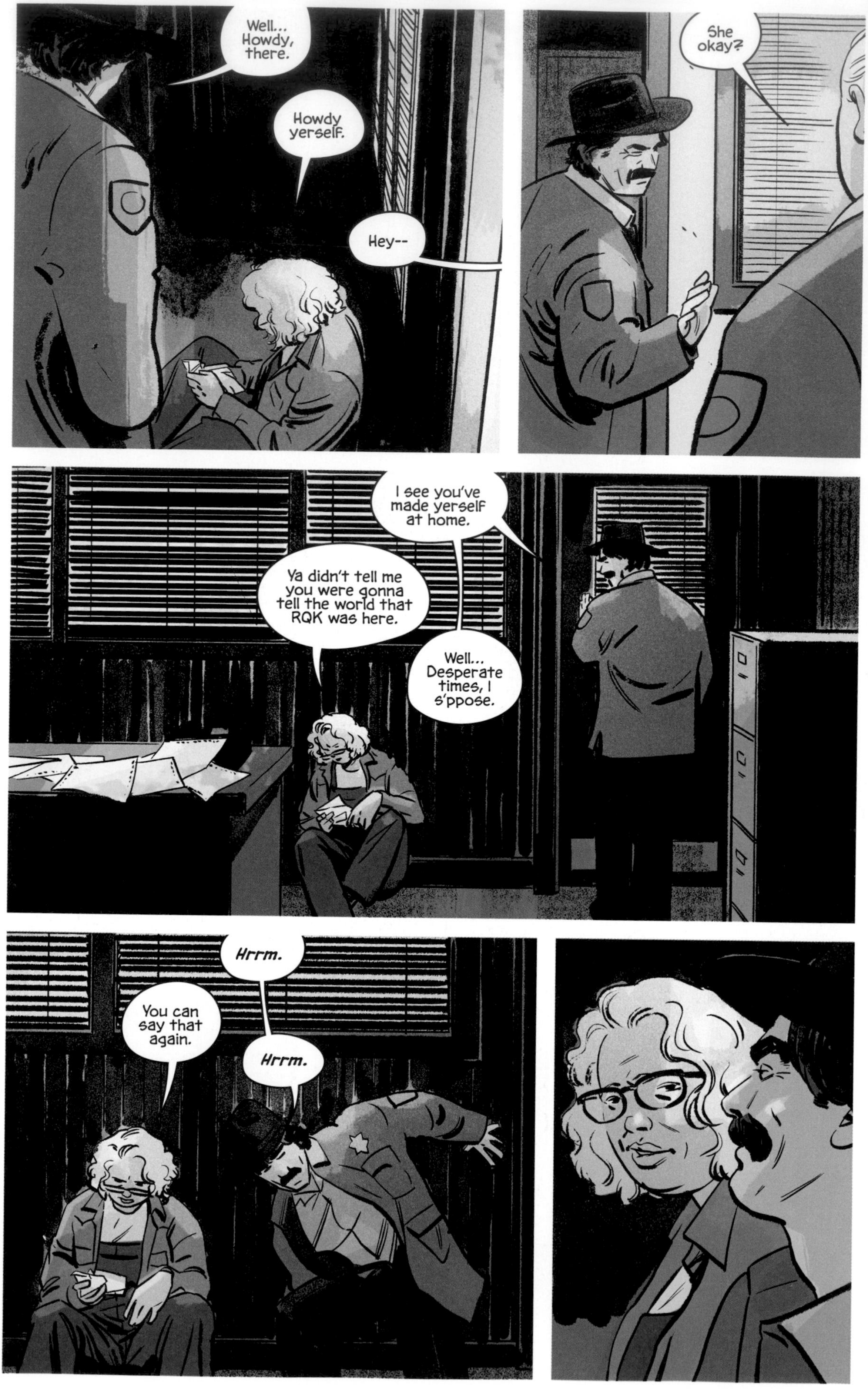
Well... Howdy, there.
Howdy yerself.
Hey--
She okay?
I see you've made yerself at home.
Ya didn't tell me you were gonna tell the world that RQK was here.
Well... Desperate times, I s'ppose.
Hrrm.
You can say that again.
Hrrm.

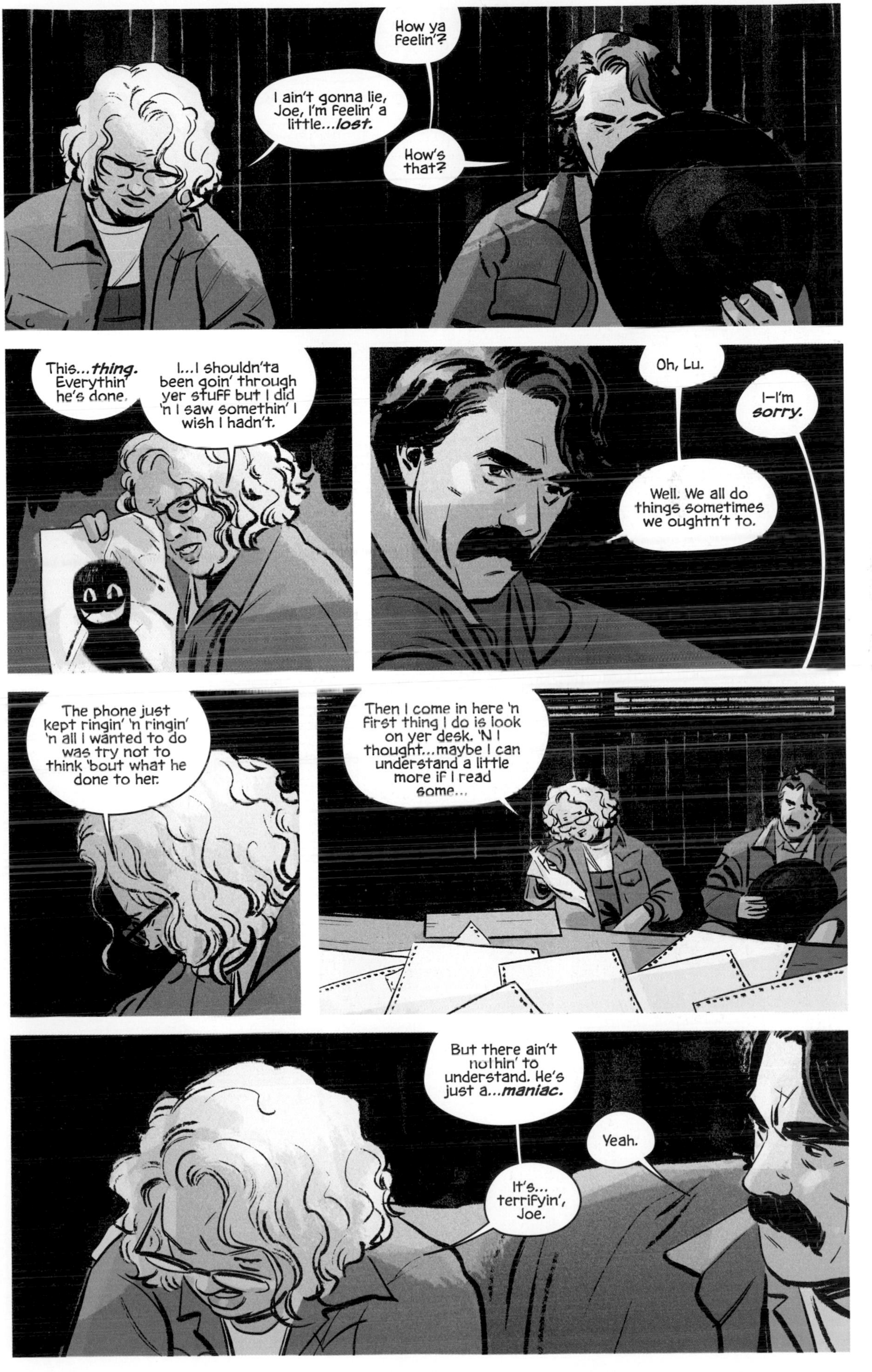
How ya Feelin'?
I ain't gonna lie, Joe, I'm Feelin' a little...lost.
How's that?
This...thing. Everythin' he's done.
I...I shouldn'ta been goin' through yer stuff but I did 'n I saw somethin' I wish I hadn't.
Oh, Lu.
I-I'm sorry.
Well. We all do things sometimes we oughtn't to.
The phone just kept ringin' 'n ringin' 'n all I wanted to do was try not to think 'bout what he done to her.
Then I come in here 'n first thing I do is look on yer desk. 'N I thought...maybe I can understand a little more if I read some...
But there ain't nothin' to understand. He's just a...maniac.
Yeah.
It's... terrifyin', Joe.

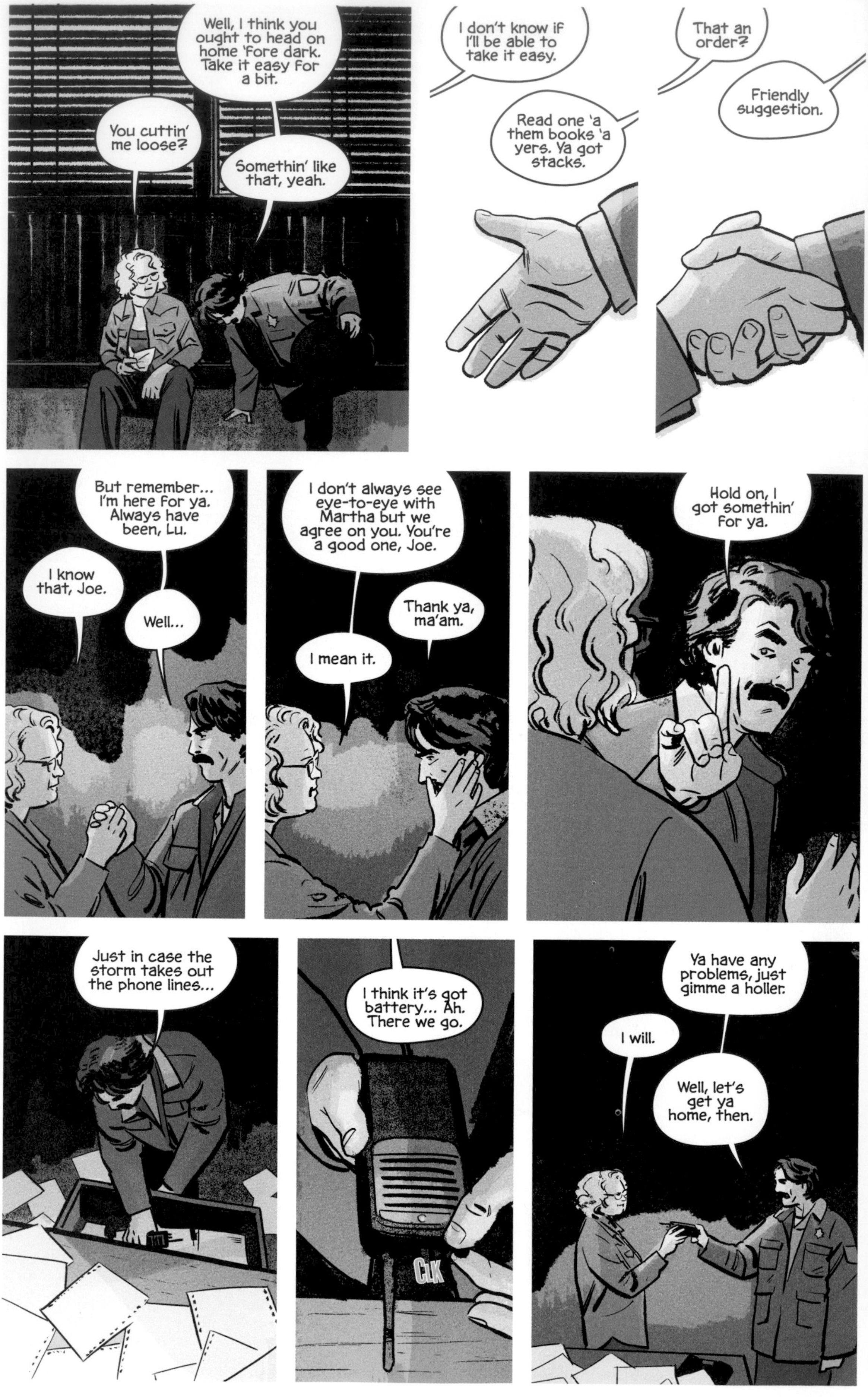
Well, I think you ought to head on home 'fore dark. Take it easy for a bit.
You cuttin' me loose?
Somethin' like that, yeah.
I don't know if I'll be able to take it easy.
Read one 'a them books 'a yers. Ya got stacks.
That an order?
Friendly suggestion.
But remember... I'm here for ya. Always have been, Lu.
I know that, Joe.
Well...
I don't always see eye-to-eye with Martha but we agree on you. You're a good one, Joe.
Thank ya, ma'am.
I mean it.
Hold on, I got somethin' for ya.
Just in case the storm takes out the phone lines...
I think it's got battery... Ah. There we go.
CLK
Ya have any problems, just gimme a holler.
I will.
Well, let's get ya home, then.

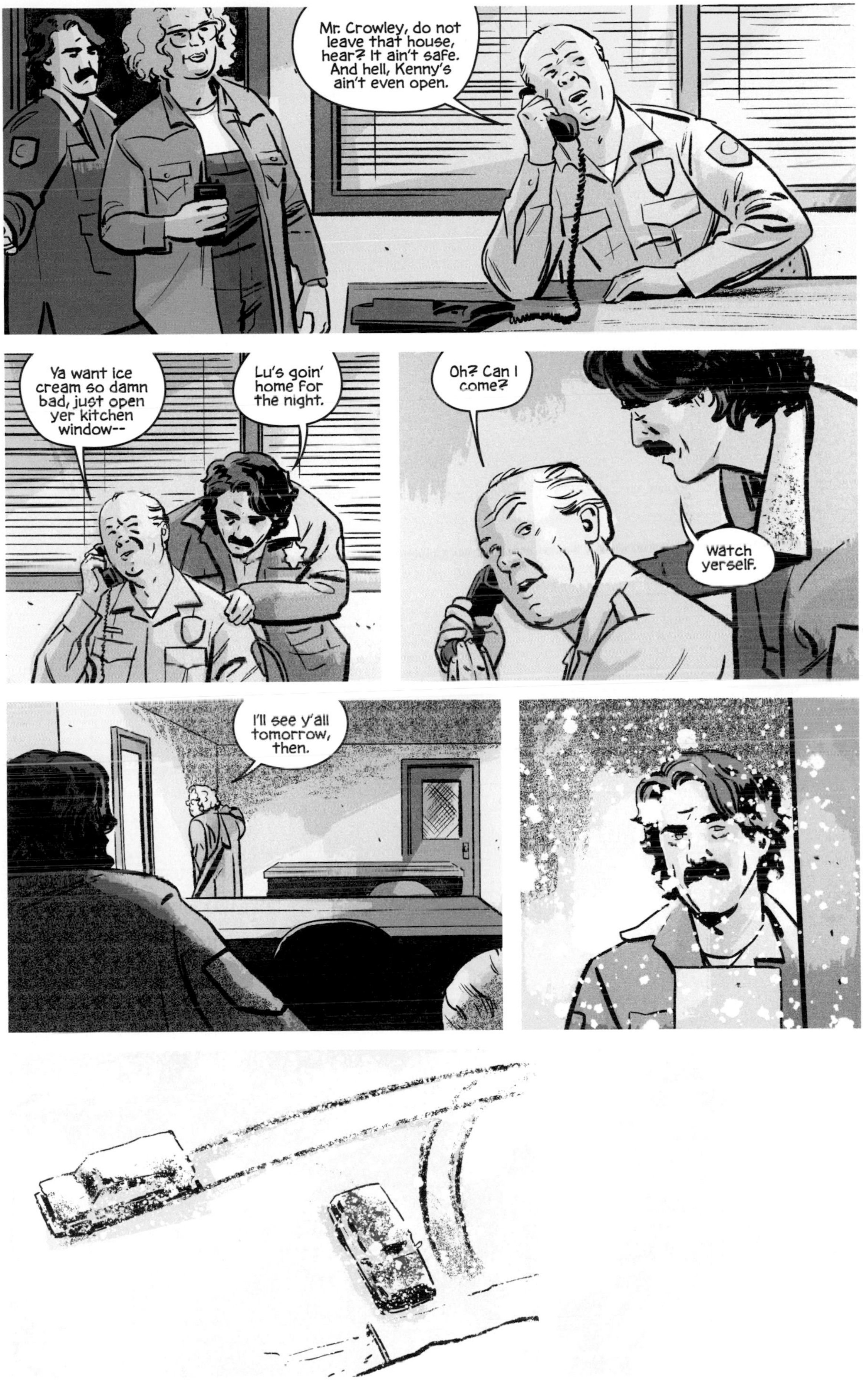
Mr. Crowley, do not leave that house, hear? It ain't safe. And hell, Kenny's ain't even open.
Ya want ice cream so damn bad, just open yer kitchen window--
Lu's goin' home for the night.
Oh? Can I come?
Watch yerself.
I'll see y'all tomorrow, then.

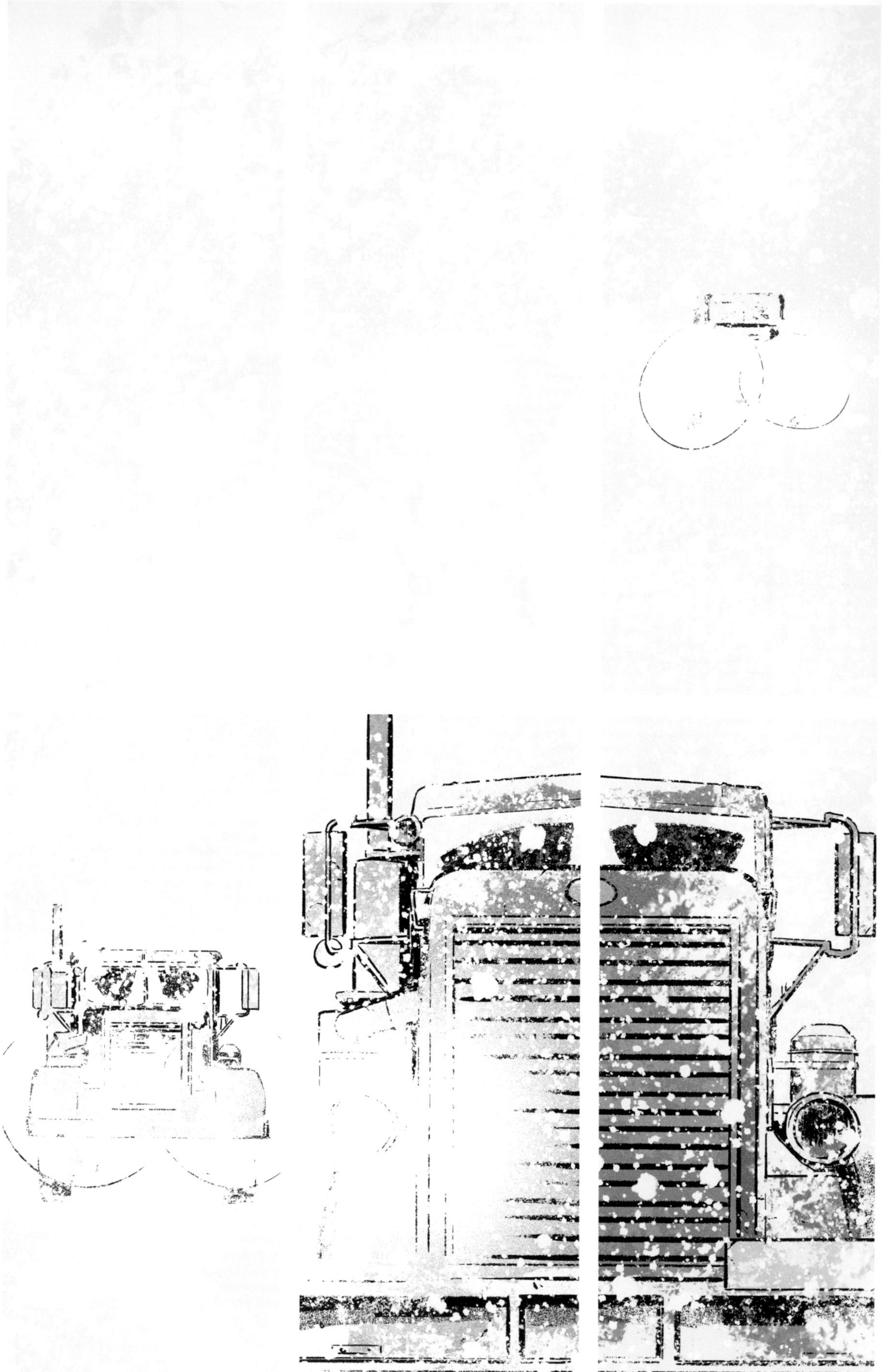

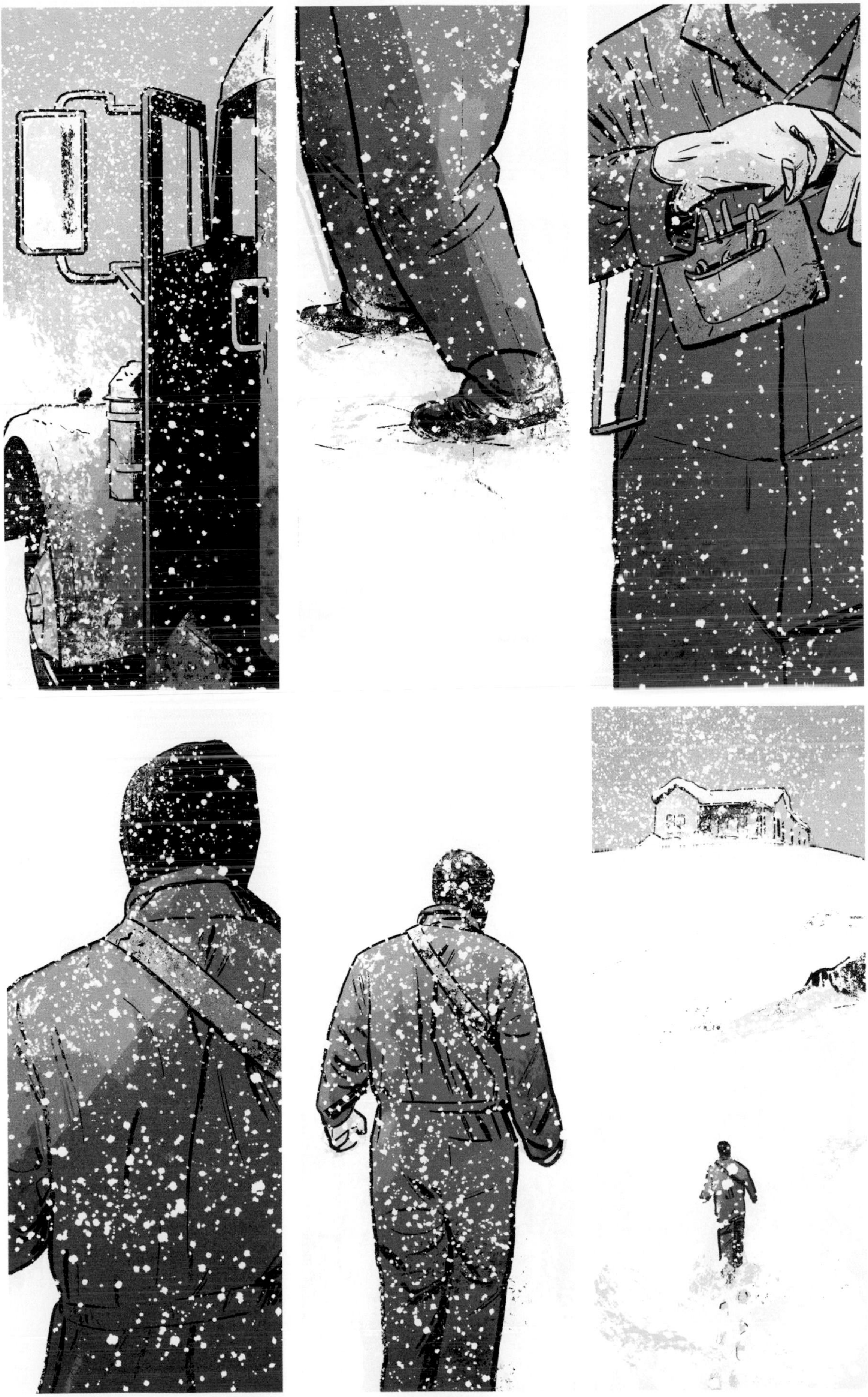

WHAT HAPPENED TO SAM AND THE HOME INVASION

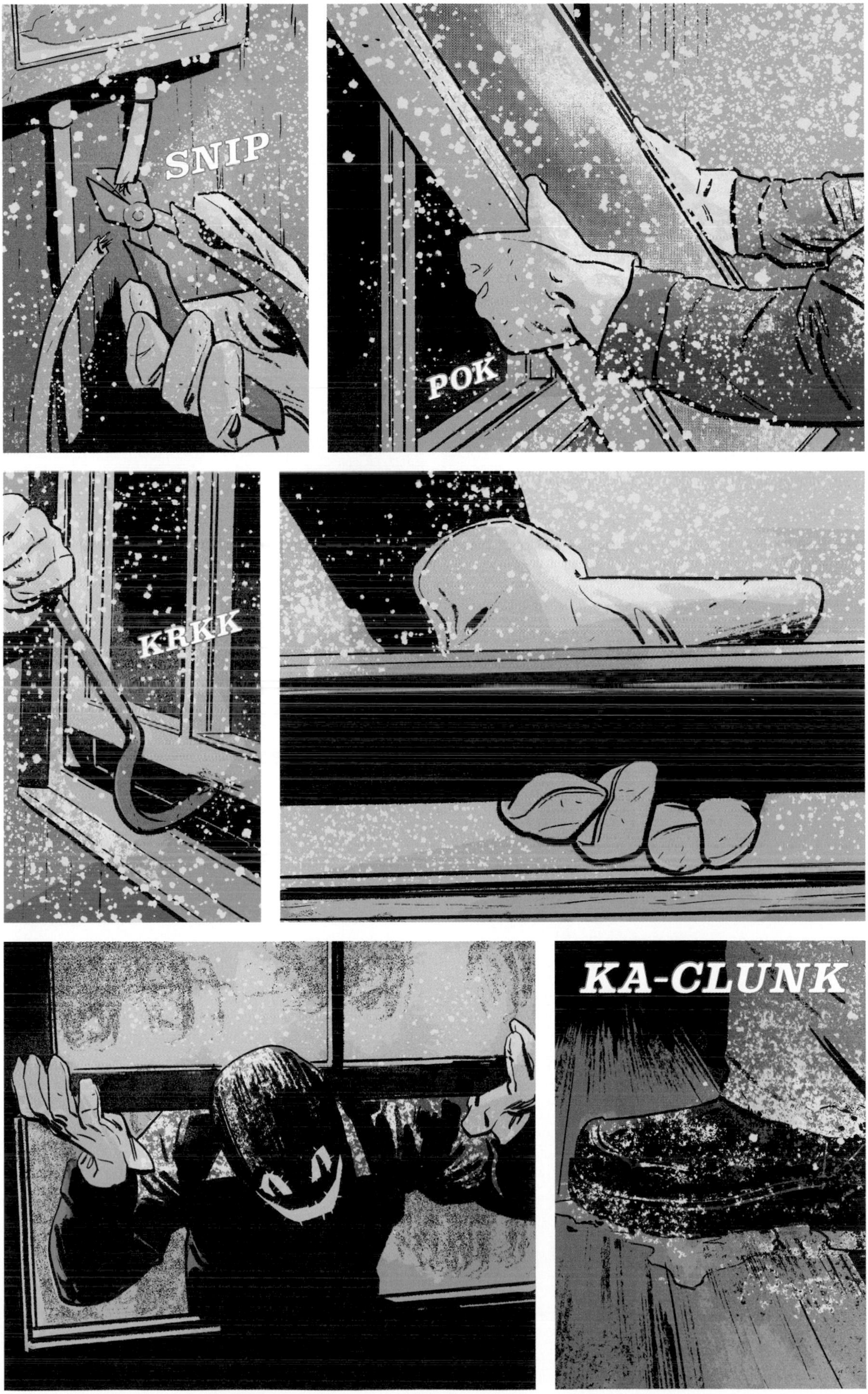
SNIP
POK
KRKK
KA-CLUNK

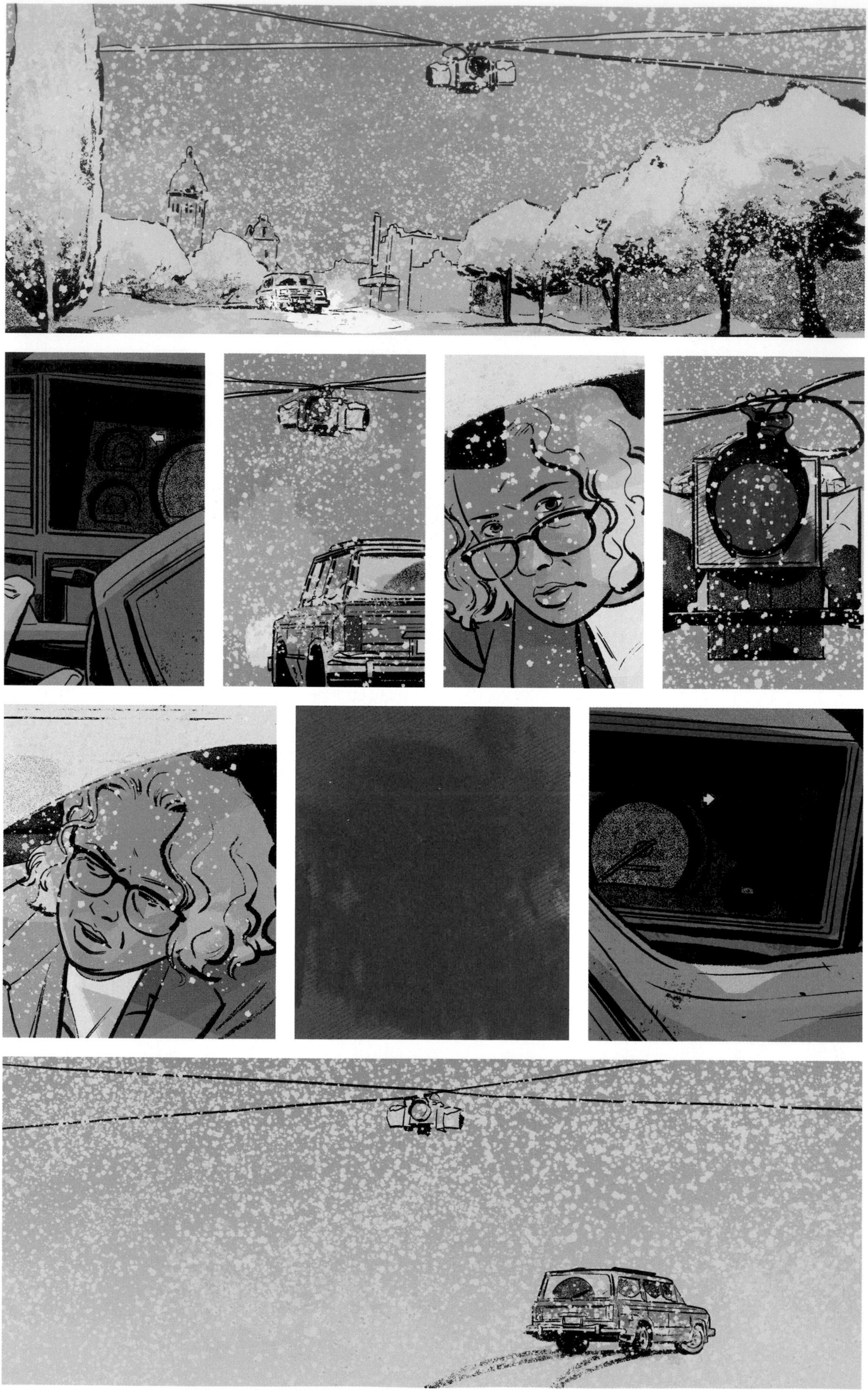

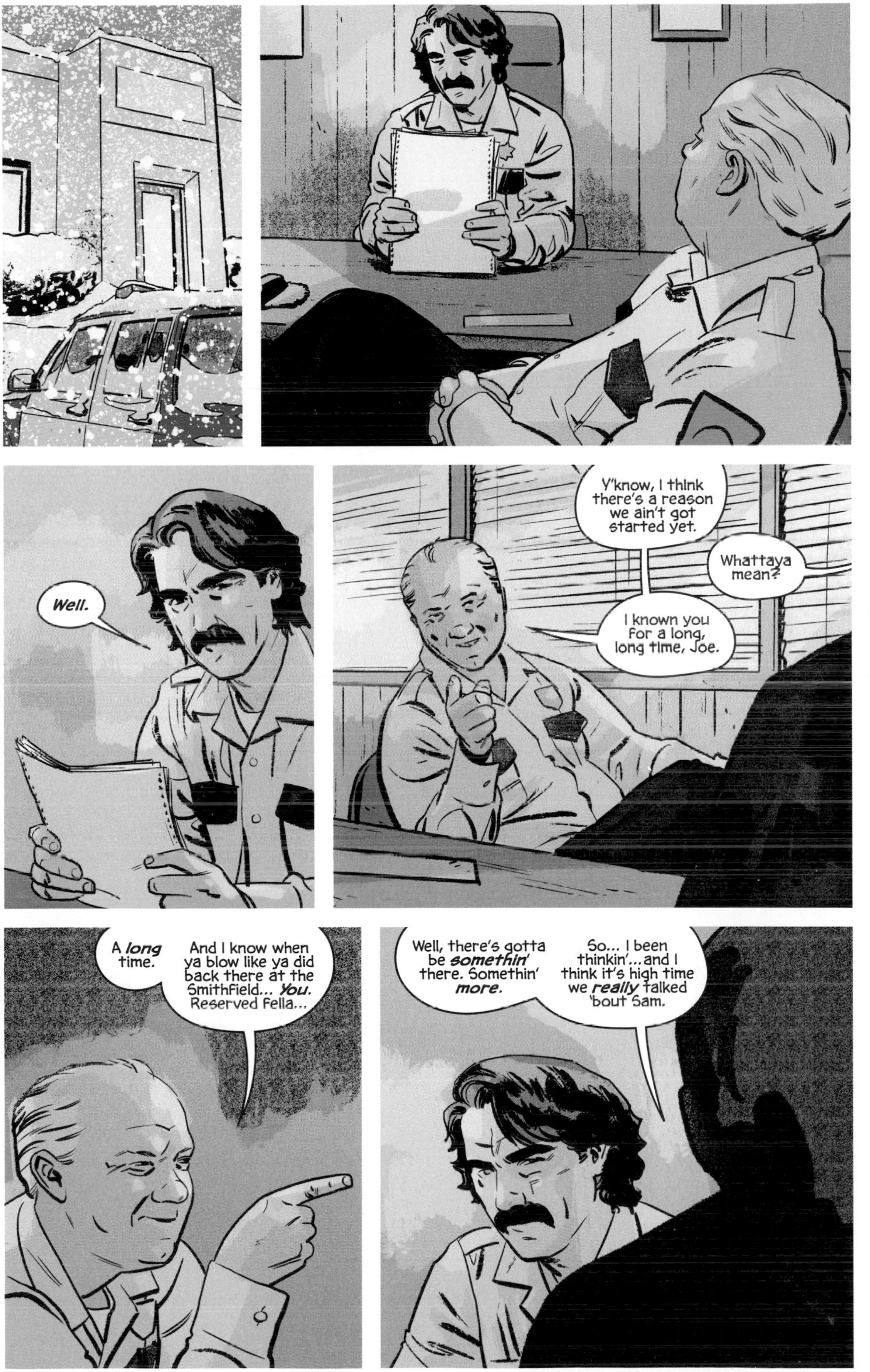
Well.
Y'know, I think there's a reason we ain't got started yet.
Whattaya mean?
I known you for a long, long time, Joe.
A *long* time.
And I know when ya blow like ya did back there at the Smithfield... *You.* Reserved Fella...
Well, there's gotta be *somethin'* there. Somethin' *more.*
So... I been thinkin'... and I think it's high time we *really* talked 'bout Sam.

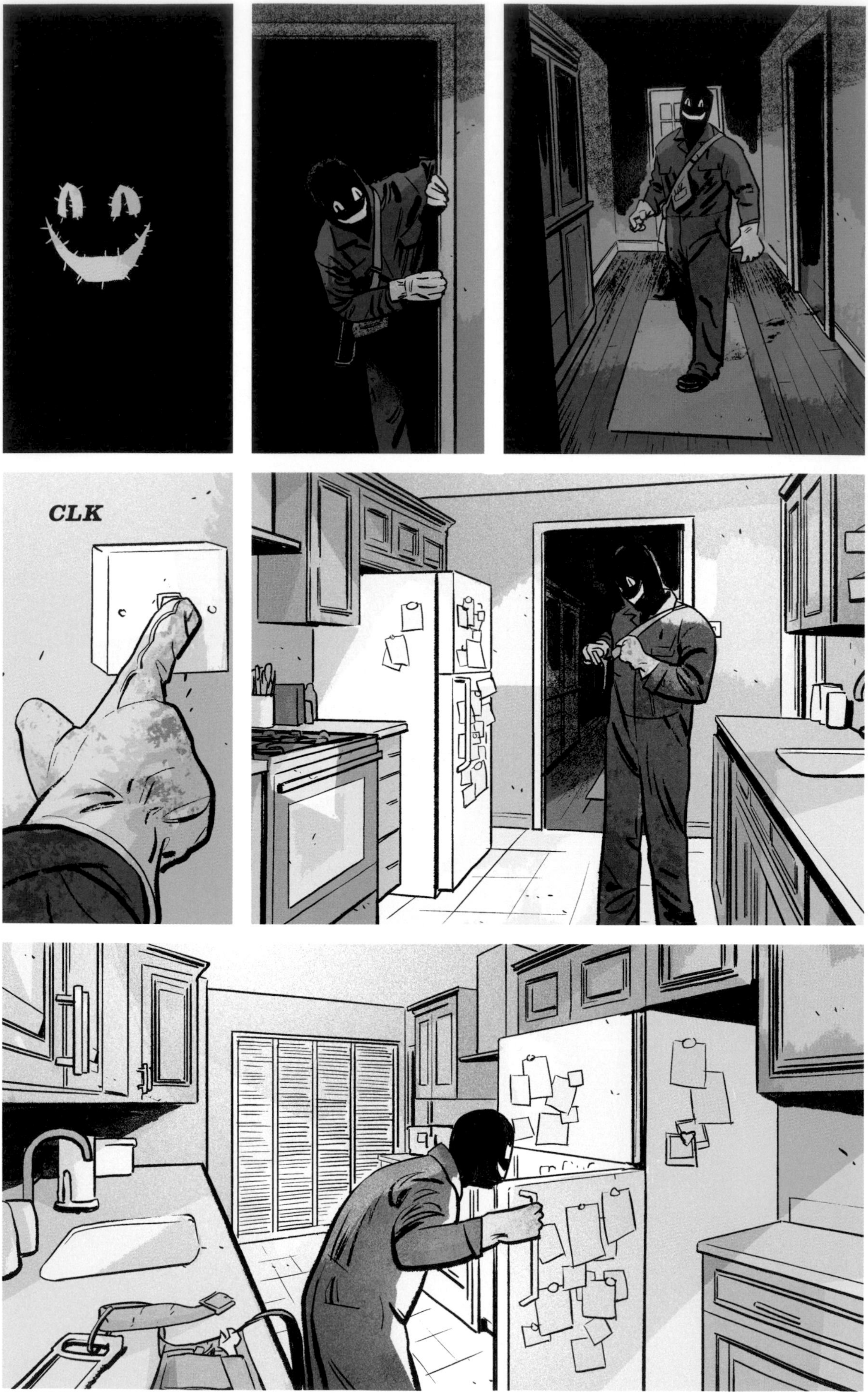
CLK

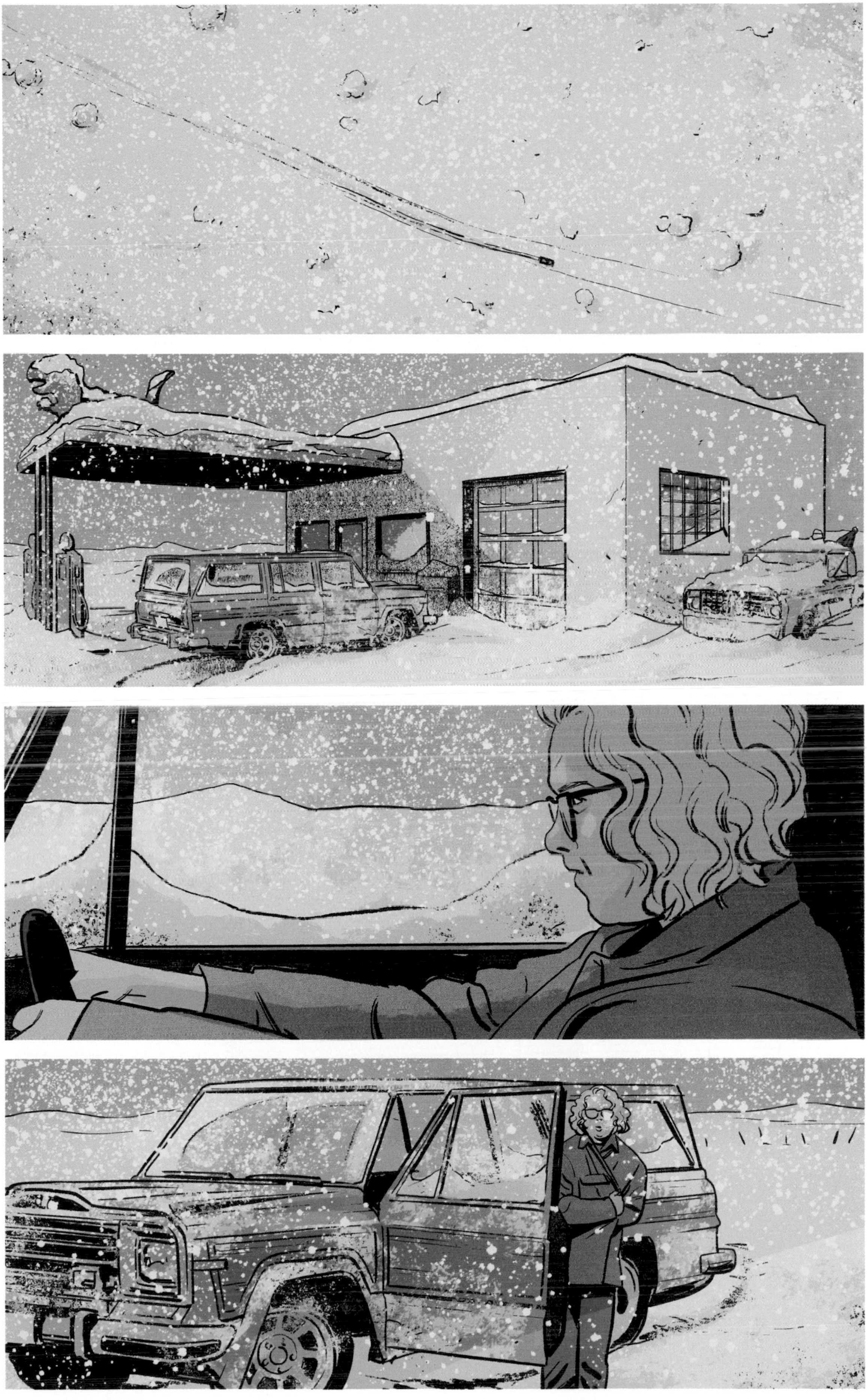

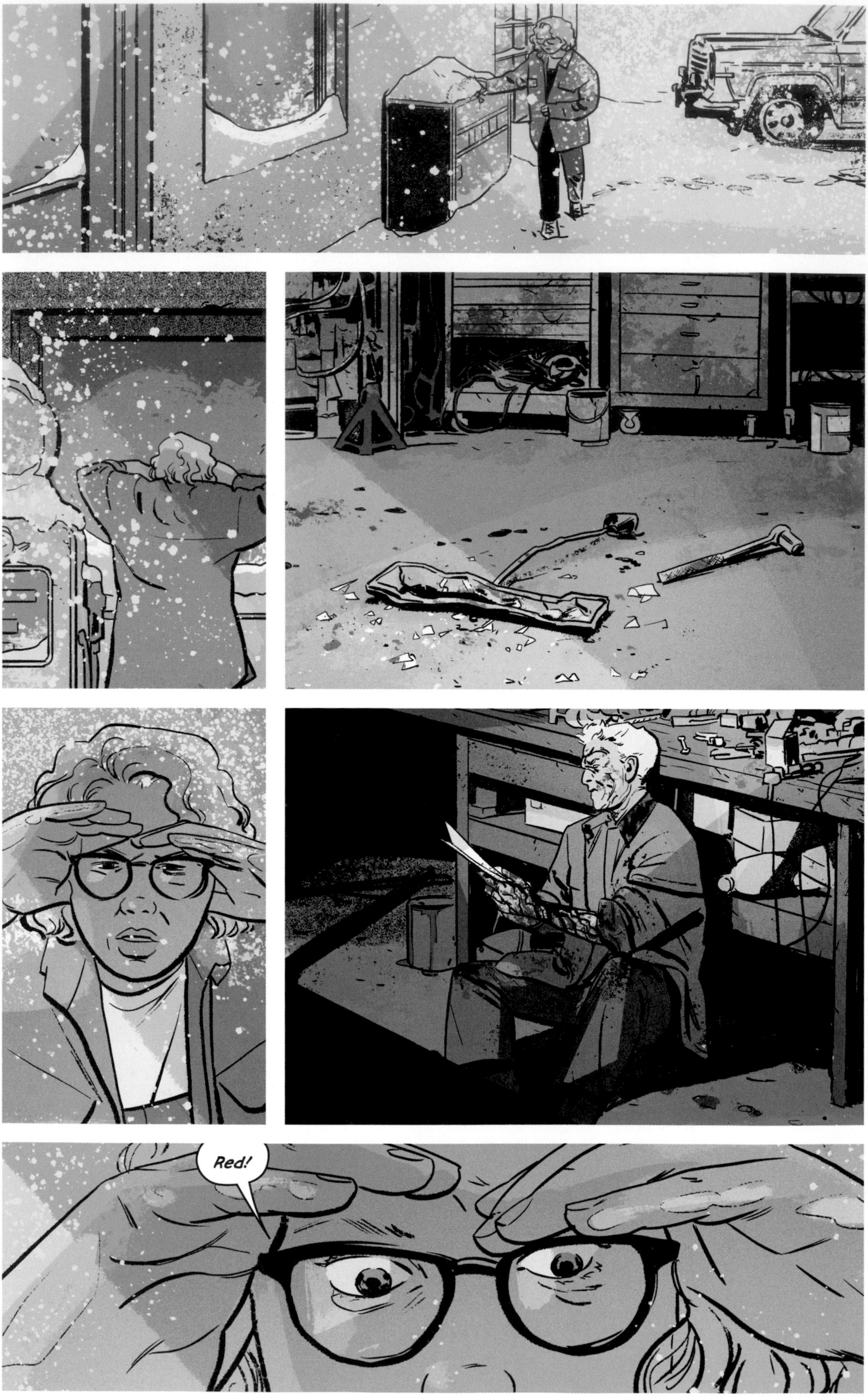
Red!

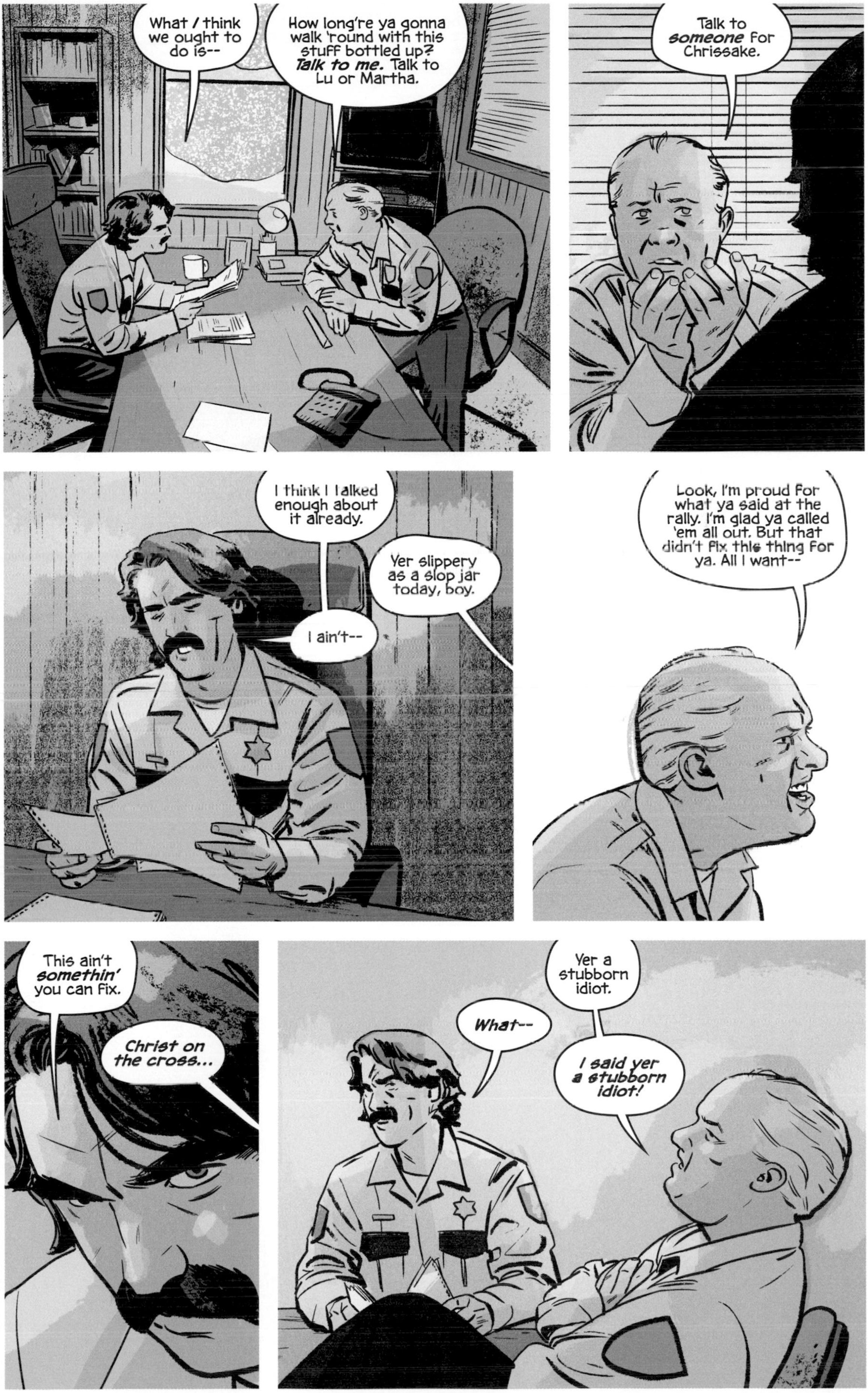

What *I* think we ought to do is--
How long're ya gonna walk 'round with this stuff bottled up? ***Talk to me.*** Talk to Lu or Martha.
Talk to ***someone*** for Chrissake.
I think I talked enough about it already.
Yer slippery as a slop jar today, boy.
I ain't--
Look, I'm proud for what ya said at the rally. I'm glad ya called 'em all out. But that didn't fix this thing for ya. All I want--
This ain't ***somethin'*** you can fix.
Christ on the cross...
Yer a stubborn idiot.
What--
I said yer a stubborn idiot!

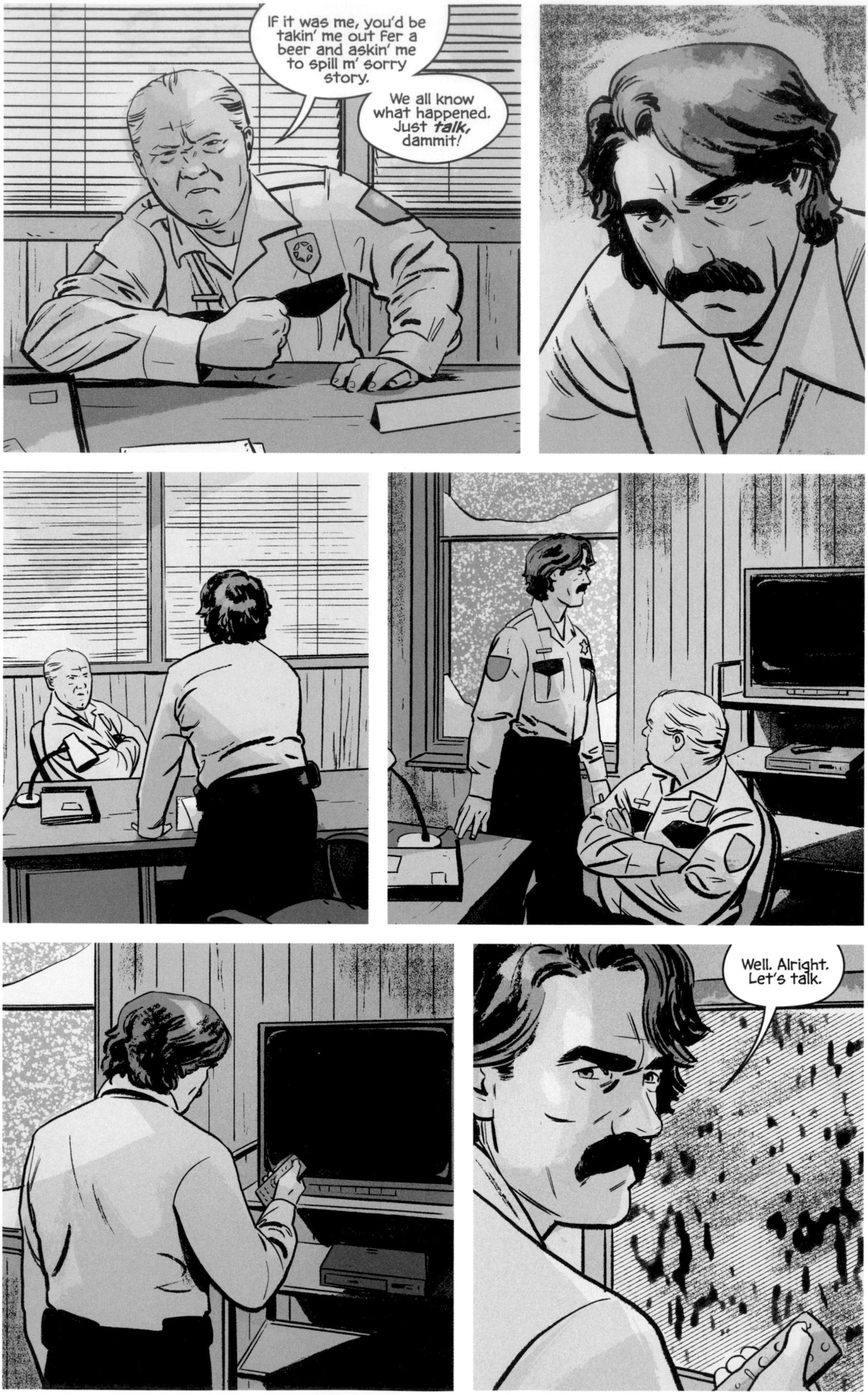
If it was me, you'd be takin' me out fer a beer and askin' me to spill m' sorry story.
We all know what happened. Just *talk,* dammit!
Well. Alright. Let's talk.

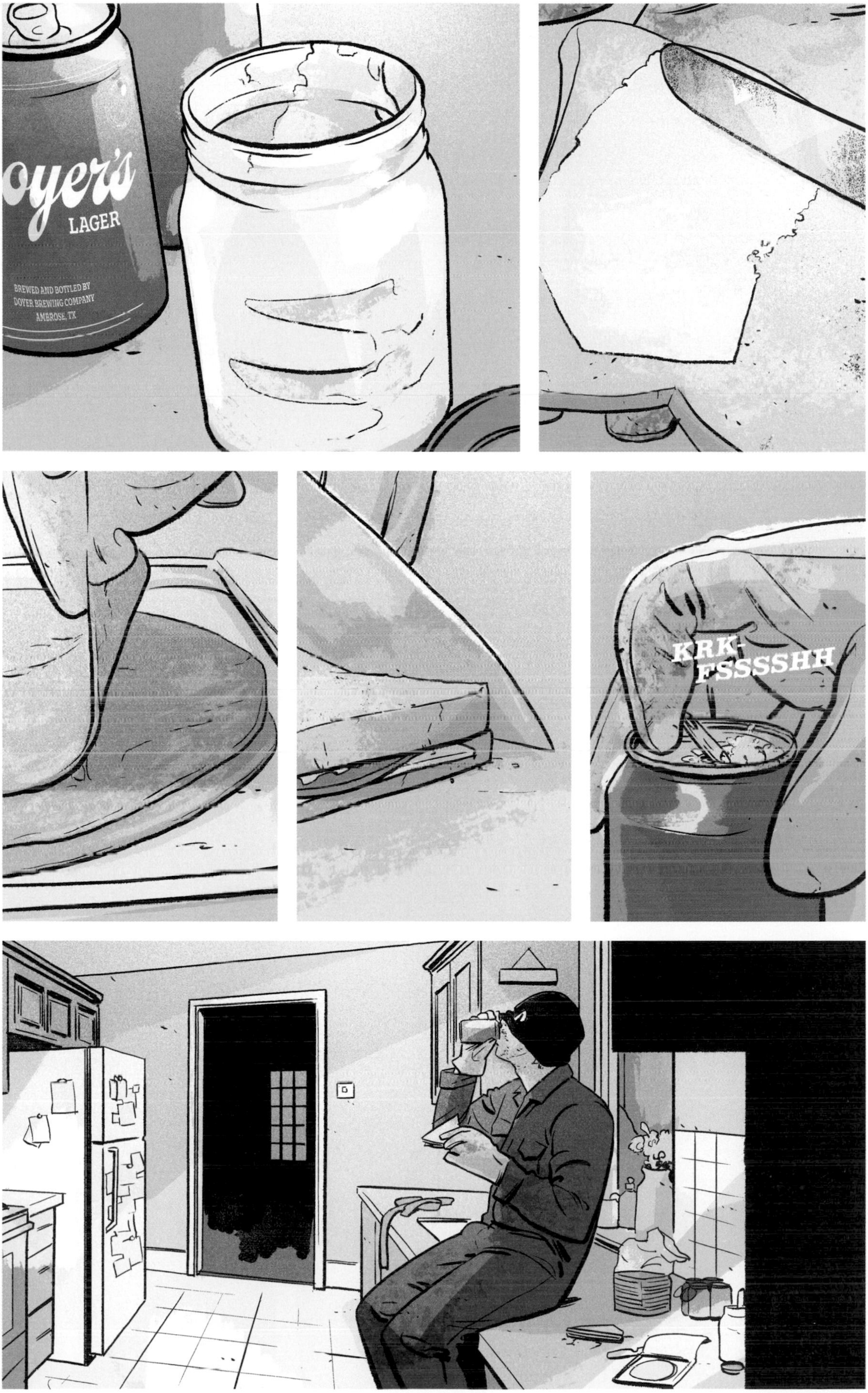
oyer's
LAGER
BREWED AND BOTTLED BY
DOYER BREWING COMPANY
AMBROSE, TX
KRK-
FSSSSHH

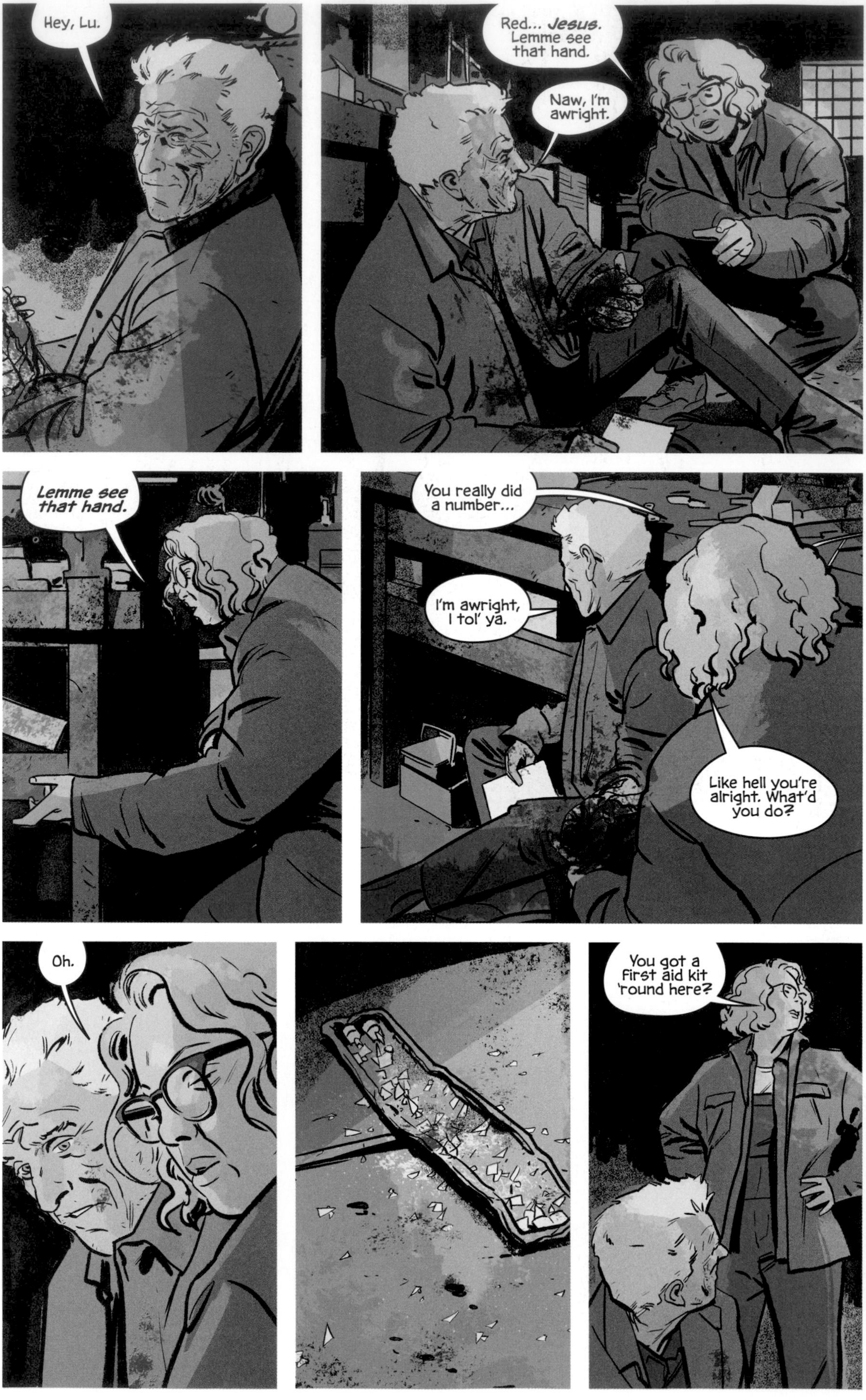
Hey, Lu.
Red... *Jesus.* Lemme see that hand.
Naw, I'm awright.
Lemme see that hand.
You really did a number...
I'm awright, I tol' ya.
Like hell you're alright. What'd you do?
Oh.
You got a first aid kit 'round here?

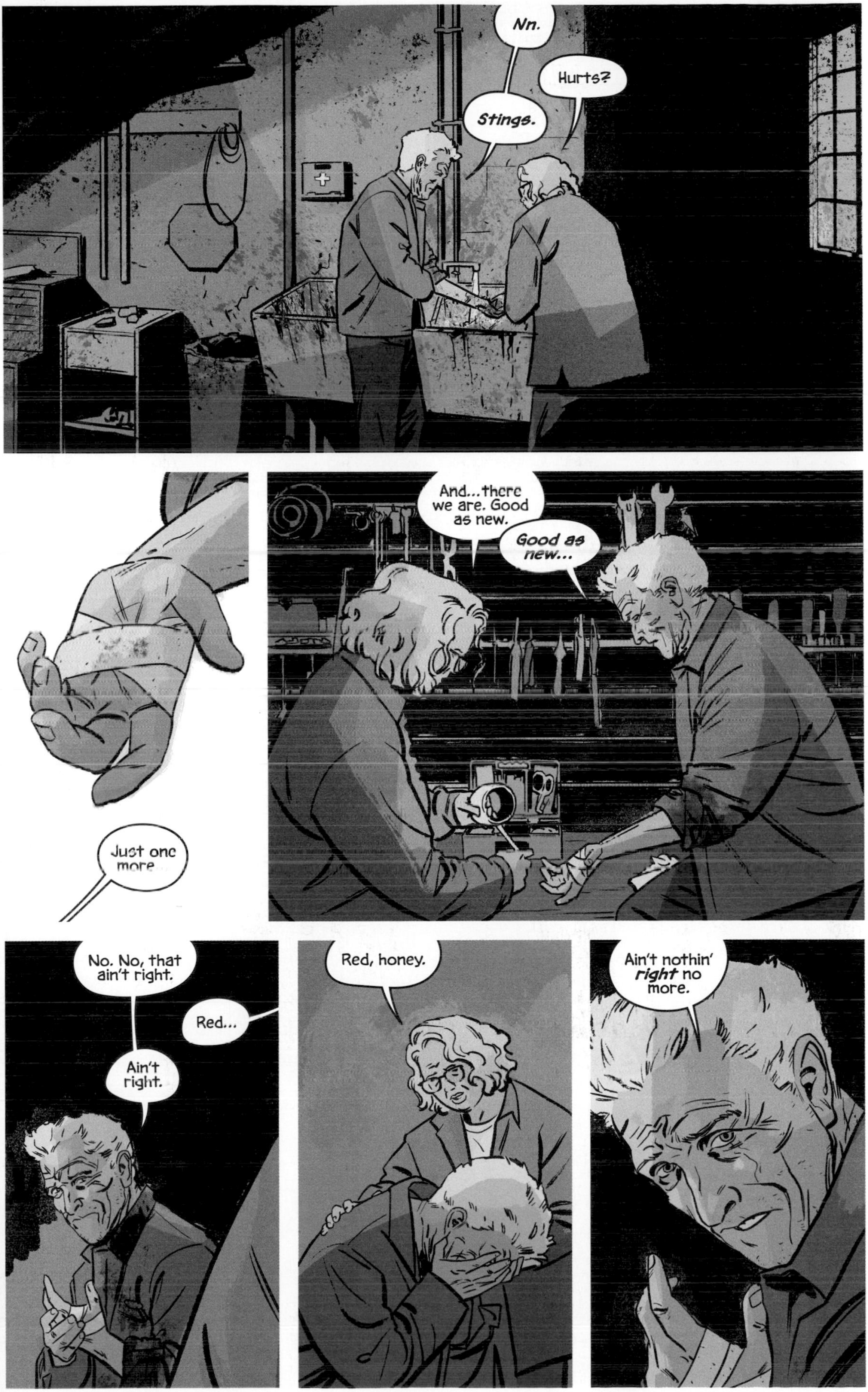
Nn.
Hurts?
Stings.
And...there we are. Good as new.
Good as new...
Just one more...
No. No, that ain't right.
Red...
Ain't right.
Red, honey.
Ain't nothin' *right* no more.

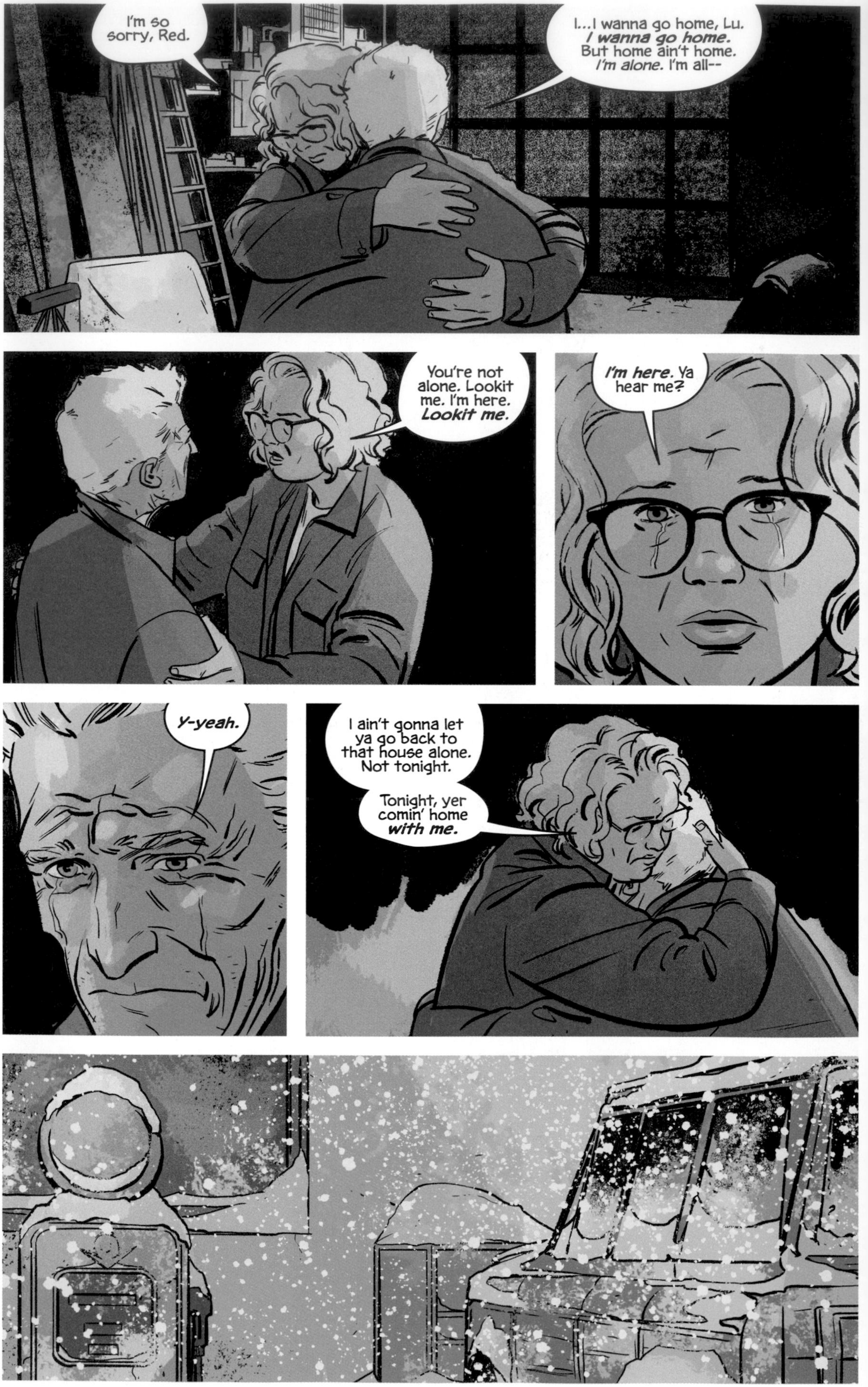
I'm so sorry, Red.
I...I wanna go home, Lu. *I wanna go home.* But home ain't home. *I'm alone.* I'm all--
You're not alone. Lookit me. I'm here. ***Lookit me.***
I'm here. Ya hear me?
Y-yeah.
I ain't gonna let ya go back to that house alone. Not tonight.
Tonight, yer comin' home ***with me.***

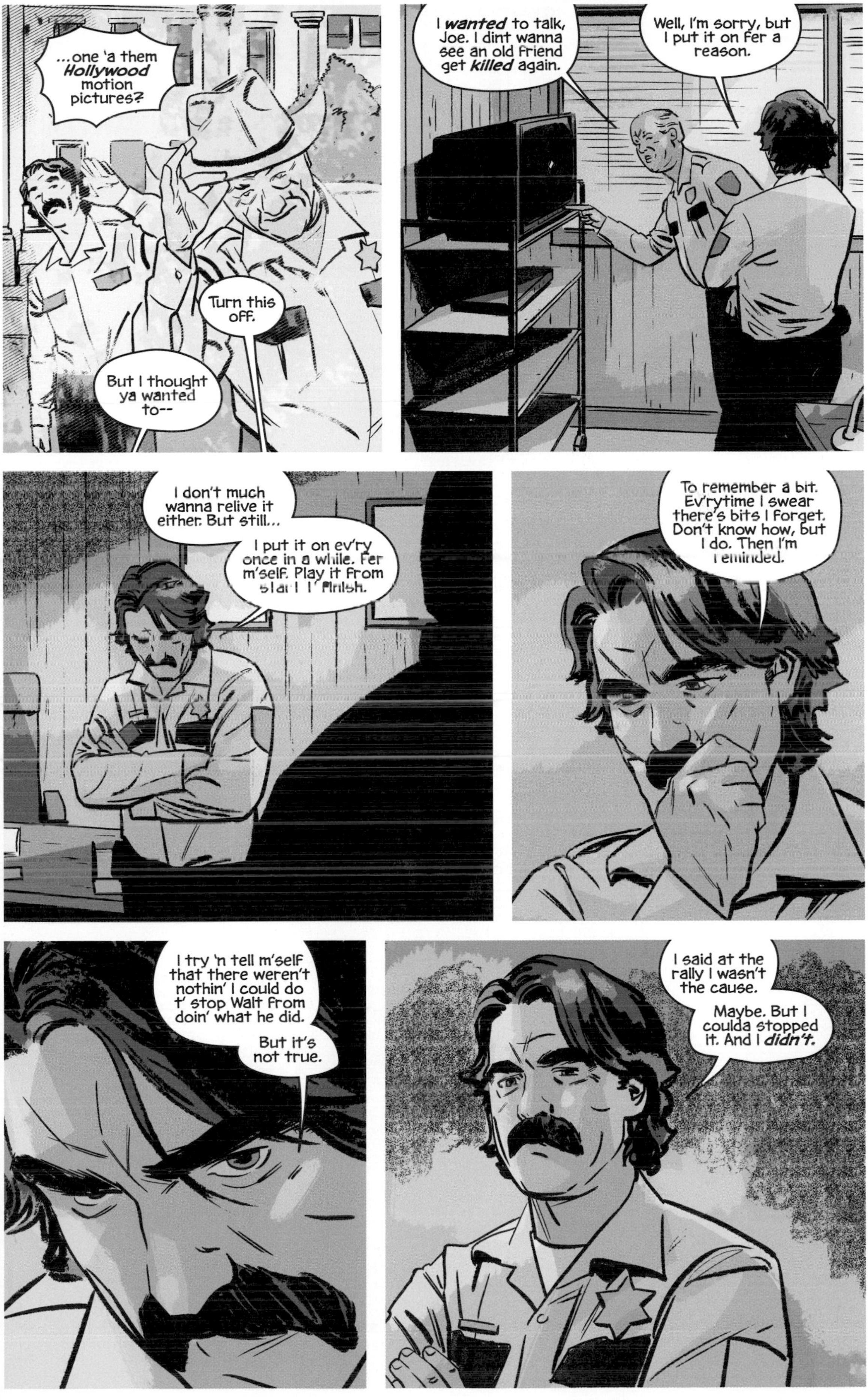
...one 'a them Hollywood motion pictures?
Turn this off.
But I thought ya wanted to--
I wanted to talk, Joe. I dint wanna see an old friend get killed again.
Well, I'm sorry, but I put it on fer a reason.
I don't much wanna relive it either. But still...
I put it on ev'ry once in a while. Fer m'self. Play it from start t' finish.
To remember a bit. Ev'rytime I swear there's bits I forget. Don't know how, but I do. Then I'm reminded.
I try 'n tell m'self that there weren't nothin' I could do t' stop Walt from doin' what he did.
But it's not true.
I said at the rally I wasn't the cause.
Maybe. But I coulda stopped it. And I didn't.

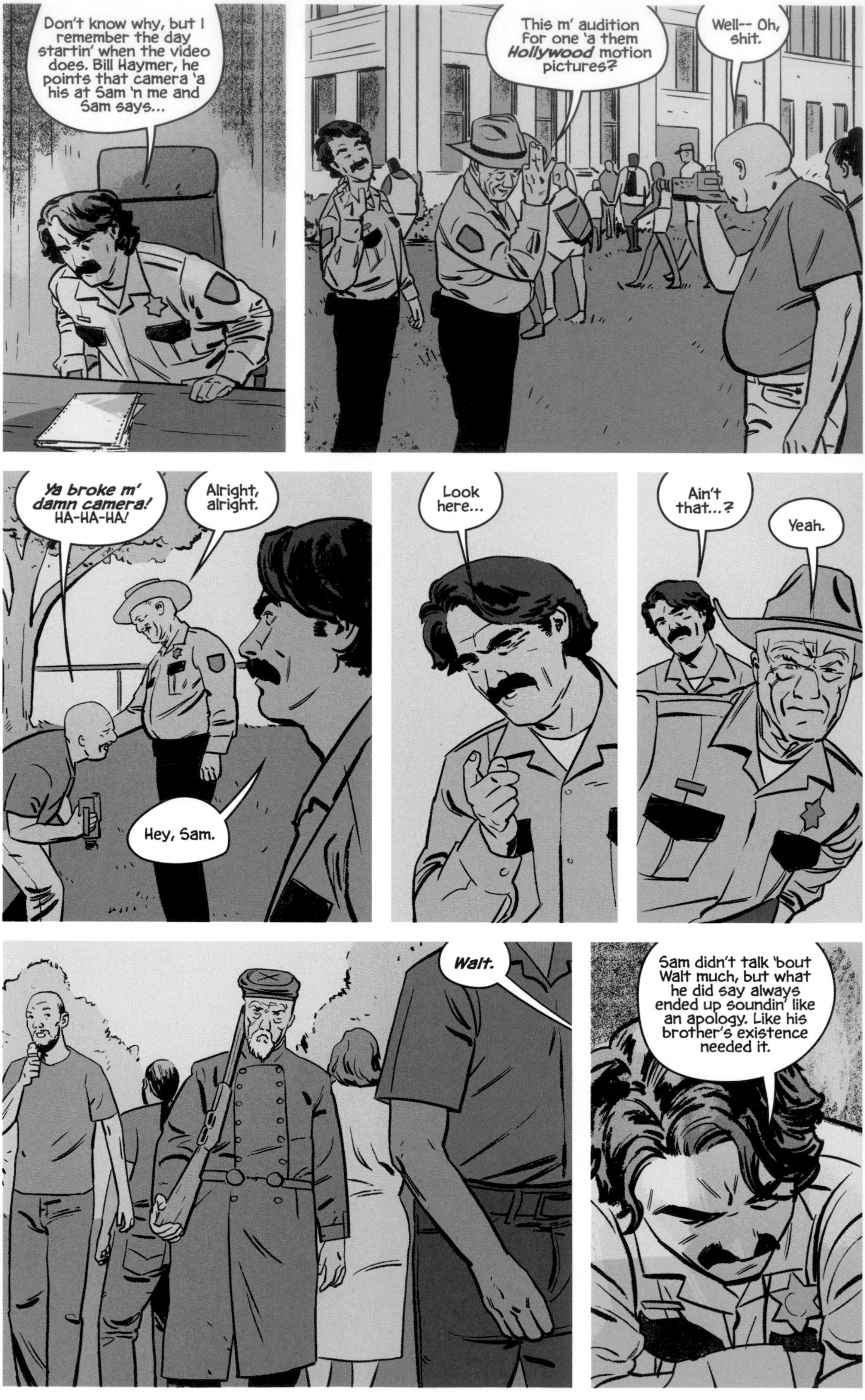
Don't know why, but I remember the day startin' when the video does. Bill Haymer, he points that camera 'a his at Sam 'n me and Sam says...
This m' audition for one 'a them *Hollywood* motion pictures?
Well-- Oh, shit.
Ya broke m' damn camera! HA-HA-HA!
Alright, alright.
Hey, Sam.
Look here...
Ain't that...?
Yeah.
Walt.
Sam didn't talk 'bout Walt much, but what he did say always ended up soundin' like an apology. Like his brother's existence needed it.

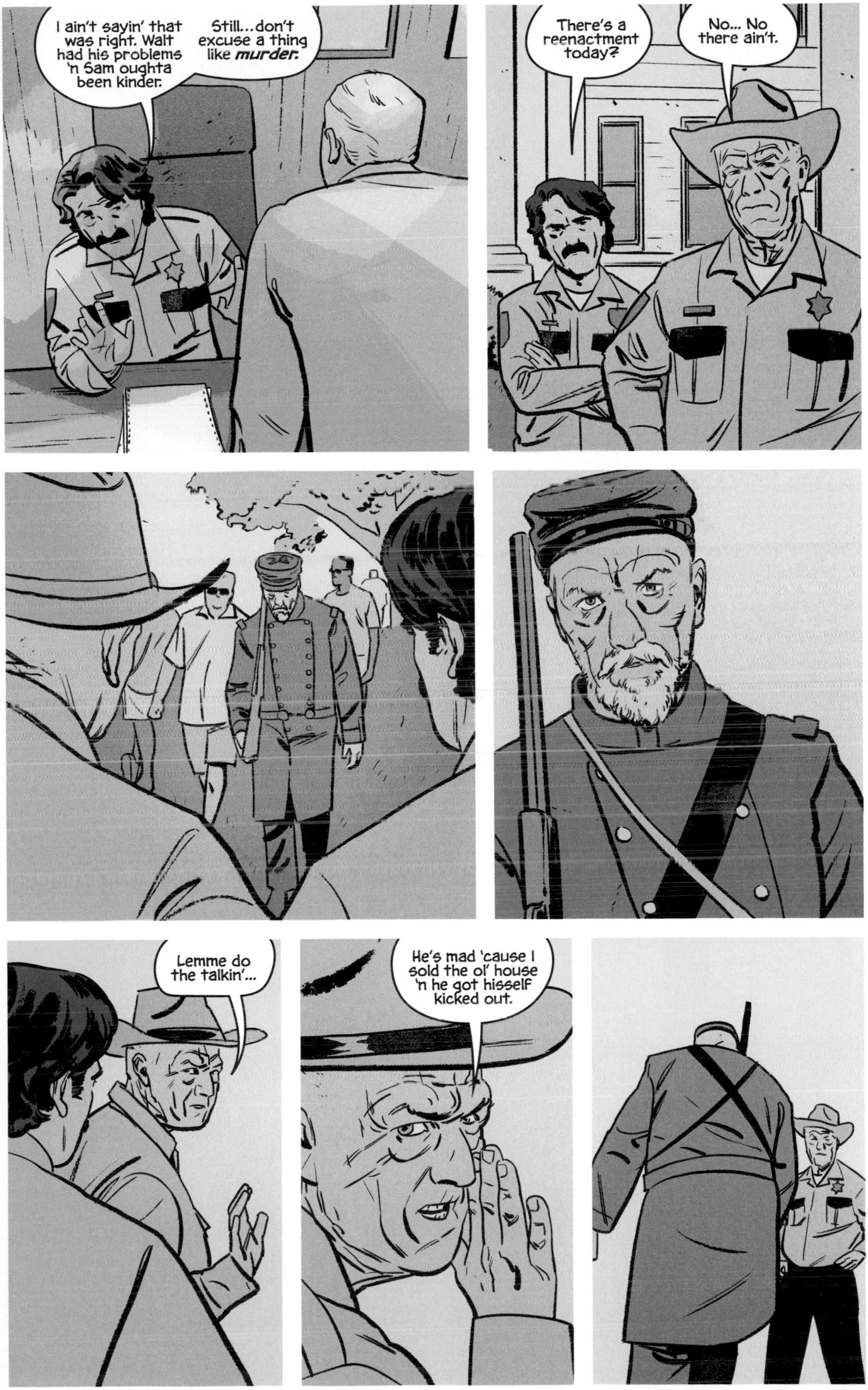
I ain't sayin' that was right. Walt had his problems 'n Sam oughta been kinder.
Still... don't excuse a thing like *murder.*
There's a reenactment today?
No... No there ain't.
Lemme do the talkin'...
He's mad 'cause I sold the ol' house 'n he got hisself kicked out.

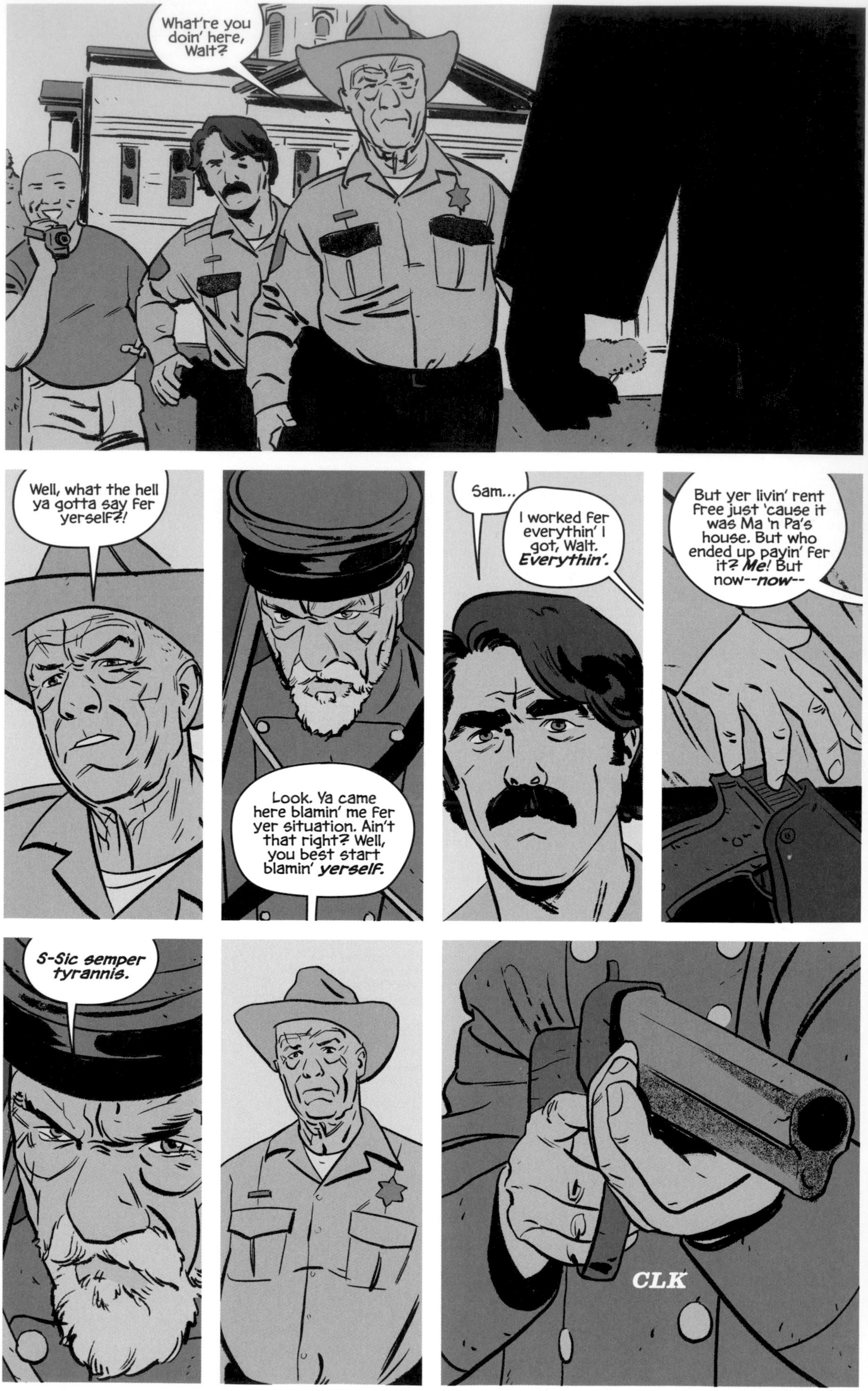
What're you doin' here, Walt?
Well, what the hell ya gotta say fer yerself?!
Look. Ya came here blamin' me fer yer situation. Ain't that right? Well, you best start blamin' *yerself.*
Sam...
I worked fer everythin' I got, Walt. *Everythin'.*
But yer livin' rent free just 'cause it was Ma 'n Pa's house. But who ended up payin' fer it? *Me!* But now--*now*--
S-Sic semper tyrannis.
CLK

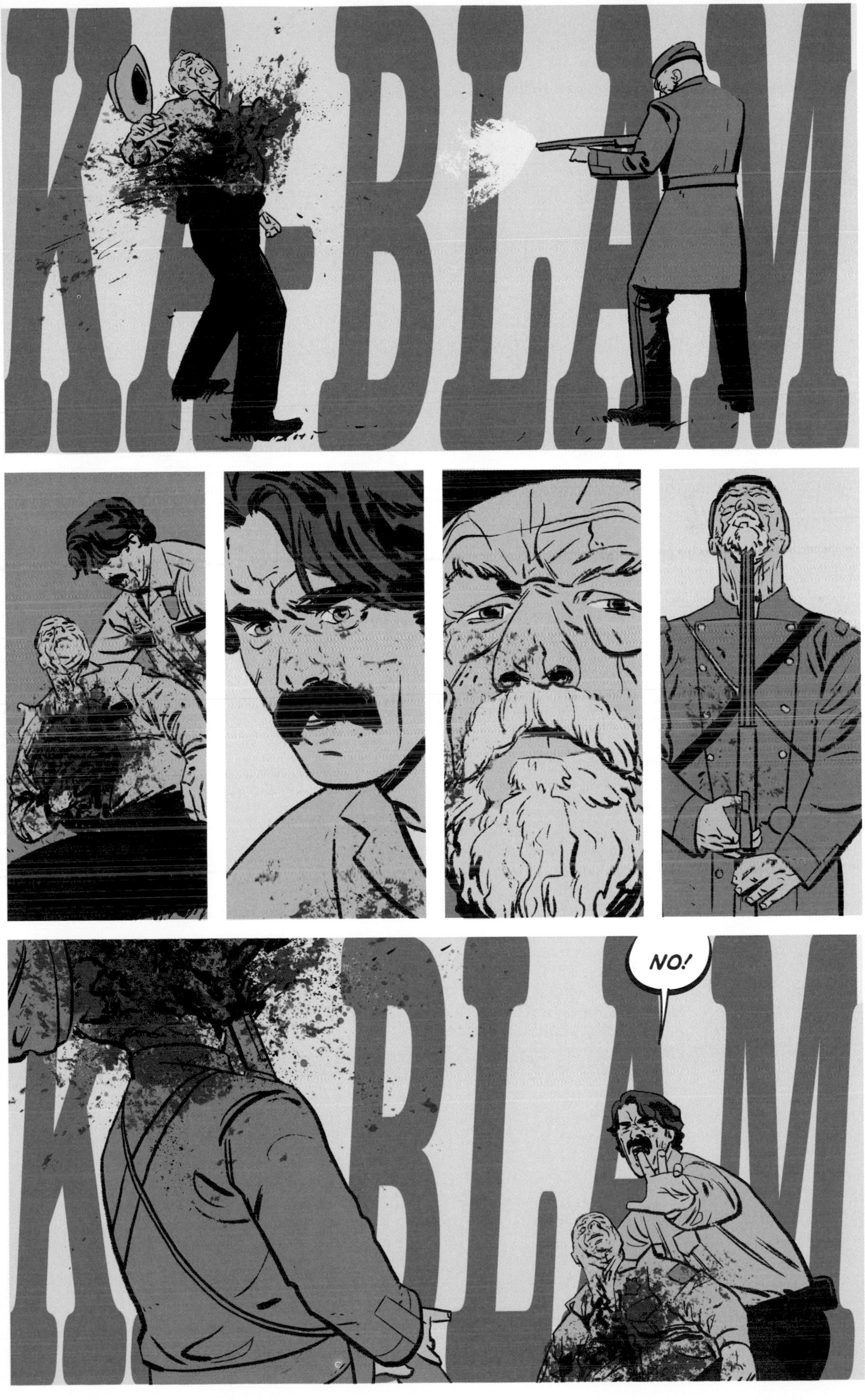
KA-BLAM
NO!
KA-BLAM

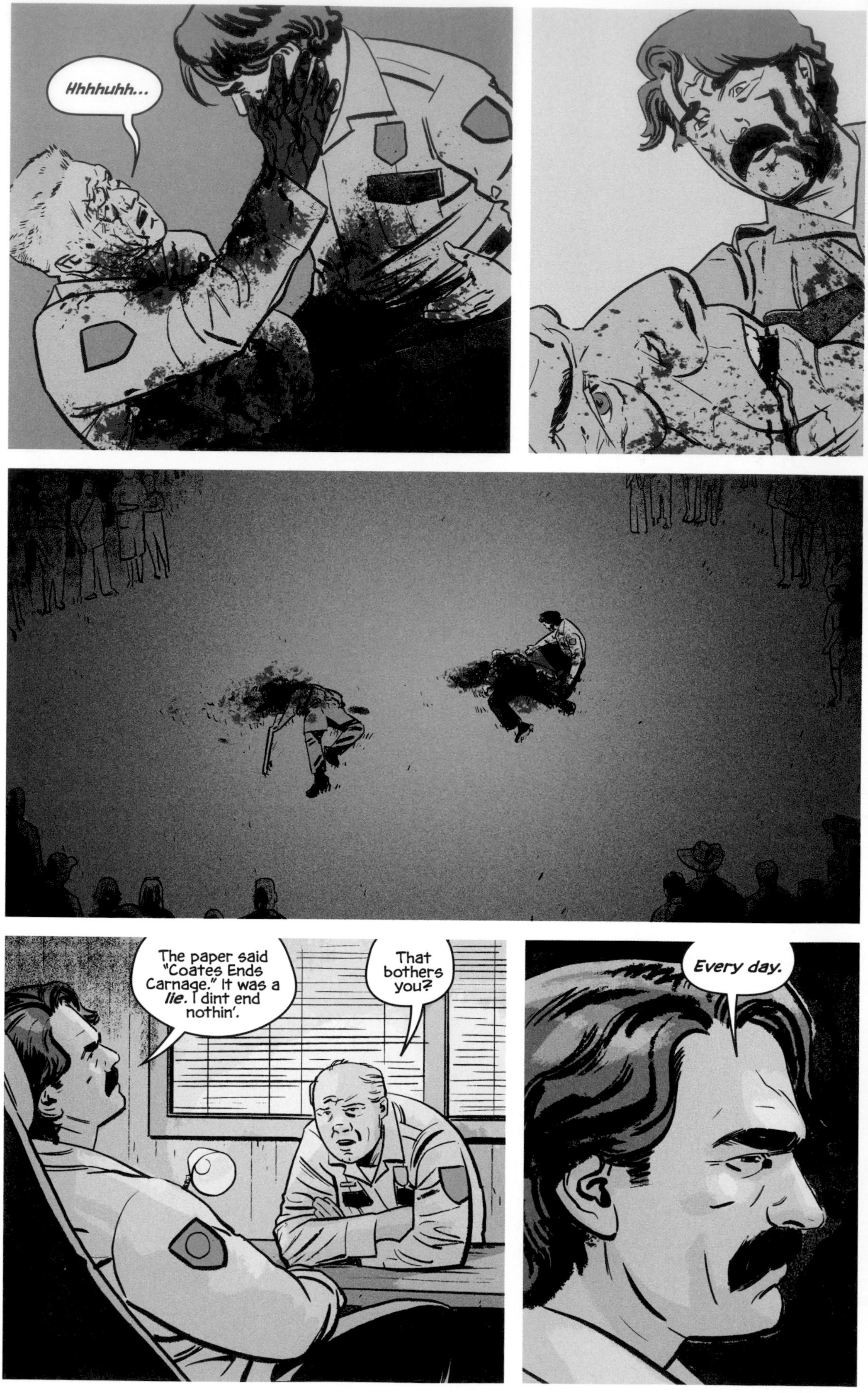
Hhhhuhh...
The paper said "Coates Ends Carnage." It was a lie. I dint end nothin'.
That bothers you?
Every day.

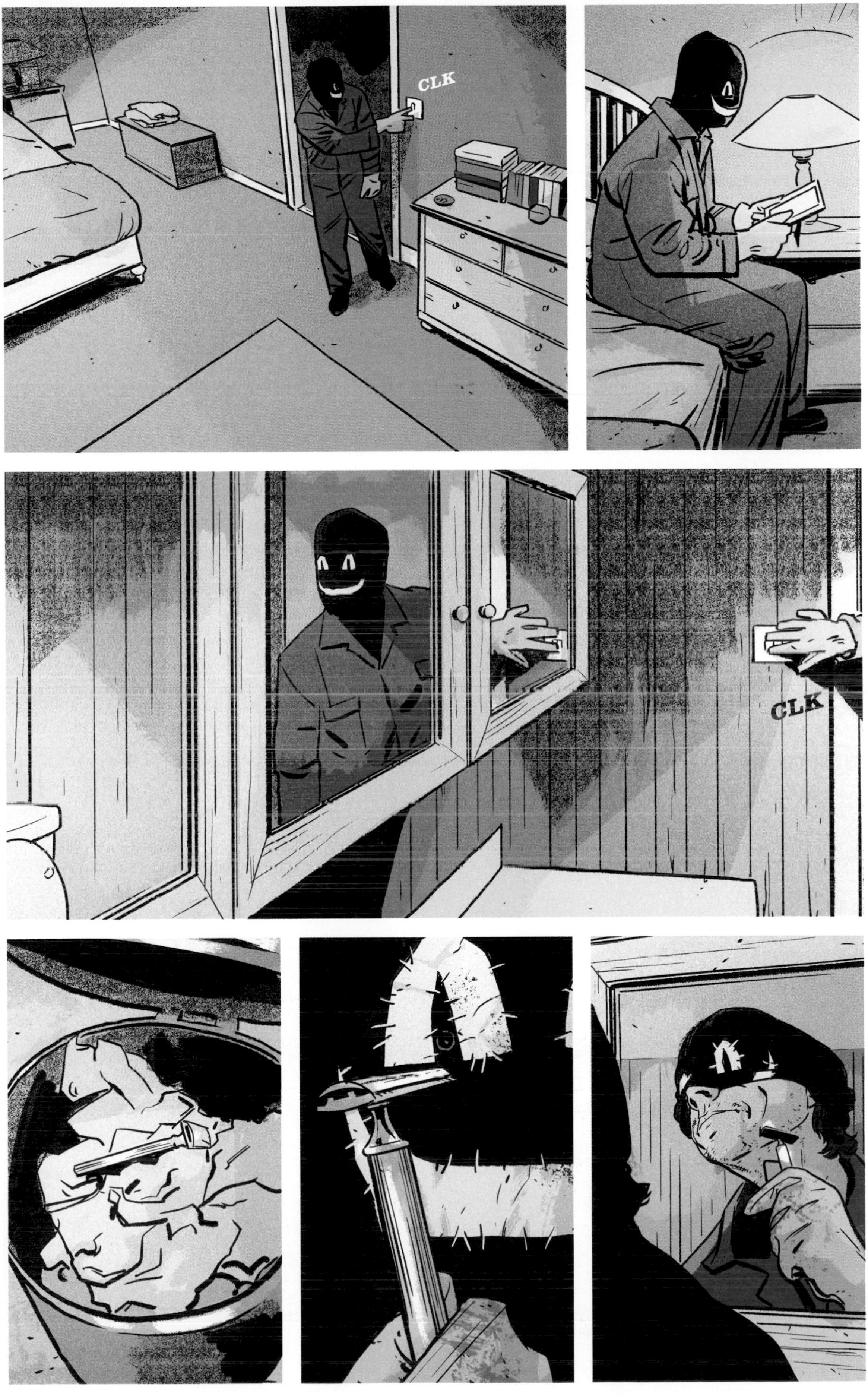
CLK
CLK

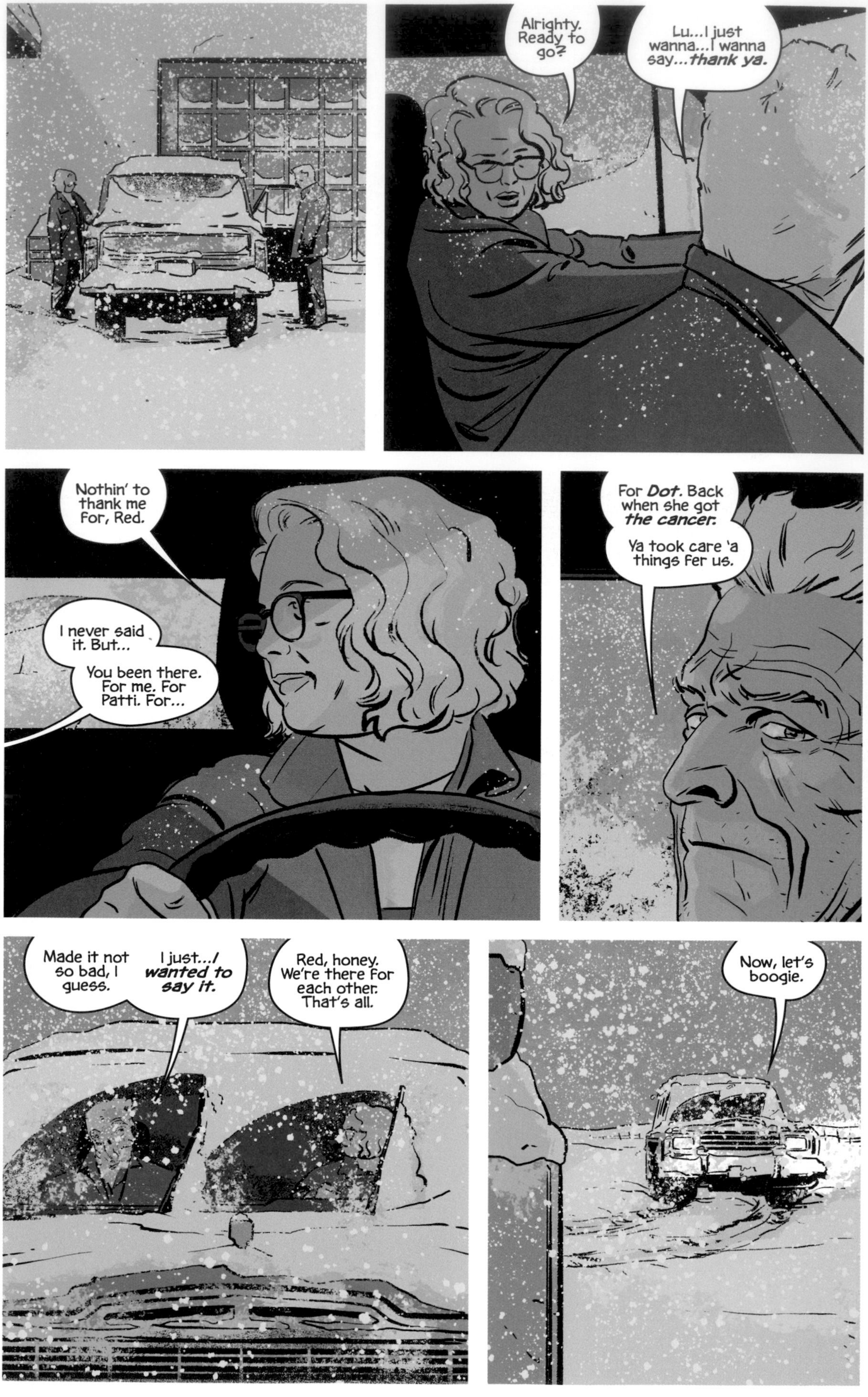
Alrighty. Ready to go?
Lu...I just wanna...I wanna say...*thank ya.*
Nothin' to thank me for, Red.
I never said it. But...
You been there. For me. For Patti. For...
For *Dot.* Back when she got *the cancer.*
Ya took care 'a things fer us.
Made it not so bad, I guess.
I just...*I wanted to say it.*
Red, honey. We're there for each other. That's all.
Now, let's boogie.

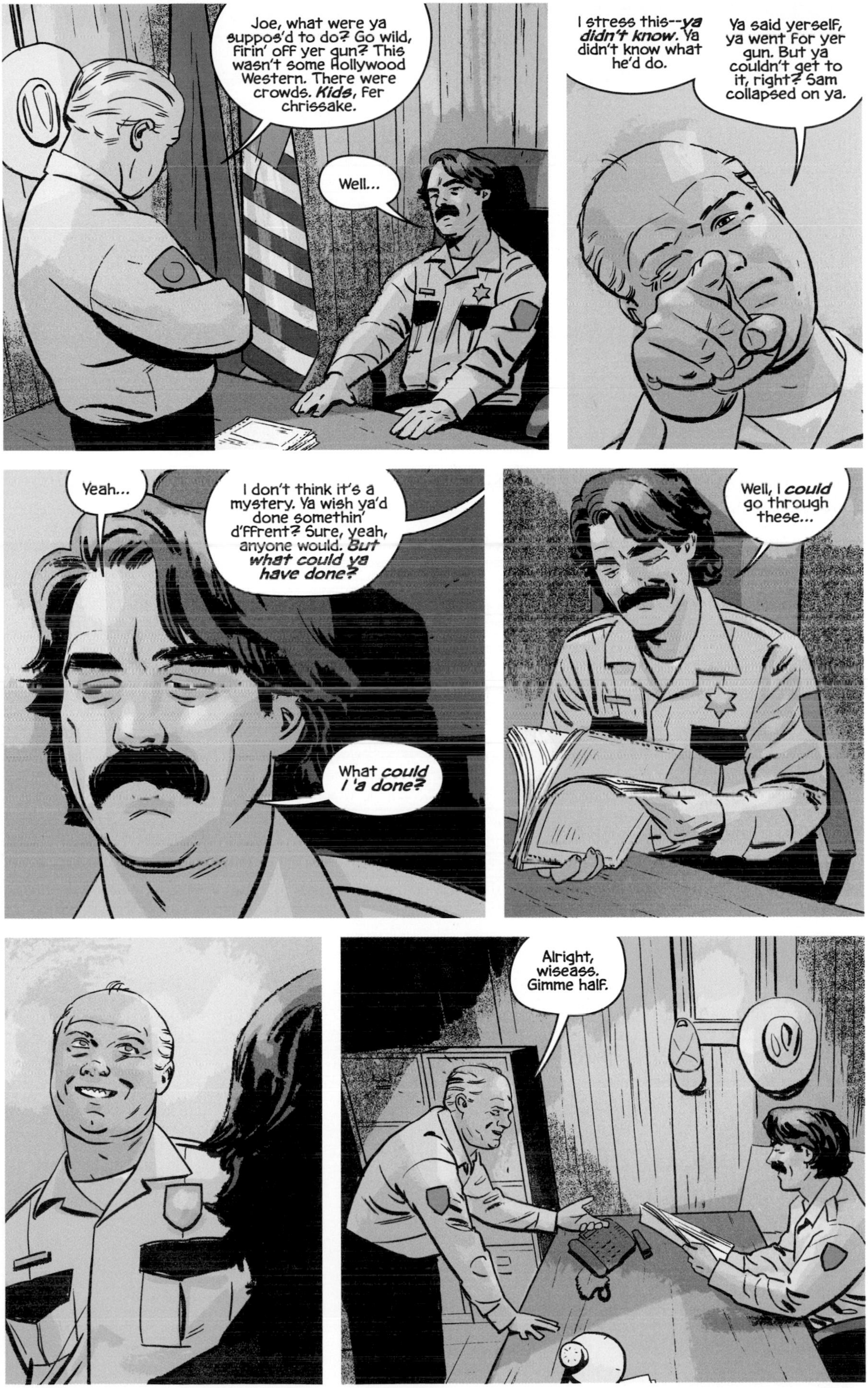
Joe, what were ya suppos'd to do? Go wild, firin' off yer gun? This wasn't some Hollywood Western. There were crowds. Kids, fer chrissake.
Well...
I stress this--ya didn't know. Ya didn't know what he'd do.
Ya said yerself, ya went for yer gun. But ya couldn't get to it, right? Sam collapsed on ya.
Yeah...
I don't think it's a mystery. Ya wish ya'd done somethin' d'ffrent? Sure, yeah, anyone would. But what could ya have done?
What could I 'a done?
Well, I could go through these...
Alright, wiseass. Gimme half.

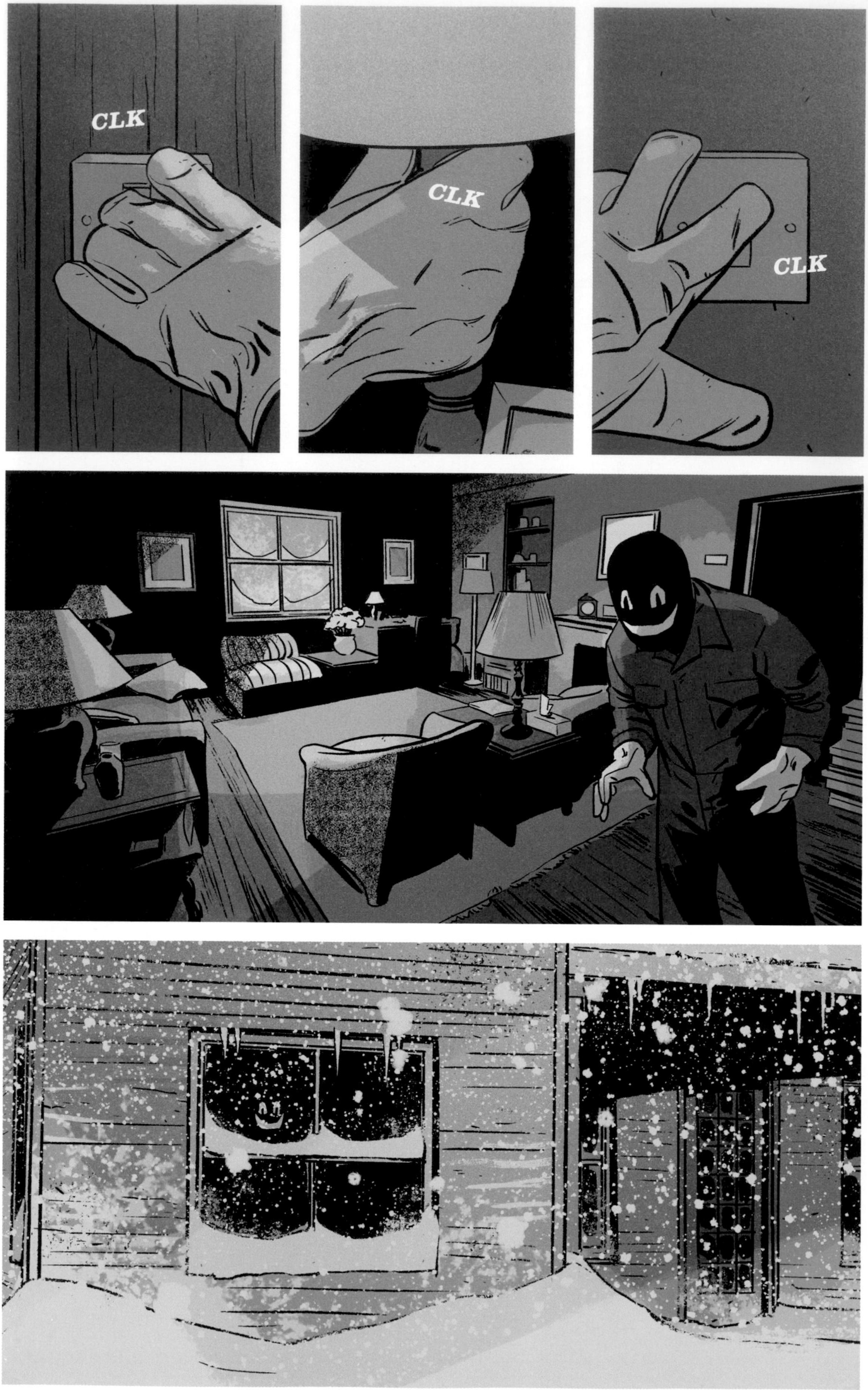
CLK
CLK
CLK

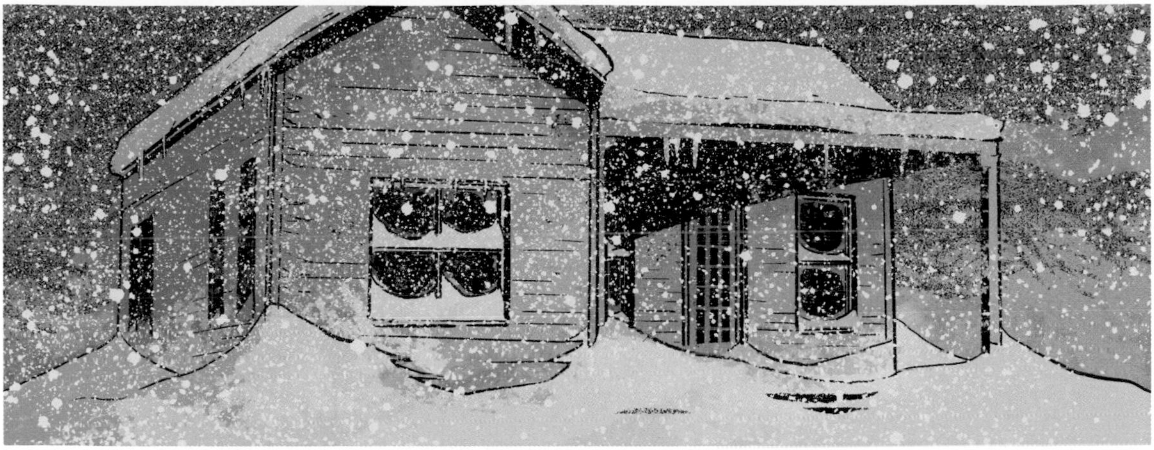
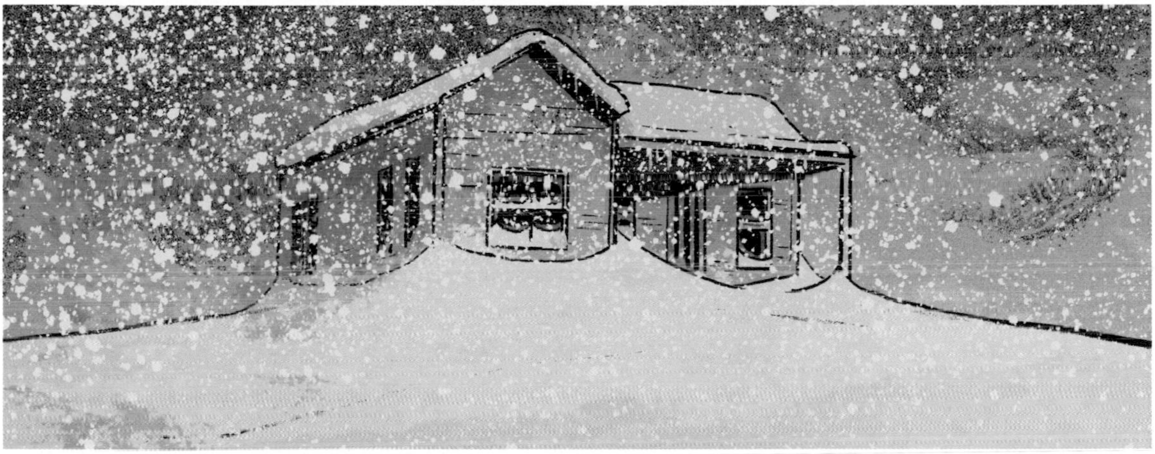
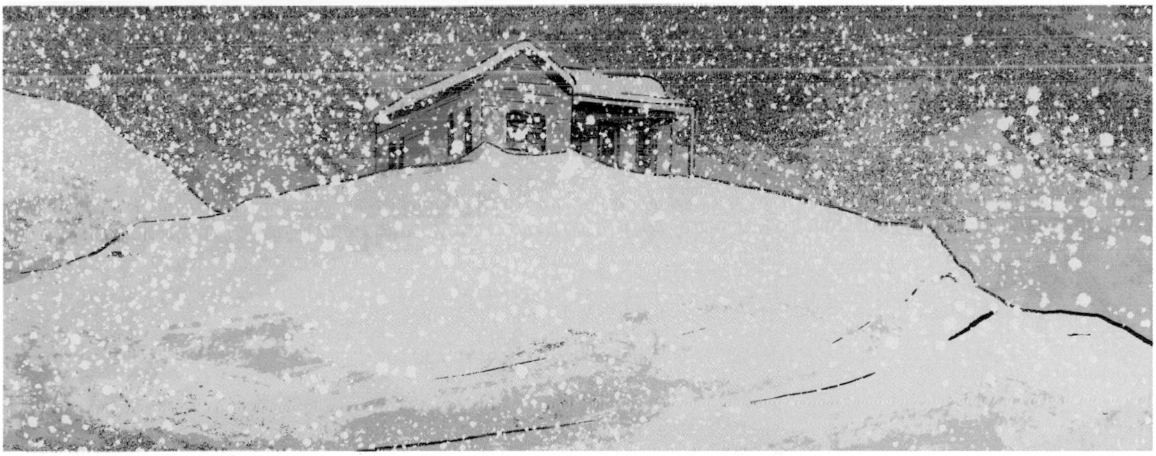
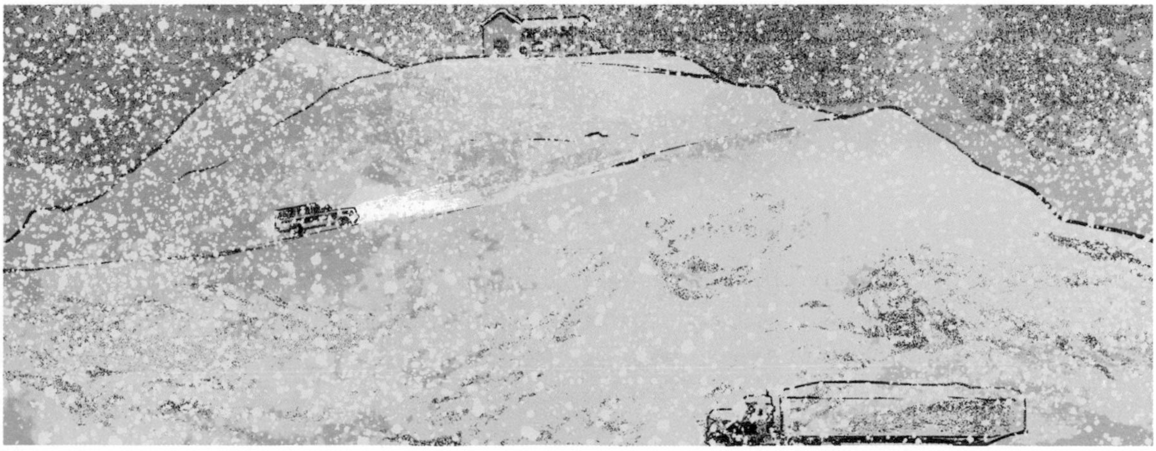

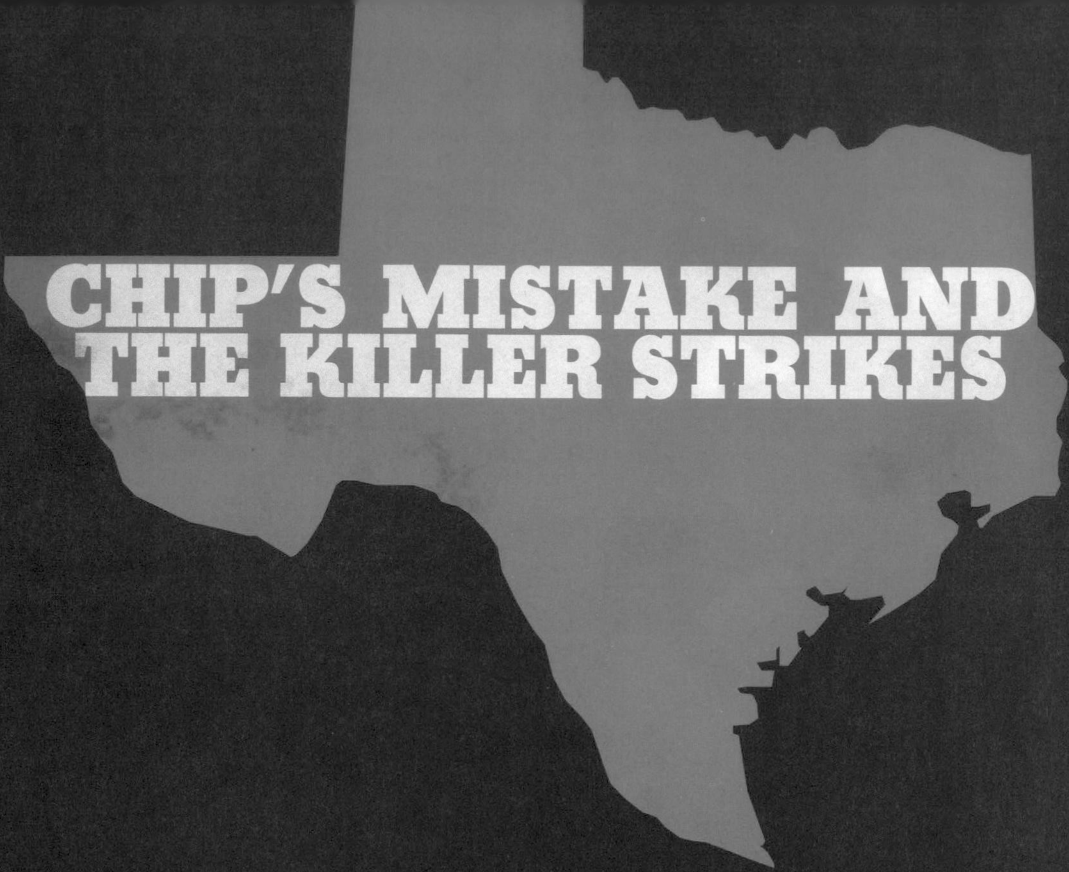

CHIP'S MISTAKE AND THE KILLER STRIKES

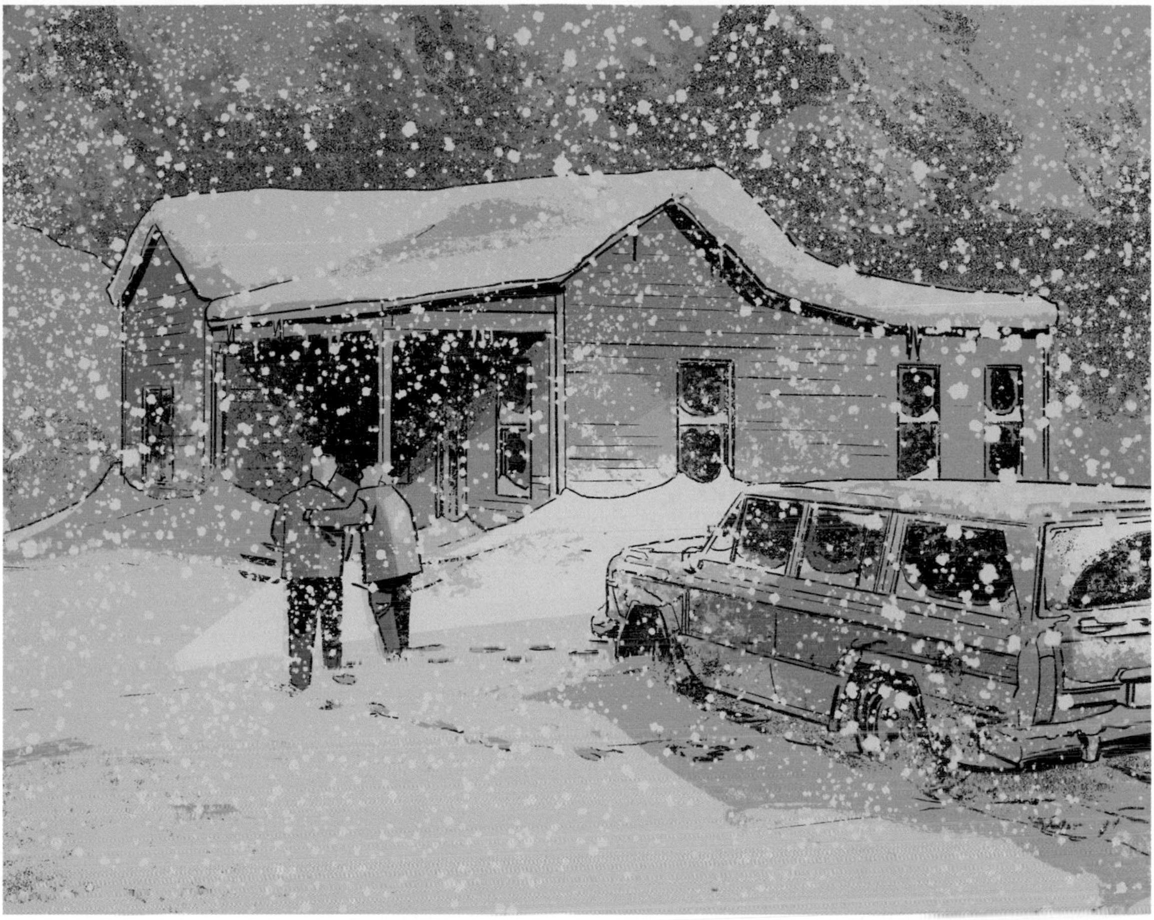
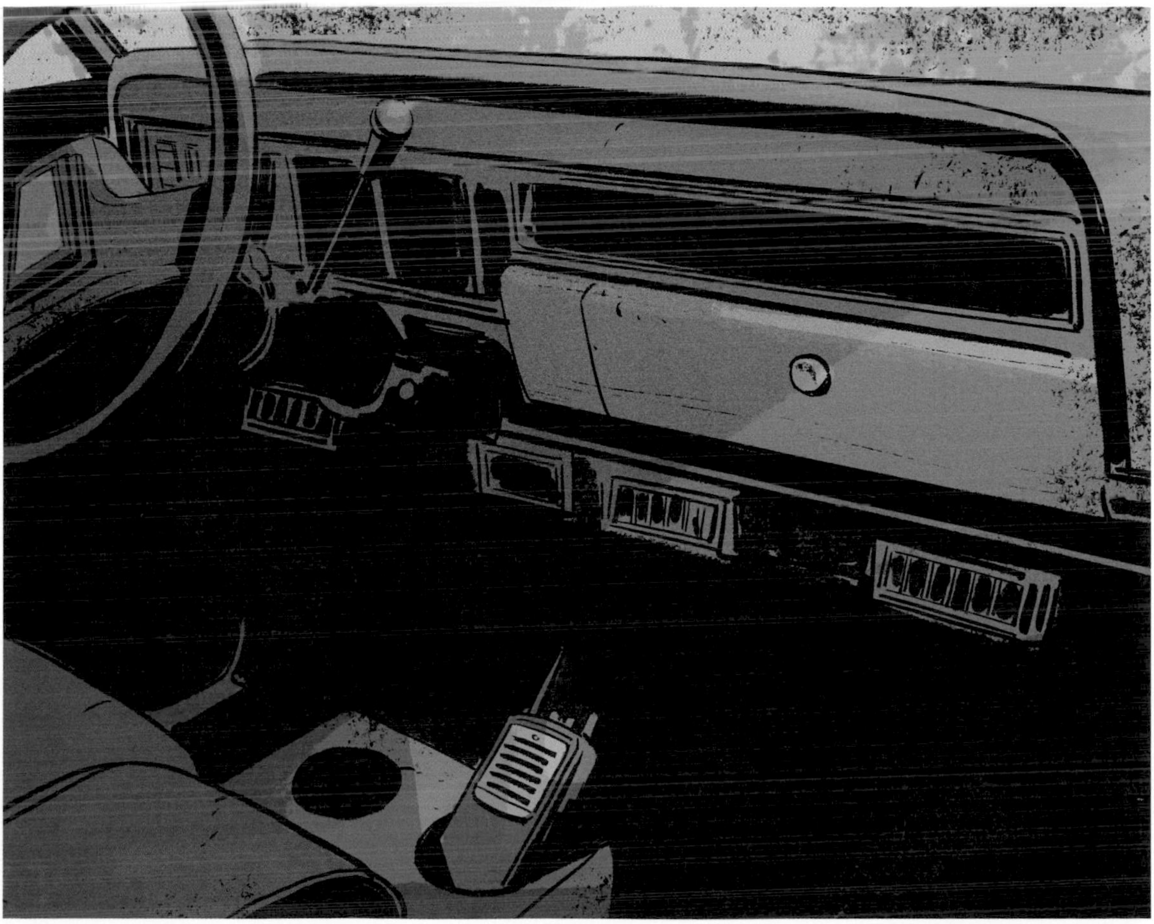

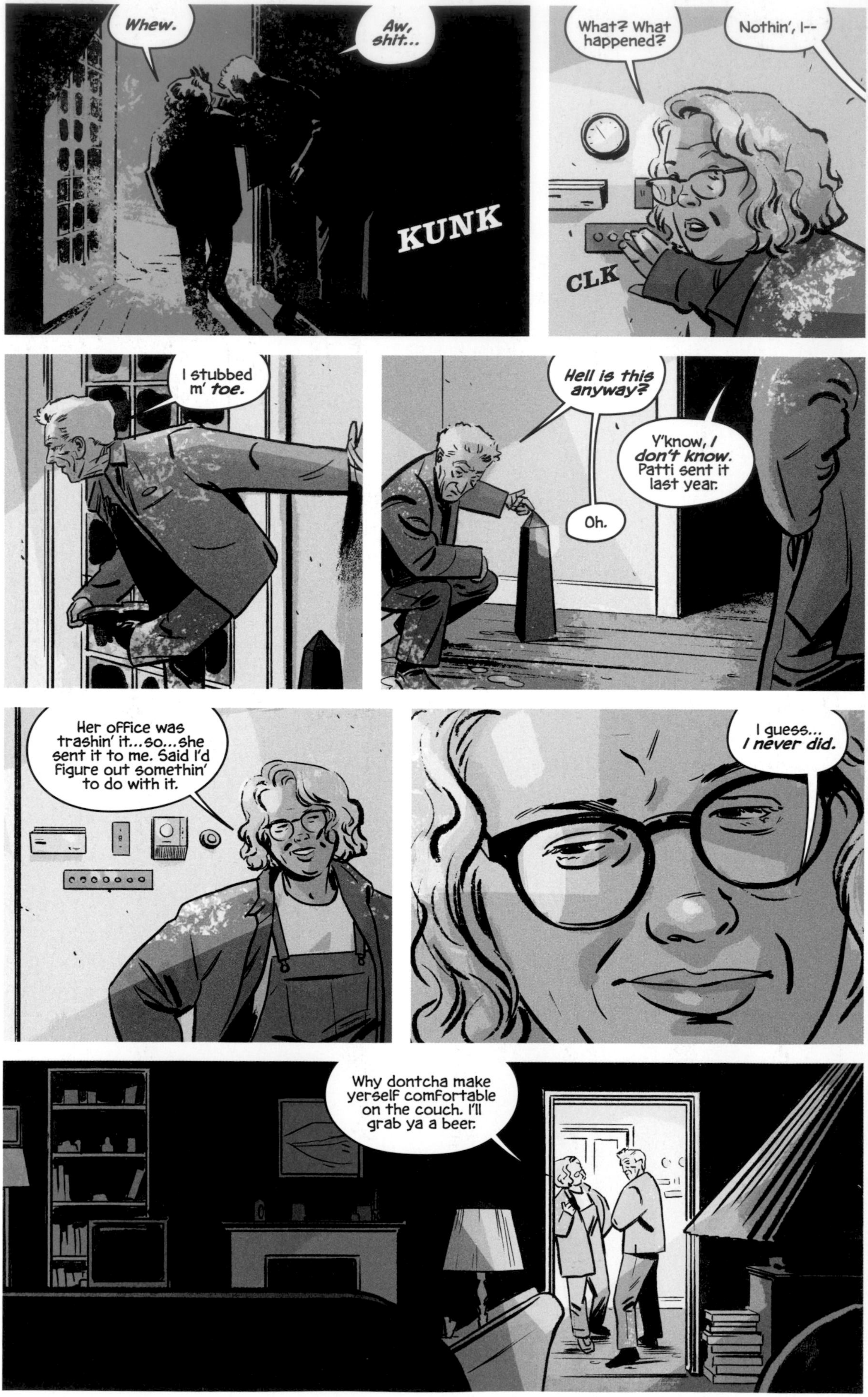
Whew.
Aw, shit...
KUNK
What? What happened?
Nothin', I--
CLK
I stubbed m' toe.
Hell is this anyway?
Y'know, I don't know. Patti sent it last year.
Oh.
Her office was trashin' it...so...she sent it to me. Said I'd figure out somethin' to do with it.
I guess... I never did.
Why dontcha make yerself comfortable on the couch. I'll grab ya a beer.

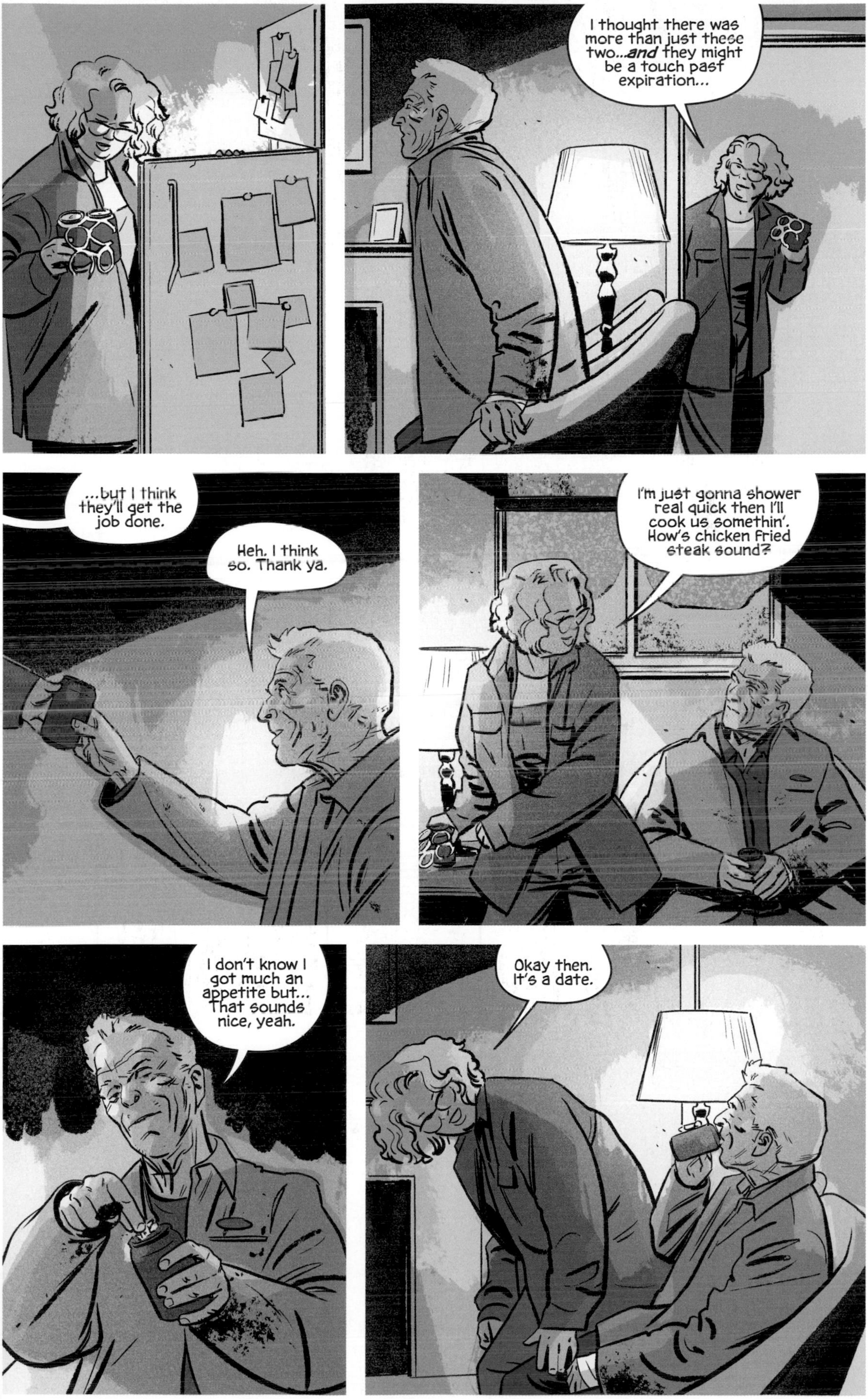
I thought there was more than just these two...*and* they might be a touch past expiration...
...but I think they'll get the job done.
Heh. I think so. Thank ya.
I'm just gonna shower real quick then I'll cook us somethin'. How's chicken fried steak sound?
I don't know I got much an appetite but... That sounds nice, yeah.
Okay then. It's a date.

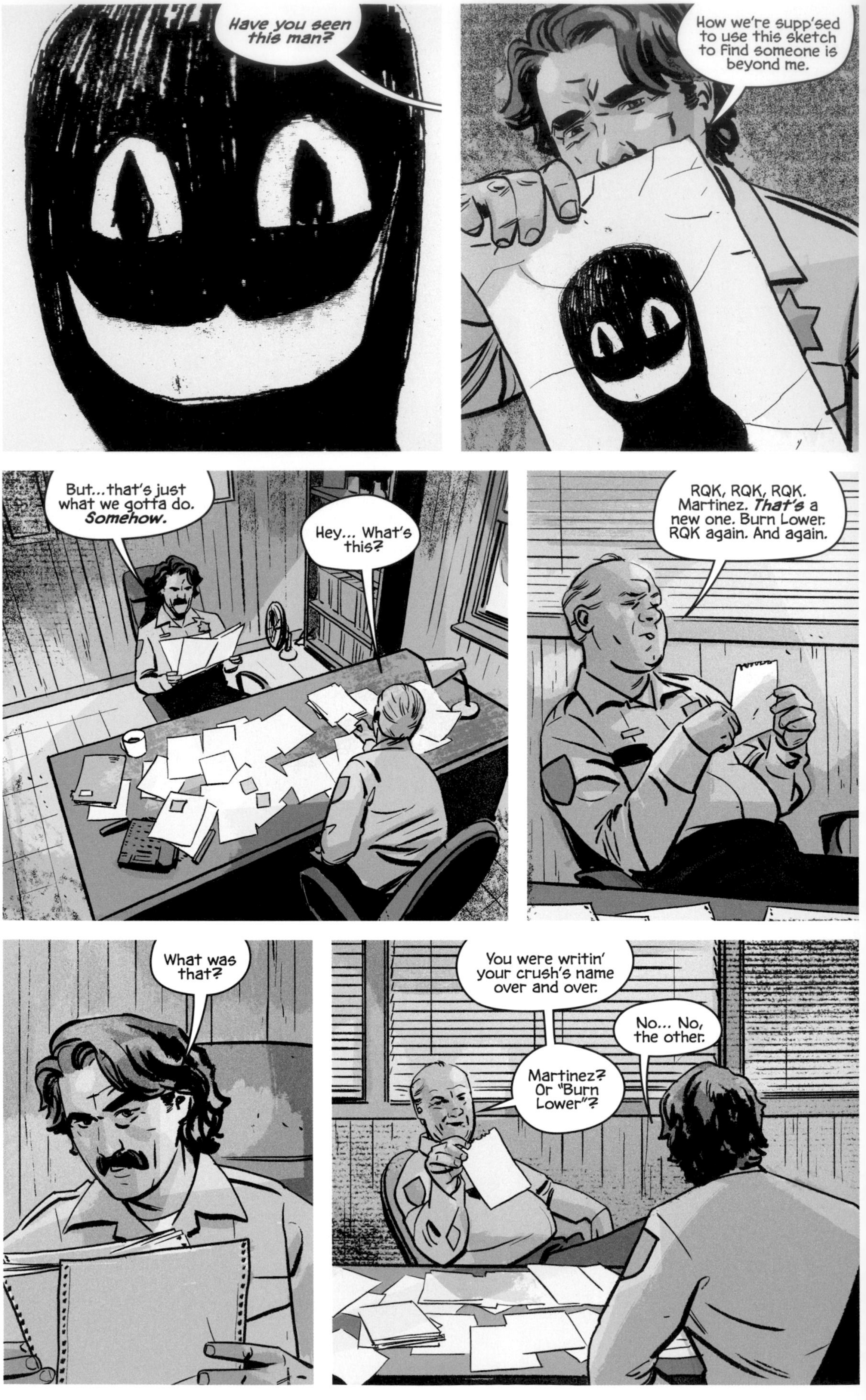
Have you seen this man?
How we're supp'sed to use this sketch to find someone is beyond me.
But...that's just what we gotta do. Somehow.
Hey... What's this?
RQK, RQK, RQK. Martinez. That's a new one. Burn Lower. RQK again. And again.
What was that?
You were writin' your crush's name over and over.
No... No, the other.
Martinez? Or "Burn Lower"?

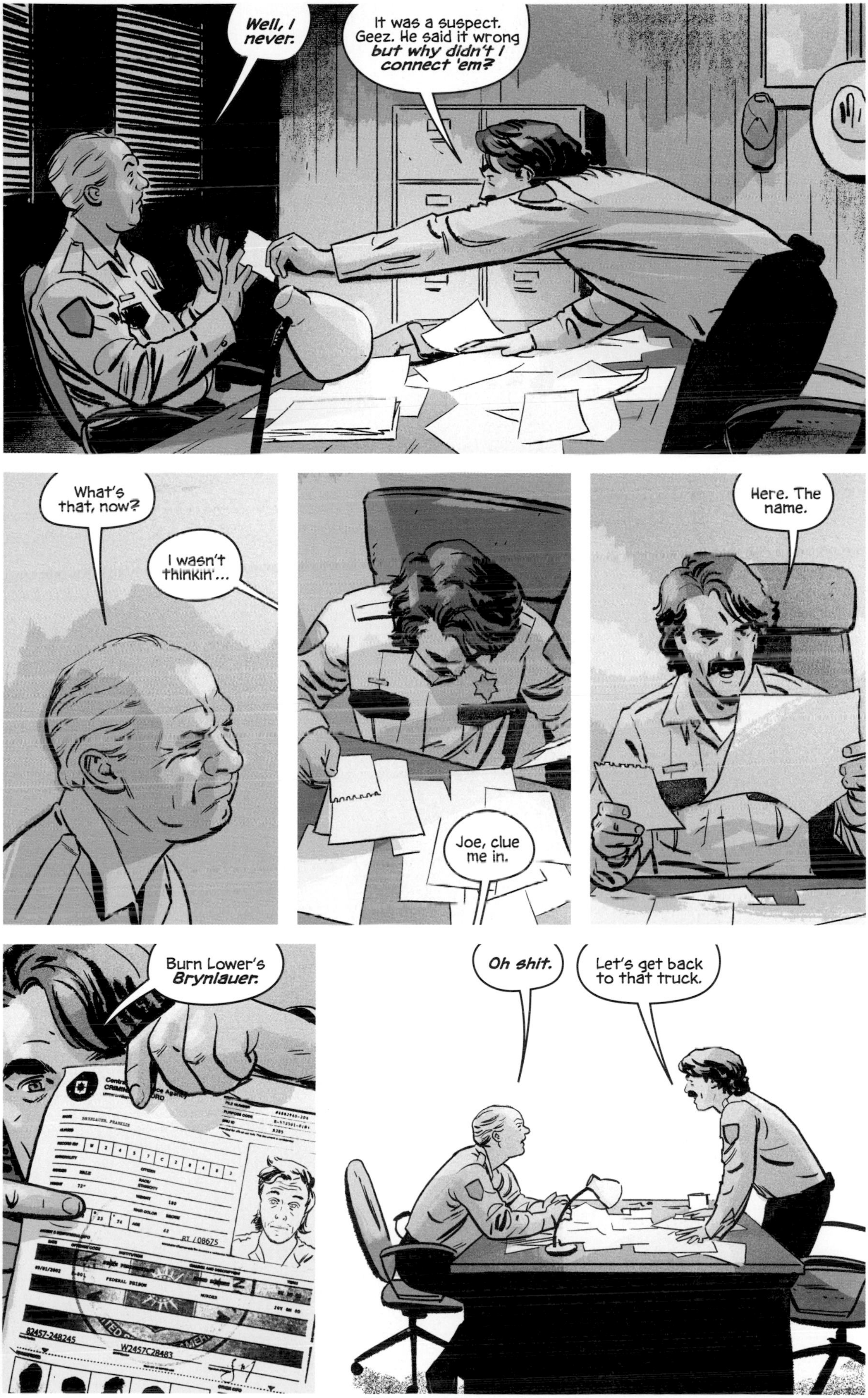

Well, I never.
It was a suspect. Geez. He said it wrong *but why didn't I connect 'em?*
What's that, now?
I wasn't thinkin'...
Joe, clue me in.
Here. The name.
Burn Lower's *Brynlauer.*
Oh shit.
Let's get back to that truck.

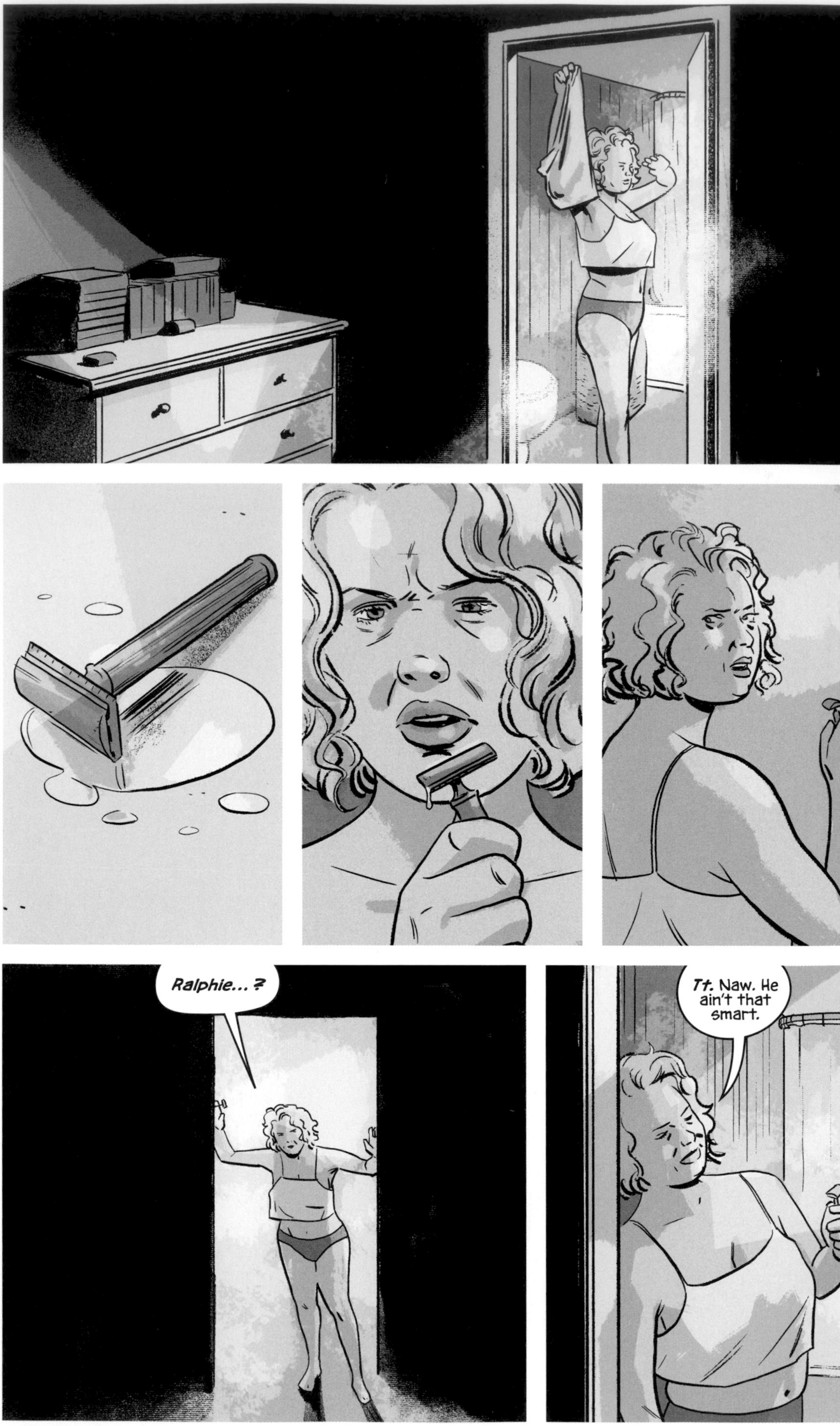
Ralphie...?
Tt. Naw. He ain't that smart.

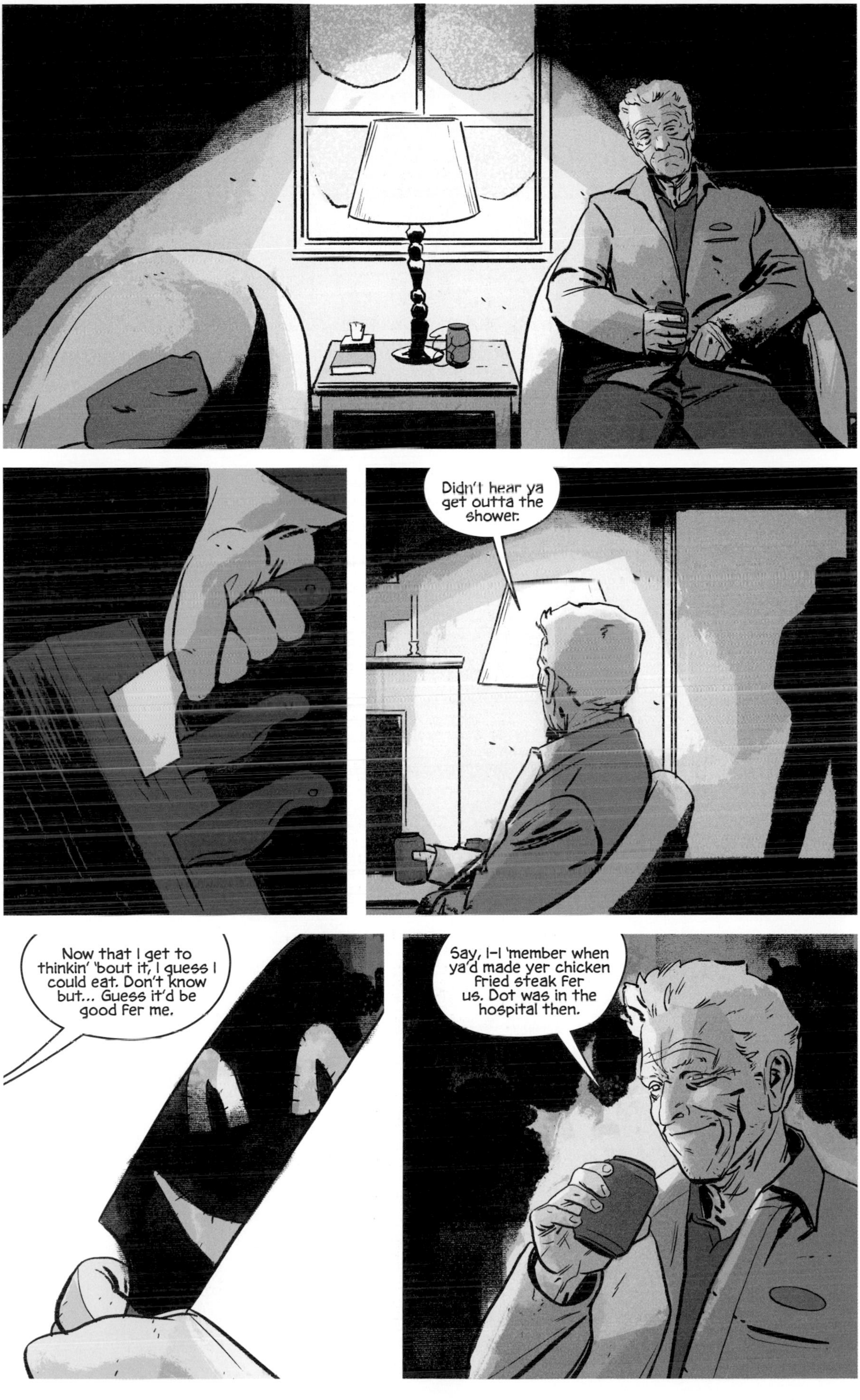
Didn't hear ya get outta the shower.
Now that I get to thinkin' 'bout it, I guess I could eat. Don't know but... Guess it'd be good fer me.
Say, I-I 'member when ya'd made yer chicken fried steak fer us. Dot was in the hospital then.

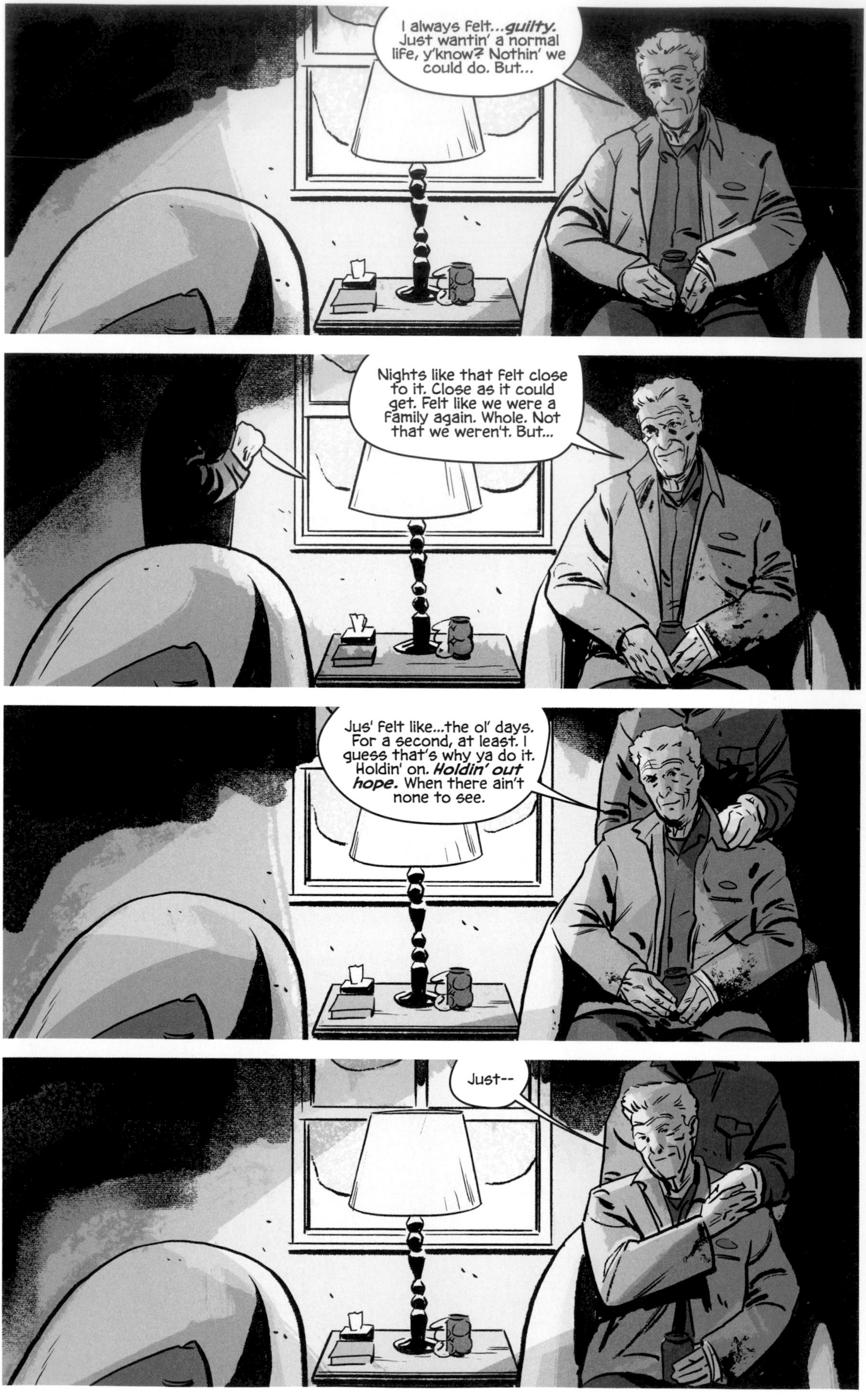
I always felt...*guilty.* Just wantin' a normal life, y'know? Nothin' we could do. But...
Nights like that felt close to it. Close as it could get. Felt like we were a family again. Whole. Not that we weren't. But...
Jus' felt like...the ol' days. For a second, at least. I guess that's why ya do it. Holdin' on. *Holdin' out hope.* When there ain't none to see.
Just--

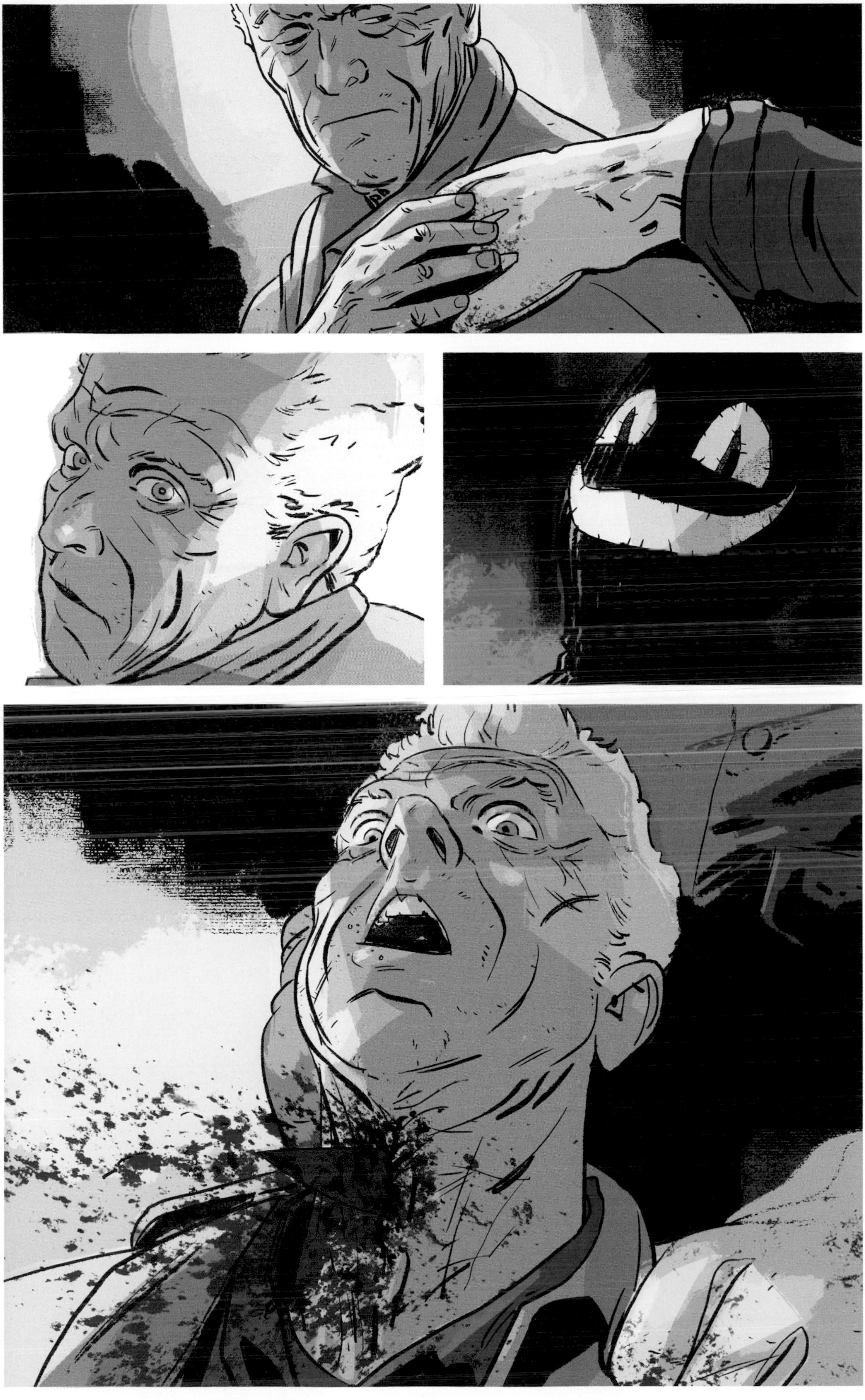

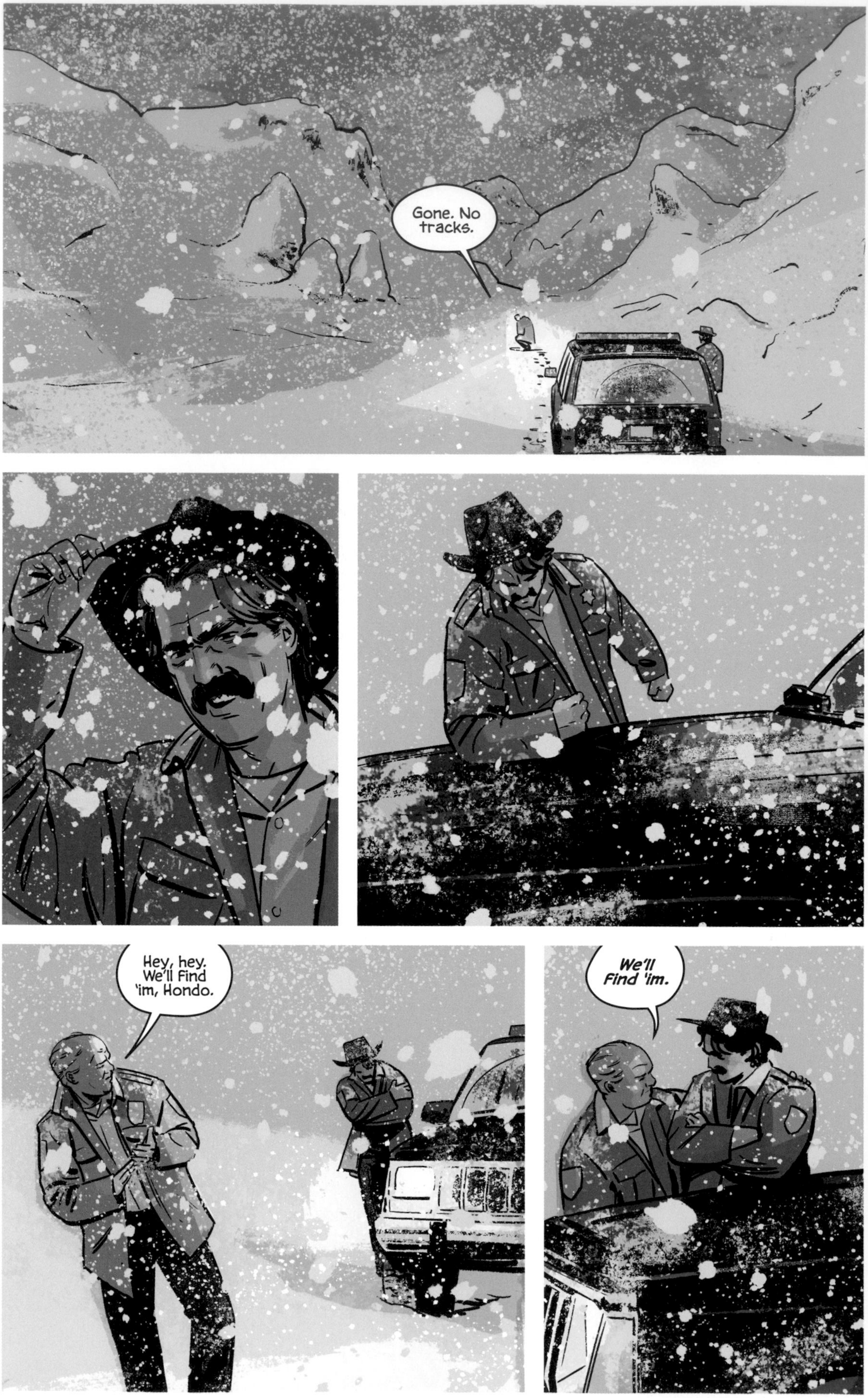
Gone. No tracks.
Hey, hey. We'll find 'im, Hondo.
We'll find 'im.

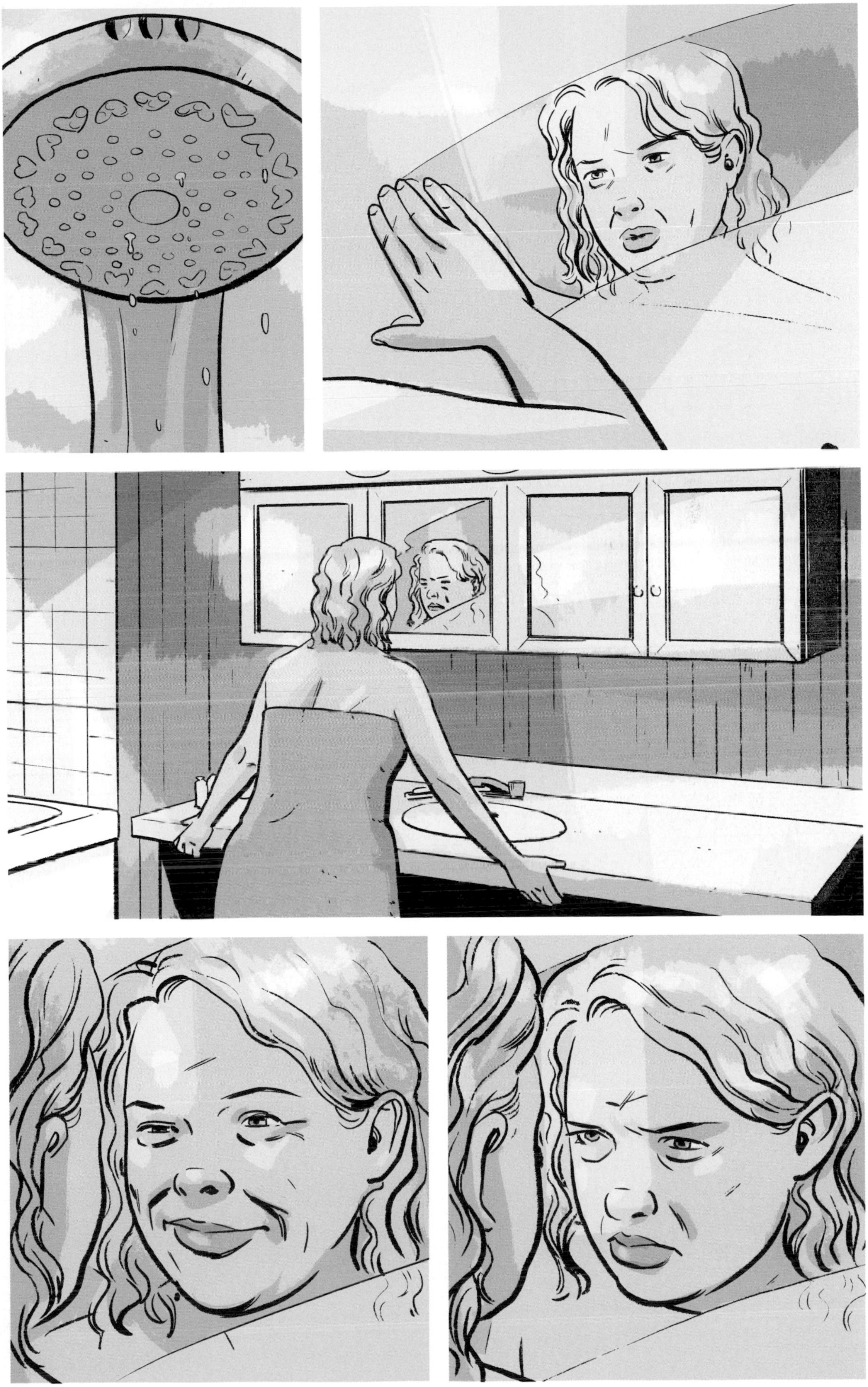

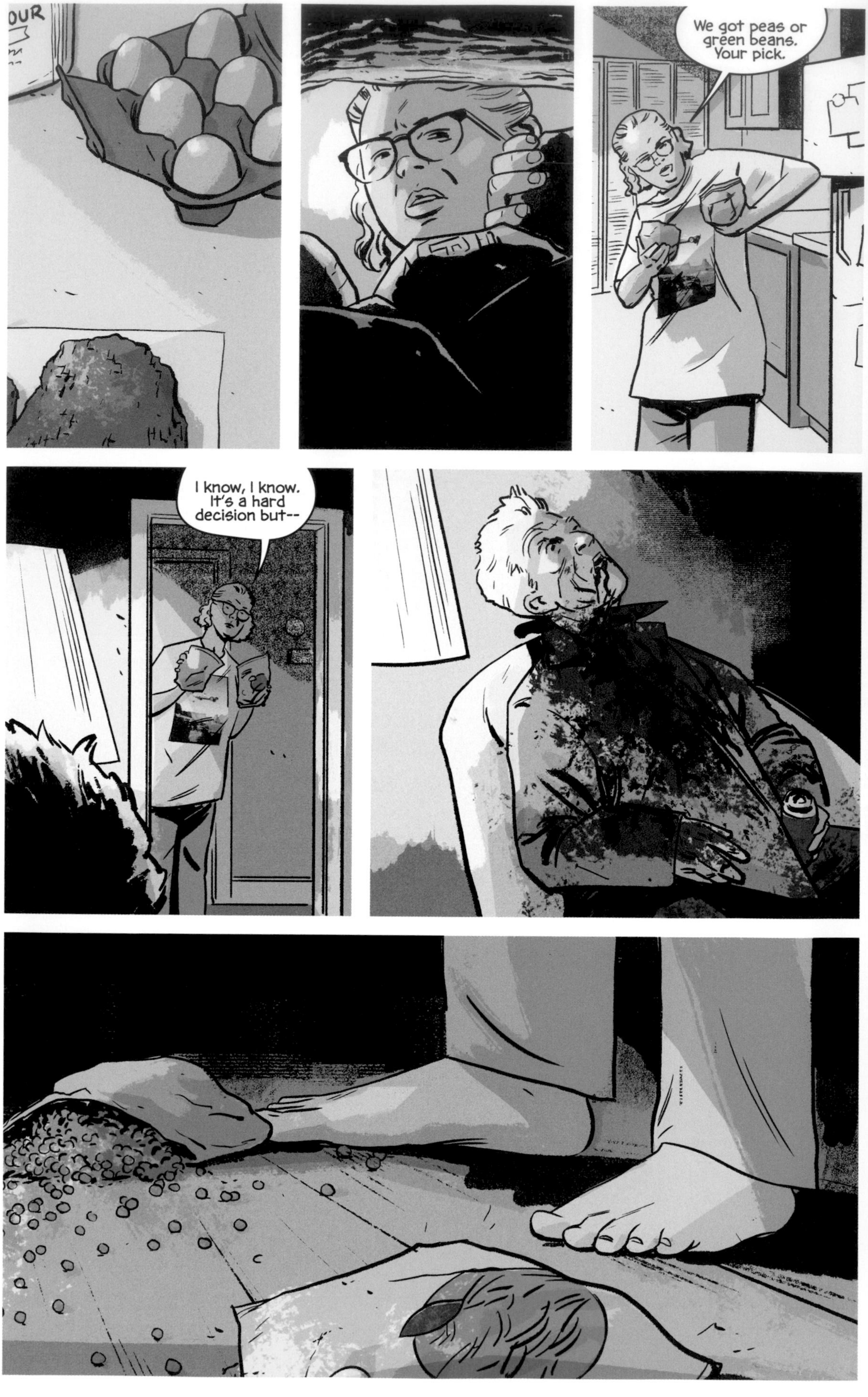
OUR
We got peas or green beans. Your pick.
I know, I know. It's a hard decision but--

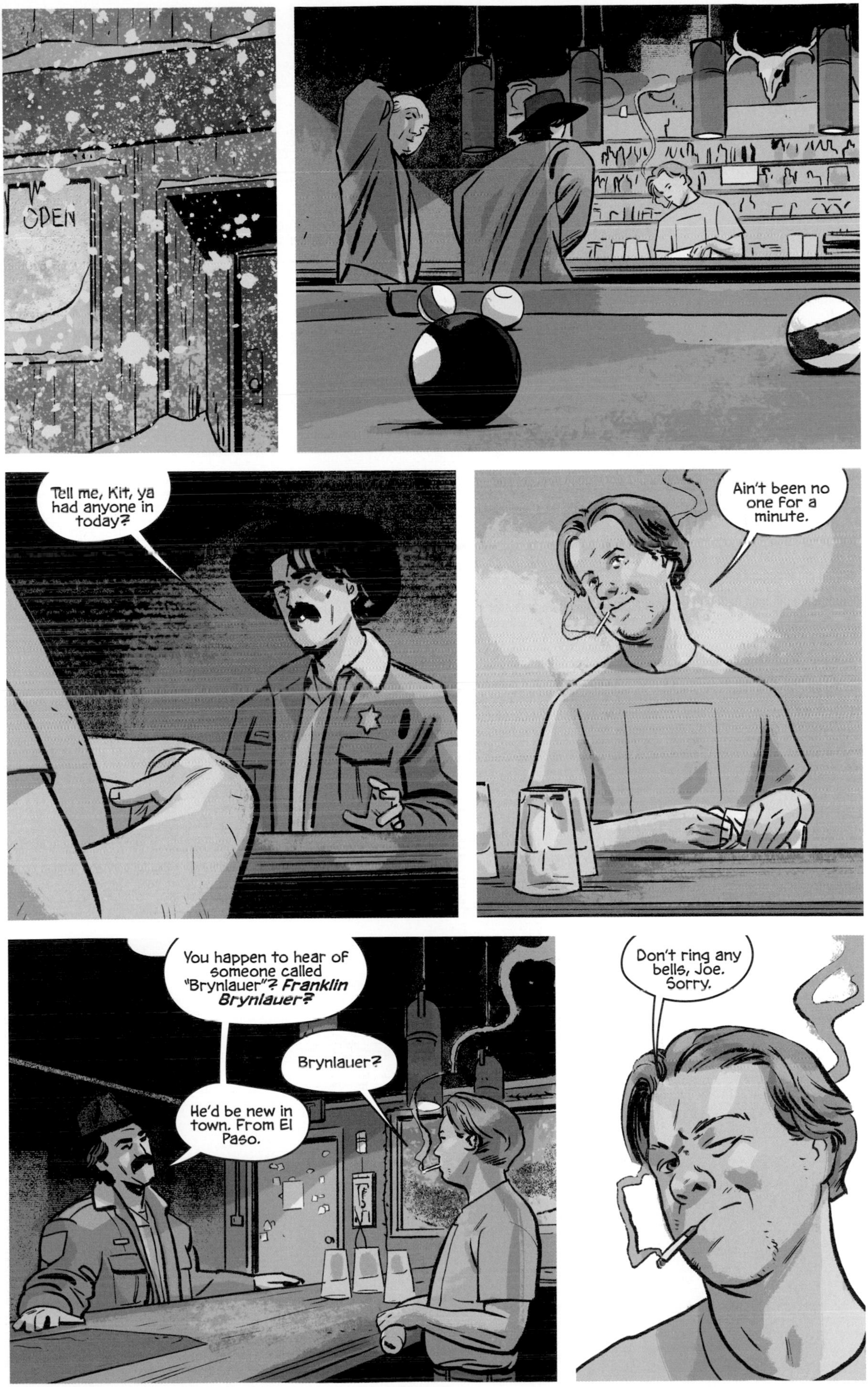

OPEN
Tell me, Kit, ya had anyone in today?
Ain't been no one for a minute.
You happen to hear of someone called "Brynlauer"? *Franklin Brynlauer?*
Brynlauer?
He'd be new in town. From El Paso.
Don't ring any bells, Joe. Sorry.

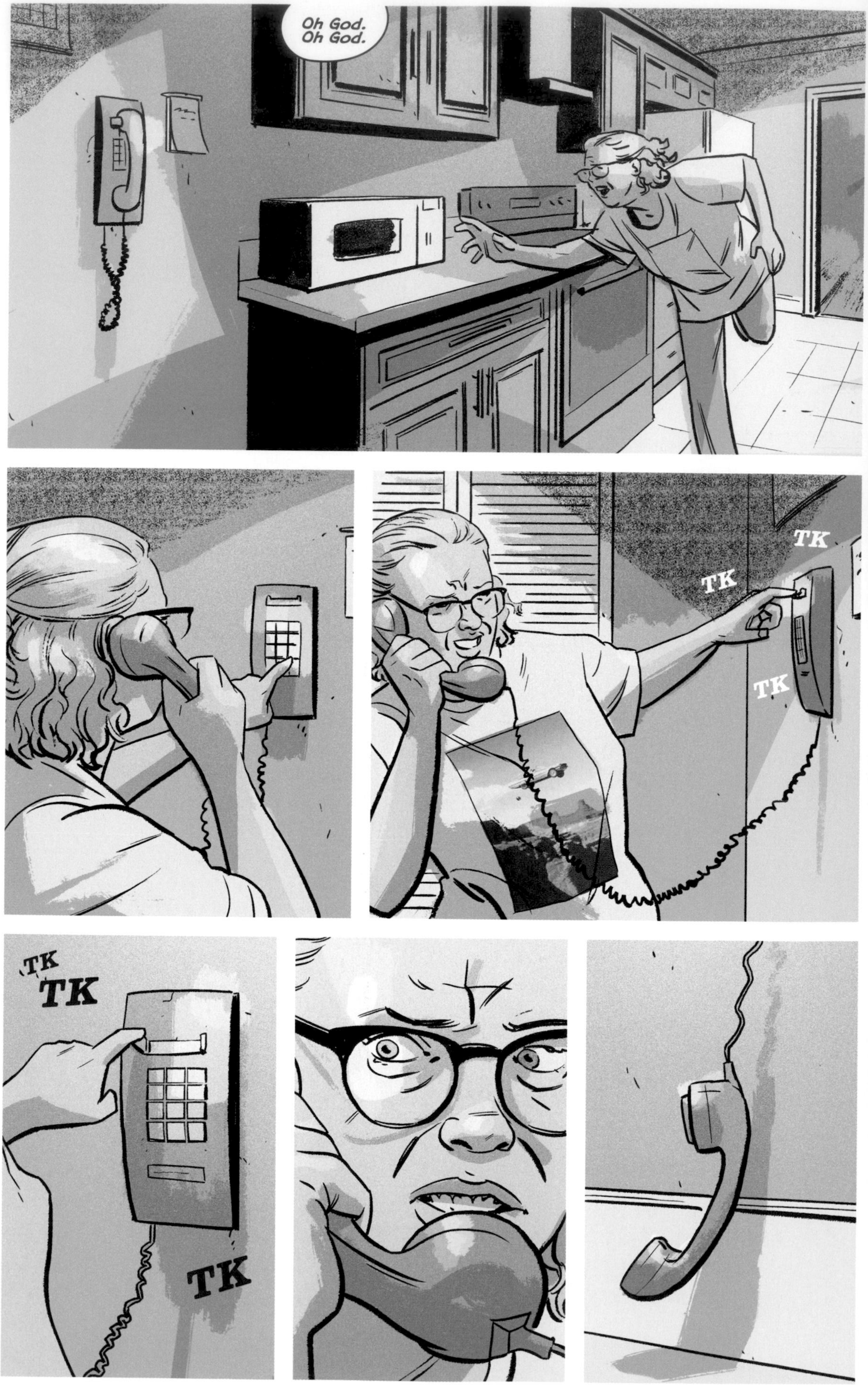
Oh God.
Oh God.
TK
TK
TK
TK
TK
TK

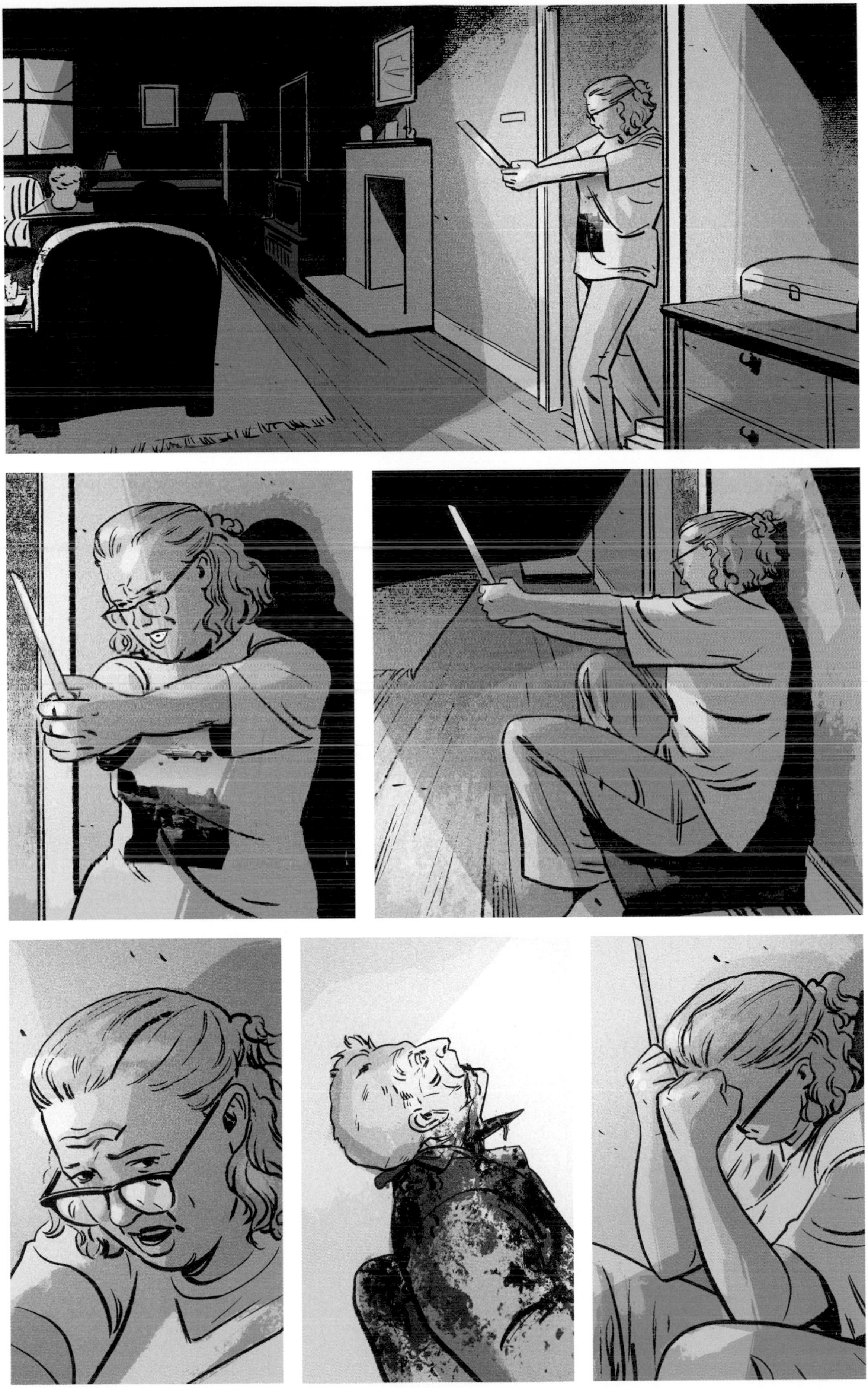

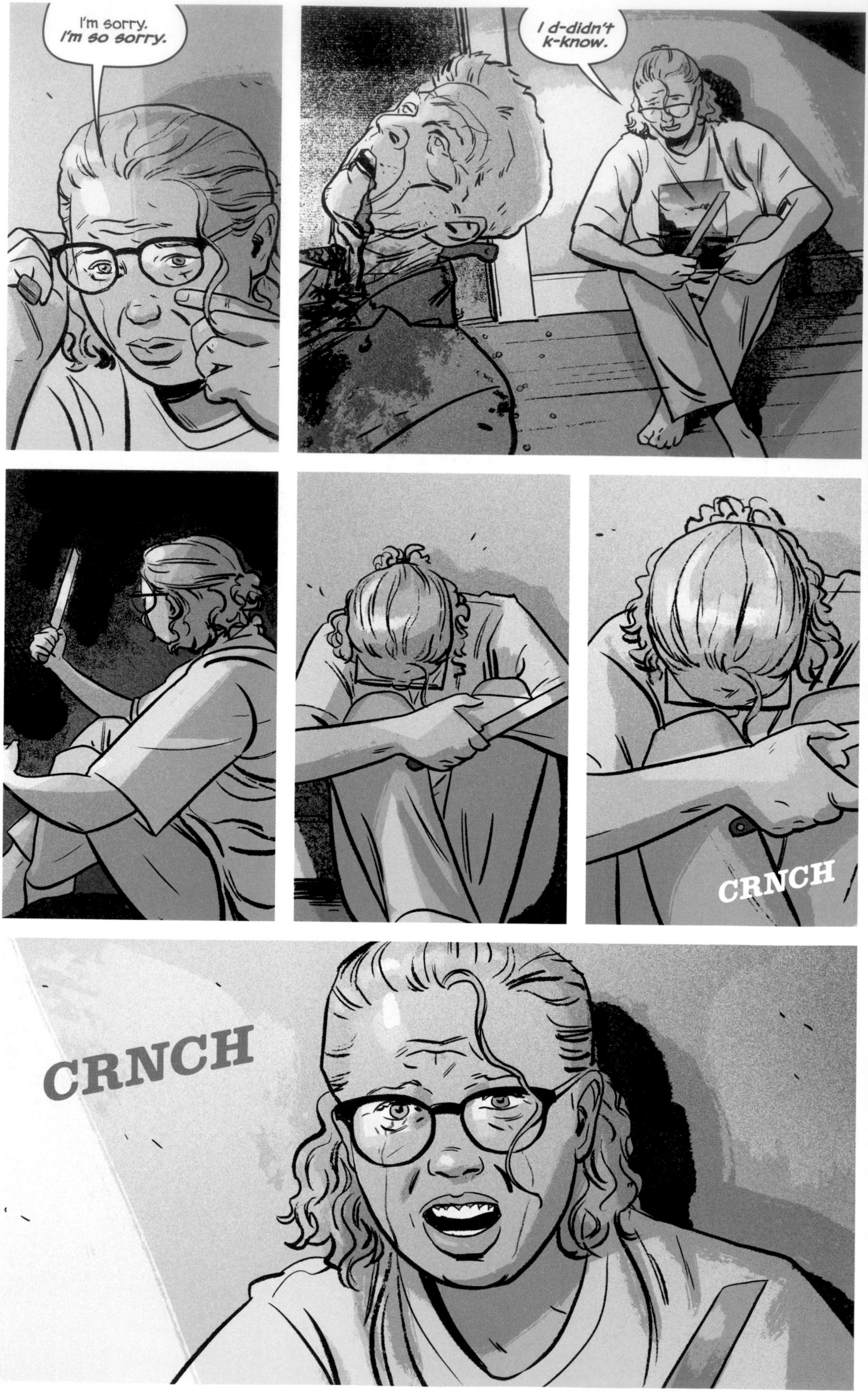
I'm sorry. *I'm so sorry.*
I d-didn't k-know.
CRNCH
CRNCH

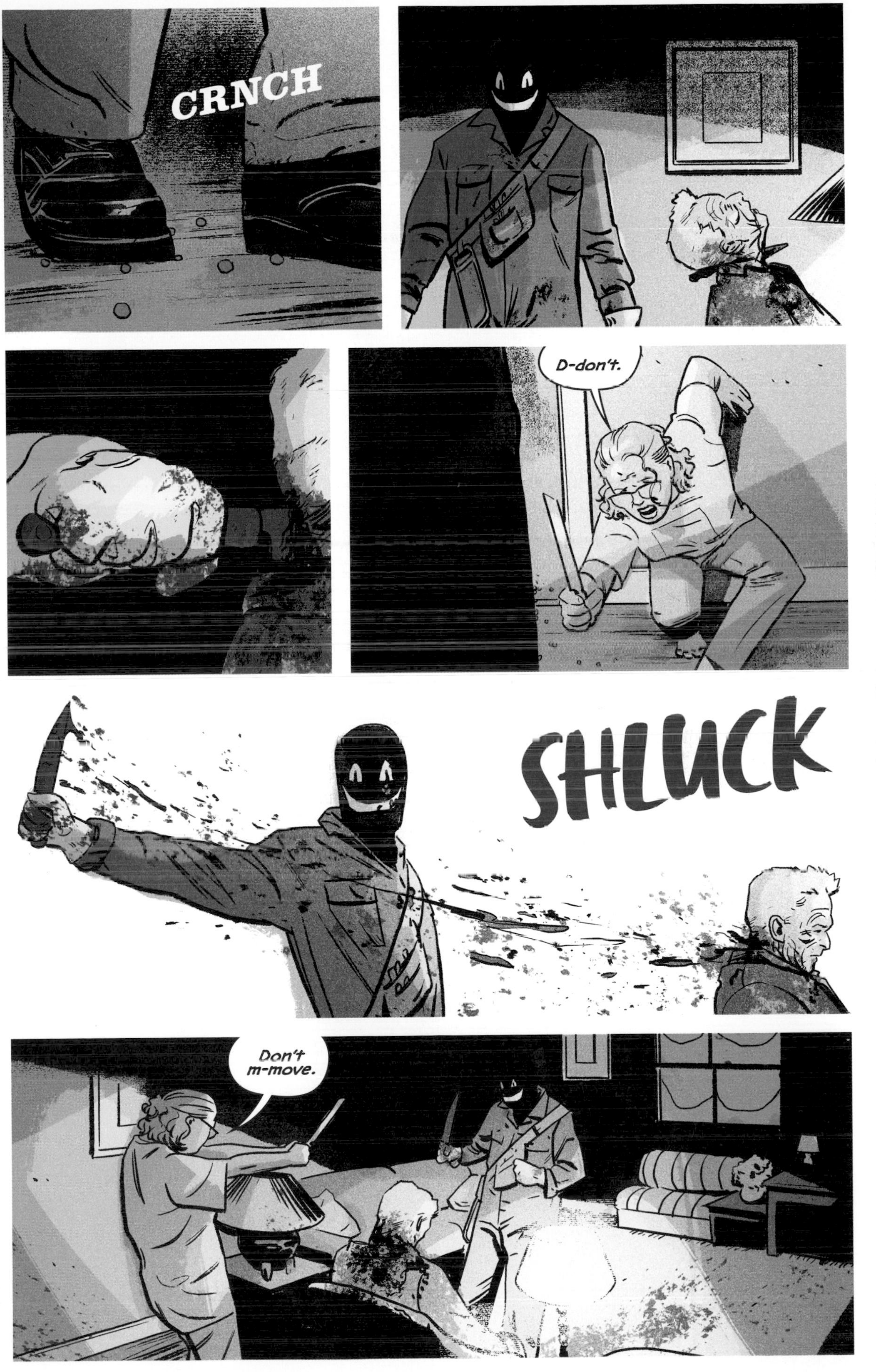
CRNCH
D-don't.
SHLUCK
Don't m-move.

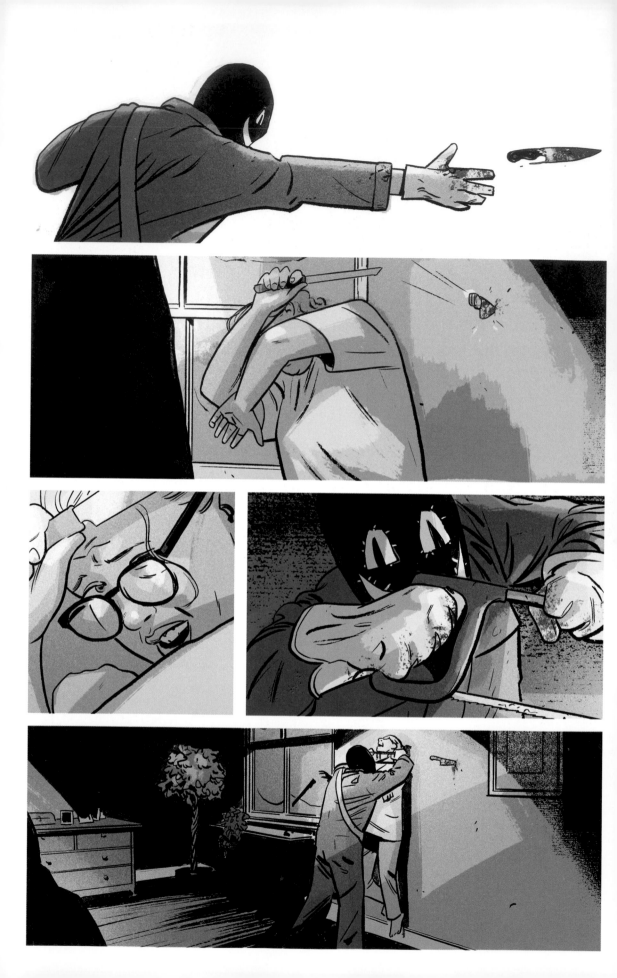

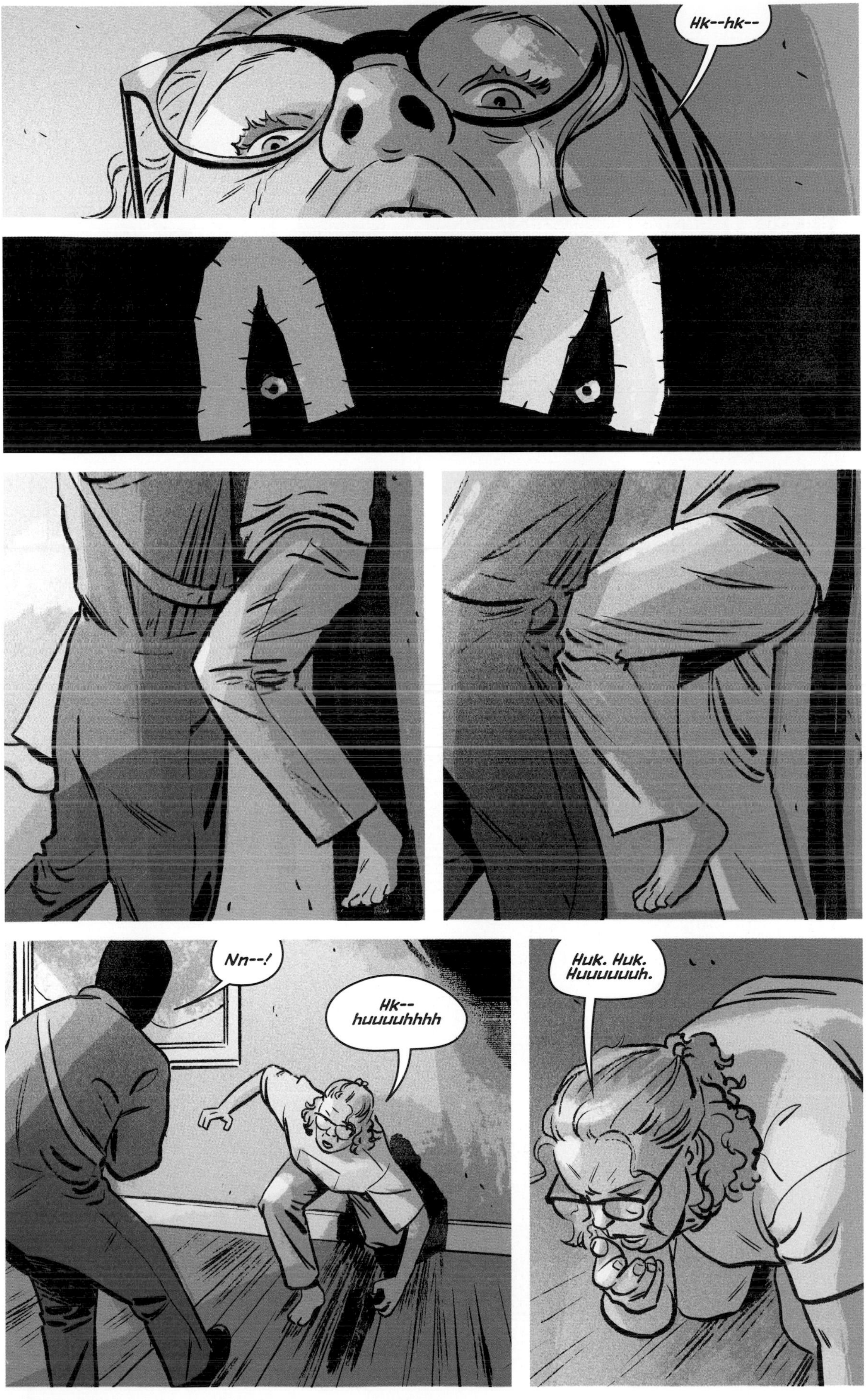
Hk--hk--
Nn--!
Hk-- huuuuhhhh
Huk. Huk. Huuuuuuh.

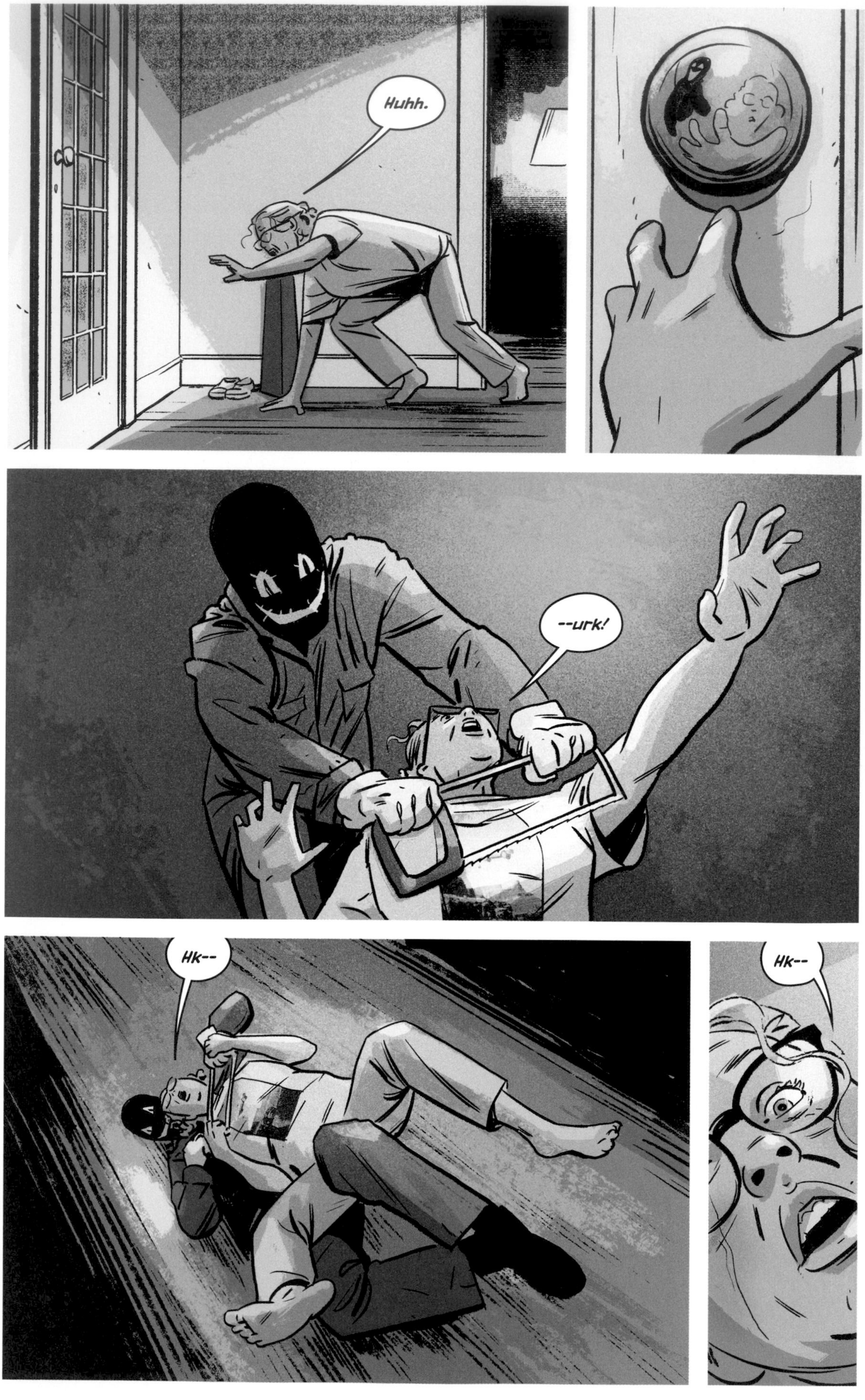
Huhh.
--urk!
Hk--
Hk--

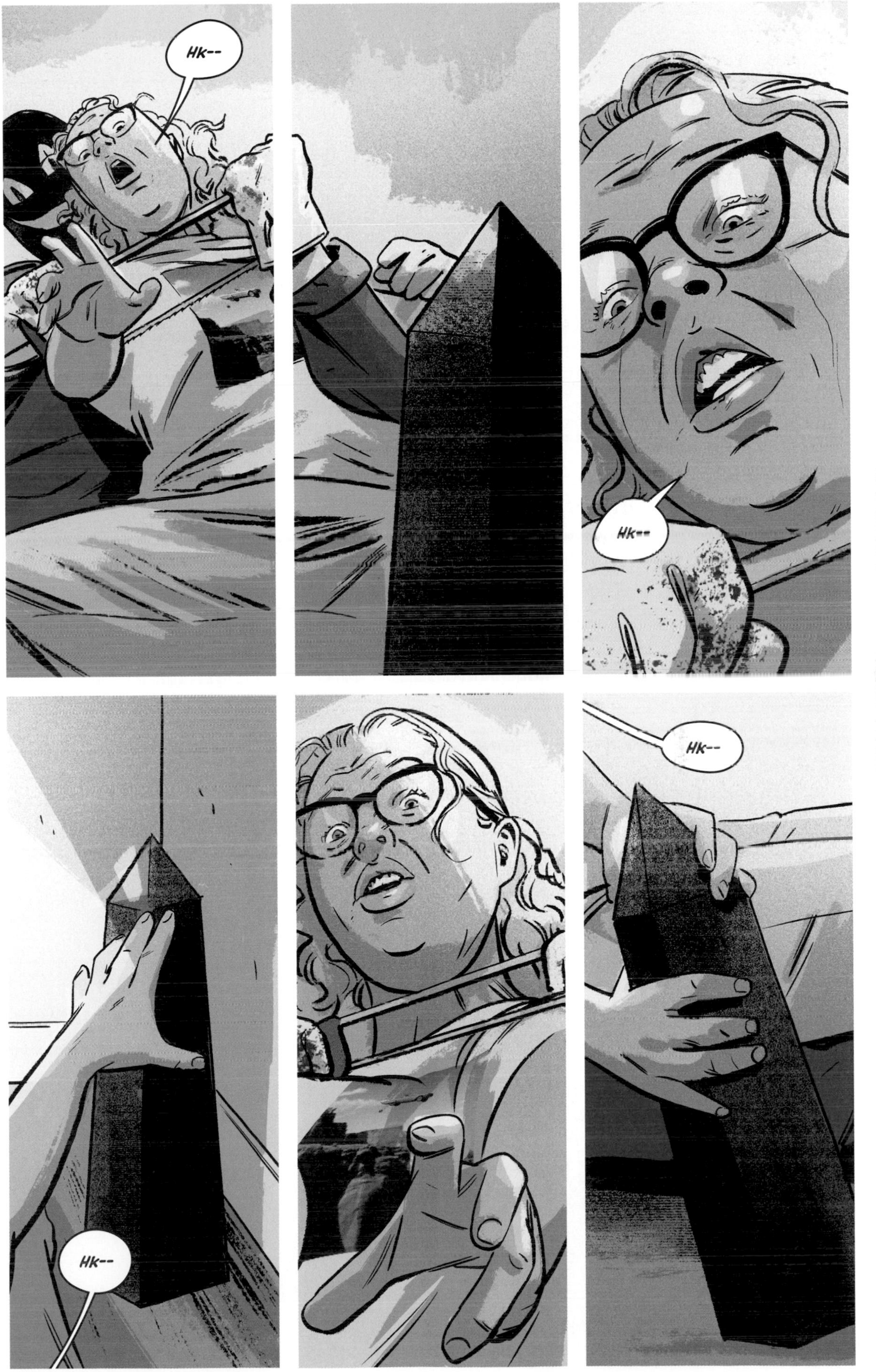
HK--
HK--
HK--
HK--

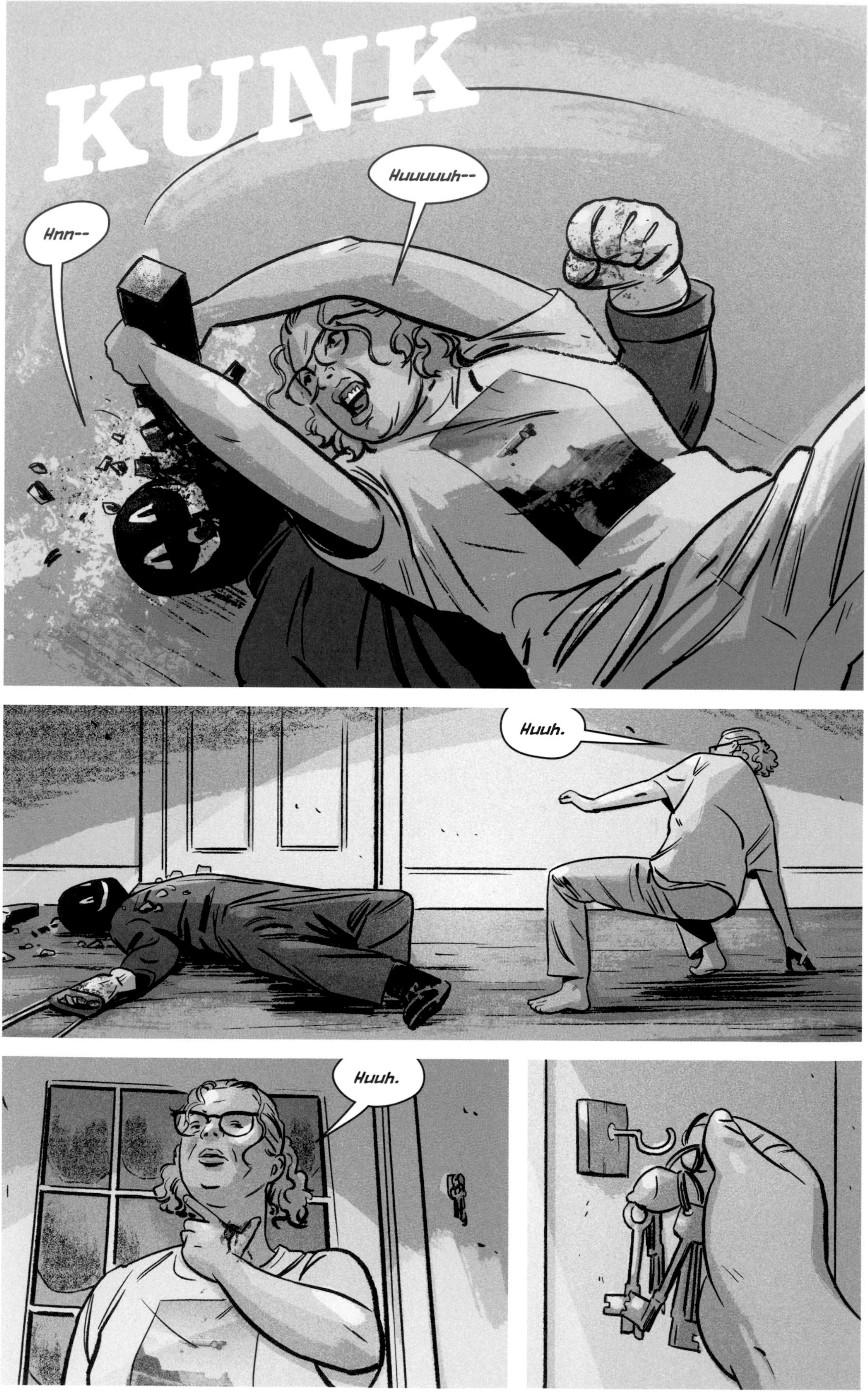
KUNK
Hnn--
Huuuuuh--
Huuh.
Huuh.

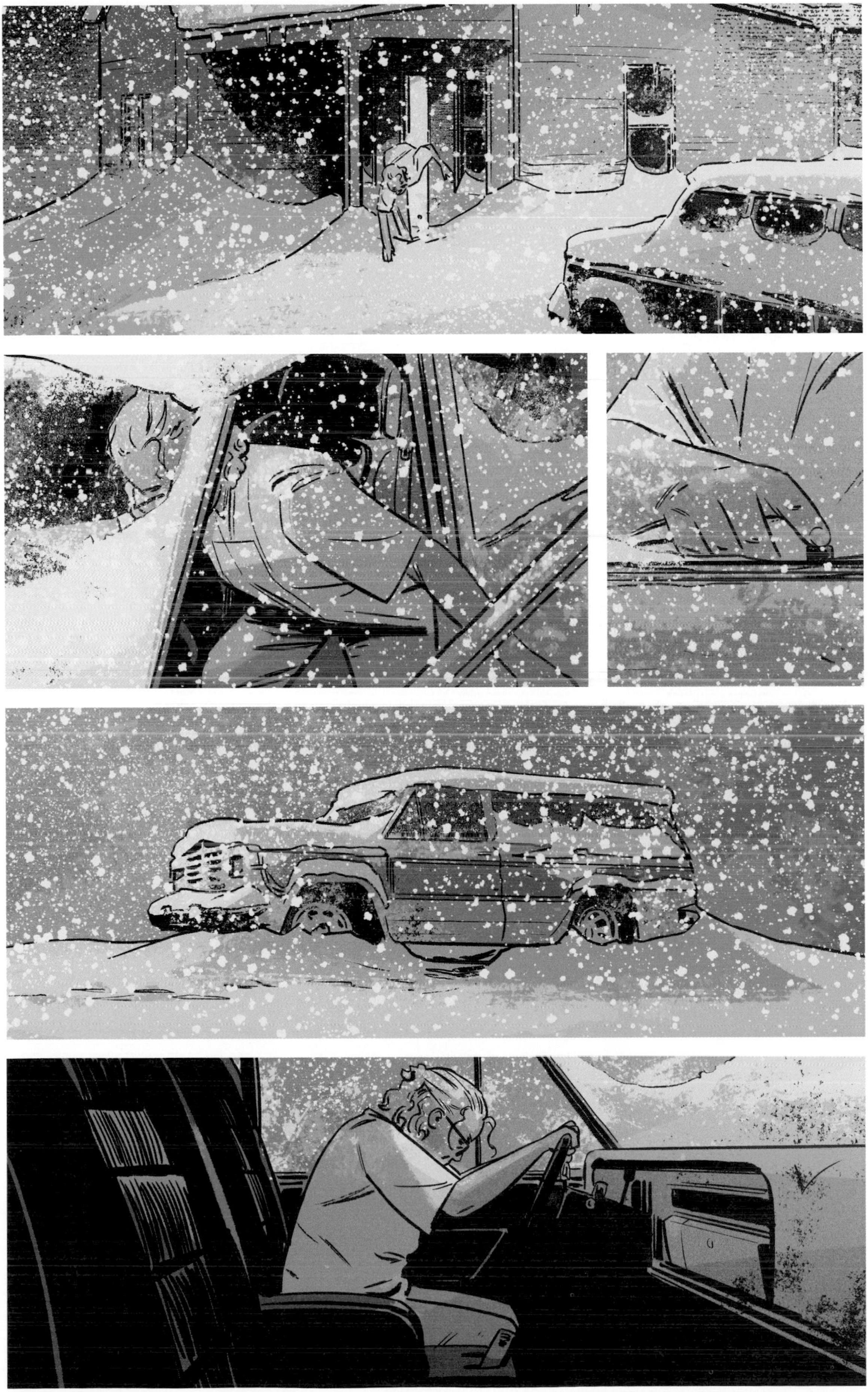

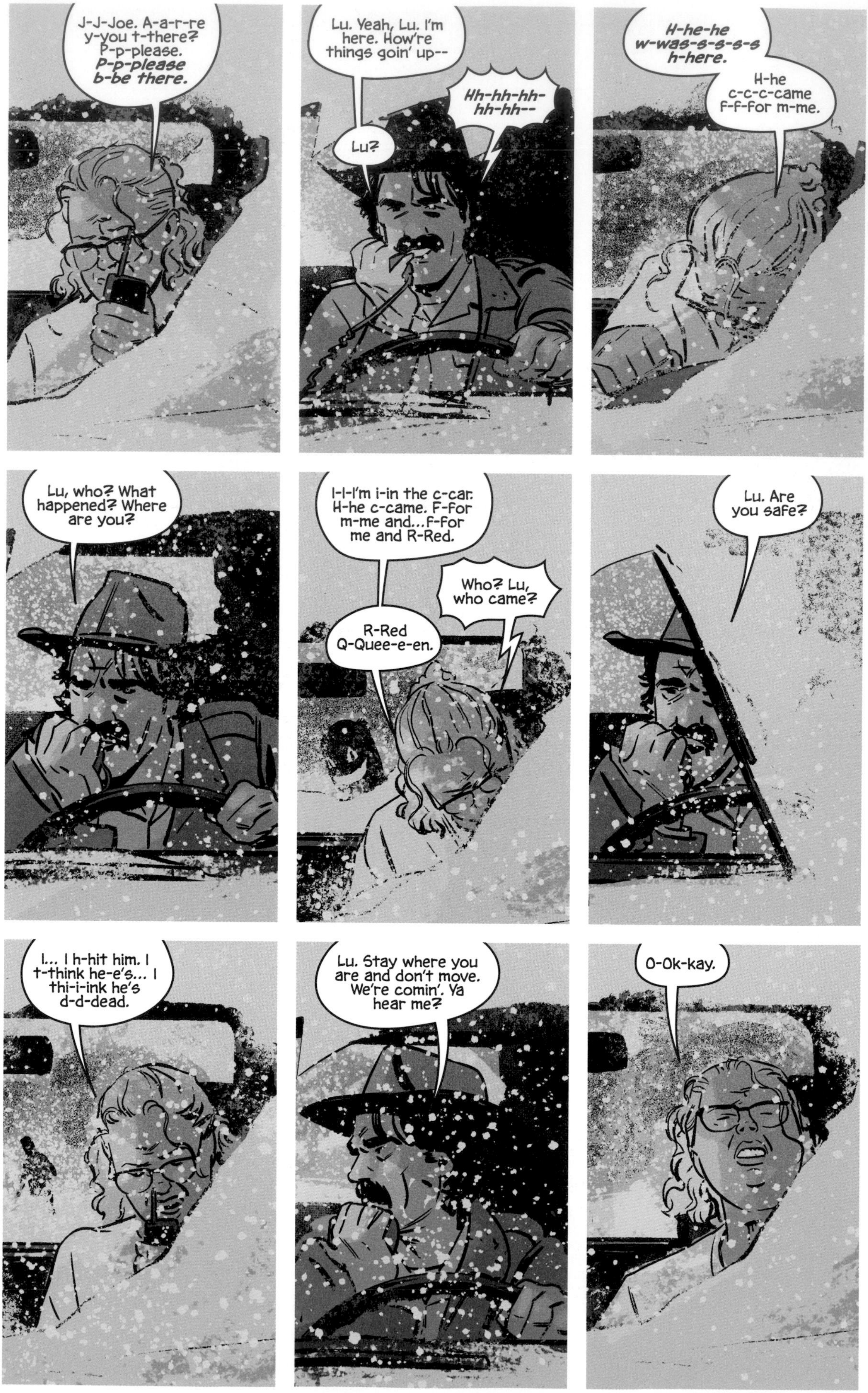
J-J-Joe. A-a-r-re y-you t-there? P-p-please. *P-p-please b-be there.*
Lu. Yeah, Lu. I'm here. How're things goin' up--
Hh-hh-hh-hh-hh--
Lu?
H-he-he w-was-s-s-s-s h-here.
H-he c-c-c-came f-f-for m-me.
Lu, who? What happened? Where are you?
I-I-I'm i-in the c-car. H-he c-came. F-for m-me and... f-for me and R-Red.
Who? Lu, who came?
R-Red Q-Quee-e-en.
Lu. Are you safe?
I... I h-hit him. I t-think he-e's... I thi-i-ink he's d-d-dead.
Lu. Stay where you are and don't move. We're comin'. Ya hear me?
O-Ok-kay.

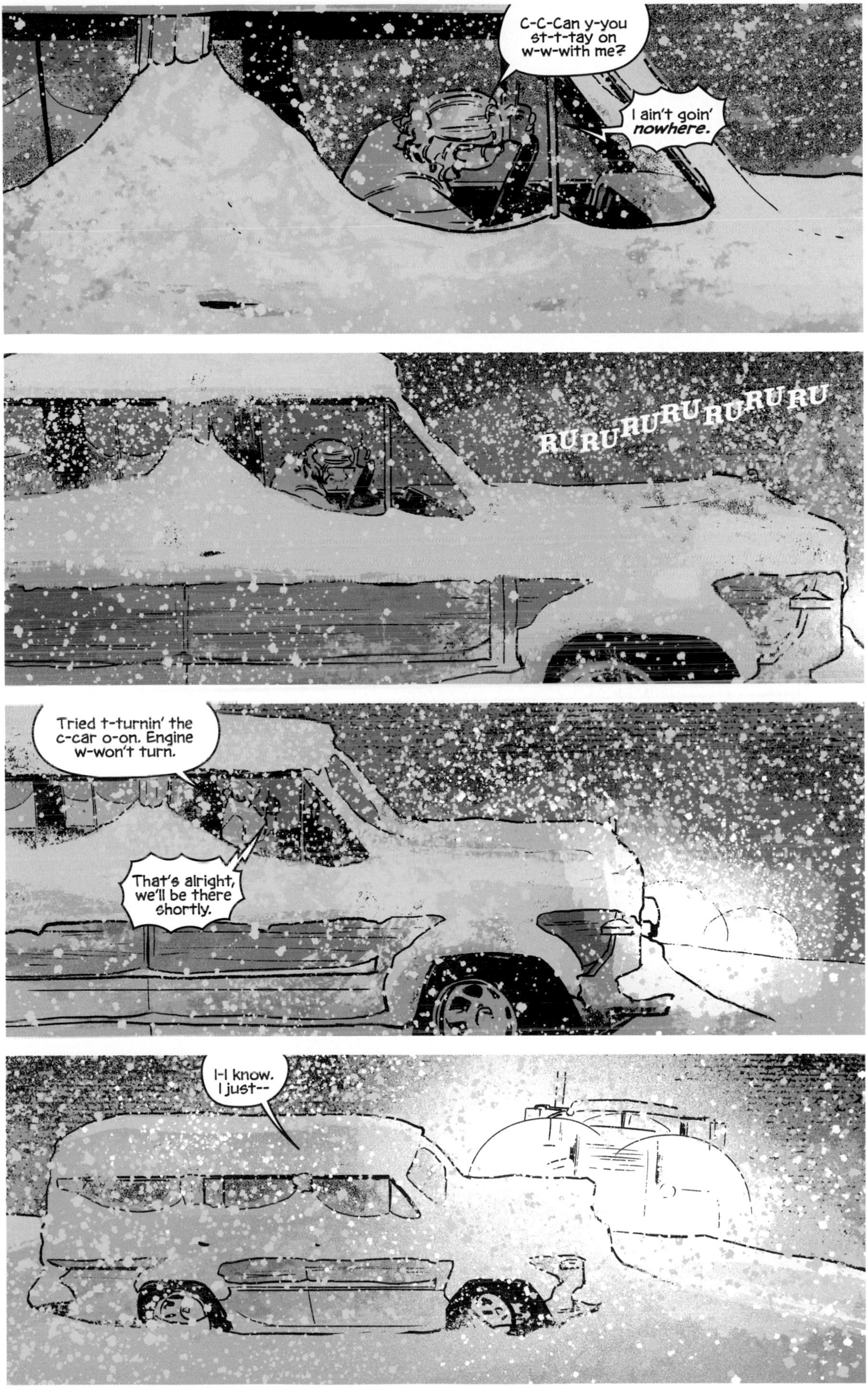
C-C-Can y-you st-t-tay on w-w-with me?
I ain't goin' *nowhere.*
RURURURU RURURU
Tried t-turnin' the c-car o-on. Engine w-won't turn.
That's alright, we'll be there shortly.
I-I know. I just--

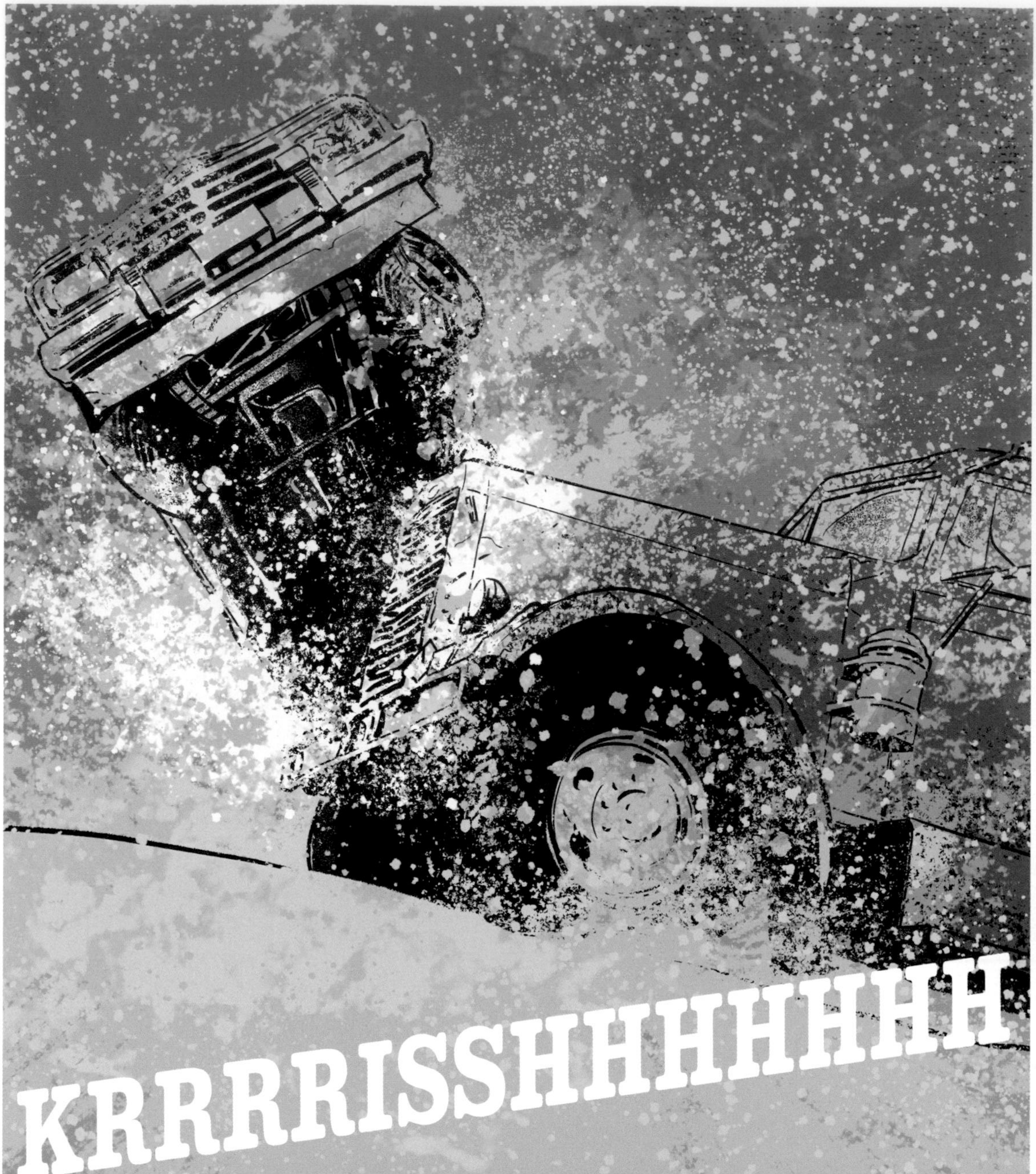
KRRRRISSHHHHHHH

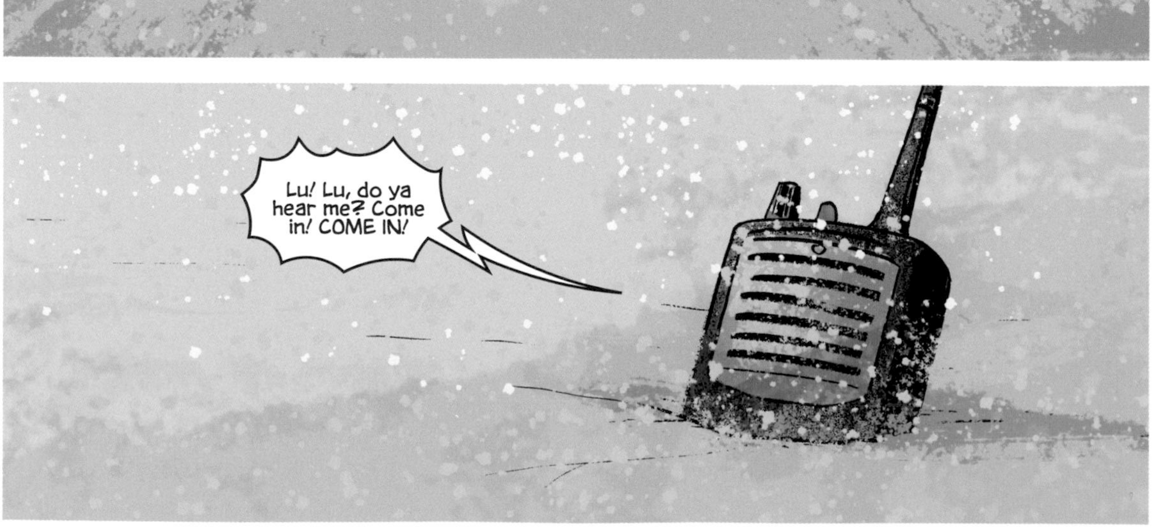
Lu! Lu, do ya hear me? Come in! COME IN!

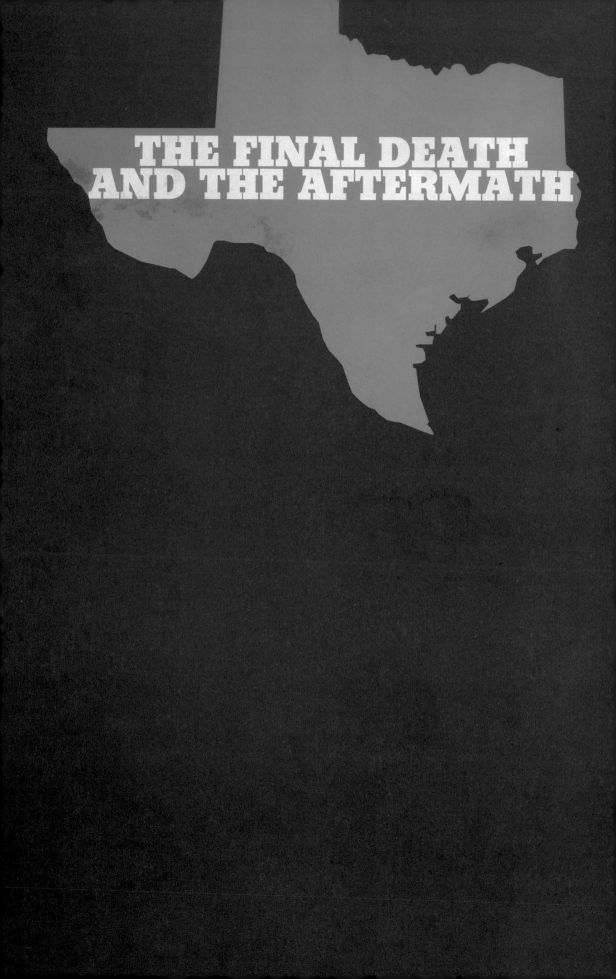

THE FINAL DEATH
AND THE AFTERMATH

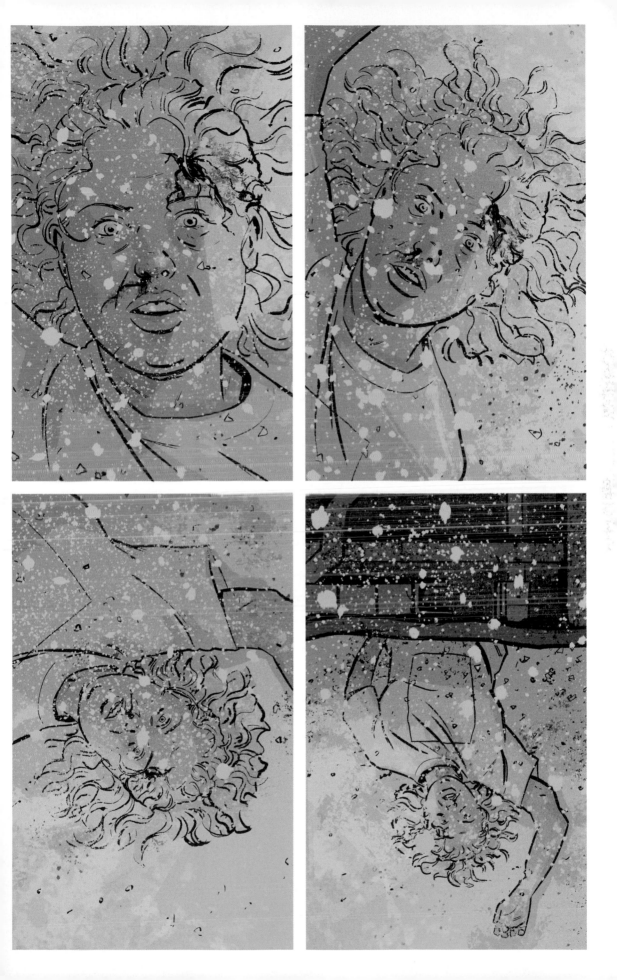

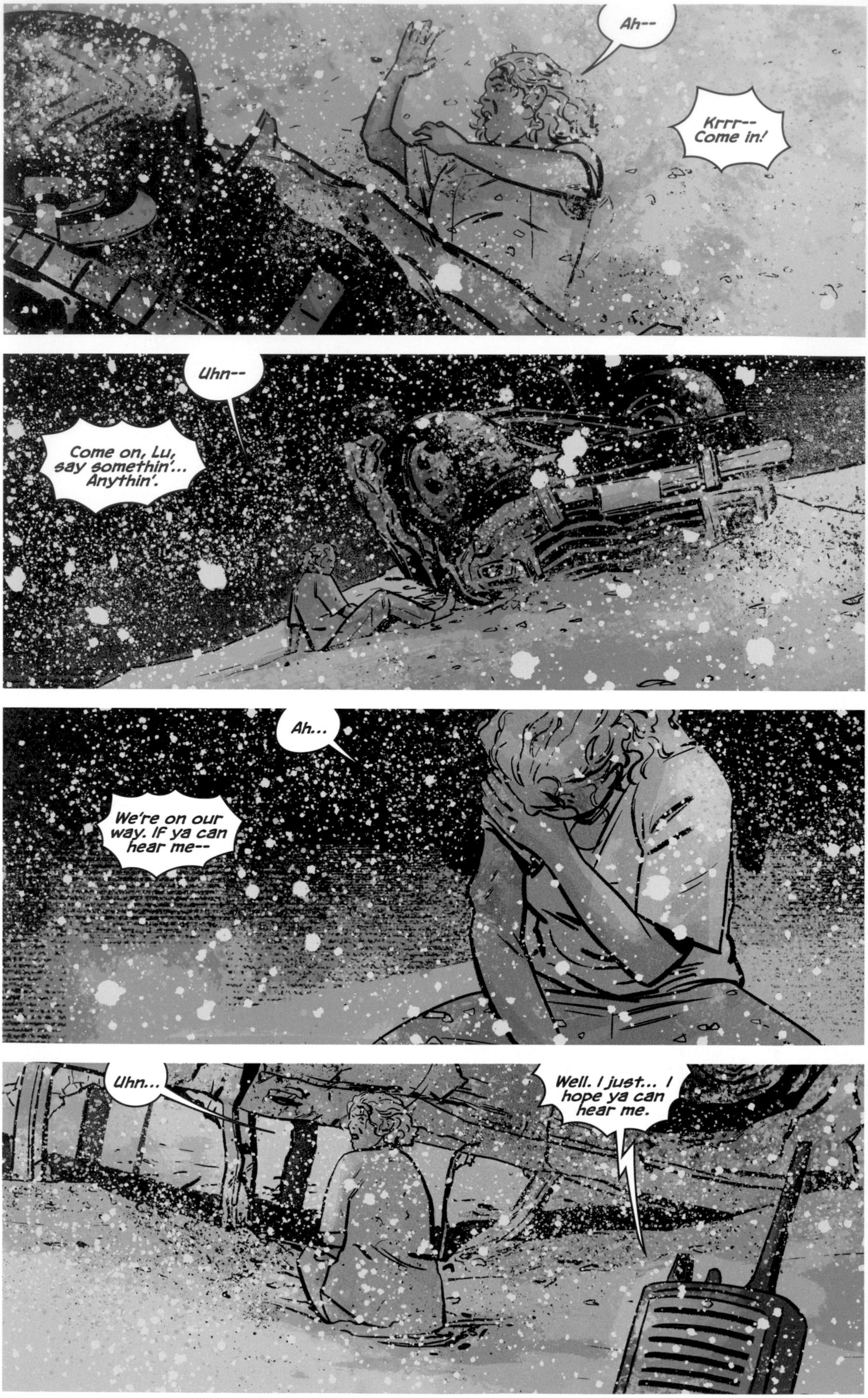
Ah--
Krrr--
Come in!
Uhn--
Come on, Lu, say somethin'... Anythin'.
Ah...
We're on our way. If ya can hear me--
Uhn...
Well. I just... I hope ya can hear me.

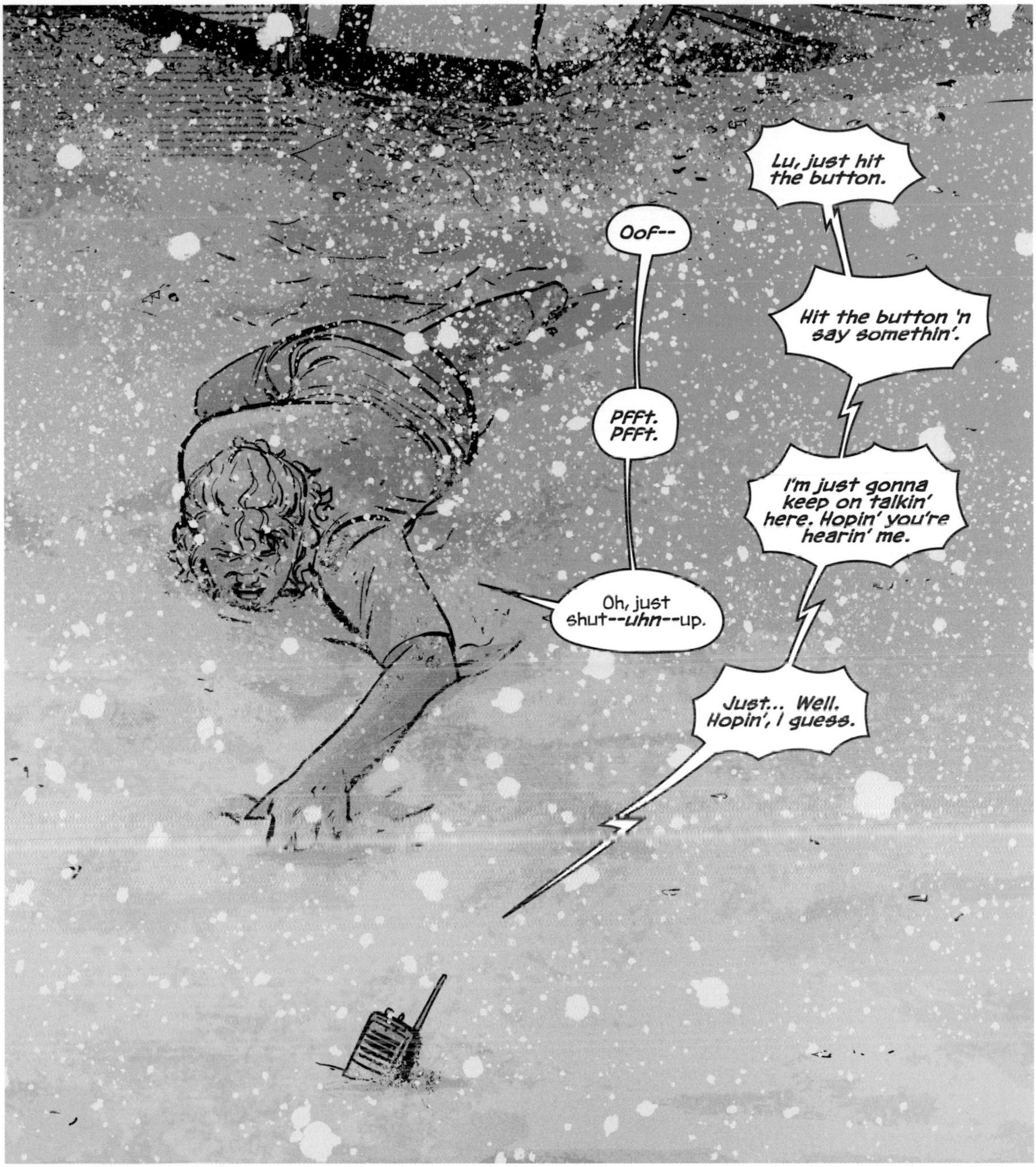
Oof--
PFFt. PFFt.
Oh, just shut--uhn--up.
Lu, just hit the button.
Hit the button 'n say somethin'.
I'm just gonna keep on talkin' here. Hopin' you're hearin' me.
Just... Well. Hopin', I guess.

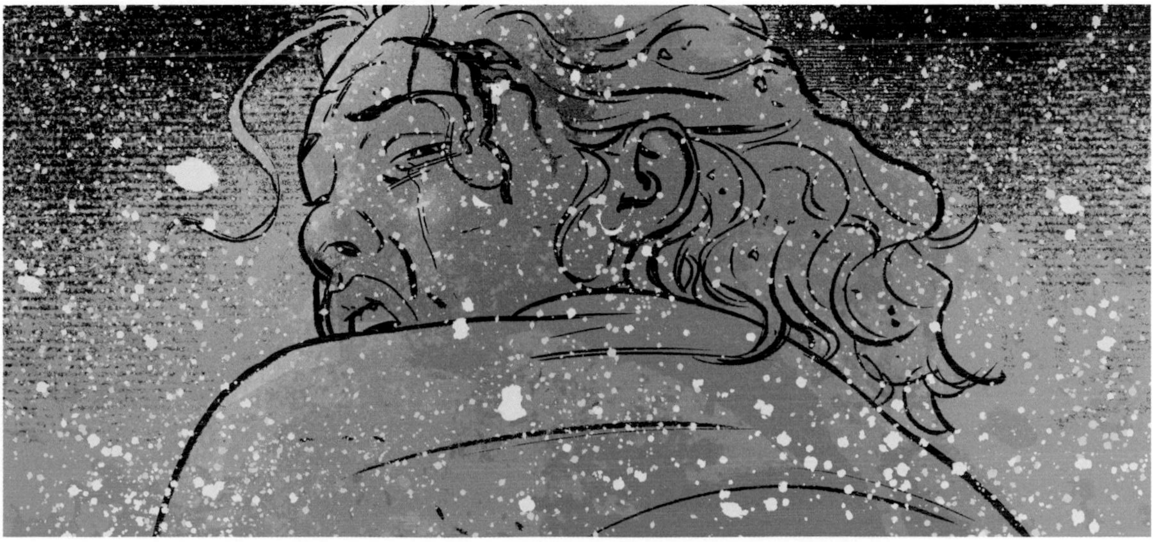

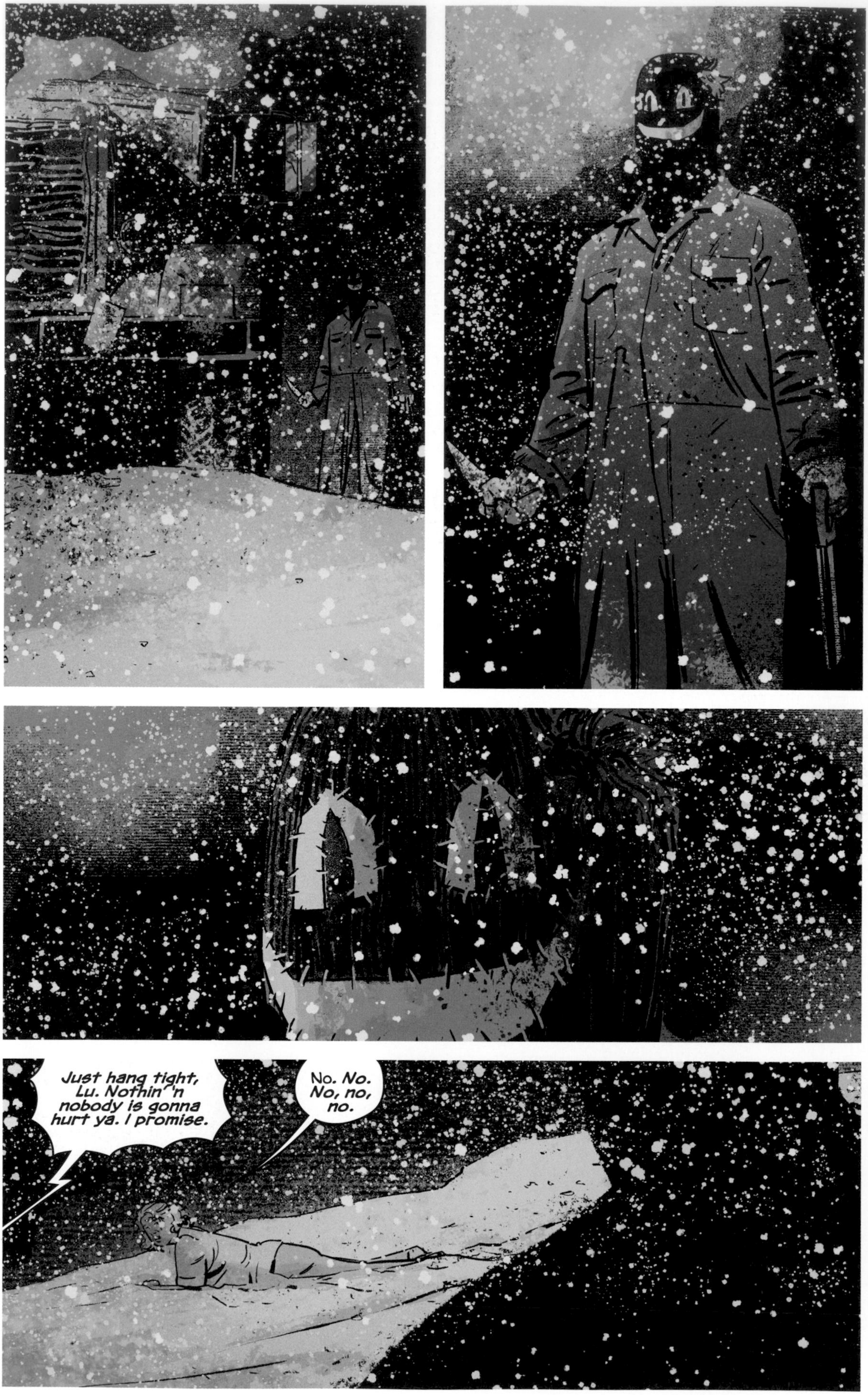
Just hang tight, Lu. Nothin' 'n nobody is gonna hurt ya. I promise.
No. No. No, no, no.

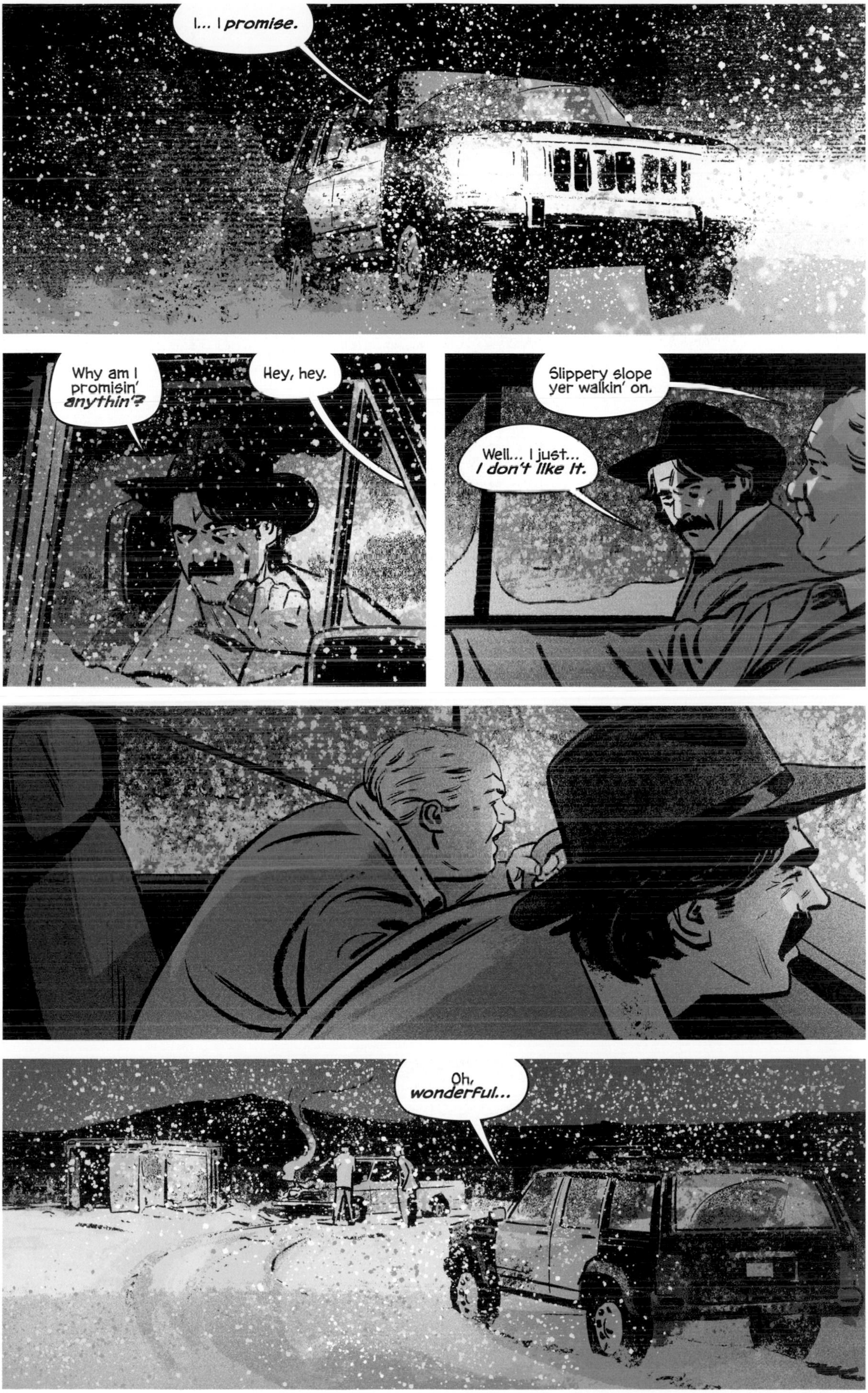
I... I promise.
Why am I promisin' anythin'?
Hey, hey.
Slippery slope yer walkin' on.
Well... I just... I don't like it.
Oh, wonderful...

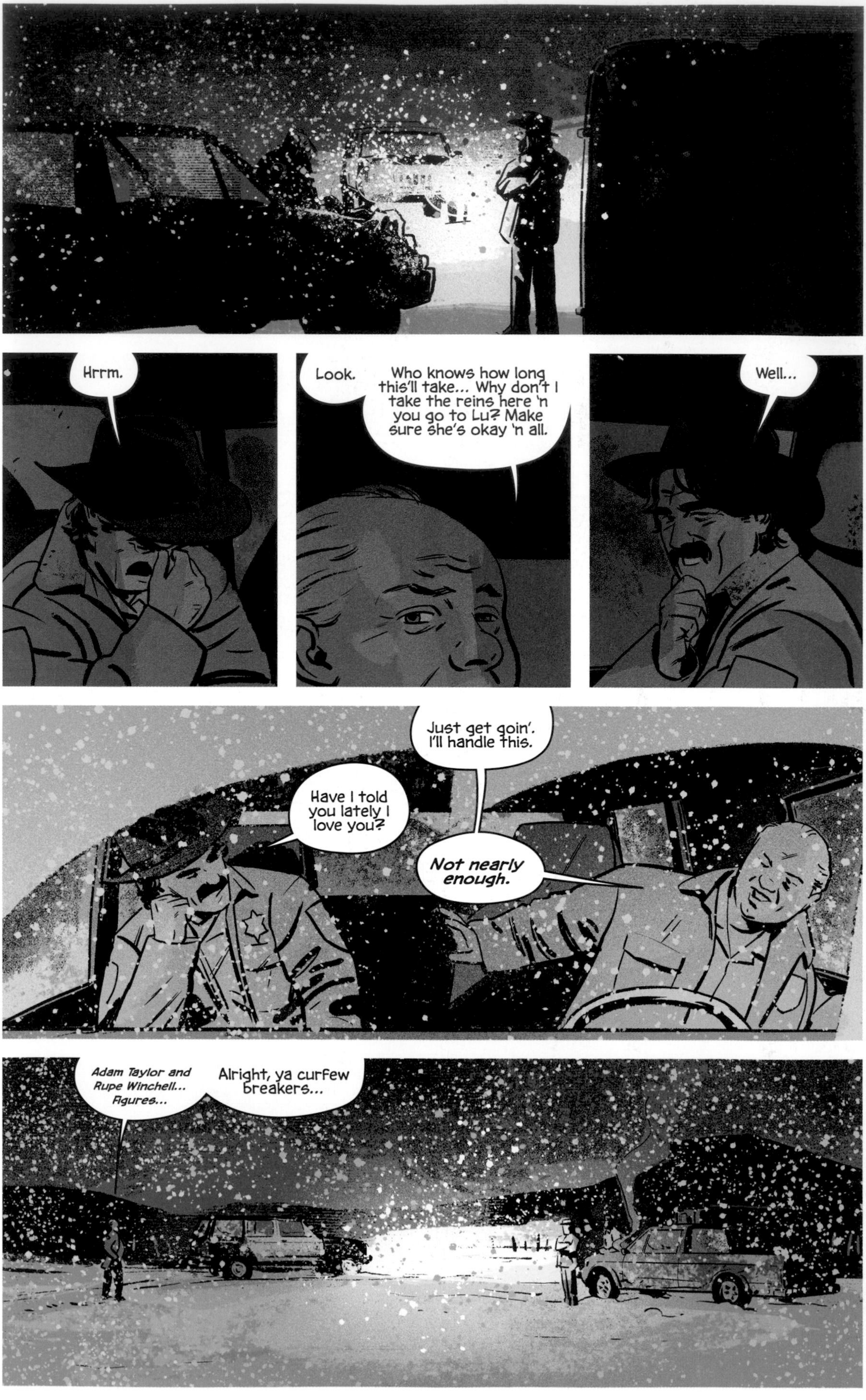
Hrrm.
Look.
Who knows how long this'll take... Why don't I take the reins here 'n you go to Lu? Make sure she's okay 'n all.
Well...
Have I told you lately I love you?
Just get goin'. I'll handle this.
Not nearly enough.
Adam Taylor and Rupe Winchell... Figures...
Alright, ya curfew breakers...

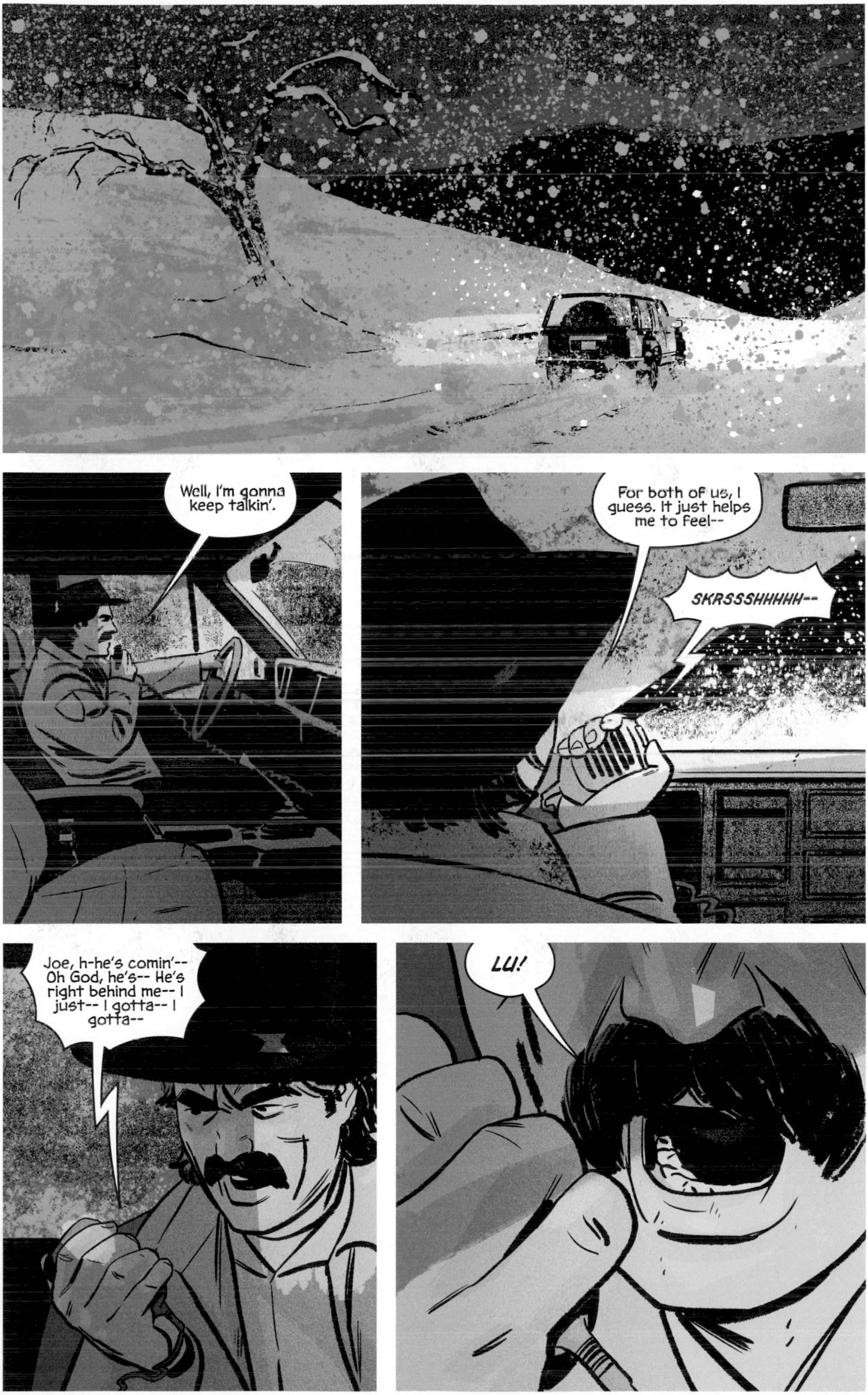
Well, I'm gonna keep talkin'.
For both of us, I guess. It just helps me to feel--
SKRSSSHHHHH--
Joe, h-he's comin'-- Oh God, he's-- He's right behind me-- I just-- I gotta-- I gotta--
LU!

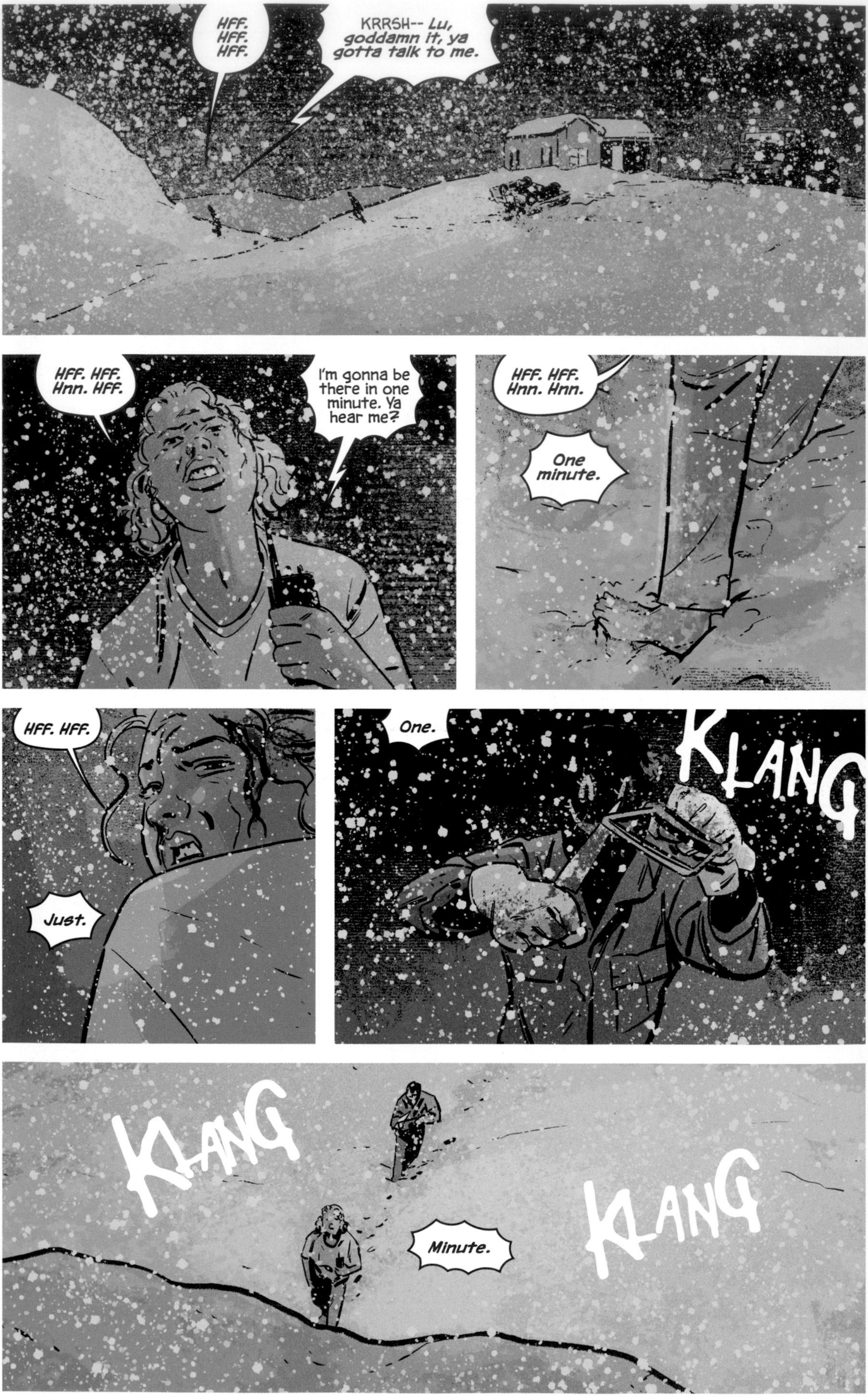
HFF. HFF. HFF.
KRRSH-- Lu, goddamn it, ya gotta talk to me.
HFF. HFF. Hnn. HFF.
I'm gonna be there in one minute. Ya hear me?
HFF. HFF. Hnn. Hnn.
One minute.
HFF. HFF.
Just.
One.
KLANG
KLANG
KLANG
Minute.

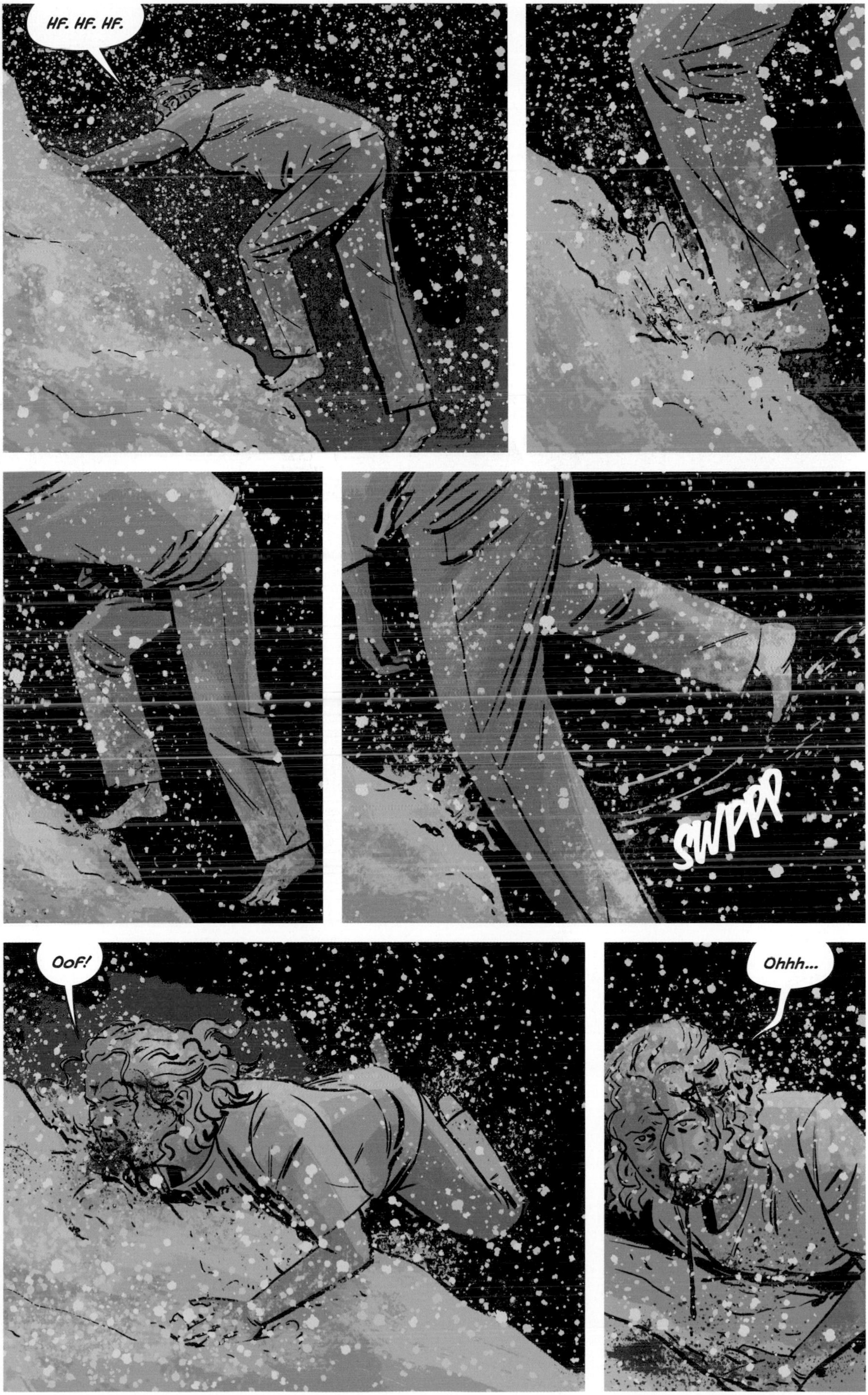
HF. HF. HF.
SWPPP
Oof!
Ohhh...

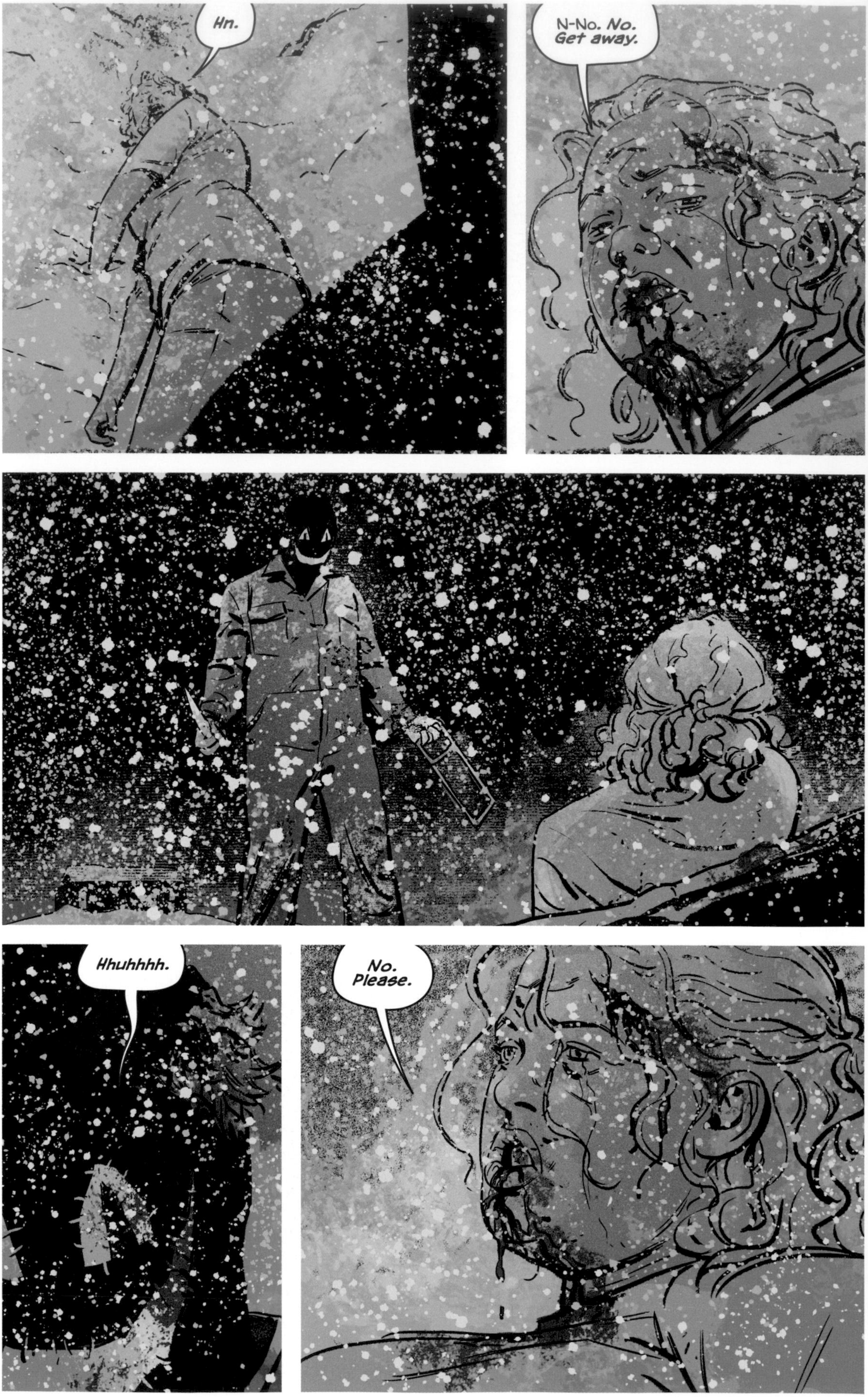
Hn.
N-No. *No.*
Get away.
Hhuhhhh.
No.
Please.

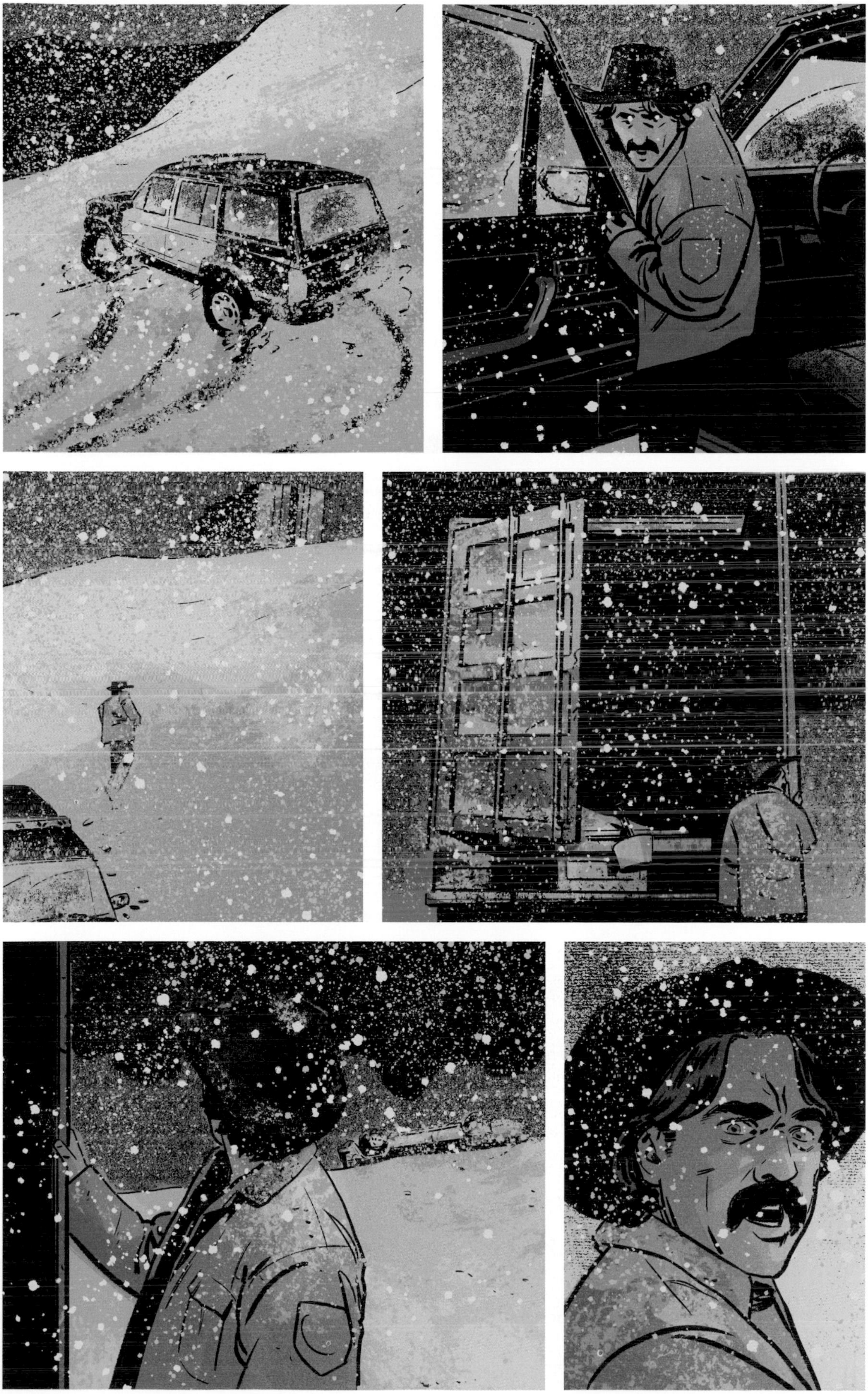

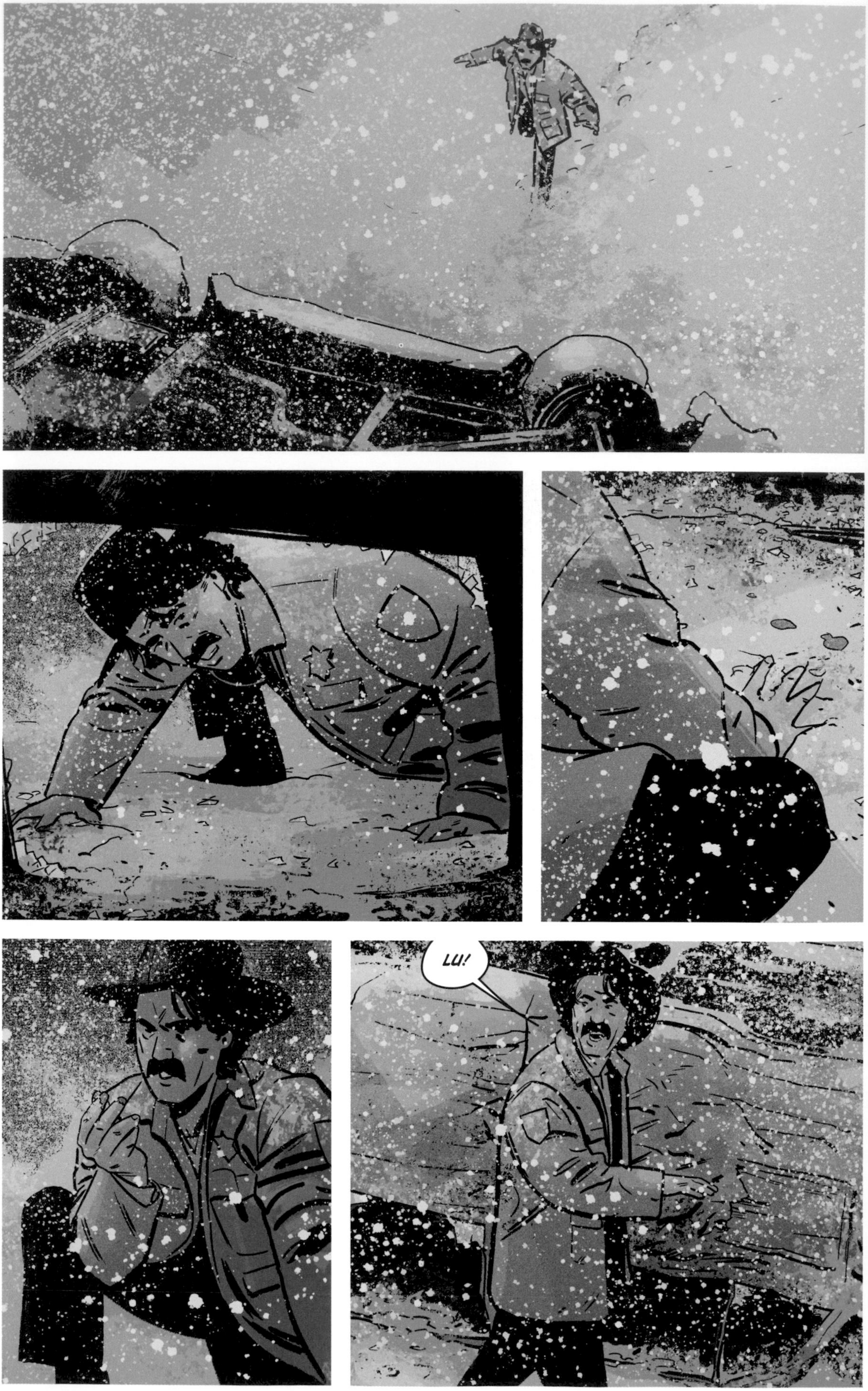
LU!

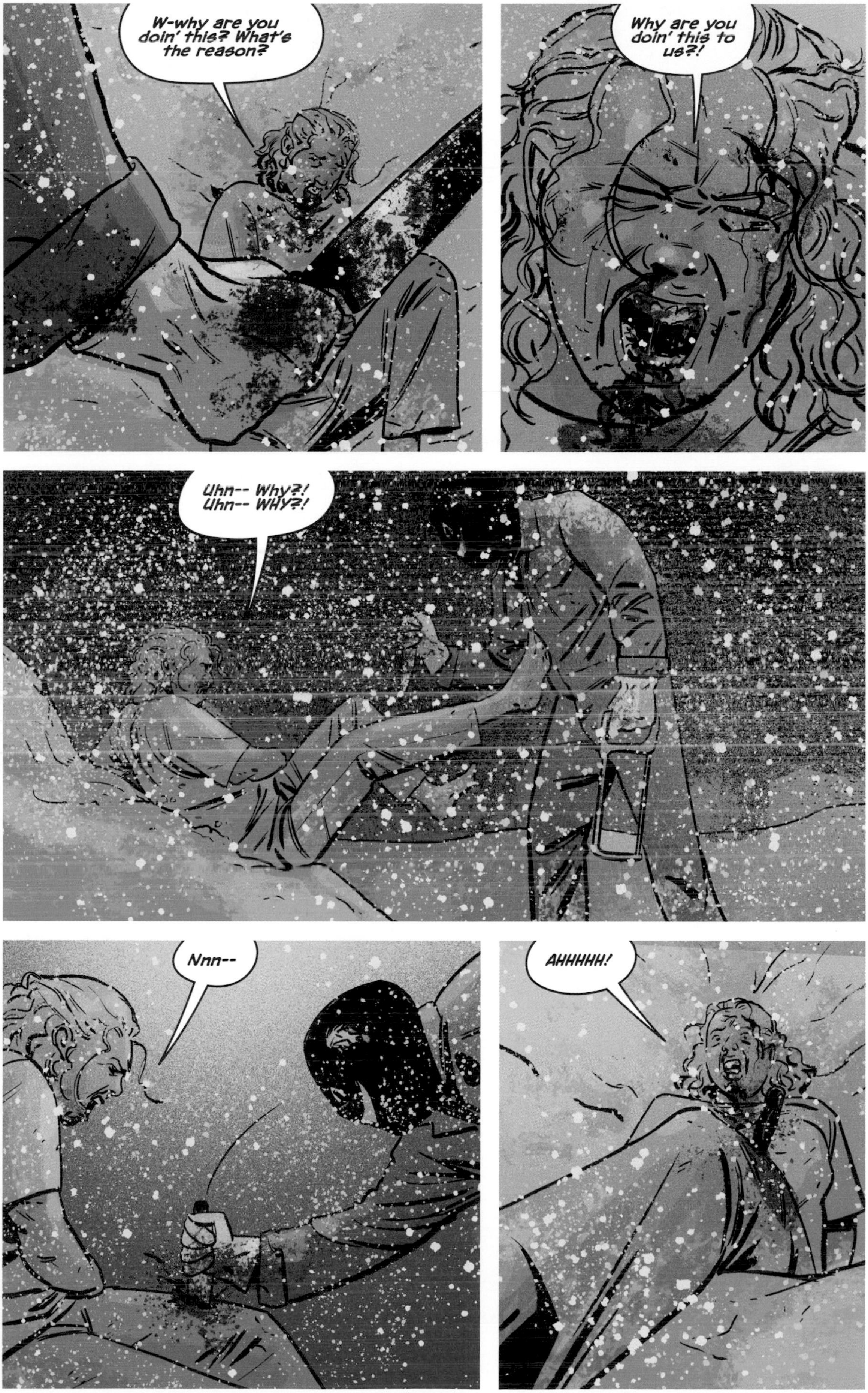
W-why are you doin' this? What's the reason?
Why are you doin' this to us?!
Uhn-- Why?! Uhn-- WHY?!
Nnn--
AHHHHH!

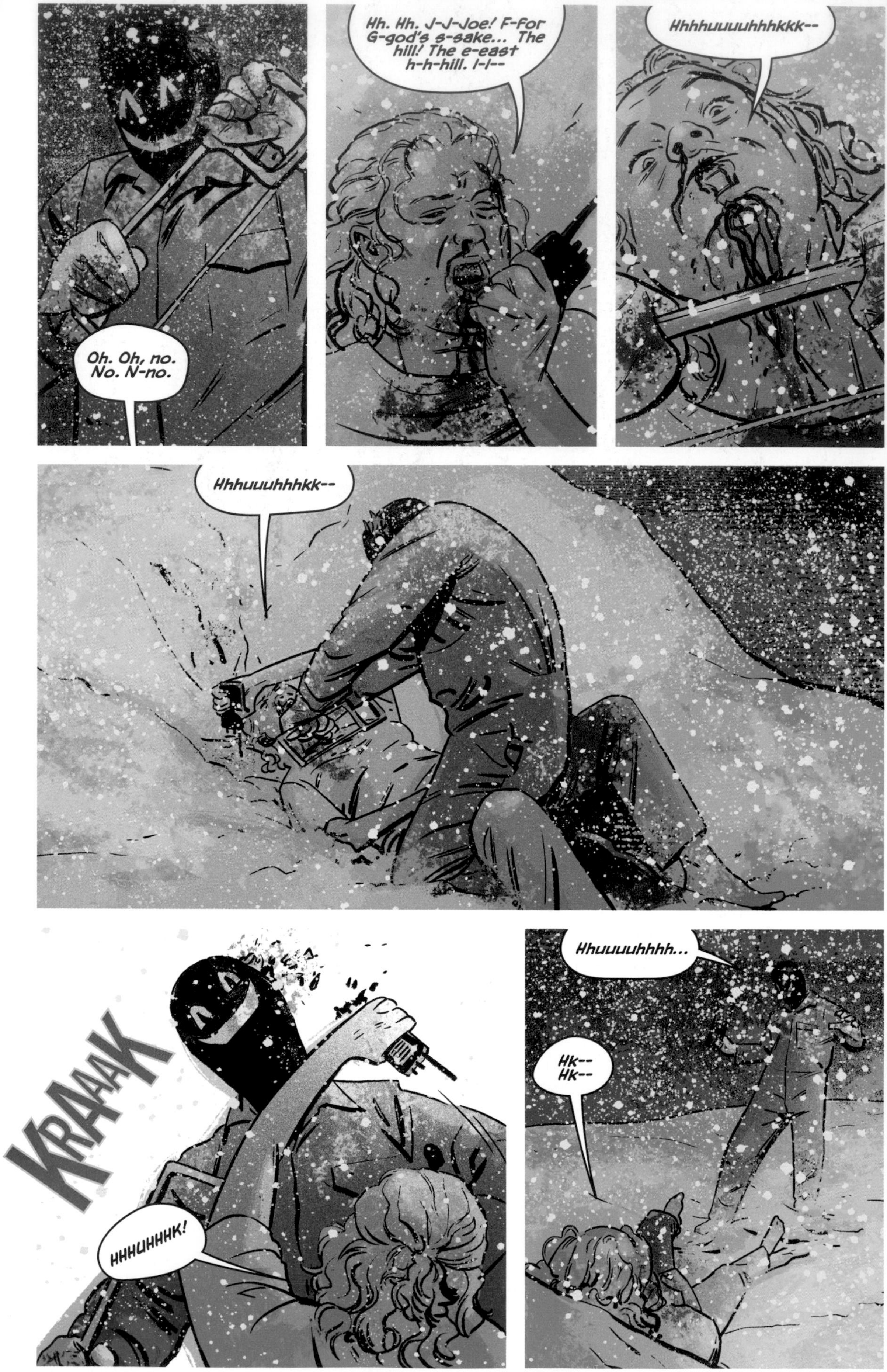
Oh. Oh, no. No. N-no.
Hh. Hh. J-J-Joe! F-for G-god's s-sake... The hill! The e-east h-h-hill. I-I--
Hhhhuuuuhhhkkk--
Hhhuuuhhhkk--
KRAAAK
HHHUHHHK!
Hhuuuuhhhh...
Hk-- Hk--

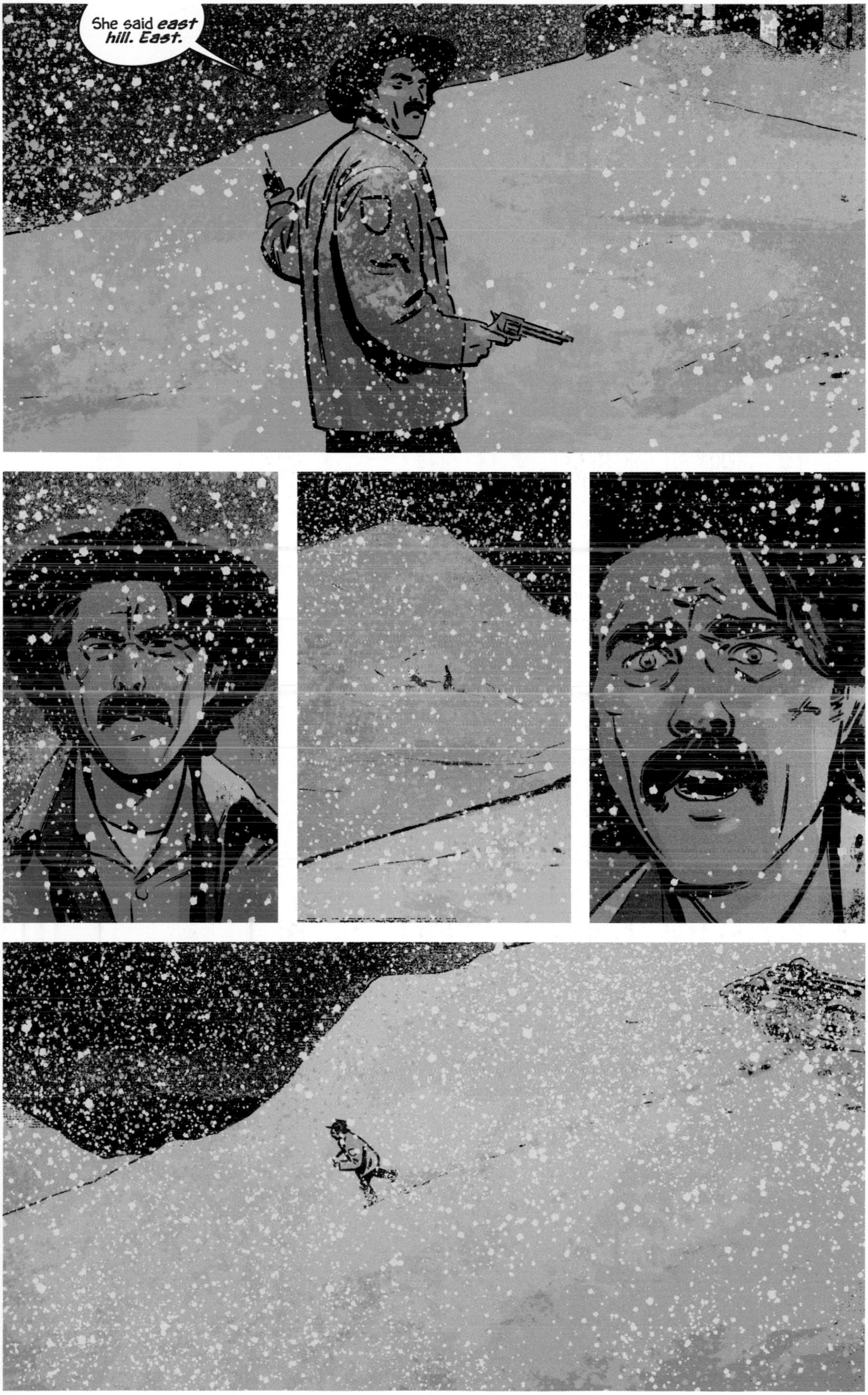
She said *east hill. East.*

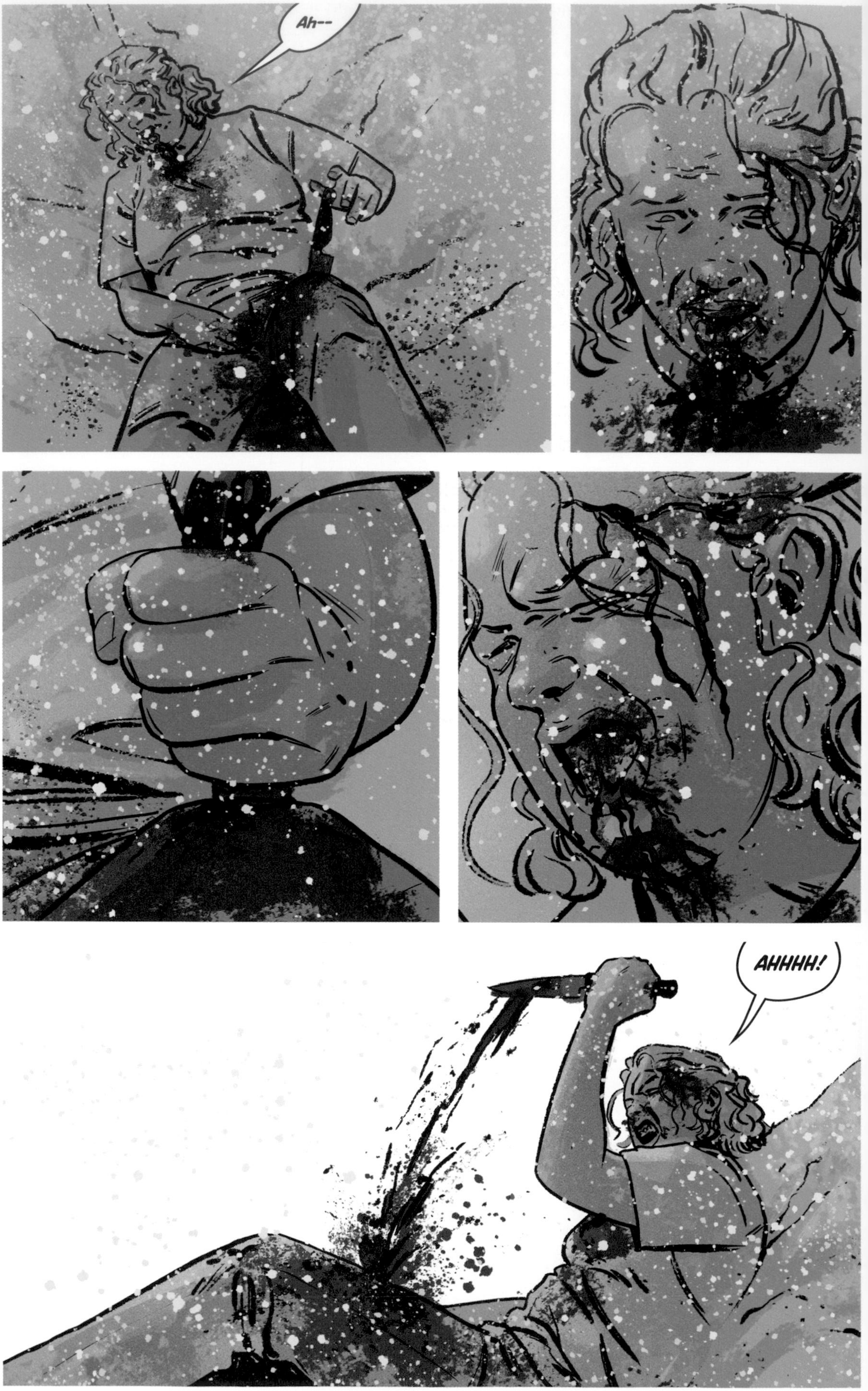
Ah--
AHHHH!

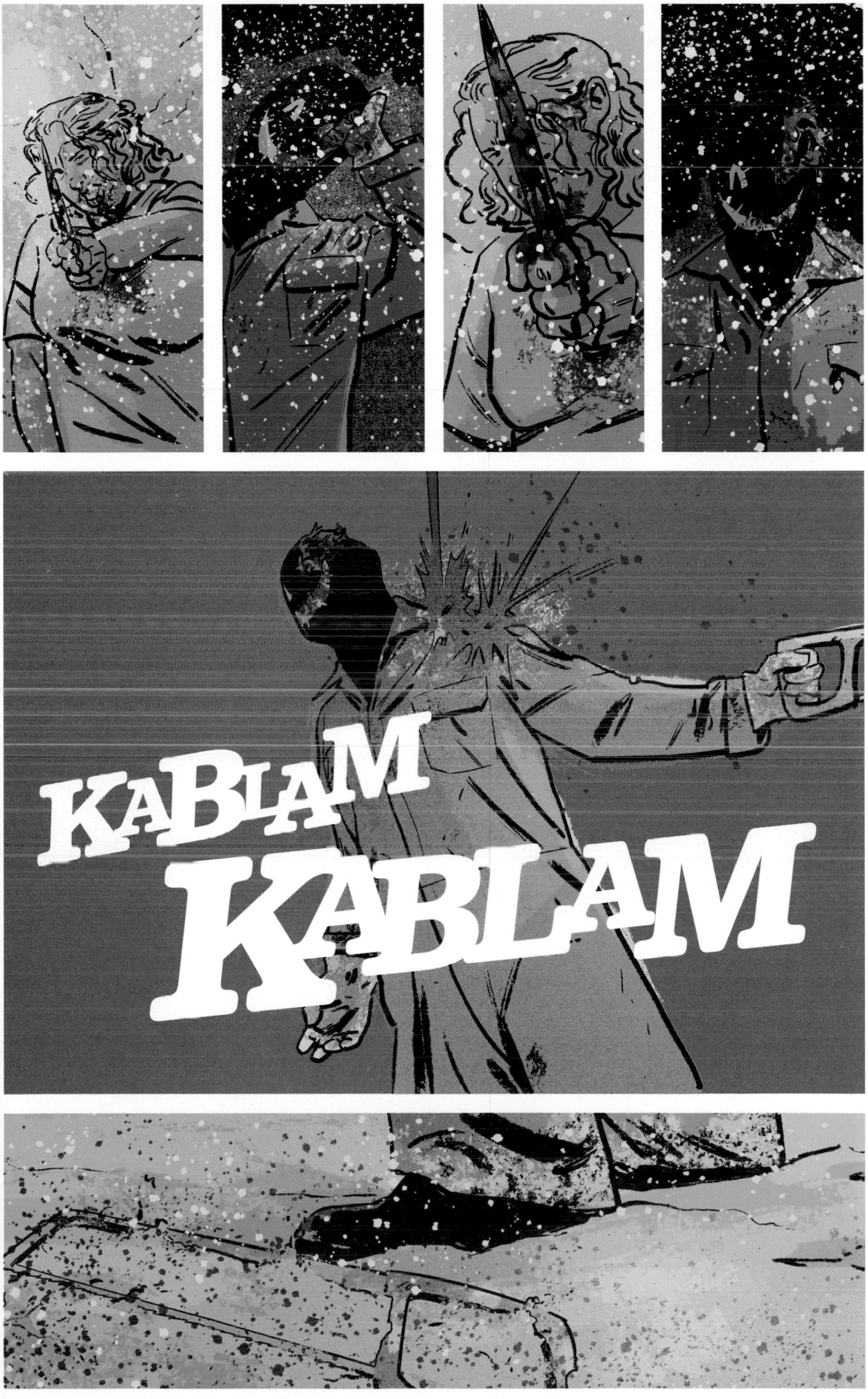
KABLAM
KABLAM

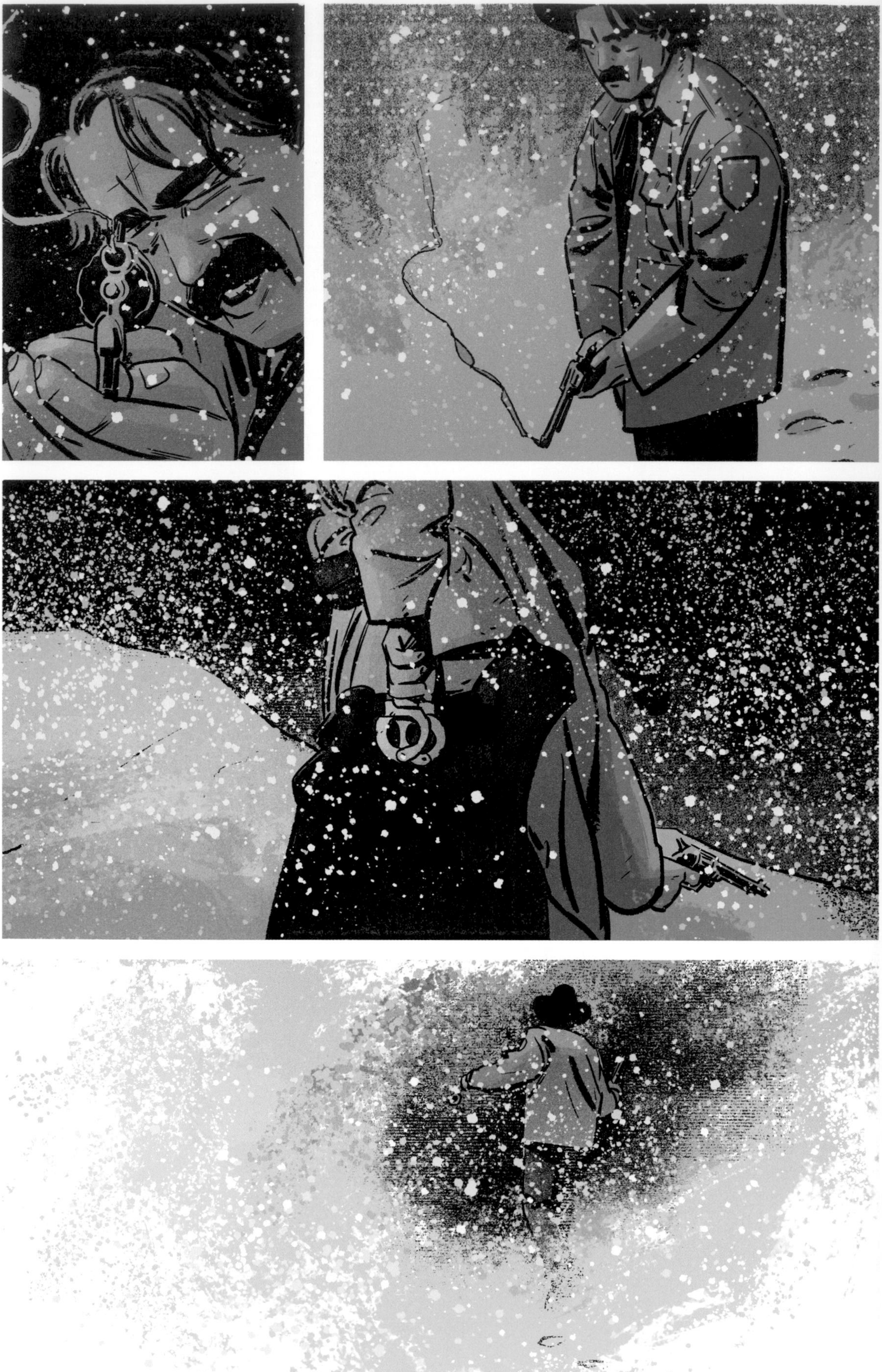

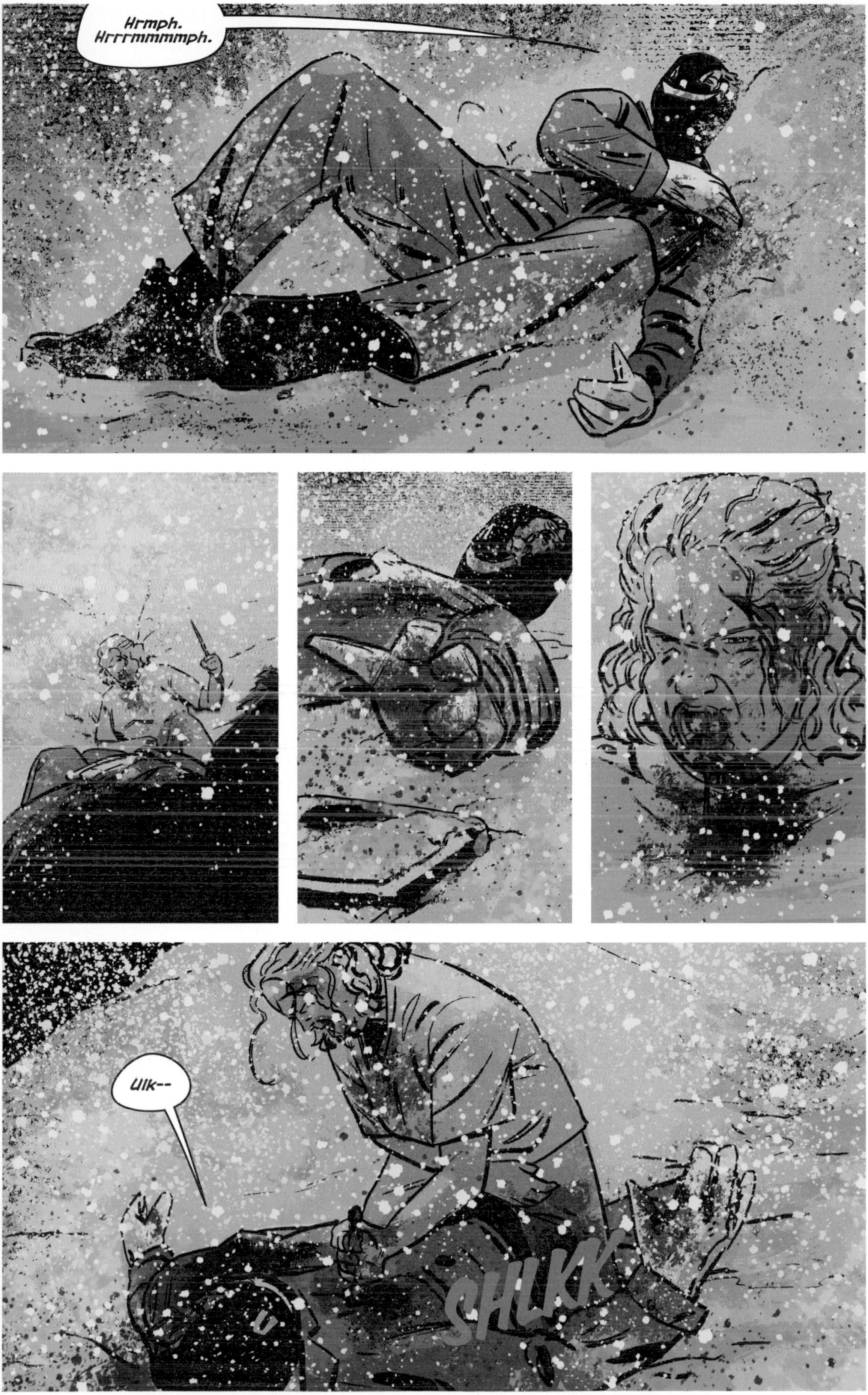
Hrmph.
Hrrrmmmmph.
Ulk--
SHLKK

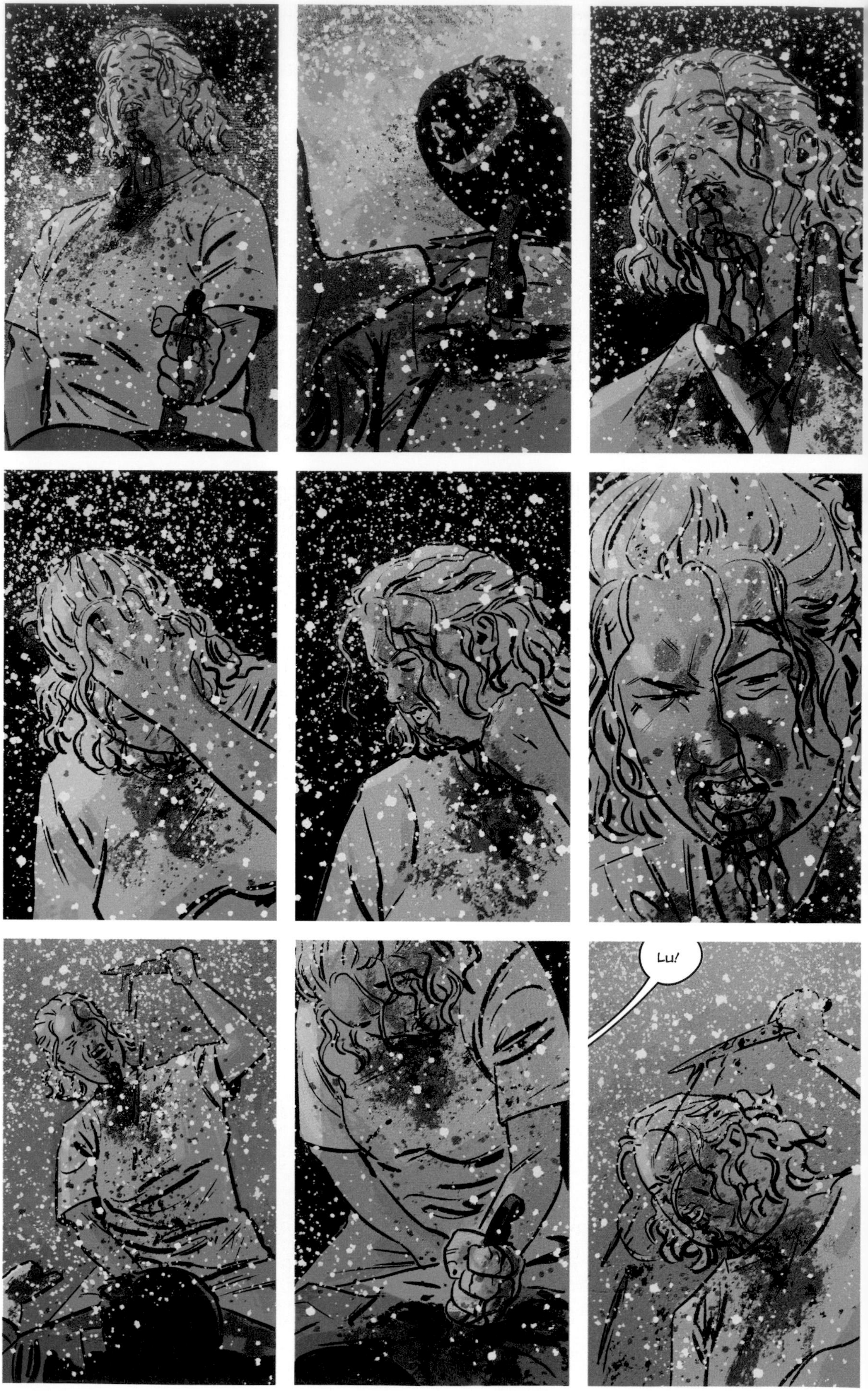
Lu!

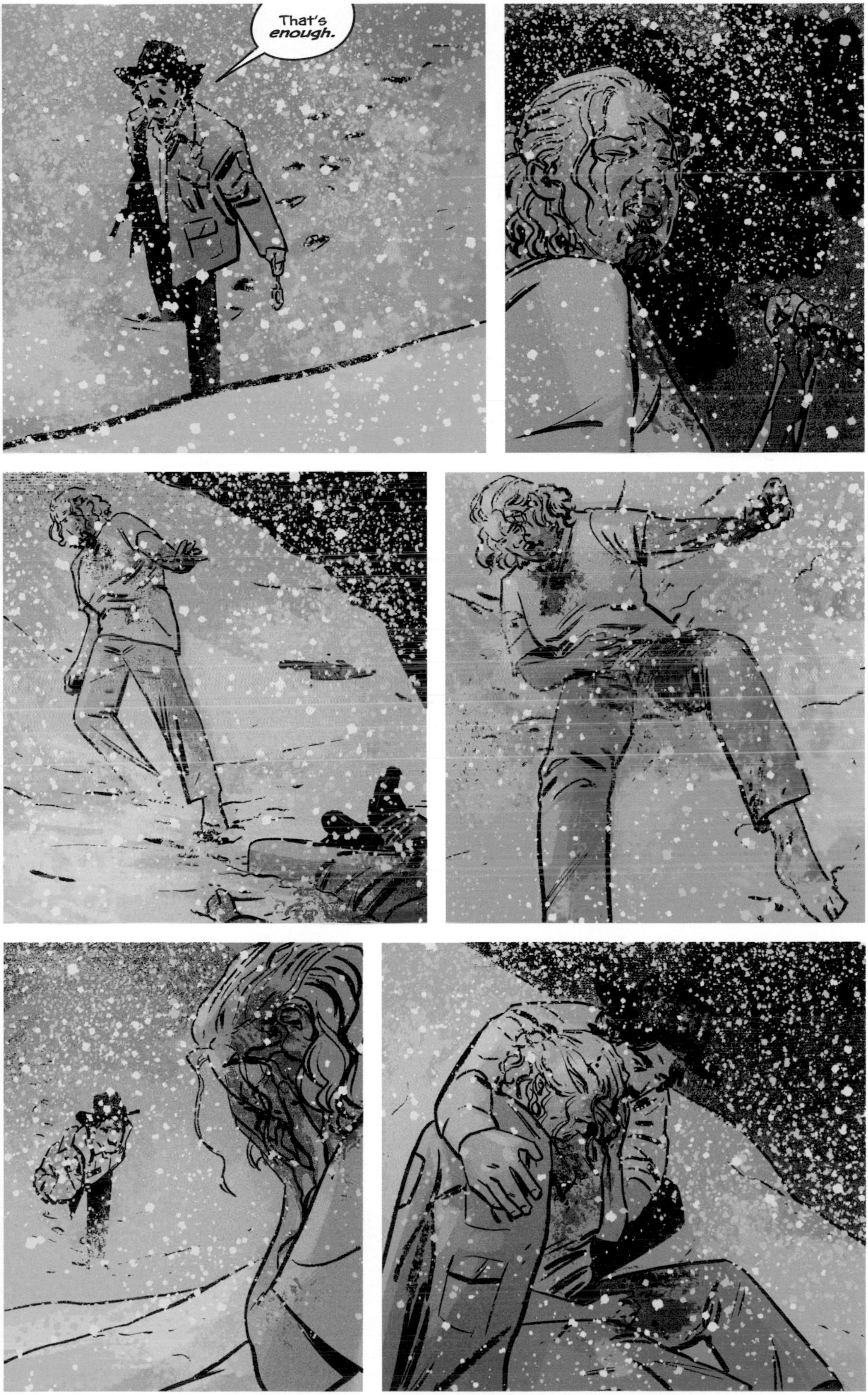
That's *enough.*

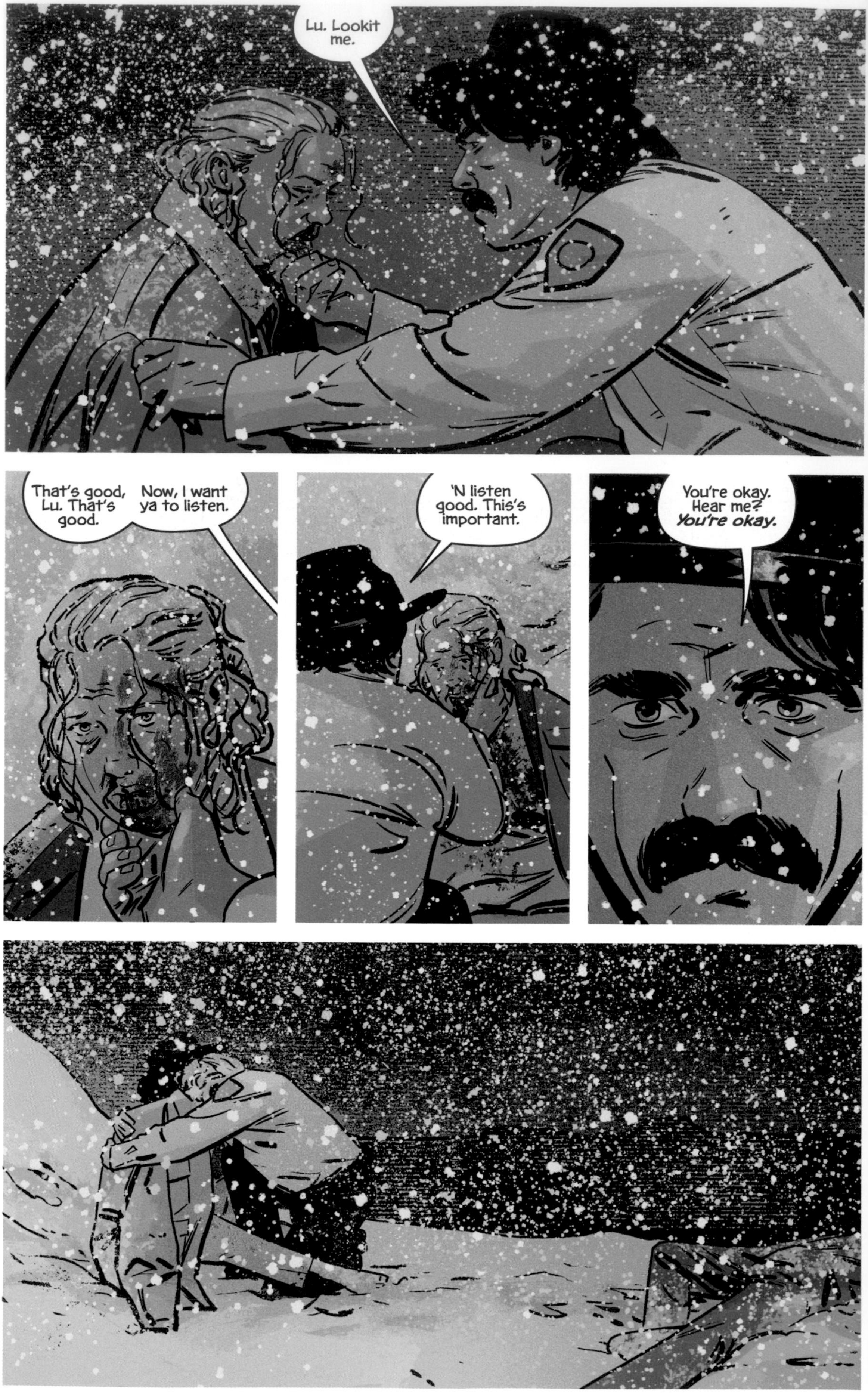
Lu. Lookit me.
That's good, Lu. That's good.
Now, I want ya to listen.
'N listen good. This's important.
You're okay. Hear me? *You're okay.*

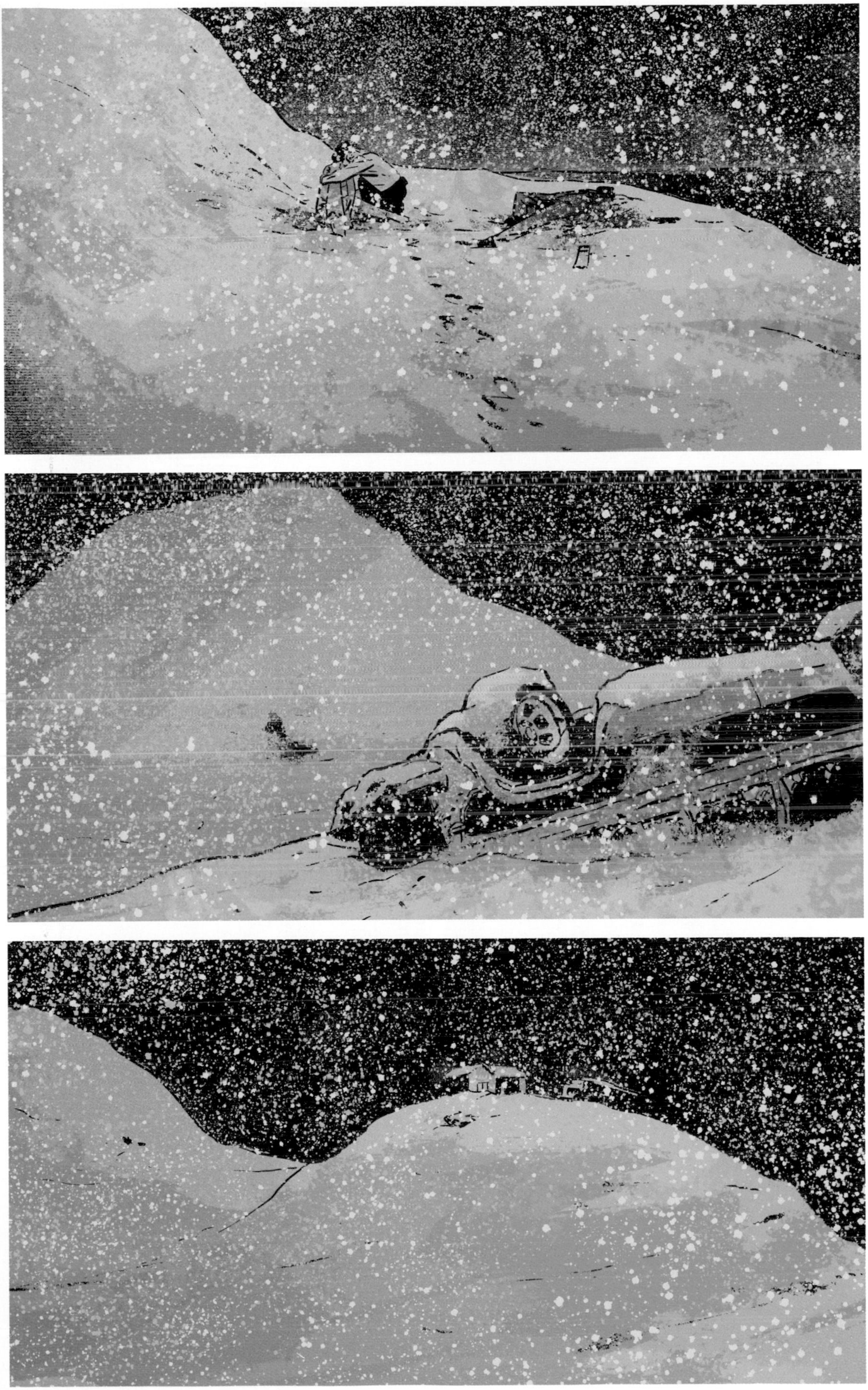

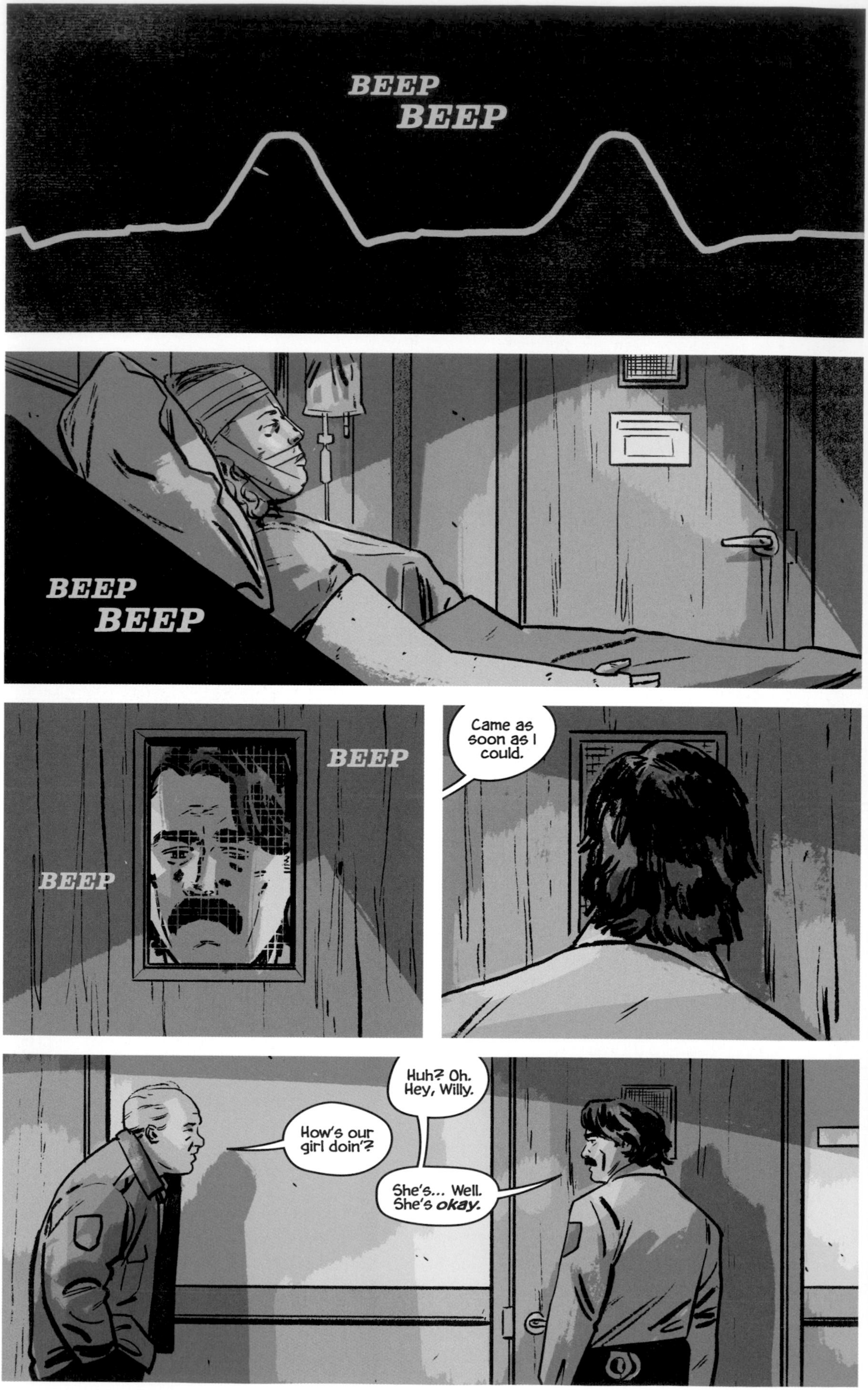
BEEP
BEEP
BEEP
BEEP
BEEP
BEEP
Came as soon as I could.
How's our girl doin'?
Huh? Oh. Hey, Willy.
She's... Well. She's *okay.*

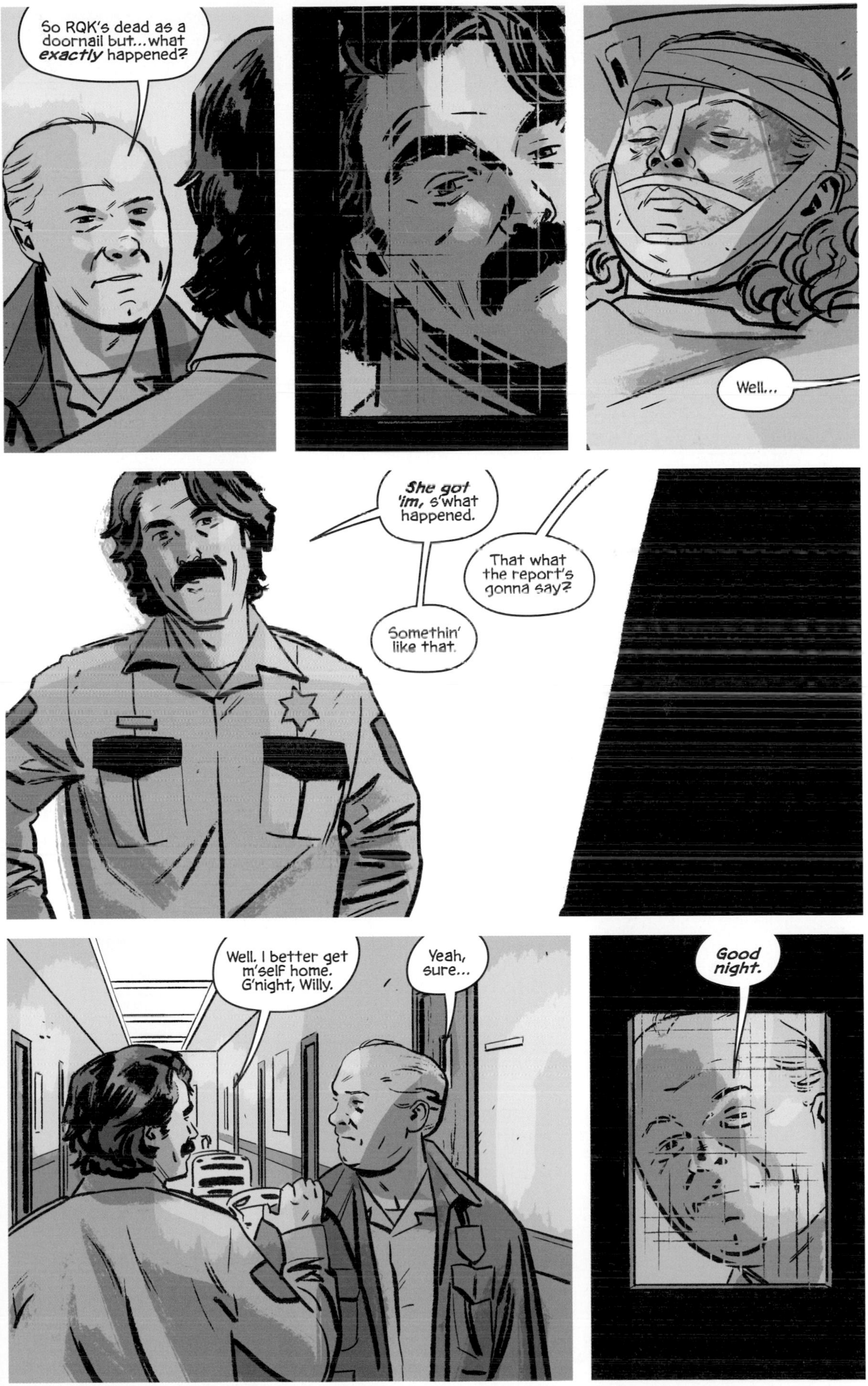
So RQK's dead as a doornail but...what *exactly* happened?
Well...
She got 'im, s'what happened.
Somethin' like that.
That what the report's gonna say?
Well. I better get m'self home. G'night, Willy.
Yeah, sure...
Good night.

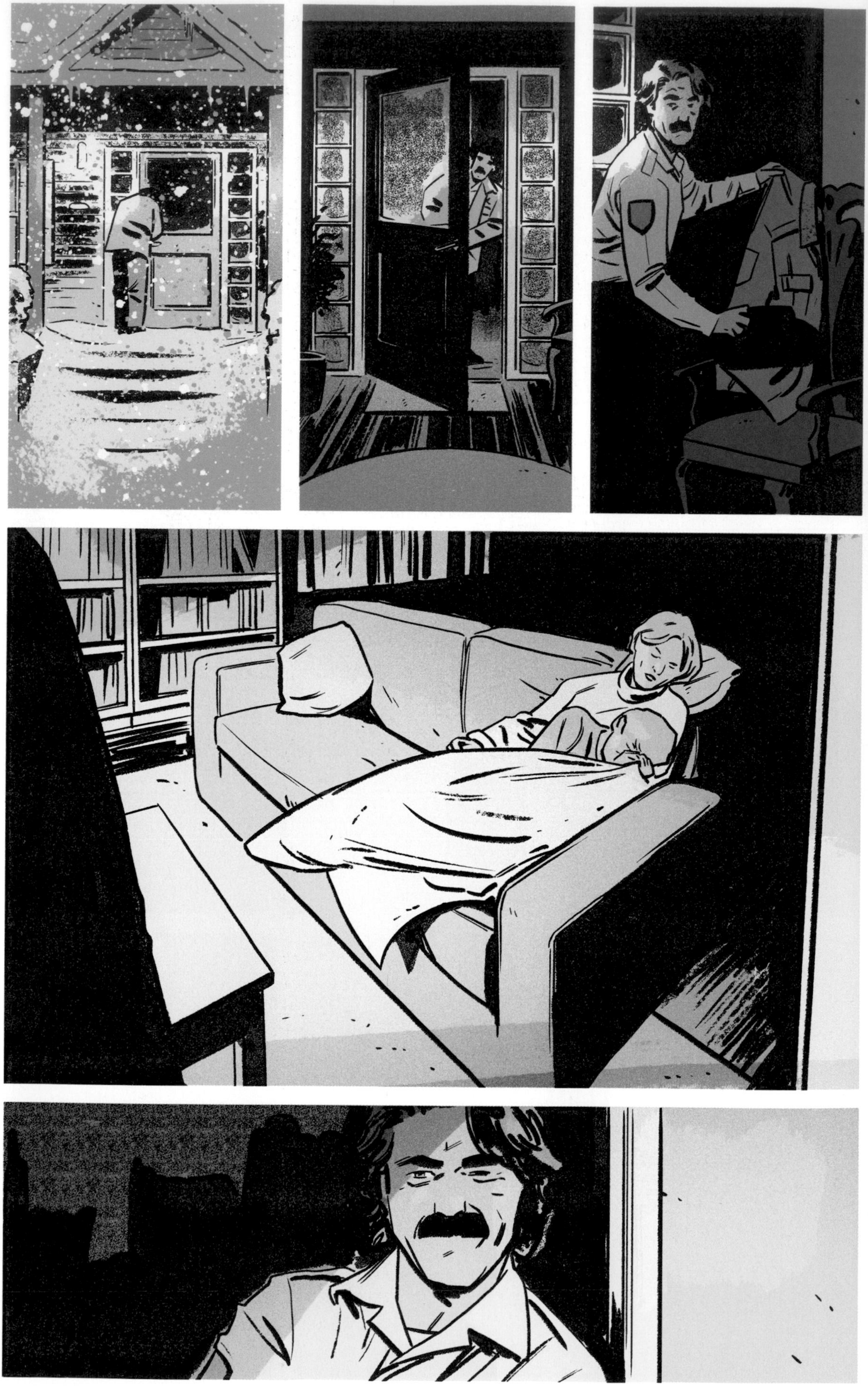

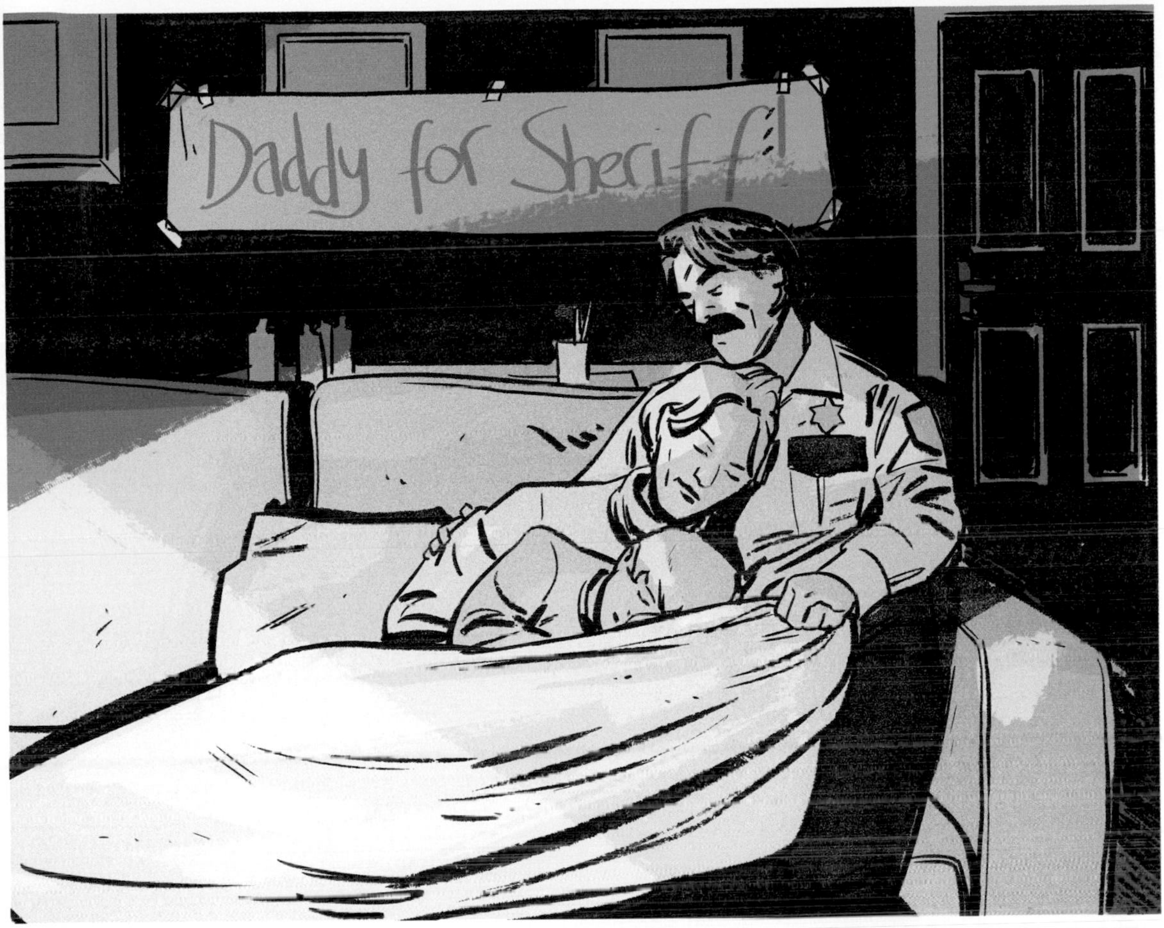
Daddy for Sheriff

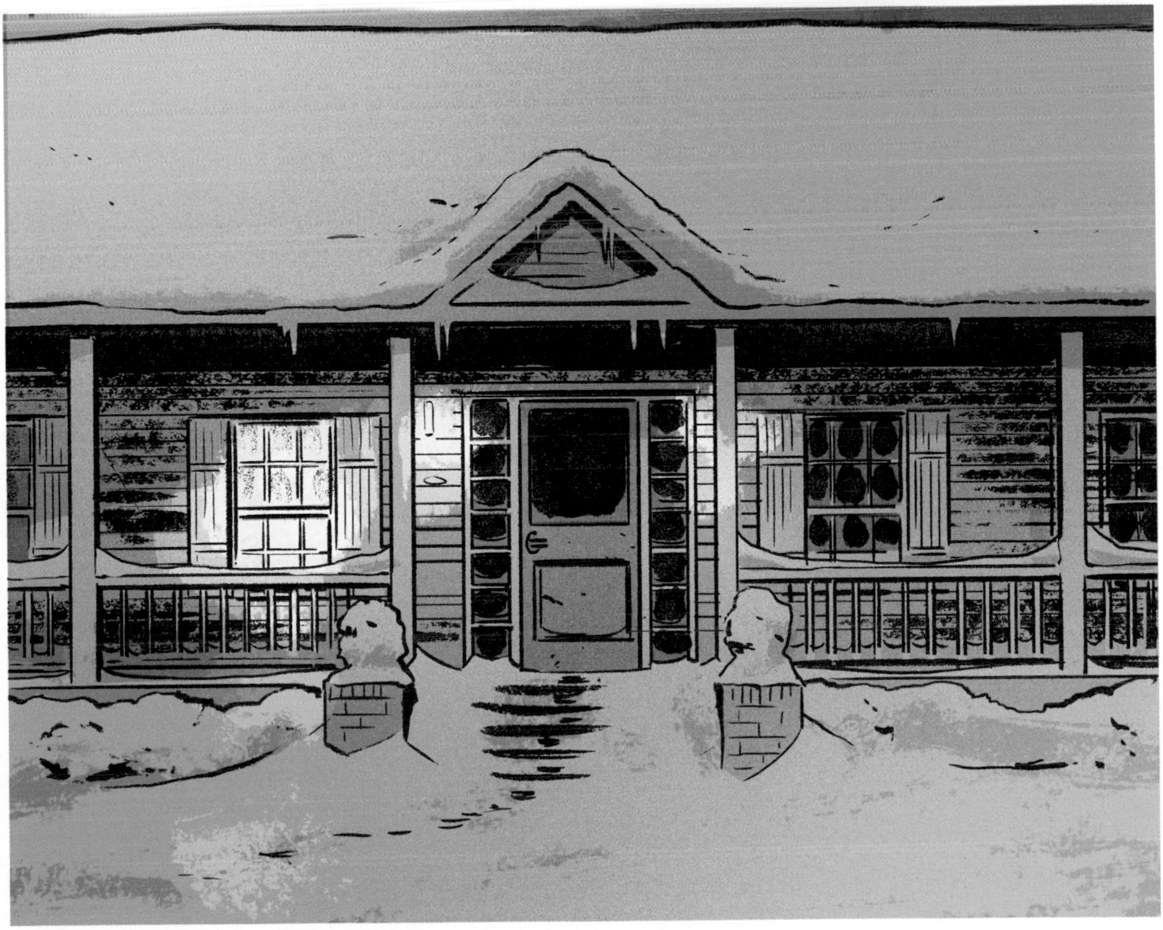

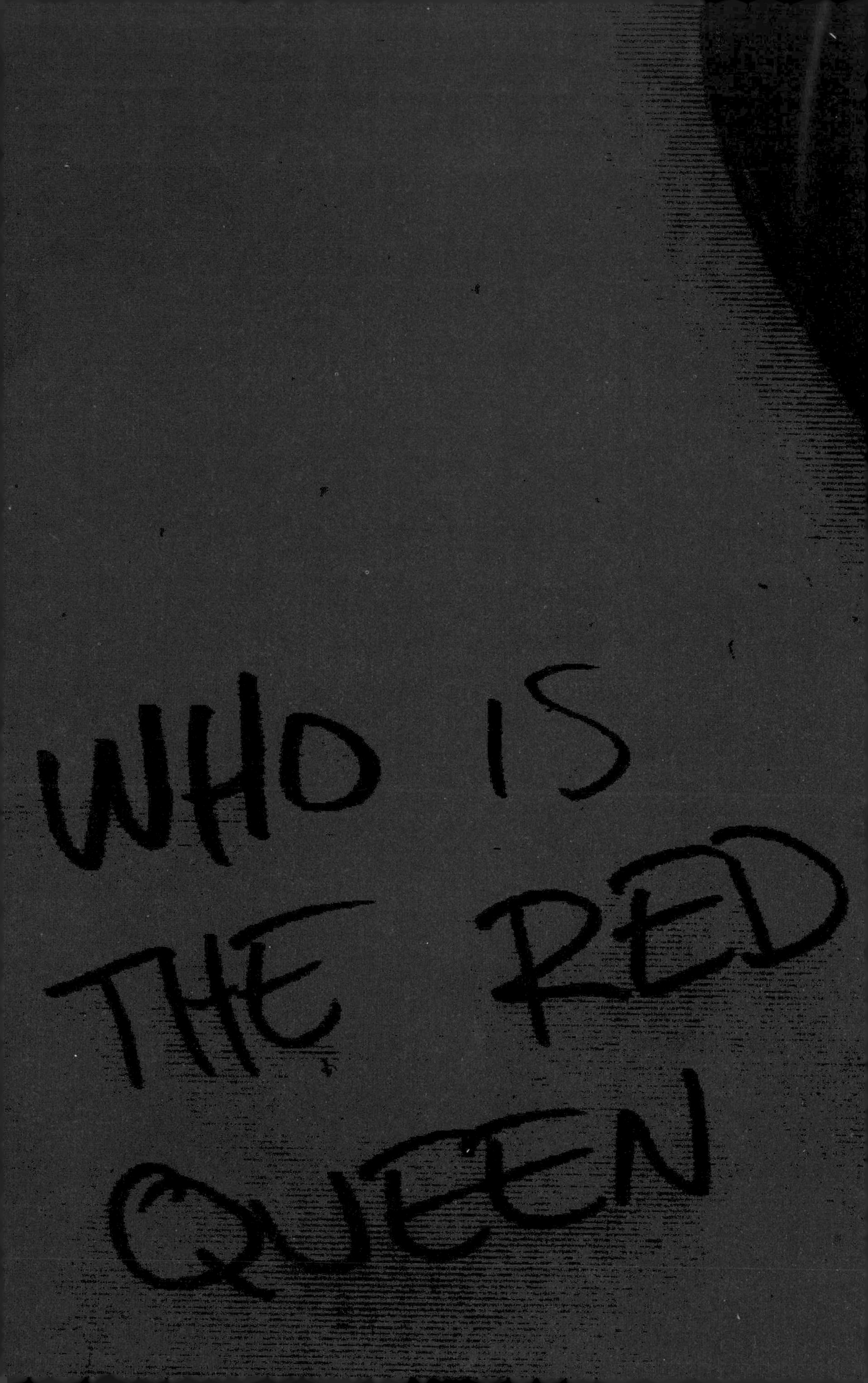
WHO IS THE RED QUEEN

KILLER?

Number Fourteen

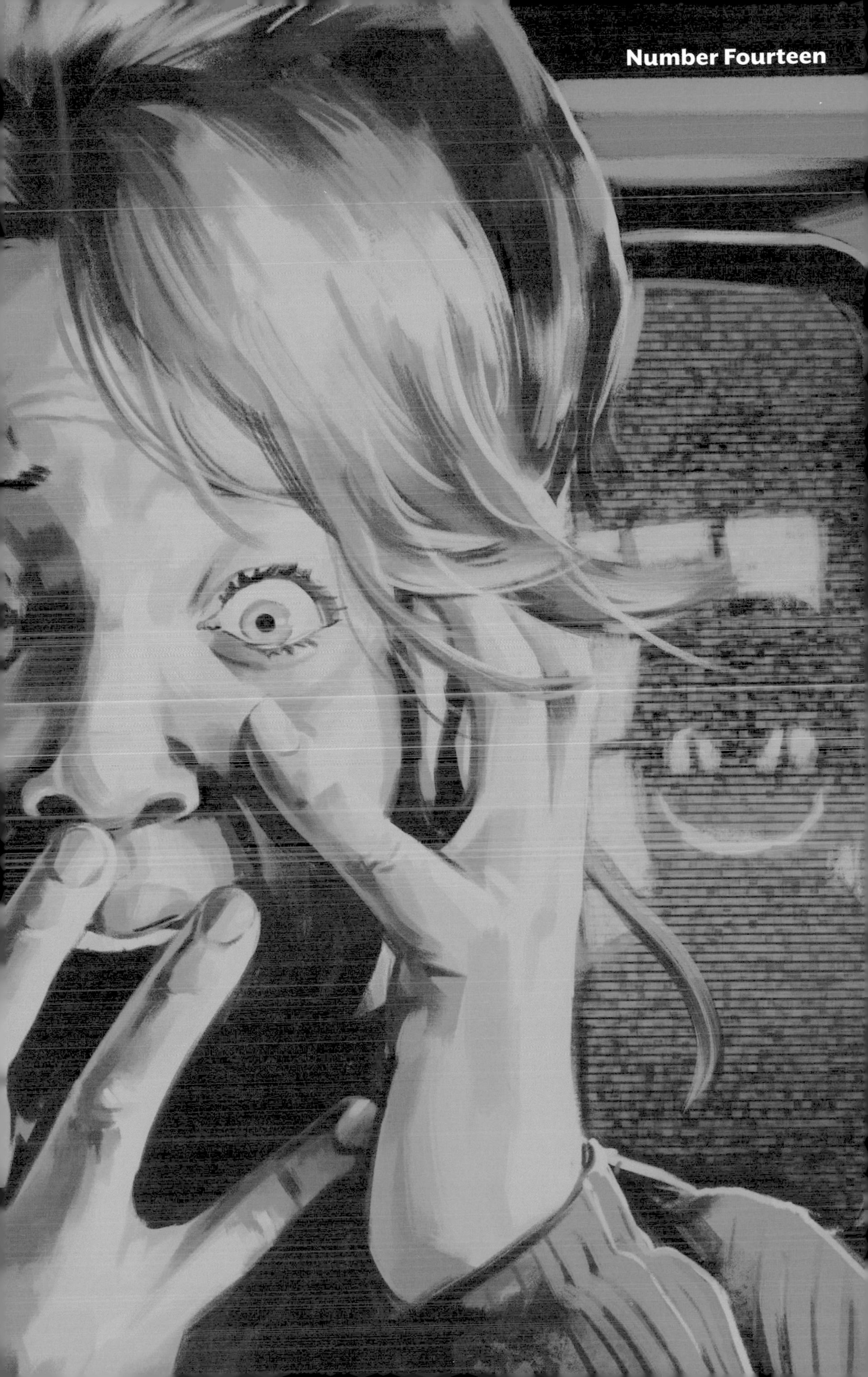

Number Fourteen Variant by Greg Smallwood

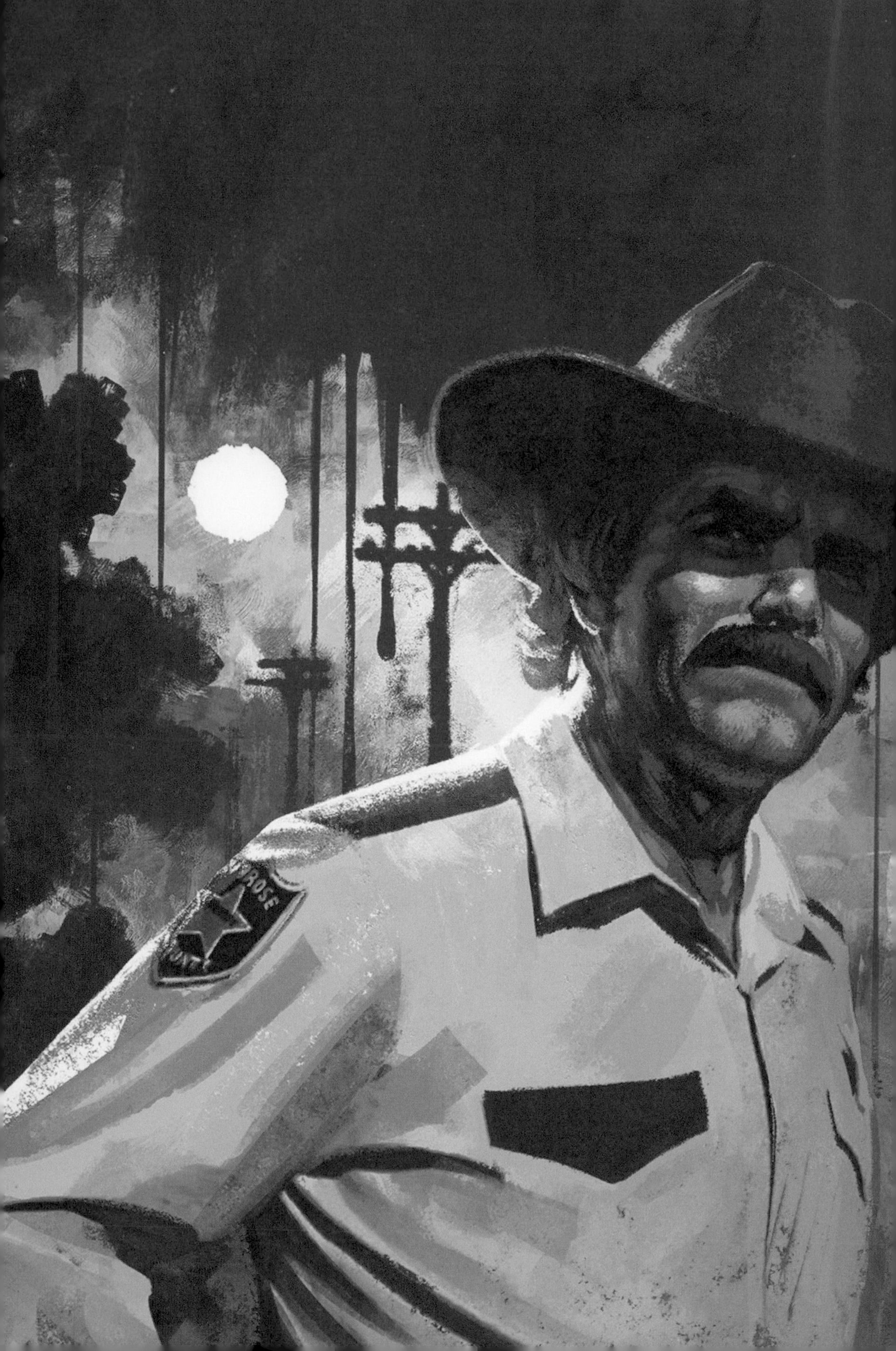

Number Fourteen Variant by Matt Taylor

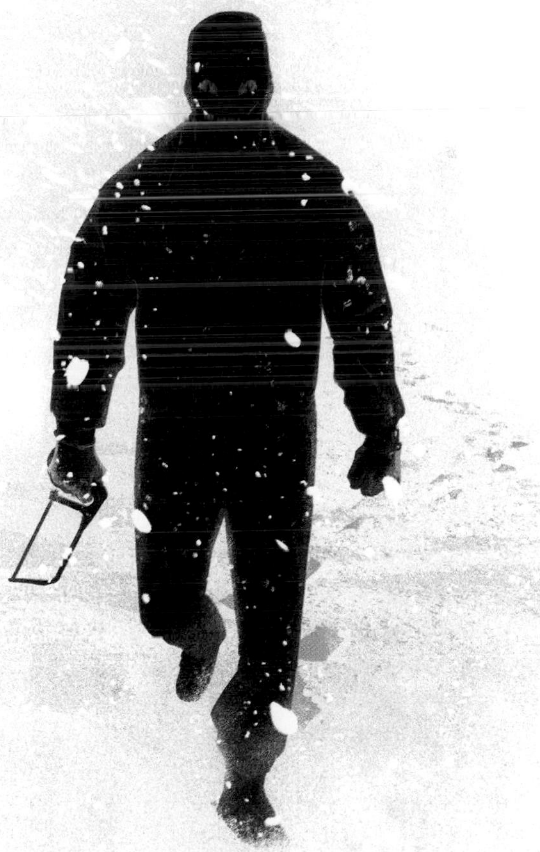

Number Fifteen

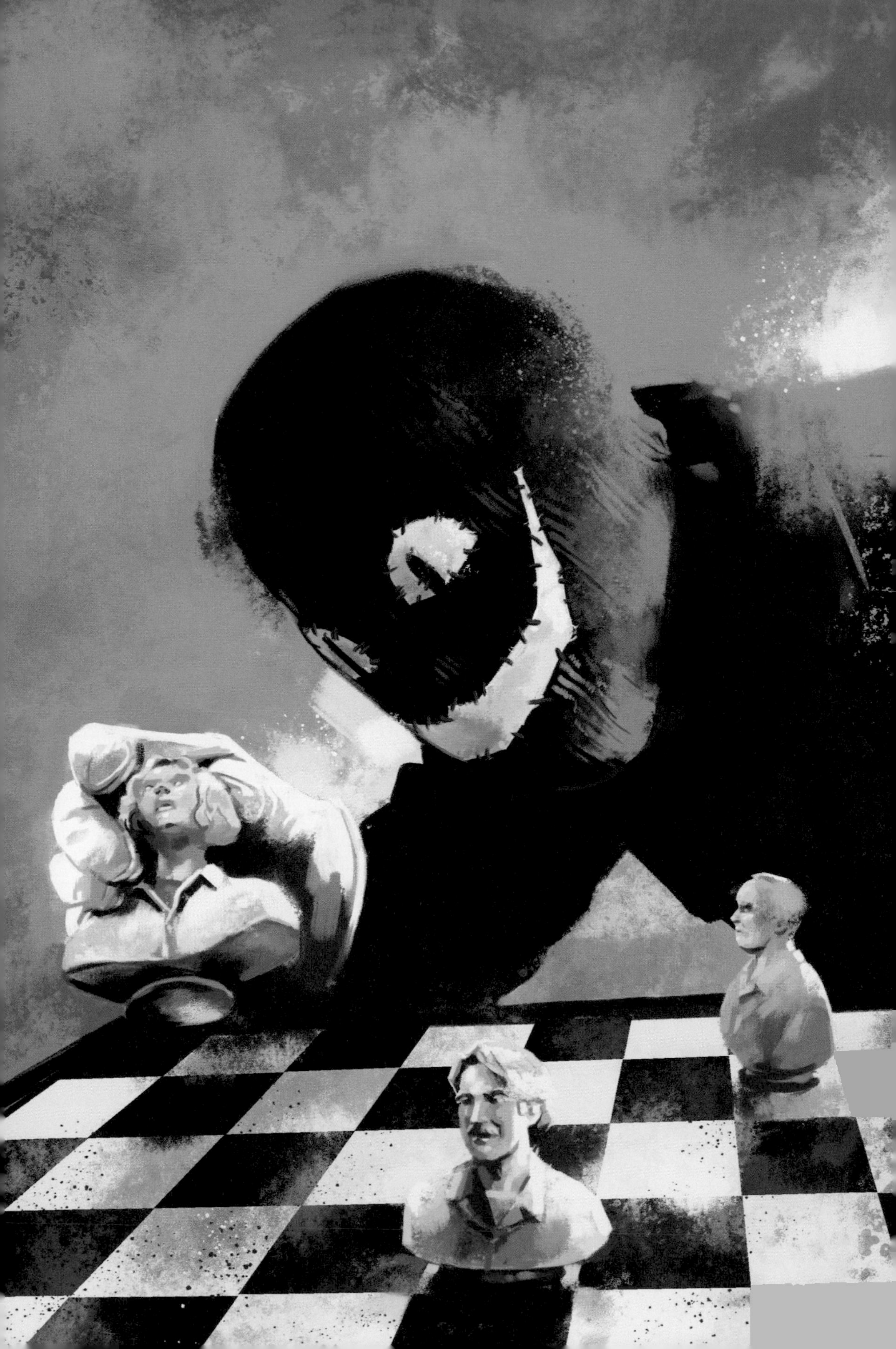

Number Fifteen Variant by DaNi

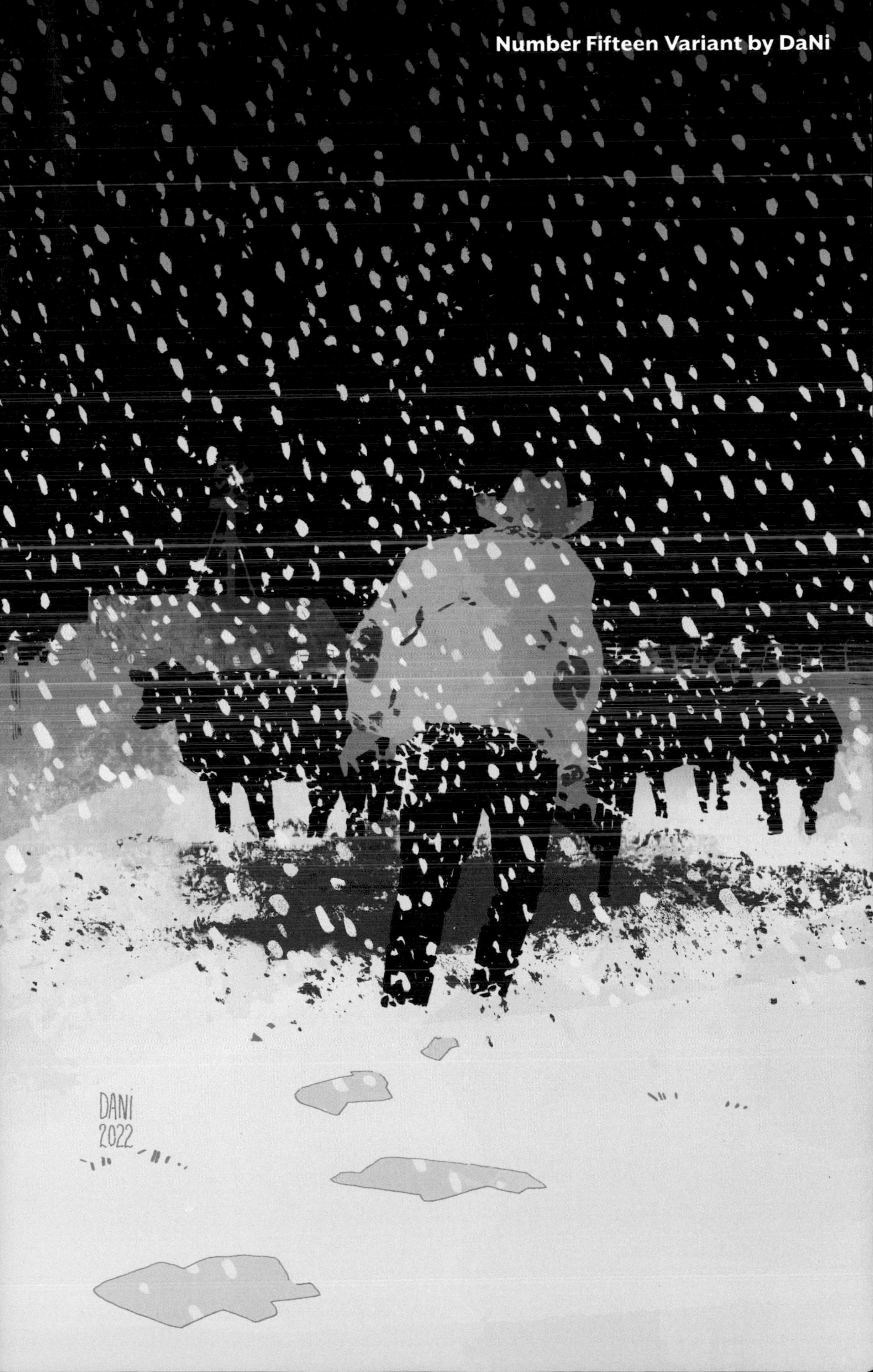
DANI
2022

Number Sixteen

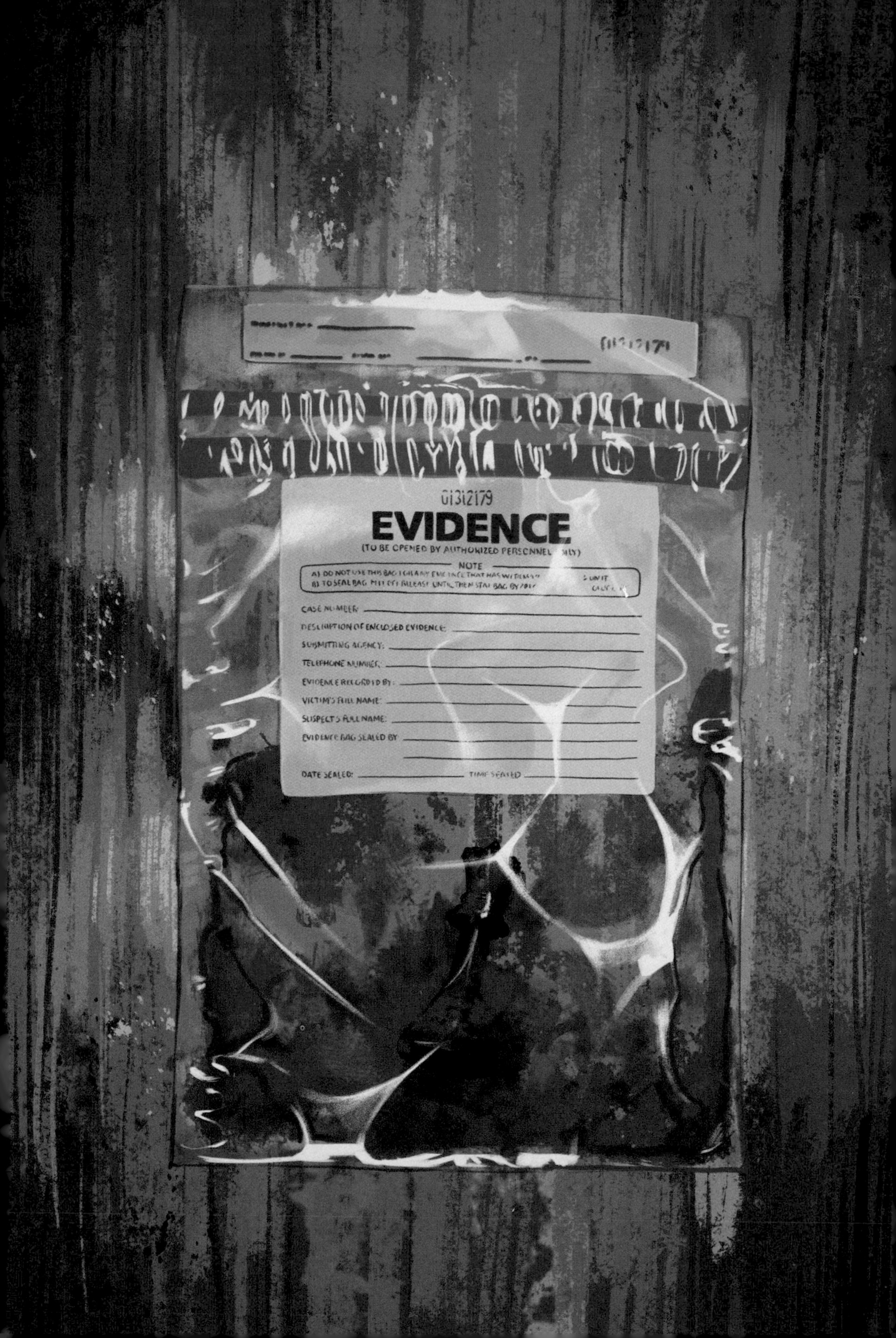
01312179
EVIDENCE
NOTE
CASE NUMBER:
DESCRIPTION OF ENCLOSED EVIDENCE:
SUBMITTING AGENCY:
TELEPHONE NUMBER:
EVIDENCE RECORDED BY:
VICTIM'S FULL NAME:
SUSPECT'S FULL NAME:
EVIDENCE BAG SEALED BY:
DATE SEALED:
TIME SEALED:

Number Sixteen Variant by Charlie Adlard

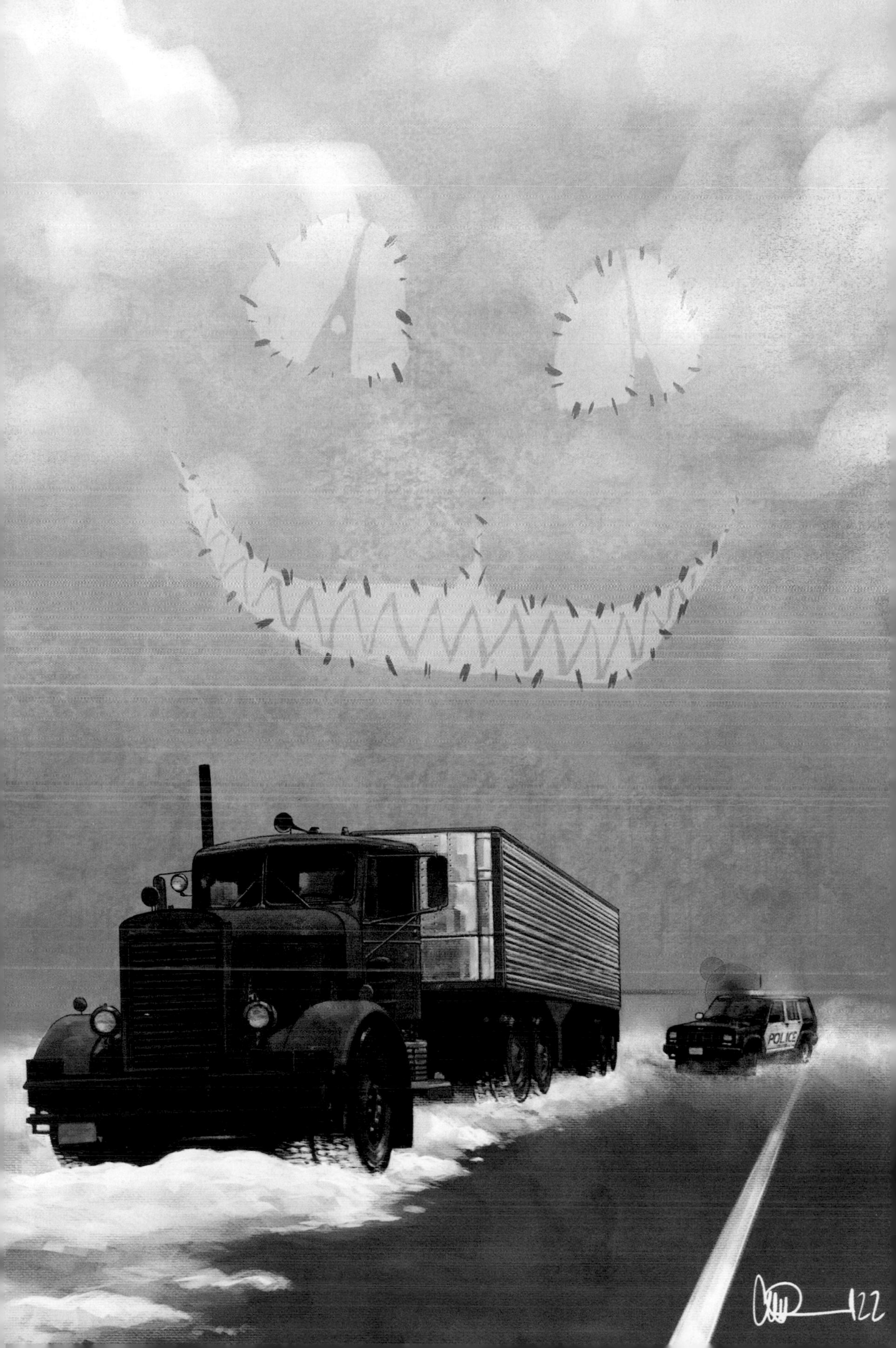
POLICE

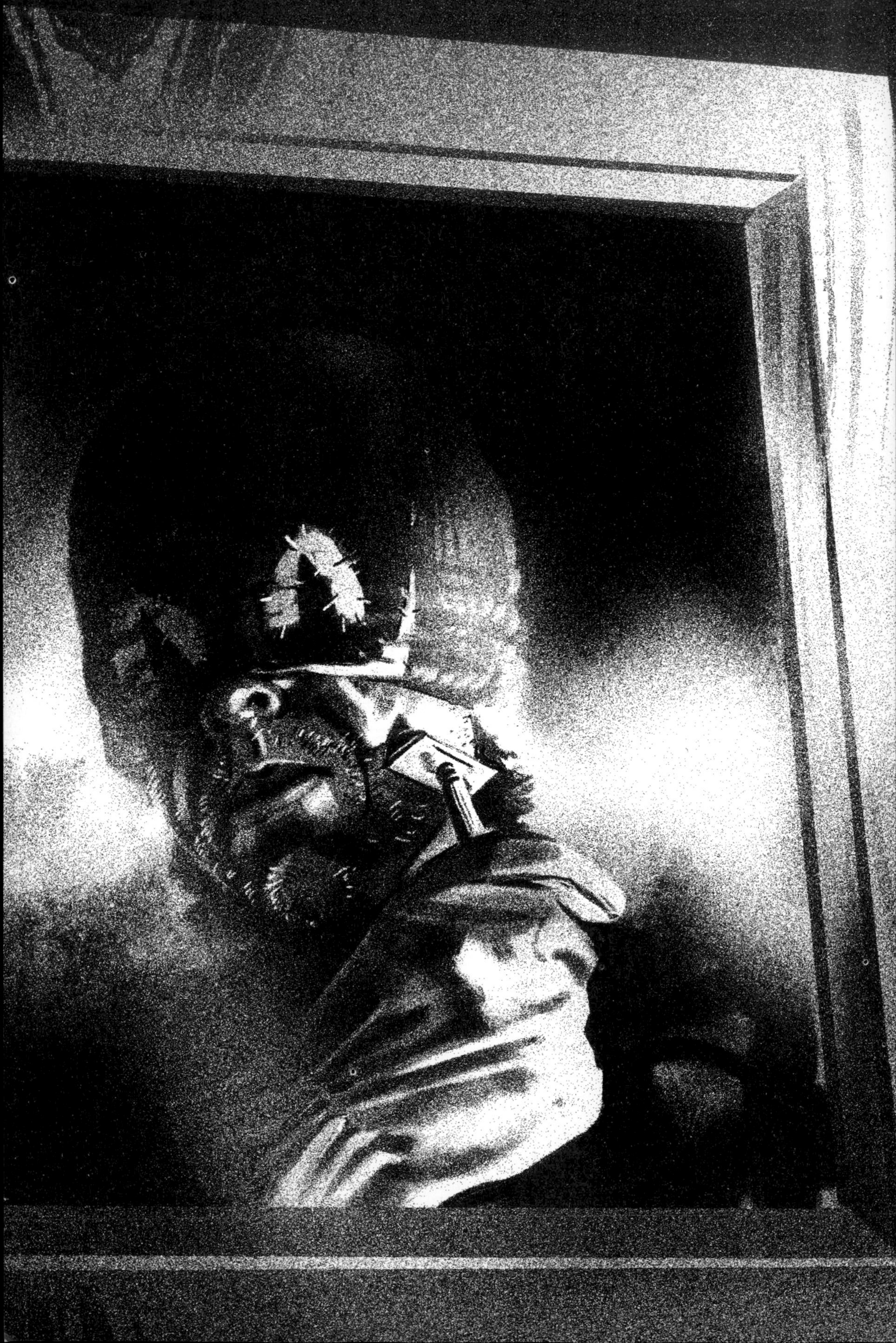

Number Seventeen Variant by Zi Xu

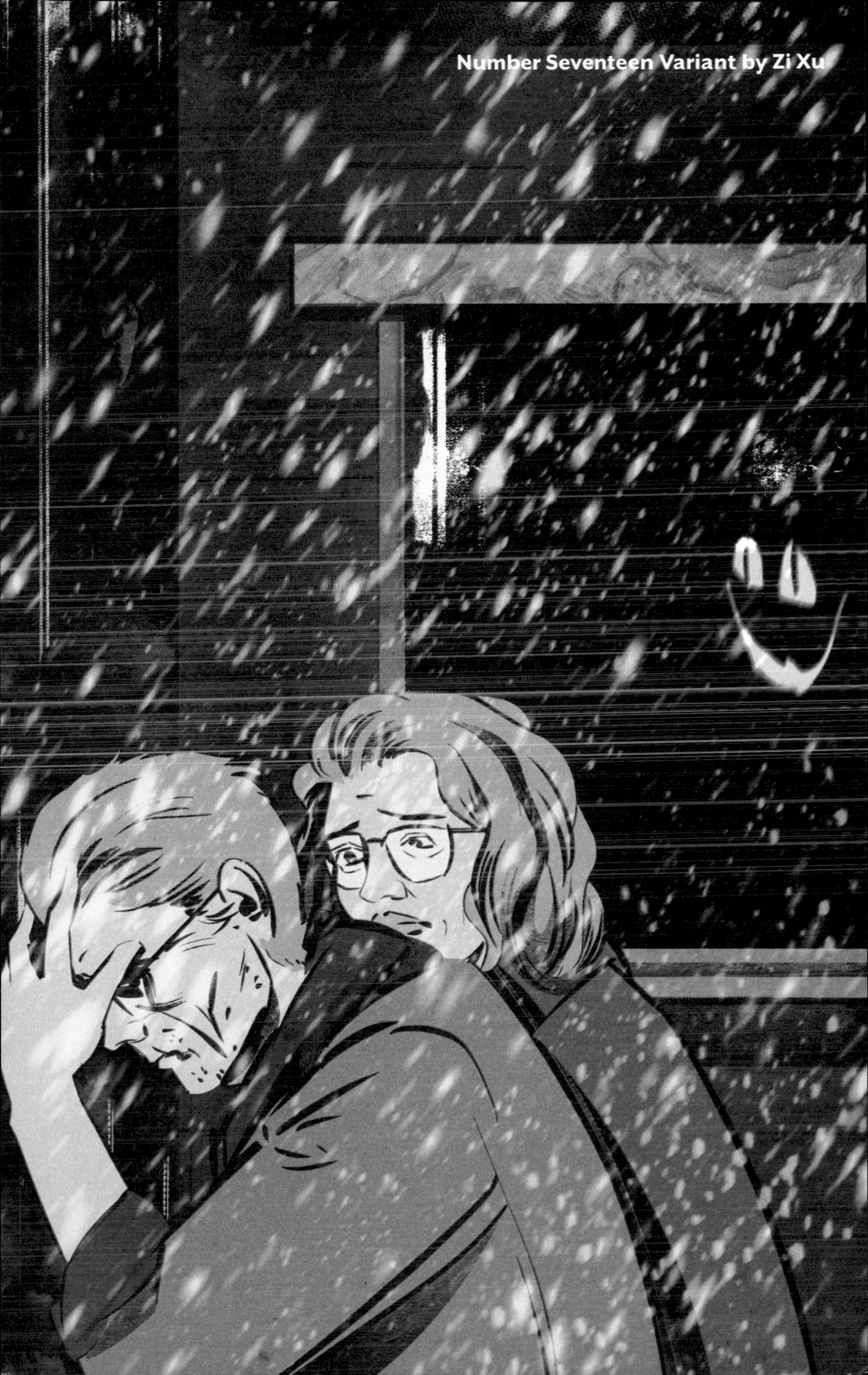

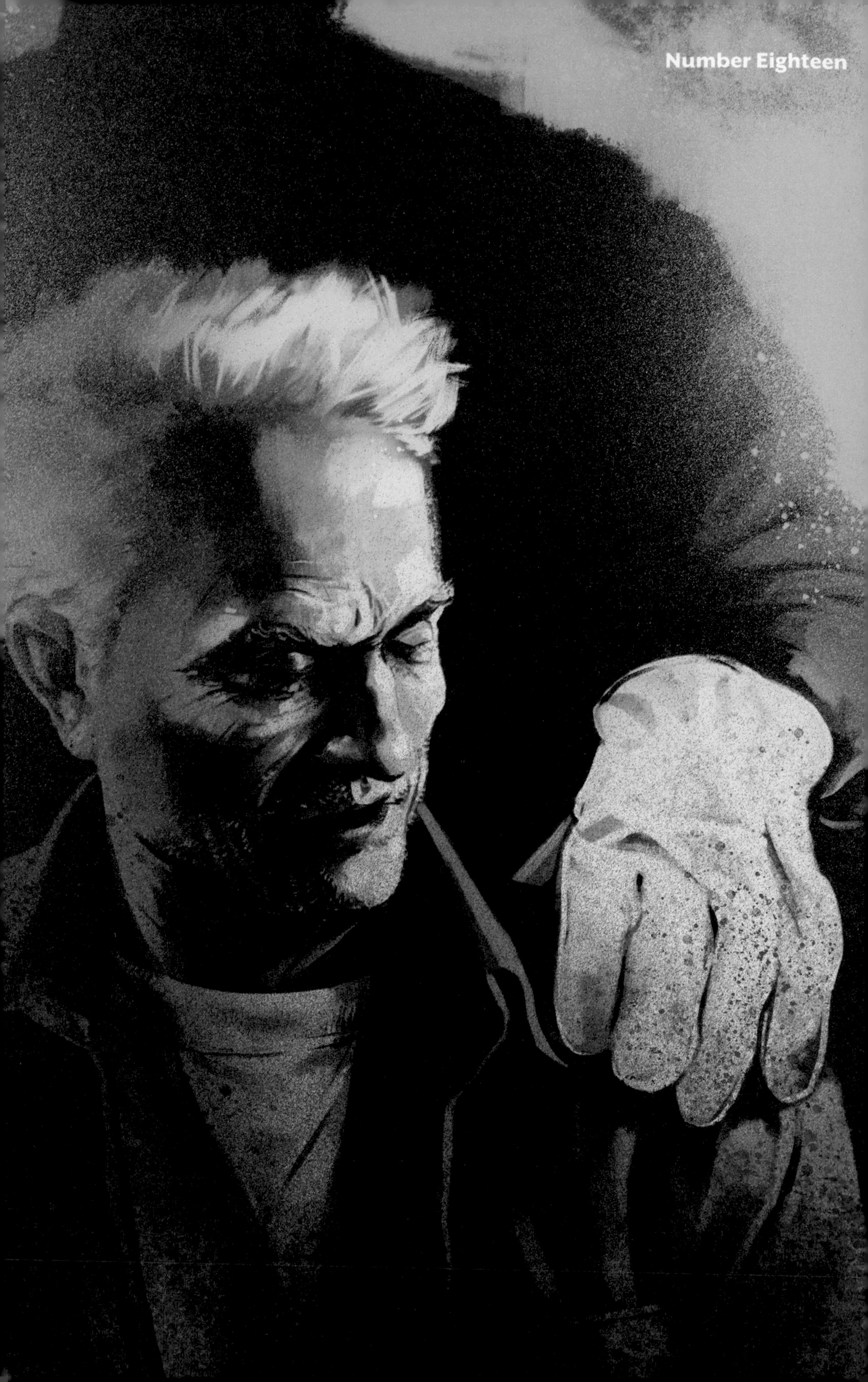
Number Eighteen

Number Eighteen Variant by Declan Shalvey

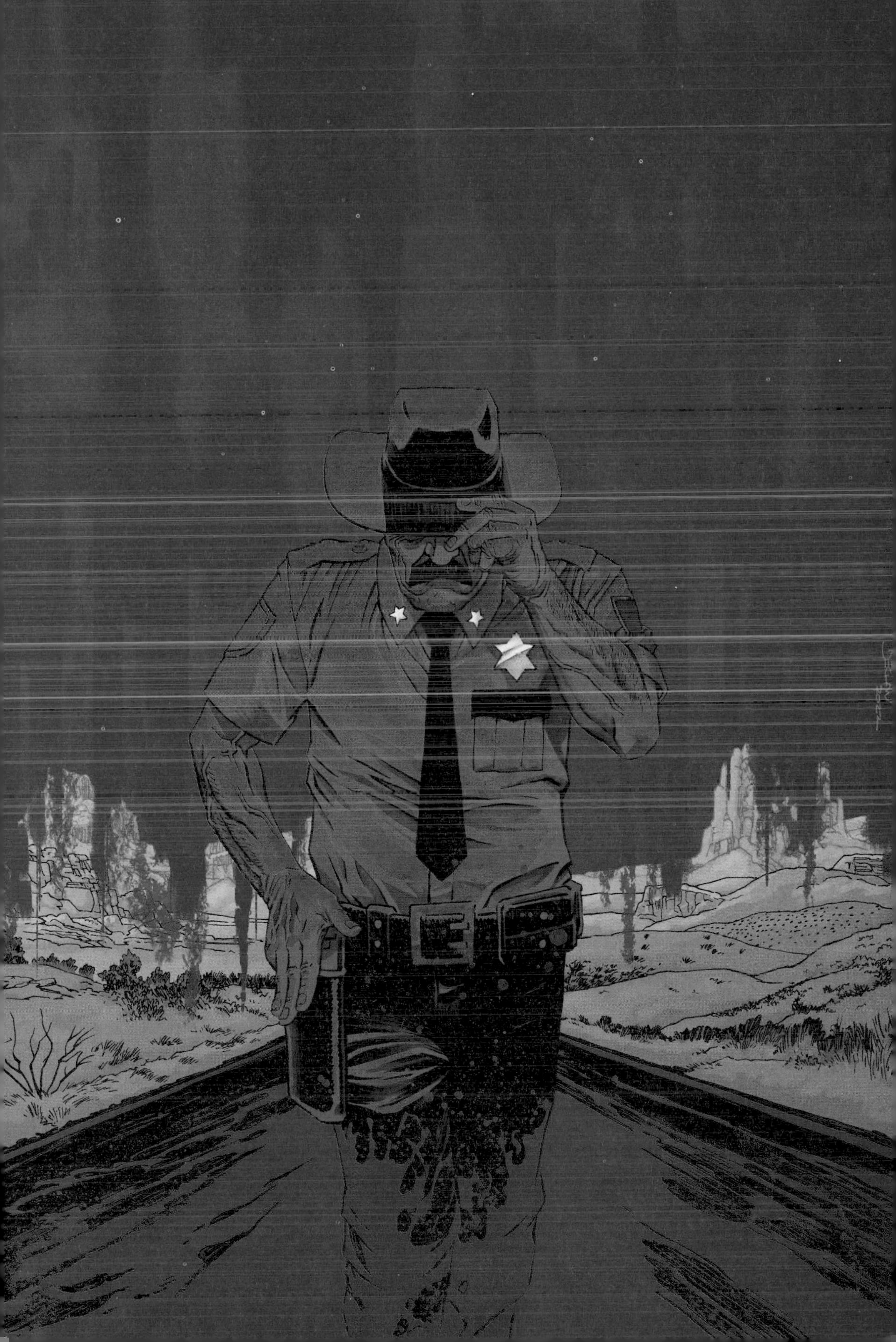

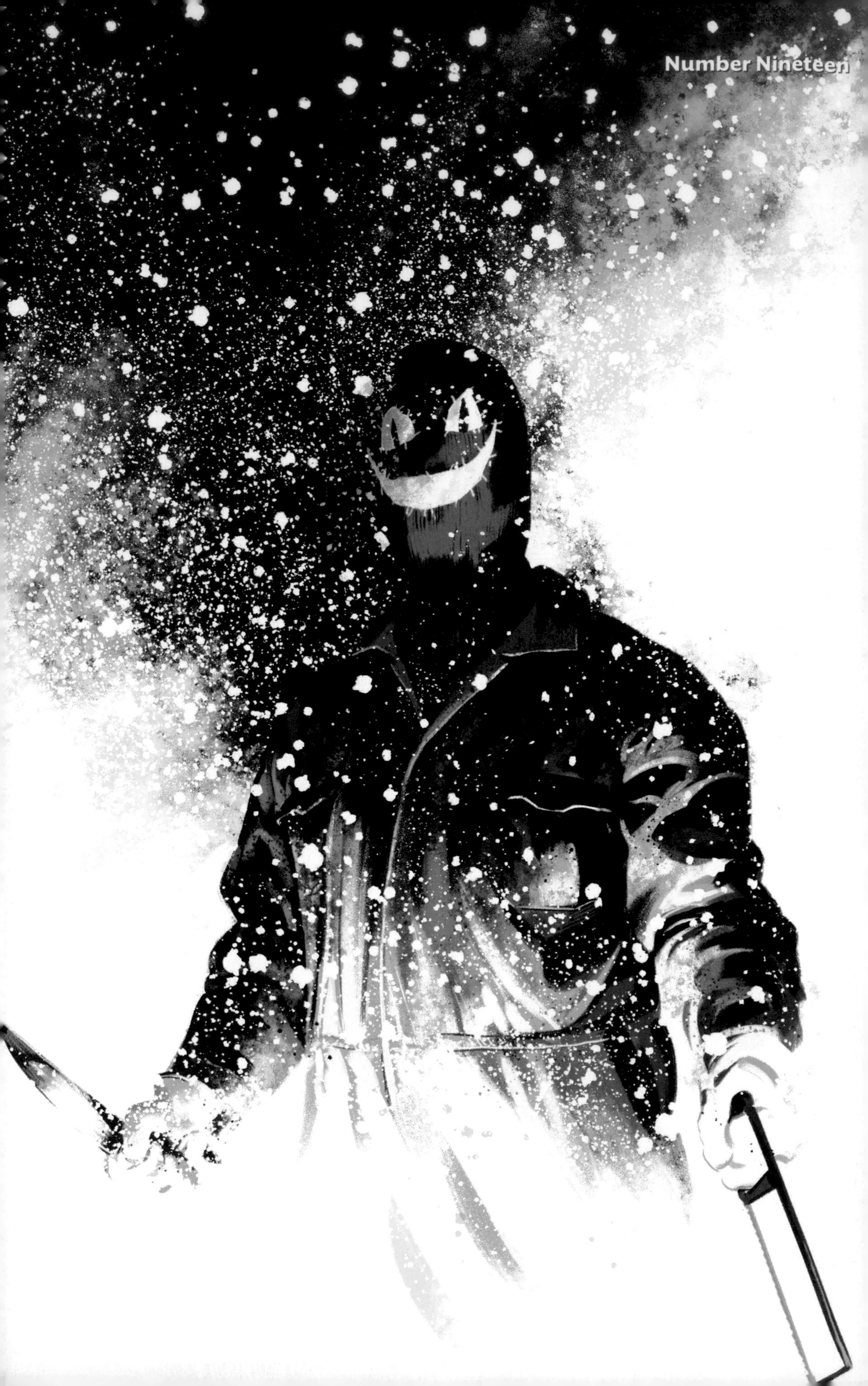
Number Nineteen

Number Nineteen Variant by Tonci Zonjic

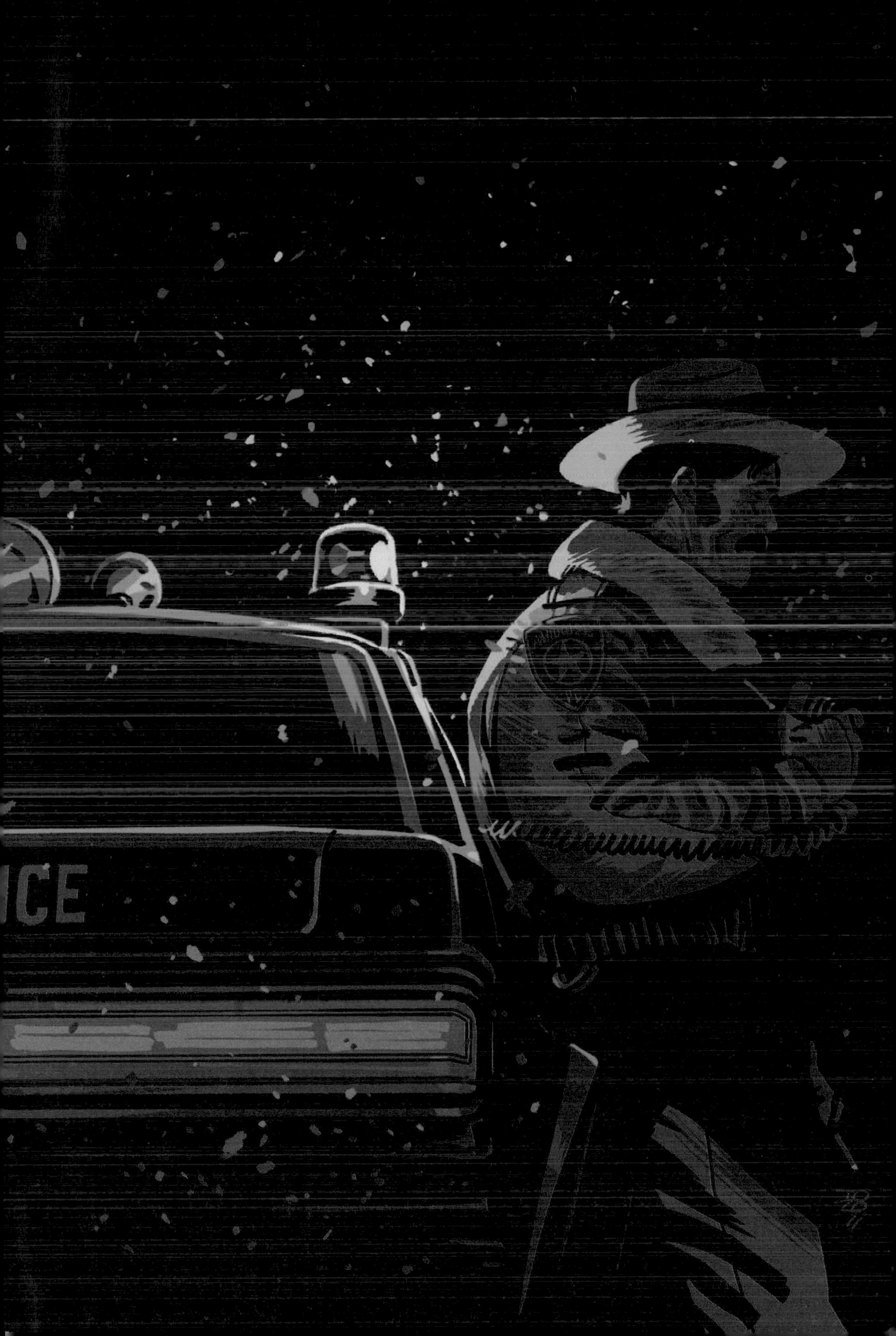
ICE